BIOGRAPHY
ALI CARTER

Ali lives in King's Lynn, Norfolk with her husband, a retired Met. Police Officer who was a great help in assuring the U.K. legalities in *Dead Girls Don't Cry* are as accurate as possible. Research regarding the New York Police Department is mentioned in her acknowledgements.

Her debut thriller – *Blood List* – has been extremely well received and this is the second in the D.C.I. Harry Longbridge series. A third is currently in preparation.

Website:- alicarterauthor.com
Twitter:- @alicrimewriter
Facebook:- @alicarterauthor

She crossed the corridor, entered the room and closed the door behind her. This had to be done fast. The window blinds were flicked shut, nurse call buzzer knocked to the floor and morphine drip switched to maximum flow (with a squeeze on the bag for good measure). 'X' was in no fit state to fight back. He struggled valiantly beneath the pillow as Carla leant heavily across his broken limbs and pushed down hard. His torso bucked and twitched... then just stopped. She lifted the pillow, placed it back behind his head and plumped it up beautifully...

To Josie,

She's back!!

DEAD GIRLS DON'T CRY

ALI CARTER

7·8·2022

Matador
9 Priory Business Park,
Wistow Road, Kibworth Beauchamp,
Leicestershire. LE8 0RX
Tel: 0116 279 2299
Email: books@troubador.co.uk
Web: www.troubador.co.uk/matador
Twitter: @matadorbooks

ISBN 978 1838593 391

British Library Cataloguing in Publication Data.
A catalogue record for this book is available from the British Library.

Printed and bound by CPI Group (UK) Ltd, Croydon, CR0 4YY
Typeset in 12pt Adobe Garamond Pro by Troubador Publishing Ltd, Leicester, UK

Matador is an imprint of Troubador Publishing Ltd

To all my wonderful readers
who loved *Blood List* enough
to want the sequel…

Just for you

She's back!!

PROLOGUE

RAMPTON HIGH SECURITY PSYCHIATRIC HOSPITAL
NOTTINGHAMSHIRE, DECEMBER 2019

Ex-G.P. Charlotte Peterson stood outside Rampton cuffed between two women prison officers as she waited to be put into the van. She'd been given leave to attend her mother's funeral and it felt good to be on the outside at last, *two years was a long time – too long.* It had been really difficult to knuckle down and accept everything at first, but she'd managed to get along with most of the other patients *most* of the time, and had one friend in particular who would do absolutely anything for her. Eventually she'd be able to show her appreciation to that friend in the way criminals prefer to receive their loyalty payment – *cold hard cash.*

Her not quite millionaire father had died the previous year due to a weak heart that had followed multiple illnesses, all as a result of the shock at his only daughter's hideous crimes, the macabre murders of five women and one man, and the attempted murders of three others. Sadly she hadn't been given permission to attend *his* funeral owing to an unfortunate kitchen incident…

Her mother, who had been constantly unwell and in and out of hospital for the past two years, had lived with what she felt was an eternal family shame, then followed by the loss of her husband it was just all too much to bear. So now, Charlotte found herself on this surprisingly warm December day outside in the fresh air, grateful for a breeze through her mid length floppy auburn cut, with difficult thoughts going round and round her head as they often did… and waiting for the van.

Miles had divorced her soon after the trial, which she'd found unforgiveable, *if understandable*. He'd clearly decided no amount of her parents' colossal inheritance was worth staying with her for, but as far as Charlotte was concerned it was the ultimate betrayal – after all *he* was the sole reason she was in here – well, apart from the girls…

She glanced down anxiously at her cuffed hands and checked her watch – *Let's hope all the arrangements are well synchronised Mummy dearest, I've only got one shot at this.* The large prison vehicle came round the corner and pulled up in front of them; she thought it overly big for just the two of them and a driver. Charlotte looked briefly around her before getting in. *There's nothing left for me here any longer and… well… I've always had a hankering for New York.* A twisted smile slid over her face, a previously attractive face, but one that had hardened considerably over the last couple of years. *I wonder if those two scheming bitches are happily settled out there . . ? To be honest it really doesn't matter one way or the other, after all –* **Dead Girls Don't Cry…**

ONE

SOUTH LONDON

JANUARY 2020

She took the towel off her head. The short black pixie crop that looked back at her was still a bit of a shock. A shock – but not unpleasant, she would get used to it. As usual she turned her head to the left and then to the right, no, not unpleasant at all – just different. Different enough to not be recognised which was of course the whole point. The mobile hairdresser who'd created it had been paid heavily and sworn to secrecy *– well, blackmailed to keep her mouth shut – to Charlotte that was the same thing.*

The crisp new passport lay on the dressing table, she glanced at it as she picked up the hairdryer; *Dr. Carla Preston.* Yes Charlotte definitely approved of that, she *was* after all a doctor – or used to be. Her lips moved into the shape of a tight smile, but her eyes did not. *They* hadn't smiled for years, not since the first time he'd let her down, *and certainly not since her incarceration.*

1

There had been a hell of a lot of cell hours, days, weeks and months, only two years of the allotted thirty admittedly, where she'd mulled over what she would do to Miles if she… *when* she caught up with him again.

She scrabbled about the dressing table drawer for a non-existent roller brush before remembering, yet again, she didn't need a big blow dry number anymore – and slammed it shut in annoyance. Old habits die hard, especially lifelong ones.

She was surprised at how quickly a fake passport had even been made up, let alone delivered. Once her Rampton contacts had sprung her on the special day release, everything seemed to go full steam ahead. She had never actually made her mother's funeral that morning, Carla had felt a bit bad about that, but needs must. It was the only way, given her freedom was literally in other people's hands. People she'd had to listen to, people she'd had to trust on sight, people who could get fake documents… *none of it had been easy.*

The hairdryer hummed noisily even on low as she wafted it back and forth over… frankly not a lot. Carla sighed and reached for a comb instead. Who was she kidding – *it looked crap.*

Reaching forward for the little white plastic case Carla popped the left lid, carefully picked up the blue lens on her left-hand ring finger and gently inserted it into her left eye. After blinking a few times she repeated with the right, looked in the mirror and blinked again. This was going to take practice. A short 'black' and sides was one thing, learning to wear bits of plastic on her eyeballs was quite another. If she were in a Bond film no doubt some bent cosmetic surgeon would've been assigned to reconstruct her face completely. However she was not in a film, Bond or otherwise and there was only so much a mobile hairdresser could achieve in a couple of hours.

She checked her watch. The taxi would be arriving in the next fifteen minutes and she needed to get a move on. A quick glance around the motel room revealed little of her last three weeks' presence; the wardrobes were empty, the bed was made, suitcases by the door, the bathroom cleared and her new passport now snapped securely inside her handbag. Picking up a pair of dark glasses from the dressing table and putting them on, Carla looked back in the mirror. *"Goodbye Charlotte – it's time I took over…"*

KIRKDALE: CUMBRIA

When the call came, Harry was at the nineteenth nursing a pint of Ruddles having just played another round of golf… *badly*. It was apparently one of the top hobby choices for retired police officers, golf that is not Ruddles, although the latter was distinctly easier to get his head around. Right now he couldn't imagine why anyone with half a gnat's cock of common sense would want to wander across a ridiculously large expanse of green, trying to knock small balls into what in his experience always appeared to be even smaller holes. Tennis hadn't gone much better. Perhaps he should try fishing… or maybe archery? *Anything that didn't involve bloody balls.*

Basically Harry Longbridge was bored. He was still only fifty-one and had done thirty years in the force, twenty-five in the Met.; the last five in the Cumbrian Constabulary. *He refused to use the 'modern' term 'service' on account of the fact he hated the names of things being mucked about with.* Now he was out – and hobbies weren't really delivering where his mind was concerned. The cryptic crossword in the paper barely scraped the surface of a mental replacement, so when the call came he was ready – *more than ready.*

To hear that the Peterson woman had been sprung on a compassionate day release from Rampton was almost music to his ears, although he'd immediately felt bad re-examining that thought given her crimes. Like everyone else he'd seen the news and read the papers. To know they were asking him to come out of retirement to assist with the case was a feather in his cap. *The Magpie was wanted back, they needed him and they'd called him – this was one feather he intended to plump up and fly straight back in on. Thank the Lord for criminals…*

At the tail end of that thought, Steve Caudell, his partner for the day, reappeared and sat down next to him, his G&T not quite so sparkling as it was half an hour previously. A former Chief Super, and with ten years retired 'green walking' practice on his side, Caudell had endeavoured to persuade Harry that golf five mornings a week was the retired officer's perfect lifestyle. Harry on the other hand had only enjoyed the watering hole, and he shouldn't have been enjoying it quite so much. Certainly not that second beer given the diabetes diagnosis he'd received a couple of years ago.

"So what do you reckon then, another round tomorrow?" beamed Steve behind newly crafted perfectly white teeth. He reached for his drink and waved at the barman for a top-up.

Harry smiled, well half-smiled, he didn't want to encourage this little meet up – "No you're alright Steve, think I'm gonna give that one a miss if you don't mind, had a call from my old crime team whilst you were in the little boys' room. The Peterson woman got sprung from Rampton 'bout three weeks back, all hell's broke loose, been all over the news, you must've seen it?"

"Sure, but how does that affect you – and more to the point, *golf?*"

"They want me back to shed some light on it, new D.I. on the case. To be honest I'm missing the job, two years of hanging about the house and playing various ball games, *not very well*, has just about run its course – if you'll pardon the pun. I need something to get my teeth back into."

"Well for what it's worth I think you're crazy," Caudell replied, downing his gin and tonic and picking up its replacement. "And don't be too disappointed if they've 'bigged' it up a little – you'll probably find it's a once only conversation they could've had on the phone." Steve stood up abruptly then; he'd caught sight of someone entering the bar. *Maybe similar to why the bathroom trip had taken so long?* "Look, must grab Geoff – he's just walked in and I need a word. Catch you later."

Harry lifted his pint in acknowledgement and turned back to concentrate on his beer. If Caudell found someone more interesting or important to talk to he would. It was his way and Harry had got used it. Geoff was the president of the club and Steve probably wanted an 'in' on the committee.

He knew there was some mileage in what Steve had said though, just hoped he could spin a reunion out for a bit. Most of his old crew were still there, he knew that because he still kept in touch occasionally with Joe Walker and Suzanne Moorcroft. It was Joe who'd rung him, and if Joe's new D.I. was who Harry thought she was, there may be more than a single conversation to be had. Either way, he was going to go as shit crazy as the Peterson woman if he didn't sort something fast. He drained his glass, grabbed his jacket off the adjacent chair and nodded to Steve and Geoff as he passed them on the way out – *no time like the present.*

As he pulled out of the club car park, Harry reflected on the Charlotte Peterson case from two years before. A local G.P. turned serial killer she'd made Harold

Shipman look like Ronald McDonald. Having initially started with hammering ice stakes into the hearts of any young women she *suspected* of bedding her practice partner and husband Miles – Dr Peterson female had begun to add *any women at all* she thought could attract his attention to her ever growing list. On top of that, one girl's journalist boyfriend had also narrowly escaped death, and another's schizophrenic brother hadn't. That didn't include two other failed attempts on women both men had known. She'd been sent to Rampton Psychiatric Hospital indefinitely, and Jenny Flood, the schizophrenic boy's sister, had fortunately (although not for her) witnessed one of the murders. That had made for an easy conviction, but it had rocked the community – this was the Lakes, not Peckham. Now she was on the run – but for Harry, as luck would have it, D.I. Fran Taylor had recently relocated from Canon Row and was running the current operation. If she was the same Fran Taylor, a D.S. he'd left behind when he'd relocated seven years ago, he wasn't at all surprised he'd received the call – *but Harry hadn't forgotten she was also one of the reasons he'd left – and he was betting that neither had she.*

Fran wondered if she'd done the right thing by having Harry contacted re the Peterson case. She knew exactly what he'd think – that he was back in, and not necessarily just with regard to the team. She drummed her fingers on the desk as she looked over at Joe Walker and Suzanne Moorcroft through her office window, recalling how their eyes had lit up when she'd asked one of them to give Harry a call. He'd clearly left on a high note after working with these two youngsters, *not always been a sarcastic bastard then.* She grinned, remembering their time together in London. He hadn't been all bad, there'd been some fun times at Canon Row, and she'd missed him like mad after discovering he'd suddenly put in for a transfer and left for the Lakes the same fortnight she'd spent on an Italian beach. But at the end of the day Harry was married and she'd been in the middle of a messy divorce, everything about it, *whatever 'it' was,* had been unspoken, and he'd never made any contact since. Yes it was going to be interesting at the very least to see him again, she just hoped it didn't open everything up... *oh crap... who was she kidding, of course she did. That's exactly why she'd got Joe to call him in...*

It felt strange sitting in reception waiting to either be called up or the S.I.O. (Senior Investigating Officer) to come down. Nothing much had changed since Harry had retired, but then it *was* only a couple of years ago. He noticed the new paint job was still waiting as his eyes circled the reception, hallway and the double doors leading off it. The two fresh-faced female sergeants on the front desk weren't familiar to him though, obviously there'd been some new blood transferred in, maybe along with Fran...

Just the fact he couldn't walk straight past the W.P.O.s, through those doors, down the corridor to the lifts, bagged sarnie hanging from his mouth, coffee in one hand case files in the other… *it irked him considerably.* Instead, he leaned forwards head down, arms on his knees hands clasped – today would prove to be very telling. At that moment the doors swung open and gave their usual double backward thud.

"Sir – it's great to see you!" Joe Walker strode through, his hand held out ready. Harry noticed his young rookie walked more purposefully but still owned that daft gawky smile – it used to annoy him at times but not today, not anymore. Today he welcomed it. He stood up, lifted praising eyebrows, and with a nod at Joe's new stripes, held his own hand out and warmly received the new *Sergeant* Walker's greeting. Harry gave an equally broad grin, now he would discover just how much he was actually needed, how much they really wanted him to contribute. Ex-D.C.I. Longbridge was so wrapped up in the happy reconciliation, he hadn't noticed another familiar face had followed Joe through the doors – *this one a Scottish D.I. from Canon Row…*

TWO

FLIGHT BA173 TO NEW YORK

Carla sat by the window, seat tilted back and eyes closed behind a copy of the *Telegraph*. The fact that facing outward was a fairly large (*now outdated*) photo of her, beneath a heading of '*Chiller Killer Still At Large*', was truly evocative of her macabre sense of humour. She no longer looked anything like Charlotte Peterson. It was quite ironic really given she'd always hated overly short, overly dark hair, yet here she was sporting a black pixie crop, the absolute epitome of the style she disliked the most.

"Excuse me… er… *Madam?* Would you like a drink?" Carla pulled the paper down from her face and placing it on her lap, flipped her seat back up, not that it had flipped very far down in pleb class… she'd made a mental note to upgrade on the return trip – *if* she came back of course…

"Yes – thank you, a large gin and tonic would be *lovely*," she breezed smiling up at the flight attendant, swiftly scanning the girl's appearance and just as quickly dismissing her as a plain Jane. Not that young attractive women were an issue at the moment – Miles had divorced her and she was single again, all that… *business* was behind her. Well… apart from the unfinished agenda in New York of course.

Carla swirled her drink thoughtfully as she looked at her watch. They were due to land at 6.00 p.m. so only another couple of hours. She knocked back her G&T in two short gulps and placed the empty cup on the back tray of the seat in front. *Definitely flying first in future, G&T in a plastic cup is just rank, and sardine city even worse.* Carla sighed at a memory that hovered briefly, a long-ago trip to Hong Kong with Miles… *that* had been so much more glamorous, a happy life… she winced. *Better try to get some sleep, the jet lag's going to be bad enough as it is.* She was just about to flick the switch to recline – *ish* again, when a very attractive man began to walk up the aisle. He appeared to be looking straight at her, but she also knew there was a very pretty and very *young* blonde in the seat behind. Raising the newspaper slightly, Carla watched him covertly as he got closer. When he drew level she thought a flicker of recognition tugged at the corner of his eyes, just a flicker, then his gaze shifted quickly forwards as he carried on up the aisle. In that fraction of a second she went cold. *Did he actually look at her? Who was he and who could know she was on this flight anyway?*

Despite her recent drink her mouth now felt quite dry, it had been the airport check-in procedure she'd worried about; once she'd passed that and was aboard she thought she'd be safe. The loud thumping of her heart brought back uncomfortable memories. A small drop of sweat slid slowly from her temple, past a perfectly chiselled cheekbone and down the side of her neck. She sat rooted… still bolt upright.

KIRKDALE POLICE STATION
CUMBRIA

Harry and Joe had exchanged a couple of nostalgic jokes before the older man had realised who'd followed Joe through the double doors.

"Hello Harry – it's been a long time." Fran Taylor smiled and tentatively held out her hand. Harry shook it warmly, holding her longer than necessary as the air seemed to depart from his lungs. Eventually he spoke.

"It's… good to see you Fran," he said, a slight break in his voice. His eyes held hers as he continued to encase her hand, now with both of his, and a surprised Joe noted definite atmospheric changes in that corridor. His old D.C.I. and new D.I. certainly hadn't noticed anyone else passing them in either direction at that moment. *Fran broke the spell.*

"Thank you for stopping by Harry, we appreciate it," she said suddenly, removing her hand and snapping out of her frozen demeanour. Harry noticed it was 'we' – not 'I', *and smarted a little.* "I asked Joe to contact you regarding Charlotte Peterson's escape from Rampton as you were the Senior Investigating Officer on the case. We thought you could shed some light on one or two things."

"Yes of course, only too glad to help!" he said, brightening up – "It was a ghastly time; Sergeant Walker here was a considerable asset." Harry threw a faint smile at Joe who hadn't lost the art of blushing over the previous two years. As a rookie he'd made quite a few silly mistakes on that case which had exasperated his senior officer. However, as it had proceeded, Joe had also made a couple of important discoveries and suggestions that had contributed to solving exactly how the female victims had been murdered.

"I'm sure he was," said Fran, smiling. "Which is why he's here now." She checked her watch. "Look, it's nearly three and I've not eaten, shall we find a quiet corner in a café somewhere? I don't really know my way around yet but I'm sure you two have a favourite filling station?" Both men answered together.

"Brenda's Buffet?" offered Harry instinctively…

"Café Calisé?" countered Joe with a knowing side glance… Fran laughed.

"No change in your eating habits then Harry," she said smiling at him wryly. "Come on Joe, you can drive us to the Calisé – sounds slightly more my style."

Sitting at a corner table away from the service area and the door, Fran and Joe tucked in to a bowl of carbonara each, Joe's smothered in grated cheese, whilst Harry stuck with what he knew best – bacon and egg baps and a strong mug of PG Tips. The Calisé was very flexible and adaptable, *unlike Harry.*

"So what was she like then?" asked Fran. "I mean – *really like?*" She lowered her voice slightly. "Apart from being a totally crazy psycho murdering bitch I mean." Harry leant forwards, one elbow on the table, thumb and forefinger stroking his chin with one hand, as he stirred his tea with the other. A glazed expression fell across his face as he recalled all the photographic images. All the dead women who'd been neatly lined up on his meeting room's white board two years previously, images he knew would stay with him the rest of his life.

He tapped the spoon on the rim of his mug and took a sip. *"Harry?"* pressed Fran, waving a forkful of pasta in front of him. "I want to get a *feel* for her, understand what she's really like, what she's likely to do, think, plan, where she's likely to go." Fran raised her eyebrows in anticipation. Harry bit into his roll and glanced up briefly at Joe who was now looking a bit tense as he too brought back those images. Harry thought for a moment, but not about Fran's question, he knew the answer to that and didn't need to ponder it. No, he was thinking about how Fran had always been the psychoanalytical side of their partnership at Canon Row, he was the practical weight thrower. They'd fitted together perfectly, and could fit together perfectly again now if only she'd give a little. Officially he couldn't be let back in; he knew that in all reality, although there was a huge deficit of police out there all over. But there was nothing to stop her letting him do a little private detective work on the side… and reporting back to her. He needed that – *at least that*. And he needed an excuse to be working with her again…

He swallowed his mouthful and took another gulp of tea before answering.

"Charlotte Peterson was – *is* – the coldest fish I've ever had the misfortune to meet. She's hard, relentless, bitter and scheming. She has lead-eyed, dead-eyed, eyes of a shark that can see right through to your very soul. They never smile and they never shine. She's a chameleon. She can change her personality at will. The elderly? *They all loved her.* But when we interviewed the staff who worked for her at her G.P.s' surgery, every single one said they felt uncomfortable to some degree. Her only real emotion was shown to her horses, yet when she was cornered and eventually arrested near Keeper's Cottage at the bottom of Kirkby Pike…" he looked at Joe again, "it was like the demon that lived inside her just slipped away into the ether, to leave an empty shell. By the time she reached court, the demon had slithered back into residence and all but physically glowed through her skin. *That* is what Charlotte Peterson is like – what she's *really* like." He picked up his roll again and began to munch, whilst Fran's fork remained in mid air – holding a cold portion of carbonara.

Annie Longbridge sat nursing a mug of tea in her kitchen flipping a glossy monthly with no enthusiasm whatsoever – she didn't even know which one it was. There was a smell of burning coming from the oven and the dog was asking to go out... *again*. She may have been a rubbish cook, and more of a cat than a dog person, but she felt she'd been a good wife to Harry over the previous twenty-three years.

She got up to let the Lab out, turned the oven off and sat back down again. Annie was feeling empty. Empty, flat and worse still – *ignored*. She'd put up with the 'Job', put up with the shifts interfering with their social life (such as it was), put up with Harry's constant stressed-out personality, periodic foul temper and moods, and reminded herself that if it wasn't for her he'd never have got his diabetes sorted out. To be fair to him that *had* reduced the grouchiness quite a bit, but apart from a fortnight at Lake Como when he'd first retired two years ago, they'd only had one holiday and one weekend away in the last ten years. And things had got more than a bit sparse in the bedroom department – not that she cared much about that side of their marriage anymore, or she'd convinced herself she didn't – she wasn't quite sure which.

It hadn't helped when her hairdressing business had gone down the pan six months earlier either, and when adding up all of the above, in her mind it pretty much made her a saint. So when Harry had been on the phone one evening and Annie had overheard Fran

Taylor was back on the scene, her bitch radar was well and truly flipped back on.

She sipped her tea as she kept half an eye on Baxter through the kitchen window, and idly turned over the last page of the magazine to reveal the *Kirkdale Courier* lying beneath it. She lifted it up a little and studied the photo on the front page. Charlotte Peterson's icy expression looked up. Whilst the woman was clearly wired like a tin of spaghetti, Annie couldn't help admiring her. *Just a little.* That tiny part of Annie's mind, the dark side (and we all have one), whispered to her now and then – and right now it was saying; *'Well at least she did something about them…'*

She shivered every time that dark side woke up, made her wonder about her *own* sense of sanity. She was shivering now.

The whimpering and scratching hauled her away from the edge of Lord knows where… Baxter's goofy black face looked hopefully through the glass door and she got up to let him back in, then groaned as half the flower bed followed. After quickly brushing up the earth, complete with newly planted seedlings, and depositing it outside in a heap, she picked up her mug and put it in the sink, all the while feeling Charlotte Peterson's eyes looking up from the page and following her every move. Irritably, Annie returned to the table, swept the paper off it and into the recycling bin. *'I don't need **your** approval lady…'* she muttered tightly, and walked through to the hall where she grabbed her keys off the side table, catching her reflection in the mirror above it. A distinctly flustered yet preoccupied Annie opened the door, and looking back paused briefly before reaching for her jacket on the stand. She swore as her perfectly layered hair blew sideways with a sudden gust of wind, *and behind her the front door slammed more loudly than usual.*

When Harry arrived home he found a snoring Baxter, legs akimbo in his bed in the kitchen, a faint smell of burnt... something, and no Annie. Considering it was January, blowing a hooley and she didn't go anywhere by choice in filthy weather, he was surprised not to find her stretched out on the sofa reading the latest copy of *Hair* magazine. Then as he stood in the lounge he remembered – the salon had gone tits up six months previously and she'd cancelled her subscription. His wife had become distinctly reticent following the loss of her business, and he'd probably not helped much with moaning about how bored he was since retiring from the 'Job'. He flushed then, Harry knew just how much Chique had meant to her, and he also knew he'd been less than supportive when it had folded – he just couldn't seem to find the right words to console her.

He checked his watch, it was 6.00 p.m. Where the hell was she? Baxter, whose welcome had been delayed (probably by some random bunny-chasing dream), now bounded into the room, launched himself at his favourite person in the whole world and nearly knocked him flying. Harry gave him a friendly fast head and shoulder rub and eased him off his waist.

"Hello Bax where's your mother then – hmm?" The black Lab answered with his standard anti-clockwise dance, tongue hanging out and stupid grin on his face. "No clues with you then old boy, as per…" At eighteen months, Baxter wasn't old at all, but Harry referred to all dogs as 'old boy' – even the female ones he sometimes met with their owners in the park. However Baxter *did* lead him back into the kitchen where the smell of Annie's latest burnt offering was even more evident, and it was then that Harry realised he'd be eating pizza for the second time that week, and his wife was likely out picking it up. Not that he disliked pizza, but given his diabetes he wasn't supposed to be eating fast food, and as Annie harped on about it so much even *he* had started to take note.

Sighing, he went over to the kettle and switched it on to make a cup of tea whilst he skimmed through the post left on the side. As it came to the boil and he reached into the cupboard for his favourite Arsenal mug – *it was then… then that he heard her unearthly scream.*

THREE

KIRKDALE
CUMBRIA

When Harry had heard that blood-curdling yell he knew without a shadow of a doubt who and where it had come from, and had reached the front door (with Baxter in hot pursuit), just as Annie was frantically trying to put her key in the lock.

"Oh my God Harry get it out... get it OUT!!" she screamed hysterically, arm up her back and flinging herself at him as he opened it. "It's gone down my neck, I can FEEL it!!" When Harry had opened the door, Annie Longbridge was in a permanently growing state of panic, her face, like her body, in a complete contortion. With the correctly guessed pizza now flung in the flower bed, and his wife screaming like a banshee, he'd had to try and restrain her from stripping off right there on the doorstep. *Not being murdered then*, he thought.

Harry manoeuvred her into the house carefully avoiding windmill arms, shooing a concerned Baxter out of the way, and grabbing the pizza box from between the shrubs and the little hooded path lights she'd insisted on buying at Christmas. One by one each layer of clothing was torn off in a frenzied display any tantrum-throwing four-year-old would be proud of, until she stood in the hall in her latest black M&S undies set... as a very small leaf fluttered quietly to the floor...

They ate their re-heated takeaway with a distinct sullen air hanging between them. Harry had operated the oven. It wasn't that Annie didn't know *how* to or wasn't capable of improving, she simply had no interest, and over the years he'd got used to her culinary abortions and knew she was unlikely to ever change. He also knew with Fran Taylor up from Canon Row, and *their* intense shared history resulting in the move to the Lakes seven years ago, his stressed, resentful and now (as she saw it) business failure of a wife was not a happy woman. Harry had hoped tonight was going to be calm and uneventful, thus enabling him to gently introduce the idea he may well be working with Fran once again. So far things weren't quite panning out...

"So love..." he said, a tiny smile hatching... "Apart from the er... leaf incident – how was..."

"You can stop that bloody smirking for a start!" Annie snapped through gritted teeth. *"How the hell did I know it was a sodding leaf??!! I was scared to death Harry you know how I hate... HATE those... those THINGS!"* Harry immediately re-assembled his face into a serious

understanding expression; she still couldn't say the word spider even after all these years, and he had to admit he wasn't entirely a fan himself.

"Yes I know, I shouldn't laugh, horrible things, nasty shock for you love." He cut and dipped a slice of Hawaiian in some ketchup and bit in guiltily... After a moment, and still working on his pizza, he opened the conversation again. "Ummm... *Annie*... you know how... *difficult* I've found it the last two years since retiring, I mean it's been great us having more time together and all that but..."

"You *are* joking Harry??" Annie threw her cutlery down causing Baxter to jump in his sleep with the jangling of metal on china. "We never do *anything* together! Either you're at that damn golf club, no doubt propping up the bar because you never liked the bloody game, or you're pretending to be Andy Murray! Actually scrap that – you gave up the tennis after a month come to think of it, so where *do* you go on a Tuesday now *anyway?*" This wasn't going well, thought Harry, it wasn't going well at all. He began shifting slightly on the uncomfortable new kitchen bar stool, Toni's *'Double Pineapple Special'* sitting like a stone Frisbee in his guts. Baxter, now awake, lifted one eye, and looked at his dad knowingly; it could be good 'lead' news for him if they kept this up much longer.

"Tuesday's changed to swimming. You said it was good exercise remember? I hate that too actually and to be honest..." *now was his chance he thought as he began to clear the plates and move them to the dishwasher...* "I won't have much time to go swimming, or the golf club come to that, because –" he took a deep breath – "I've been asked to go back in Annie, to the job – help out the new D.I. with the Peterson escape." He stood with his back to her and leant heavily on the work surface as he waited for the fallout...

"Seriously?" said Annie, eyes wide in disbelief, then narrowed again in suspicion. "So why can't Joe Whatsisname and that W.P.C. fill him in? They must have been promoted by now, and they worked the *whole case* with you." Harry walked purposefully to the key rack on the wall where Baxter's lead also hung; *the dog was beneath it before he'd even lifted it off the hook.* Harry still had his back to his wife on this side of the kitchen too as he released the bad news...

"It's not a him Annie, it's a—"

"It's her isn't it – *it's Fran bloody Taylor! She's finally followed you up here!*" Harry bent down to clip the lead to an excited Baxter's collar, and as he straightened up again, turned to face his accusing wife. "Nothing ever happened Annie," he said with a sigh. "We were just colleagues, you *know* that – anything else was all in your head." He felt a slight twinge of guilt as he said this, because although it was true, it wasn't through the lack of wanting to that he and Fran hadn't started something. They had just known it would screw things up for them professionally if they had. Both were long-term career coppers, true rank climbers who worked brilliantly together, but there was always a certain frisson between them that many a time had got too damn hot for common sense.

Harry had also exaggerated the request for his help in the new operation. There had so far been no such request; he'd merely had a bite to eat in a local café with some old colleagues. However, he fully intended to be back on it one way or another. He'd always been known as the Magpie in the Job, and as it turned out *Magpies weren't very good at golf.*

Annie's face was thunderous.

'I'm taking Bax out for his evening run, we'll discuss it when I get back,' he stated firmly. Baxter walked down the hall with his master to the sound of the kitchen door slamming behind them followed by the crashing of china plates in the sink. They looked at each other sheepishly as Harry pulled on his coat. Before he was even out of the door, Annie had already reached up to the rack for a bottle of red and a glass, and downed a very large Pinot Noir. Her gaze fell briefly on to the kitchen bin containing the ditched local paper before she looked back at the bottle. *She just knew it was about to start all over again for her too.*

Harry had circuited the park three times. Baxter was ecstatic. He (Harry) was not looking forward to the return trip, and knew his stride would become slower and slower as he got nearer the house. It was at stressful times like these he wished he'd never given up smoking, something else Annie had insisted on with their new 'healthier life' in the *Lakes*. He was considering a fourth lap when his mobile vibrated in his pocket.

"Hey up Baxter, sit for a minute will you?" said Harry, trying to fish the phone from the depths of his wax jacket. "No Bax, nooo… woah… *sit Bax!*" The young dog had seen a walker and furry friend across the park that he recognised, and was now straining at the leash to get to them. Recalling some vague puppy training class he'd attended, Harry took the Lab's head in his hands and made him look at his face. "Bax – SIT!" He emphasised the 'T', pushed the dog's bottom downwards and produced several gravy bone biscuits in the vain hope he would remain in one place long enough for him to take the call. *If* of course it hadn't already gone to answerphone. It had. He checked the number and his heart leaped. It was the station. With one eye on Baxter and the gravy bones diminishing at an alarming rate, he quickly rang directly through to his old office and waited.

"Fran Taylor."

"Fran, it's Harry – you rang."

"Yes – thanks for getting back to me. Harry… there's been a development. God knows how but we think Charlotte Peterson's got of the country. Considering all air and sea ports were covered it's a complete mystery – *and failure on our part.* Look, given our radically reduced numbers, the Chief Super has okayed your return – *temporarily* and just for *this* case." Harry was so bloody happy he was absolutely beaming and could barely speak. He hadn't even had to *ask; they* had finally come to him – *formally*. Even Chief Superintendant Chris Hitchings had accepted the need to get Harry back in – *that* must've hurt he thought grinning. There were times he and the Super hadn't exactly seen eye to eye – both men were pretty stubborn, Harry in particular... Punching the air, he hadn't even noticed Bax had been busy digging a giant hole... "Harry?" Fran questioned. "Are you still there?"

"Yes, yes I'm here, out with the dog and just – *whoaah... damn it!*" One step backwards and he was sitting in the middle of the Lab's hard work, Baxter now leaping all over him and licking his ears – but he didn't care. "Sorry 'bout that – Lab just upended me!" He could hear Fran trying to suppress a laugh on the other end despite the severity of the call. "I'll be in first thing Fran – it'll be good to be back. And – *thanks.*"

"How do you think Annie will take it?" Fran had always known Annie Longbridge had a big downer on her, she also knew it was at Annie's insistence they'd moved to Cumbria whilst she was on holiday that fortnight seven years ago.

"Put it this way," said Harry. "She won't be inviting you to dinner anytime soon." Fran smiled drily on the other end of the phone. She guessed Harry's wife would always be suspicious of them, to be fair with good reason. But Fran hadn't been about to ruin her career at Canon Row back then and nothing had changed since her move to Kirkdale.

"Well we'll just have to make sure she's got nothing to worry about then won't we?" There was silence from the other end. "Harry? I *mean it*." She didn't.

"I'll see you first thing at 7.00 a.m.," he said softly. Fran smiled, warmly this time – she knew he'd say that.

"Meet me for breakfast at Brenda's Buffet," she said teasingly. "I'll have a bacon butty waiting."

Annie Longbridge glanced up at the clock on the lounge wall. Nursing the second bottle of red, a myriad of thoughts ran through her mind. *Why has that damned woman relocated up here? It's been seven years, why now? Why here?* She took a large gulp and drained the glass, immediately refilling it to the top and drinking deeply again. *Just how close **were** you to my husband Fran? Is he telling me the truth or did you in fact steal him from me years ago?* She ran a finger around the rim of the glass as her eyelids began to blink more slowly. Despite feeling stressed over the arrival of her own past adversary, the wine was doing its job. Leaning her head back, Annie was beginning to feel calm, relaxed and comfortable on her favourite sofa. That was until there was a knock at the door. She was brought sharply out of her hazy zone then which always irritated her – *especially when she was sulking…*

"*Forgotten your bloody key again Harry?!*" she yelled from the sofa. "*This is NOT a sodding hotel!*" The knocks continued, this time a bit louder. Resignedly she placed her glass on the table, unfurled her legs and stood up,

27

swaying slightly before wandering into the hall. She saw a shape through the glass door that even after nearly two bottles of red, she couldn't identify as her husband. *Maybe it's one of the new neighbours who moved in last week?* She pondered this hopefully… *Sandy, or maybe Kate? I could do with a bit of company.* And with that thought she brightened up considerably.

That was, until she opened the door.

FOUR

BROOKLYN
NEW YORK

It would never cease to amaze Charlotte how despite the security, it was still possible to slip through passport control at any airport with fake documents, let alone one in the most powerful country in the world. Clearly the people who created hers were going to want a very big pay-off indeed. Good job her Rampton inmate had been so in awe of her; and more importantly, still in contact with some of her very creative family members. Family members who were prepared to wait a long time in return for treble their usual remuneration.

The bank account, credit cards and work permit in her new name of Dr. Carla Preston were obviously also crucial, and as she rolled the trolley case beside her and walked towards the baggage carousel for the rest of her luggage, she thought of the likely character traits of the people who had made all this possible. Although clearly not an angel herself, none the less she shivered slightly and pulled her coat collar up as a cold January blew in through the permanently open exit doors. *The collar adjustment was not entirely down to the season.*

With startling clarity, Carla realised that given the surprisingly delayed pay-off agreement, 'they' would almost certainly not be letting her out of their sight anytime soon. It was then that her brain clicked into gear. *The man on the plane... Had* he been eyeing up the blonde behind her on his walk up the gangway – or was he keeping tabs on his money... o*n her?* She glanced around nervously whilst checking and re-checking the carousel for her bags. *Why did the damn thing take so long?! Surely they should be arriving soon?!* It would be just her luck if they got lost and she'd not only have to keep her eyes peeled for *Mr. Hawk*, she'd be doing it just in the clothes she stood up in. At that moment the two familiar black and red leather cases swung down and around the shoot into view, and Carla retrieved both to reunite them with her small matching wheeler. Having already found a baggage trolley to load all three, with a deep breath she pushed her entire worldly goods out into the wind of a New Year, New York evening.

"Where to ma'am?" anticipated the first guy hanging out the window of the nearest queuing cab in the taxi rank.

"Errr... hold on..." Carla rummaged in her handbag, fished a piece of paper out of its depths, unfolded it and turned it around before bending down to open the rear door as she read out the address given to her by her 'contacts'. "Thirty-five Cranberry St., Brooklyn Heights." She looked up as the driver clocked her luggage and got out to help her. He opened the boot and gesticulated to her bags.

"Ma'am?" Carla nodded and added a thin smile in acknowledgement to let him load the trunk, her head slightly lowered against the wind as she slipped into the rear of the cab. Opening her handbag again, she produced a small make-up mirror and flicking it open checked her face. Would she ever get used to what was looking back at her? Charlotte seemed to have gone forever. *Well – maybe on the surface*, she thought snapping the mirror shut, *never in her heart… or in her soul – if she still had one.*

"How long will it take to get there?" she asked, speaking loudly above the crashing drums of someone she'd never heard of emanating from the radio.

"'Bout twenty minutes give or take depending on traffic." He glanced up in the mirror at his customer. "You here on vacation from the U.K. ma'am?" There was a long silence in the back. "Sorry, I er… just assumed with your accent an all…"

"Something like that," said Carla crisply, her steel-blue gaze lost through the window as the freeway snaked past them and the first few January snowflakes danced beyond the glass.

Manny Berkowitz' concentration was on the highway. He was a good cabby and had made his living for the past thirty years at it. Next to bass fishing and

31

a good barbeque, driving was his favourite thing to do. But now his eyes flipped sporadically up to his rear view mirror that 'held' his passenger, and for no apparent reason he could fathom, felt a distinct and uncomfortable chill despite the heated seats and warm air system. At that exact point Carla's shark-eyed stare had left the Brooklyn skyline and flicked onto cab officer Berkowitz' eyes in the mirror. He dropped his gaze, leaned forward to turn up the radio and put his foot down on the accelerator. This was one fare he wanted delivered in double-quick time with a swift return to the airport – and he wasn't bothered about a tip either…

Gina Rowlands relaxed with a large glass of diet Pepsi in the lounge of her mother and stepfather's luxurious Bay Ridge home. When Gareth's father, Raymond, had died the previous year, it had enabled them to move from a less affluent (although still very nice) area of Brooklyn, to the delights of Narrows Avenue. With George McCarthy having been bought out due to gambling debts, Emily and Gareth Stone were now the sole proprietors of 'McCarthy Stone Publishing', and a serious amount of financial assets to boot.

'The Narrows', as it was affectionately called, was certainly one of the most beautiful areas Gina had ever seen, and Emily and Gareth Stone's residence positively palatial compared with what the twenty-two-year-old had been used to back in the U.K.'s Lake District.

Kirkby-over-Sands, a tiny village outside Kirkdale, and then Kirkdale itself *('not quite a town but bigger than a village')*, had been her home the whole of her life. That was until her mother had turned up out of the blue after twenty years, since her disappearance when Gina was a toddler. Not that Gina was in any way complaining about her upbringing. Her grandmother, Margaret Rowlands, had given her everything she could have wanted until Gina was fourteen, when the old lady's health had deteriorated, necessitating a move to the local nursing home. The following six years Gina had spent living with her best friend Molly Fields and her parents at their pub The Carpenters Arms, which had remained a 'family' home for her to this day. Now though, she and journalist fiancé Andrew Gale were living together, and in New York getting to know her mother better and planning their dream wedding. Emily's explanation of why she'd left Gina in the care of her own mother all those years ago had come tumbling out when she'd returned for Margaret Rowlands' funeral two years before...

Gina gazed over the deep hue in her glass to the flames beyond as she watched them jump around the interior of the huge fireplace. It had been a difficult time those last couple of years. She, Molly and Andrew had found themselves in the middle of a series of gruesome murders in the Lakes, carried out by the village doctor, a psychotic female G.P. called Charlotte Peterson. Gina had actually worked for her as a receptionist, and as if that wasn't enough, during that time she'd nearly died at her hands. Having kidnapped her, Charlotte had gone on to slash the girl's arm with a surgical knife during a terrifying fight on her husband Miles' boat, the *'Babe of the Bay'*, flinging her overboard into the lake hoping she'd drown. Luckily for Gina the river police were on scene to haul her out.

Molly too had almost become a victim of the evil doctor, and it was all part of a recurring nightmare Gina and boyfriend Andrew had worked hard over the last two years to put behind them. She was getting there gradually, and Andrew was her absolute rock, despite his own near-death experience, and difficulty of having to come to terms with a new family tree. He had always known he was adopted, but had discovered that local vagrant, Rose *(the estranged and much younger sister of Gina's grandmother),* was in fact his *real* mother, making him and Gina second cousins. That revelation took a lot of mental unravelling and relationship rebuilding for them both. On top of all this was the craziness that Gina's father was Dr. Miles Peterson, Emily having had an affair with him at the university she, Charlotte and Miles had attended in the 1980s. It was that affair which had launched Charlotte's psychotic mental episodes, although she'd no knowledge of the pregnancy or Gina's connection at the time.

Charlotte and Miles had got engaged at uni, so the betrayal ripped deep, especially as she had been best friends with Emily since childhood. Unbalanced and drowning in anxiety, Charlotte had then threatened her life and that of her mother Margaret, blackmailing her to leave the country and never return. Twenty years later however – *Emily did just that…*

At the time it had frankly all been a terrifying, emotional and confusing mess, and every now and then Gina found the nightmares returning – *like last night.* The fact she'd been rescued by the river police just in time was a miracle in itself, the chances of her completely forgetting the details of the past would be another. Andrew's colleague Rachel had been murdered by Charlotte, as had Jason Flood, brother of journalist Jenny who was also a colleague at *The Kirkdale Courier* where Andrew, Jenny and Rachel had all worked. Charlotte had been caught in the forest above Keeper's Cottage having left Gina to die in the waters across the bay, and had escaped in a power boat across the lake. But the law had prevailed, and now Charlotte Peterson was safely detained in Rampton, a high-security psychiatric hospital, serving a life sentence.

They had nothing to be worried about and everything to look forward to. Andrew had proposed the following year and they'd both been getting to know their mothers. Andrew locally in Kirkdale, Gina through phone calls to New York, Skype, FaceTime and social media, and one previous holiday. So why did she feel uneasy today? Why were the headaches and nightmares returning? *Why wasn't Molly here…?* She swallowed the last of her Pepsi and leaning forwards, placed the glass on the coffee table. Cuddling into the corner cushions, she tucked her legs up and twisted her engagement ring backwards and forwards as she rolled her lips anxiously. Molly should *be* here. She missed her. Molly had… abilities, psychic senses. She might know why these uneasy feelings had started returning. She'd ring her tomorrow and get her to fly out early so she could be included in the wedding preparations – Emily wouldn't mind.

"Gee?" Andrew had stuck his head round the doorway of the lounge. "Your mum and Gareth are suggesting a meal at the River Café on Water Street tonight, you up for that? The snow didn't settle after all, and the weather's pretty good. We've not been there yet – your mum reckons it's a great place. What do you think?" Andrew was looking keen at the prospect of trying another American restaurant. He was enjoying this wedding planning/family bonding holiday, and he also loved eating out. Gina smiled at her fiancé, she knew she was a very lucky girl. Andrew was six foot five of pure gorgeousness… and she wasn't. Not that she wanted to be six foot *anything*, but the gorgeous bit would have been nice. Despite her stunningly thick, wavy auburn hair and the clearest pale complexion, all Gina could see was that she wasn't exactly tall, willowy and traditionally size-eight beautiful – *not like Jenny Flood*. Mind you, Gina wasn't a recovering anorexic either, and she knew Andy loved her to bits. All of her size fourteen wobbly belly and arse bits…

"Yeah tell her that'll be lovely – I'll pop upstairs and get changed in a minute." She unfurled her legs from the softness of the giant black settee, and as she absentmindedly stroked the matching furry cushions thought fondly of 'Poppy dog', a small terrier cross Molly's parents had recently adopted, or rather it was Poppy who'd adopted them. She missed her too, *no chance of a 'Poppy dog' in this house,* she thought wistfully as she got up and walked from the lounge to climb the stairs to change for dinner.

Carla closed the door behind her and leant heavily against it. Her eyes closed with relief. Having slipped out of the U.K. and into the U.S., seemingly without obstruction, she was at last 'home' and dry. After getting some heating going in the house, something to eat, a shower and hopefully a good night's sleep, she could fine tune a little more succinctly *exactly* how she was going to execute her plan.

Pushing herself off the door and leaving her luggage in the hall, she walked purposefully upstairs to find the main bedroom. She knew exactly what she'd be looking for when she got there. The wardrobe concerned was where she'd been told it would be, standing against the main wall opposite the window.

From her bag she produced a black fob with two silver keys, and inserting the larger of the two into the lock of the right-hand door of the wardrobe, turned it and watched it swing open. Her eyes swept the emptiness, empty but for a number of hangers and a set of drawers standing vacant on its floor. Vacant that was, until she saw the red peeping through the long 'dip' of the bottom drawer top. Carla bent down and pulled it open to reveal the blood-red case. She lifted it out and sat on the bed with it front of her. Her heart was thumping a little in anticipation as she slipped the smaller key into the lock to open it. The click snapped sharply into the quiet of the cold room. Carla lifted the lid to reveal a flat black board, and reaching in, felt carefully along the inside until she found them. She pushed the two concealed buttons simultaneously, one either side of the case wall, and the board flipped smartly upwards. Beneath lay thousands of dollars, all in rows, all neatly bound and stacked – all ready and waiting for her needs.

She giggled slightly, *that well-known laugh*, that smile that never quite reached her eyes, and menace hovered heavily in the Brooklyn air as she picked up a wad of notes. *Yes, 'execute' being the operative word* she thought dryly as she flicked the dollars slowly through her fingers and tapped the wad on her chin. But even in that moment, the snigger fell away and the corner of her left eye began to twitch uneasily as was its habit. She chilled. The man on the plane… *would this hunter,* experienced as she was, *eventually become the hunted?*

FIVE

BROOKLYN
NEW YORK

Gina sat with Andrew, Emily and Gareth at one of the window tables overlooking the water. She'd perked up considerably from earlier and was enjoying the whole experience of discovering yet another New York restaurant in the beautiful River Café, although unusually for her, she was not overly hungry.

Sharing normal family time with her mother after all these years apart, and planning her wedding to Andy with Emily alongside, was wonderful. However, looking at the menu she'd just passed to her, she found herself longing for The Carpenters Arms, a *small* portion of Maisie Field's special spicy shepherd's pie and beans… *and home.* As she repeatedly ran her eyes up and down the choices, Andrew glanced over the top of his menu guessing exactly what she was thinking, having already decided on the crab for starters, and a sixteen-ounce chargrilled steak to follow.

"What's it to be then Gee?" he said knowingly, "given your favourite's not there." Gina raised her eyebrows at him in a *'thanks for that'* expression, at the same time wondering what Jenny Flood would choose. *A couple of prawns and a lettuce leaf probably. And she'd leave the prawns.*

"Hmmm… not easy is it…" she said, getting nowhere fast until her mother cut in.

"The organic chicken with mushrooms, pasta and Madeira wine jus *is lovely?*" Emily offered, questioning gently. Gina re-checked it for the fourth time and decided it would be as good a choice as any.

"That'll be fine – thanks Emily." She closed the menu and placed it on the table. They had decided that for her to start using 'mum' after all this time apart, *a lifetime for Gina*, might feel a little odd, at least at first. Of course there had been all the phone calls, Skype and FaceTime over the previous two years, but even so. "I'll give the starters a miss too if that's okay?" Gina wrinkled her nose slightly and raised her eyes in an unsure expression. Her mother smiled and leant over to squeeze her arm.

"Yes of *course* darling, I usually do too actually," she whispered as the waiter reached over to place a ridiculously expensive bottle of rosé and four glasses on the table, only pouring after Gareth had tasted it first. It was fantastic to have her daughter back in her life even if the reasons as to how that had come about *were* pretty horrendous. But then an awful lot of that was down to herself and Jenny, *she was well aware of that.*

Whilst Gina and Emily had been deciding on their choices, Gareth and Andrew, both steak men and easily satisfied, were talking crime thrillers in all their various guises. Andrew never read anything else, and publishing crime fiction was Gareth's business.

As Emily and Gina sipped their wine and discussed designer bridal gowns, Emily couldn't help thinking how amazing it was that they were all so easy with each other. She never thought she'd see the day when her daughter was back in her life, making preparations for her wedding, and all in a happy family setting. But she also knew it had come at a cost. Over the evening as they ate their meals, laughed together and toasted Andrew and Gina's engagement for about the fifth time that holiday, Emily couldn't help but recall just exactly what had happened two years ago. How she and Jenny had conspired together across the Atlantic, the previous three years it had taken Emily to persuade the young reporter to work with her, plotting in the tightest detail, making absolutely sure without a shadow of doubt that they would bring down their shared enemy. *Charlotte Peterson.*

Gina had gone to the ladies' for the third time since arriving. It hadn't gone unnoticed by her mother, nor the fact that her appetite seemed a little off and she was barely drinking. Just for a few minutes as Andrew and Gareth swapped murder plots by classic and contemporary authors, Emily topped up her glass and lost herself in the swirl of the river through perfectly polished windows…

It was easy to drift back to her meeting with Jenny in 2015 at an international book fair in Carlisle. Gareth had been attending it in his capacity as an overseas publicist promoting several of McCarthy Stone's authors, and she had accompanied him to network and do a bit of talent spotting – *it was also home territory*… Jenny Flood had been a junior reporter back then, shadowing a colleague working for a national newspaper.

Three years prior, Jenny had been dumped by Miles, and the two women had met in the ladies' rest room at the venue, unaware of their shared history. Eyes glazed, Emily recalled how she'd found Jenny in tears that day trying to save her make-up in the mirror…

CARLISLE
CUMBRIA U.K. 2015

"Hey… heyyyy… sweety… come on now, it can't be that bad. Can I help? You're not hurt in any way are you?" The raven-haired twenty-something had stopped dabbing at her eyes with a mascara-soaked tissue and begun to flush with embarrassment. Emily had noticed how overly slim, how long her legs were and just how utterly stunning she was, despite the mess her face was in.

42

"No, no… I'm… I'm not hurt – thank you." She had smiled weakly as she'd searched through her bag for various items to try and repair her make-up.

"Is there anything I can do to help – fetch someone, a friend, get you some water?" Emily had offered kindly. She'd been genuinely concerned. Jenny wasn't much older than her own daughter would be, what's more she knew Gina wasn't living that far from Carlisle, yet she'd never be able to see her. This fact alone had made her want to help this young girl, who although obviously a professional (she was dressed impeccably and wearing a Guardian press badge), seemed so young, desperate and alone. "My guess is it's a man thing then," she'd stated candidly, as she leant back on her heels and crossed her arms. "It usually is – we've all been there." Jenny had looked up at her in the mirror, threatening tears had begun to well up behind newly applied mascara, and her bottom lip had wobbled visibly… Then the whole story about her affair with Miles Peterson had come out in bits and pieces, slotted in between other rest room users coming and going.

"Three years we were together, three!" Jenny had steamed. "Yes I know it all finished several years ago, and I should be over him… but I'm not, and I know he was married but he wasn't happy. Miles always said I was the only one for him and he should never have married Charlotte, but he had to consider their medical careers, their future. It would be too difficult to disentangle himself from the practice. Medical careers?! Yeah right! He stayed with her because her parents are million—"

43

She had stopped dead then, turned back to the mirror and leant heavily on the sink when a couple of women had come in to use the loos. She and Jenny had stood around awkwardly in silence, waiting until the room was empty again. As soon as they were alone she'd carried on… *"Every now and again I just… fall apart, especially if I see someone who looks like him. Well today I did – just now, which is why…"* Suddenly she'd tailed off. *But at the mention of Charlotte's name Emily had stiffened, and the look on her face had clearly intrigued the younger woman because Jenny had stopped gabbling, narrowed her eyes and had begun to look distinctly quizzical. "What? Why are you looking at me like that?"*

Once Emily had established that Jenny's Miles was HER Miles, she had quickly related her own story. How she and Charlotte had been best friends at high school, how they'd both met Miles at uni; Charlotte and Miles' relationship leading to their early engagement… and Emily's own affair with him leading to a pregnancy Charlotte had no knowledge of. But the betrayal of that affair was enough to turn her mind into a very dark and twisted place – one nobody should ever live to visit… (And let's face it – several didn't.)

"Oh my God!" Jenny had exclaimed. *"What are the chances of that?! I mean… you live in the U.S. How——?"* Emily had filled her in on her own details…

"After Charlotte had found out about me and Miles the threats kept coming. Over and over. In the end, after a couple of years, it got so bad she basically forced me to leave

the U.K. Charlotte seemed beyond psychotic by then and I was scared. I'd had Miles' baby a few months after we'd left uni – Gina was only two when I left her with my mother. Neither Miles nor Charlotte ever knew about her. I told my mum the father was a fairground lad who'd quickly moved on. I could never have coped with a baby on my own in a strange country, and Charlotte swore to me she'd kill both my mother and myself if I didn't leave. So I flew to New York and eventually made a life for myself there. I lost my daughter because of her…"

Emily could still see Jenny's face, mouth open so wide she thought she'd get lockjaw. They had swapped contact cards and kept in touch by phone and social media over the following three years. It had taken that long to persuade Jenny to help her with a plot to send Charlotte over the edge, just enough to commit a serious crime to put her away for a decade or so. Emily had harboured her grudge for over twenty years; *she'd lost her daughter because of Charlotte Peterson and she'd wanted revenge for a very long time.* Jenny however, although heartbroken at losing Miles, knew deep down that she was in the wrong for seeing a married man. It had taken a great deal of cajoling to get her to go along with the whole crazy plan of two years ago. However, even Emily couldn't have envisaged the trail of ghastly murders that had finally led to Charlotte's confinement for much longer than even she could have hoped. But there was also the death of Jenny's brother, which had nearly killed her. It was the reason Emily had invited her out to New York, bought her an apartment and given her the events manager job at McCarthy Stone. She was quite good at it too, despite the anorexia that had started with Miles and escalated with losing her brother at Charlotte's…

"… and I was wondering if we could go dress shopping tomorrow. Emily. *Emily?*"

"Em?" prompted Gareth. "Gina's talking about wedding prep stuff."

"Oh… sor… sorry sweetheart… *sorry.* I was miles away! Yes, yes of *course* that would be lovely! We can grab some lunch at my favourite little Mexican place too, just the two of us." She said smiling as she leant over to give her an extended hug. She was pretty sure she knew exactly the reason why her daughter was spending so much time in the loo, reducing her alcohol intake and off her food. And absolutely *certain…* that she would make *damn* sure, no one and nobody would *ever* hurt either of them.

The following morning Carla awoke and just for a moment forgot where she was. The room was still cold. She pulled the duvet more tightly around her, and in the unfamiliar darkness began to plan. Today would be one of understanding and setting the heating system, filling the fridge, buying some more clothes and generally settling in. But first… *first she would check online for current vacancies at the local hospitals.* She needed to weave herself into Brooklyn life, make some general enquiries – *gain access to drugs…*

There was something else she was going to have to do as well, or rather *not* do, and that was not to wear any make-up whatsoever. She would also start using the non-prescription glasses she'd been given by the mobile hairdresser. Hideous of course, and a complete anathema to her, but she *had* to create an image as far removed from Charlotte Peterson as she possibly could. Black rimmed and round framed, they perfectly matched the radical black pixie crop created for her whilst hiding up in the London flat. One day… when all this difficult business was behind her, she would move on to somewhere they couldn't find her, go back to being beautiful – being elegant, *being Charlotte*. For now though she needed to not raise any alarms, to truly live as the quiet, plain Dr. Carla Preston, a single, reserved, hard-working book fan – with absolutely no social life. She would play her part to perfection. *She would ensure Emily and Jenny were sent to the very depths of hell.*

SIX

KIRKDALE
CUMBRIA

"Hello Mum."

After thirty-two years, Annie Longbridge's biggest dream (and biggest nightmare) had finally materialised... *and was now standing on her doorstep.* The sudden realisation on opening the door that it was neither of her two new neighbours, Sandy Howard or Kate Simms, sobered Annie up faster than any amount of coffee could have possibly done.

*"M... **Michael?**"* she uttered incredulously, eyes wide in disbelief. By now she was clutching the frame and had swapped her wine flush of a few minutes earlier for a distinctly grey pallor.

"Yes – yes, I'm... I'm sorry, I shouldn't have just blurted it out like that. It's just – I've been looking for you... for so *long!* Can I come in... can we talk, please, just for a little while. *Please?*" He looked anxious, desperate, pleading, but Annie's head was spinning.

With the past, with visions of a school disco, the banging of the music, the lane behind the hall… *the swaggering pushy waste of DNA that was Kenny Drew…*

Michael turned to look over his shoulder, following the furtive and rapid eye movement of the woman in front of him.

"You can't stay. *Not now*," said Annie urgently. "My husband's due back any minute – he doesn't… nobody knows. *"*

In some sort of weird dreamy re-run, she could smell Kenny's 'Paco Rabanne' aftershave – feel his eager hands all over her, feel tears spilling down her cheeks, the struggle as he tore at her tights, the beer on his breath, the flint wall jutting in her back… and she could hear herself pleading with him, begging him to stop… And yet, growing his child in her womb for nine months (thirty-five weeks and two days to be exact) meant she had bonded with an innocent. A beautiful baby boy her strict Presbyterian parents had forced her to have and then give up for adoption. The only child she would ever carry because of the fibroids that had developed ten years later…

She wiped her cheeks with the back of her hand, grabbed a notepad and pen from the hall table and passed it to him. "Here – write your mobile number down. Quickly, I'll – I'll call you tomorrow." Michael scribbled the number down as she looked agitatedly over his shoulder to the street again, and then passed it back. Annie studied her 'son' as she bit her lip nervously, if he *was* her son she would need proof. *A little of the*

'Job' had rubbed off on her over the years. "Go now," she said tears re-brimming. "Go – *please*, I'll call you in the morning." Michael dipped his head in acceptance, now appearing more than a little worried that he'd seriously upset her.

"Thank you. Are you… okay?" Annie dropped her eyes. "I'm staying at a local B&B," he continued quickly. "I'll hear from you tomorrow then – *yes?* I'm *so* sorry I – are you *sure* you'll be okay?"

"Yes." She glanced up the road again. "Now you really *must go*." Annie was getting increasingly anxious now. All thoughts of Fran Taylor had passed into insignificance in comparison with this. This magnitude of a strange man turning up late in the evening claiming to be her son, and Harry's imminent return from the park with Baxter – it had completely erased the earlier row from her mind. *For now, Fran Taylor was off the hook.*

As he turned the corner into his road with a very happy Labrador, Harry's steps began to slow. Five laps of the park, although not a huge area, had still taken its toll on an overweight, out-of-condition, retired copper. Not that this was the main reason for him slowing down. He felt like his head was in two places at once. On the one hand he was deliriously happy to be officially back in the job, albeit temporarily, and on the other… on the other *there was Annie.* If only she could find something to occupy her mind, really get stuck into, maybe she wouldn't be so obsessive about Fran. It was a damn shame about Chique going to the wall. He made a mental note to be more sympathetic about that, and to get her some flowers the next day. Annie had always liked flowers – just so long as she didn't have to be involved in planting them.

He reached the house and as he put his key in the door, realised on turning it, it was already unlocked. Strange, he could've sworn he'd locked it. Annie wouldn't have gone out again that night, not if as he'd suspected she'd had a date with a bottle of red anyway. Her drinking habit had been creeping up the scale a bit too much since she'd lost the business, something else he'd have to keep an eye on.

Once in the hall he unclipped Baxter's lead and let him run on ahead of him into the kitchen for a drink whilst he took off his coat and shoes. He didn't normally remember to take off his shoes and was constantly getting criticised for it, but tonight he was treading lightly… *literally.*

It seemed a bit quiet. No TV or music playing. His wife usually had one or the other going and there was a new series of *'Vera'* on – she always watched that. He popped his head round the lounge door to see the correctly guessed wine bottle and glass on the table, then sighed as he saw the second bottle on the floor. *But no Annie.* He checked his watch, 9.00 p.m., maybe she'd gone up already. Harry checked the kitchen, and once he saw she wasn't there either, gave Baxter his 'night night biscuit', a pat on the head and turned out the light. He rolled his eyes, *if his old squad could see him now they'd rib him rotten.*

Upstairs on the landing he saw the light under the closed bedroom door and found himself hesitating before he opened it, he really didn't want another showdown before turning in. The floorboard creaked as he reached for the handle… and instantly the light went out. Harry let his hand fall to his side and turning went across the landing to one of the spare rooms. *Probably just as well,* he thought, *I need an early shut-eye and a good night's kip – back to an early start tomorrow.* His heart sang.

Annie Longbridge waited nervously in the 'nook' section of the Carpenters Arms pub. It wasn't exactly secluded, but being central there were no windows and it had a wall around most of it, shielding her from the front door. She had already bought herself a large glass of red.

After Harry had left for the station at 6.30 a.m. that morning, surprised by her change in demeanour *(basically no shouting, scowling or banging things about),* she had rung the mobile number Michael had given her and arranged to meet him in the Carpenters at noon. He was staying close by so it was ideal, for him at least, she just hoped the landlord's daughter didn't recognise her. According to Harry, Molly Fields was very intuitive, even had a touch of the psychic about her, and despite it being the last thing he'd wanted to admit, she'd proved to be quite a help on the Charlotte Peterson case two years ago. Nearly lost her life at Charlotte's hands in the process, but Annie could see her now laughing and joking with the customers as she brought out her mother's famous spicy shepherd's pie a few tables away. She definitely seemed happy, confident and well over her near-death experience. Annie wondered if *she* had flashbacks.

"Mrs. Longbridge?" She looked up to see Michael standing in front of her with a pint in his hand.

"Hi – ermm…" She waved at the chair opposite her for him to sit down.

"I feel I must say again, how *very* sorry I am for the way I announced myself last night, I should've known better."

"Forget it – it's… done," said Annie, taking in his facial features properly for the first time, now she wasn't under the imminent threat of Harry turning up.

"You look like him – your dad." *Pity, she thought.*

"Do I?" He sounded pleased. *He wouldn't be if he knew what he was like, she thought dryly.* "I tried to find him, thought I was close once, but it turned out to be another Kenneth Drew, same date of birth and area, and… well, London's a big place isn't it. I guess it's not such an uncommon surname either." Annie played with a beer mat.

"I'm sorry to have to ask you this but—" Michael anticipated her question.

"It's okay, yes, yes I have it here." He reached into his inside jacket pocket, pulled out a brown envelope and slid it across the table. Annie looked at it, threw back a large mouthful of wine and breathed in deeply. She picked up the envelope with trembling hands, pulled out the contents and unfolded it. And there it was – in all its non-glory…

Name & Surname: Michael Liam McMahon
Sex: Male
Date & Place of Birth: Twenty-eighth September 1988
Whitstable & Tankerton Hospital, Kent
Father: Unknown
Mother: Andrea Mary Frances McMahon
Place of Birth: Penge, London
Occupation: Unemployed.

It was all there, and tears began to prick behind her lids as she remembered all the rows, the accusations, the recriminations, the shame… *and all the unending heartache.* She had never told anyone what Kenny Drew had done that night, and had remained tight-lipped every time her parents tried to force her to reveal the father's name. In the end she'd been shipped off to an aunt's in Kent to see out her labour and have her baby adopted, ironically by a couple back in London. She would never forget the salty 'woody' smell of the Whitstable docks and the fishing boats bobbing on the water. She had hated boatyards and the smell of raw fish ever since.

Annie re-folded the birth certificate, slid it back into the envelope and handed it back to him. She said nothing.

"What now?" he said quietly. "Do you want to get to know me or do you want me to walk away? I'll understand if it's all too much." He was gripping his beer glass like his life depended on her only giving him one answer. The one she knew he wanted. Right at that moment Annie didn't feel he would understand anything at all – and why should he? He must have felt, *still feel* that she'd given him up, abandoned him to strangers, although given her age... *surely* he wouldn't resent her – *would he?*

"Michael, you must have questions for me. Have your parents told you anything, anything at all?"

"Not a lot – just that you were only sixteen or seventeen and your parents were very religious, so anti–abortion, but wouldn't let you keep me either. I don't blame you if that's what you're thinking." *It wasn't. Well it was a bit. Stop lying to yourself Annie, of course it was, but how could you have kept him – how? Your parents refused to allow it, wouldn't support you, it had all been a totally impossible situation.*

"Were you happy with them? Did they give you a good childhood?" she asked. Somehow it seemed even more important *now* than it was back then that everything had been done for the best. She lifted her glass up to drain it when the blow came...

"Actually... no they didn't." Annie choked and coughed a little as her wine went down the wrong way. Putting the glass down she looked at him searchingly.

"But… but surely they *loved* you, *wanted* you? They wouldn't have adopted you otherwise!"

"Probably – in the beginning, I don't know. All I remember is that Dad never paid me much attention, always away on business somewhere, quite often abroad. He was a bit secretive about it to be honest, I learnt to stop asking. My mum drank – *a lot*. It wasn't great…"

Annie now felt guiltier than ever and twice as uncomfortable. Like Harry, she also now felt she was in two places at once. On the one hand this was her only chance at being a parent (the phrase 'chance at motherhood' felt odd considering his age – and hers), and she was longing to embrace him, bring him into her life. On the other… every time she looked at him she was back in that lane, *her shoulders scraped by jutting flint…*

They agreed to leave it a few days for her to think things over, and also for Michael to leave ten minutes ahead of her so they weren't seen leaving together. In theory it shouldn't have mattered, she wasn't having an affair for heaven's sake, but it was a small town and she wasn't prepared for even the most innocent of questions yet. At that thought Annie glanced up at the bar and noticed Molly Fields drying a glass, whilst looking over at her table… it was then a text came through on her phone. It was Harry.

Annie, can you meet me at Café Calisé for a quick lunch? I have something to tell you. H.

Annie glared at the screen for a few seconds before replying that she'd leave home in ten minutes and see him in half an hour. *This was the official 'back to work'* chat wrapped up in a bowl of cheap Italian pasta then. She sat fuming looking at her watch. Still five minutes to wait before she could leave.

Outside in a discreetly chosen parking bay, Michael McMahon *(now Michael Morton)* sat low in his car with one eye on the pub entrance. He opened his mobile, brought up the name and tapped the phone icon. It connected immediately and the contact picked up…

"It's me. Yep – she swallowed it… *hook, line and sinker.*"

SEVEN

KIRKDALE
CUMBRIA

Harry had run over in his head a million times how he was going to explain to Annie he was back on the Charlotte Peterson case *again* – and full time. He'd even driven the long way round to Café Calisé to give him time to think of some way to soften the blow. But that wasn't even the main event. It was likely the Peterson woman had skipped the country – and when they found out where to, he and Fran Taylor would be on the next flight out to bring her back.

Annie Longbridge wasn't a stupid woman in fact she was pretty astute. As she waited, now sipping coffee in place of wine, for her (as usual) annoyingly late husband, she churned over in her mind everything that had occurred with Michael since the previous evening. If Harry was going to be back on a case, maybe it could work to her advantage. With the demise of Chique she would no longer be going to work every day, Harry would be busy sleuthing, and it would mean she could get to see her son, get to know him a bit. At the end of that thought Harry appeared round the door of the café and she noticed he was looking suitably nervous. He ordered himself a tea and his second bacon roll of the day *(not as good as Bella's Buffet but considering it was a pasta place...),* and sat down opposite his wife. Annie made a show of looking at her watch and then back at him.

"Did you want me to get you any—"

"You said lunch – a spag bol would be nice," she interrupted pointedly at his afterthought. Harry got up, went to the food bar and added her meal to his ticket and sat down again.

"Annie..."

"It's okay Harry, no need to make a meal of it, you're officially back in the Job, on the Peterson case number two, and you're working with your favourite Scottish detective. So what's new? You were determined to achieve it and now you have – *congratulations.*" She took a gulp of her cappuccino, banged it back down on the saucer and looked out of the window. The girl on the till looked up worriedly from behind the counter whilst Harry shifted uncomfortably in his chair, and then leant back so the waitress could put his order on the table. She glanced at his companion and back to the till girl – both staff hoping a domestic wasn't about to kick off. Harry thanked her edgily...

"It's a bit more than that love, and can you please keep your voice *down*." On hearing this Annie Longbridge turned back to look at her husband and narrowed her eyes slightly.

"Go on." She was all ears now.

"We think Charlotte Peterson has managed to get out of the country after being sprung during a day release for her mother's funeral. Appears she's literally disappeared off the face of the earth – well the U.K. anyway. This is pretty embarrassing for us if nothing else, even the Met. can't find her. Once we get any leads as to where she might be…" Harry bottled the next bit by taking a large bite out of his roll whilst also managing to have the good grace to look sheepish. Annie waited, her face giving an impression of patience, her brain on the other hand racing like a computer programme on speed. Harry swallowed – *several times after the mouthful had gone down.*

"We – that is to say, myself and…"

"Let me finish it for you," said Annie, *all computer cogs in her brain now clicked firmly into place.* "You and the Scot are flying off into the sunset together to hunt down and bring back the big bad witch of the Lakes." *She* now leant back for the nervous waitress to put a plate of spaghetti bolognese in front of her.

"That about sums it up – yes," said Harry, relieved that she'd said it for him, not that it really made much difference. Annie just stared at him. If it wouldn't have been a waste of her favourite dish, *albeit not cooked by Gino D'Acampo*, she would have tipped the whole bloody lot over his head. Instead she picked up her fork and started twirling spaghetti.

"Fine," she quipped. And to Harry's complete surprise, Annie simply began to eat.

BROOKLYN & MANHATTAN
NEW YORK

It was her first morning in Brooklyn and Carla had a lot to do. She'd found the laptop in one of the other bedrooms and immediately googled the local hospitals. Once she'd ascertained where they all were, and what they had available, she applied to Bellevue on 1st Avenue. Luckily for her, she'd discovered they were very short staffed when phoning through to check vacancies were still current. In the trauma dept. (A&E), it was due to a surge in the need for maternity cover, a high level of sickness from a particularly virulent bug generally, and a couple of senior doctors who'd gone long-term sick with stress. In addition they'd begun their 'Plant Based Lifestyle Medicine Programme' the previous autumn for patients who were interested, and were looking for more clinical staff to join their new natural diet health centre. At home, in Carla's experience, skills-gap numbers at that level meant CVs mightn't be quite so vigorously followed up given the staff depletion – particularly in winter. *It would be extremely convenient if that was also the case in New York.* She had thanked the H.R. representative and said she would complete the application form on line as per their website instructions.

Thankfully, a false work visa had also been obtained and supplied by her 'benefactors'. This wasn't a strictly accurate description of the secret group supplying her with fake papers, bank accounts, credit, cash and temporary accommodation. She was seriously in debt to them and would need to repay every penny. Exactly how, she wasn't quite sure yet considering her parents' sizeable inheritance had been immediately frozen, along with her real bank accounts and all other assets following her incarceration at Rampton. She had after all been found guilty of six murders and three attempted murders. Until she could think of a better name though, *benefactors* would have to do. At least she had enough cash available to use cabs everywhere, every need and convenience had been thought of – *'they'* were obviously highly experienced in their line of work. Her Rampton inmate *(well, ex-inmate)* was certainly a good contact to have, which reminded her – *she* would need paying off as well.

As she picked up her bag and coat to go into town for milk, her favourite muesli and a few fresh groceries, she hoped it wouldn't be long before she heard back with an interview date. If she didn't pull this off it was going to make things very difficult indeed. *Difficult – but not impossible.*

A trip into Manhattan for a selection of less glamorous clothes to embed her new *'plain Jane'* look was also on the cards. Well no time like the present, she would need a basic but smart outfit for her Bellevue interview anyway.

Gina had just thrown up. She was indeed pregnant and couldn't face the Mexican restaurant Emily had mentioned at the River Café the night before. She and Andy were ecstatic about the baby, although Gina hoped she wouldn't be showing in her wedding dress. Right now she just wanted to get her best friend Molly Fields out to New York earlier than planned, she'd not really been in touch since leaving the U.K. they'd been so busy. Since Gina was fourteen she'd lived with Molly and her parents following her grandmother's retirement to a nursing home, and Molly was like a sister to her. She didn't know if it was the hormones, but much as she was happy about carrying a new life inside her, she was equally afraid of it, *just wasn't quite sure why.*

Sitting on the bed she checked her watch then scrolled to her friend's name on her mobile. It would be around lunchtime in the U.K., she'd probably be working the bar as usual. Seeing Gina's photo flash up on her phone screen, Molly answered quickly, excited to hear from her...

"*Gee?* How *are* you, *how's* New York, *how's* Andy, how's *everything, have you been everywhere yet?!*" she joked, laughing and walking as she went. "Hold on I'm just leaving my Taekwondo class, it's noisy in here – the second class is coming in now." After she'd nearly lost her life at the hands of Charlotte Peterson two years before, Molly had at first taken up self-defence, but quite quickly moved on to the martial arts discipline. She had made good progress in the last two years and she'd also promised herself she would eventually reach the top 'belt'.

"Molly – are you *there?*" said Gina.

"Yes, yeah here now sorry 'bout that, just needed to get out of the leisure centre, it's so loud and echoey. Walking back to the car now – *is everything okay?*"

"Yes all good – I think. Look Molls, could you come out early? Weeks before the wedding I mean, I miss you and… well… Andy and I, I'm… *you're going to be an aunty!*" Molly nearly dropped the phone in shock as she opened the car door and squealed with surprise, absolutely thrilled for them both. The three of them had gone through so much together, they were all extremely close and anything that happened to any of them now they shared as family.

"Oh – my – God Gee – that's just… that's *fantastic!!* I'm SO thrilled for you, for *both* of you! And yes of *course* I can come out early – *try and stop me!*" She slung her kit into the back of the car and slid into the driver's seat. "Mum and Dad will be absolutely over the moon too, they can get some temp bar staff in to help – don't worry it'll be *fine!*"

The two girls chatted excitedly until Gina had to go down for breakfast, although Molly still sensed something was just a tiny bit off with her friend. She couldn't put her finger on it and she didn't mention it, but she was usually right about her gut feelings and there was definitely something. Molly had never been pregnant so she supposed it could just be Gina's dippy hormones, all the same she felt a need to get out to New York as soon as possible, and within a few days she'd booked her flight, packed and was on her way.

Over breakfast Andy and Gina had shared their baby news with Emily and Gareth, Emily exclaimed excitedly that she *knew* something was up at dinner the night before, with all Gina's loo trips, barely drinking and having difficulty in choosing what to eat. She hugged her daughter close whilst Gareth congratulated them both, awkwardly half-patted Andy on the back and shook his hand, then said he really should get off to work as he had an early meeting. Emily had booked the day off to go dress shopping with Gina, who'd decided to give her mother's favourite little Mexican place a miss. Her stomach would never have coped with the spicy food and she needed something smaller and lighter at lunchtime.

"I'll take you to Honey's," she breezed. "Honey makes *the* best cakes in the entire *world!*" Gina laughed; Emily certainly loved her cakes, now she knew where she, Gina, got it from.

And so it was that as they were happily being mother and daughter, laughing together and looking at bridal magazines whilst enjoying two of 'the world's best cakes' in a window seat of Honey's... Gina saw a woman on the street outside she thought she recognised. A woman who was looking in, a woman who was now staring directly *at* them, *a woman whose smile did not reach her eyes...*

EIGHT

BROOKLYN
NEW YORK

Gina kept seeing the woman outside Honey's inside her head. For the life of her she couldn't remember where she knew her from or why, and there was something not quite *right* about what she was remembering anyway. Even that sounded weird. All the way on the drive back to the house she was begging her baby hormones to let her brain work properly. She still hadn't said anything to Emily, who'd been sitting with her back to where the woman had been standing outside the window, but now she desperately wanted to see Andrew to tell him. She wasn't quite sure how she was going to explain what she was feeling, about what or who she'd actually *seen*, but she needed to share it with him – she knew he'd understand.

Emily had dropped her off at home at the 'Narrows' in Bay Ridge, and said she'd be back in a couple of hours as she wanted to pop in on a friend. Gina walked up the first set of red brick steps between the two stone pillars and black hand-railings, then on up the path to the second set below the square-panelled front door. The beauty of this ten-bedroomed, cream-painted and red-brick house with its landscaped front and rear gardens, red shutter-dressed windows and roof-capped skylights, never failed to deliver every time she returned. She couldn't say every time she came home – home was Cumbria and the Lakes, *home was most definitely Kirkdale.*

She found Andrew in the lounge with a James Patterson crime thriller. Andy never went anywhere without a really good read.

"Andy, something really odd happened in town today," she said, taking off her coat, and laying it across the arm of a chair. "I'm not even sure *what* really, whether I'm imagining things, but it felt kind of… well… *weird.*" He put his book on the table and held an arm out for her to come and sit down, giving her a kiss on the cheek as she sunk into the cushions beside him.

"*Really?* Tell me," he said, surprised.

"Well we were having coffee and cakes in that little shop Emily said she'd take me to today, you know Honey's?" He nodded. "We sat in a window seat and Emily had her back to this… well, strange *person* who was looking in at us through the window."

"*Looking* at you? Why? Why would anybody *do* that?" answered Andrew. "Are you *sure* they weren't just looking at a menu *on* the window?"

"No, it was a woman, and she was definitely looking at *us* and in a sort of… *pointed* way. It was really spooky

Andy, and I know it sounds ridiculous, but I felt a bit, well... *threatened.*" Andrew felt a slight chill shoot across the back of his neck. He brought his hand up to his mouth and started to pull on it, a nervy thing he'd started to do since that summer...

"I'm sure it was nothing Gina – just some sad lonely woman looking through the window..." he lied – *and he never called her Gina unless he was anxious or annoyed about something.* "What did she look like, this... *stranger?*"

"Fairly ordinary really," said Gina, kicking off her shoes, tucking her legs up on the sofa and leaning against his shoulder. "Short dark hair, glasses, plainly dressed, nothing special. It was just the way she was smiling at me – sort of *not* smiling at the same—" She twisted her head round suddenly to look at him then, eyes and mouth both open wide, realisation dawning... It came out in a rush. "*Oh my God Andy it couldn't have been! Andy, please say it couldn't have been her!*" She was shaking now – he pulled her closer and kissed her temple. He couldn't see how it *could* have been Charlotte, for heaven's sake the woman was locked up in a U.K. psychiatric hospital, and by Gina's own description didn't sound remotely like her... *except... Except for one thing. Her trademark. Her lead-eyed, dead-eyed trademark. The shark smile – nobody 'smiled' like Charlotte.*

"Forget it sweetheart – it was just an odd woman in New York having an 'off day'. They sent Charlotte Peterson to Rampton remember? She's safely locked up." He kissed her head again and rubbed his hand comfortingly up and down her arm as he stared ahead. *Maybe he should ring Harry,* he thought. *Maybe he'd heard something; maybe things weren't quite so secure after all…*

The next few days Gina wasn't feeling a hundred percent, so kept her diet light (she'd been having grapefruit cravings anyway), and stayed indoors whilst Emily went back into work with Gareth. Andrew had done a quick internet search on his phone to be met with a front page *Telegraph* headline from before Christmas; *'Chiller Killer Still At Large'.* He and Gina had come out to the U.S.A. well before the holiday season. Reading on, it looked like Charlotte had escaped around the same time, *or been sprung en route to her mother's funeral judging by the article.* They must've just missed it happening and been busy settling in and getting to know Emily and Gareth by then.

Andrew decided not to mention anything to Gina for the time being, especially with the baby news on top of the wedding preparations. He'd be glad when Molly arrived from the U.K. though – she'd be good for Gina, and with two years of Taekwondo practice under her belt, they may well need her. To have the three of them back together would be great – he just wished their celebrations weren't in the shadow of a possible psycho on the run – especially as she'd already tried to kill all three of them two years ago…

It was amazingly fortunate to have already found one major target already, *plus* the daughter – *always a bonus given she was the result of her ex-husband's betrayal and escaped the first time.* However, waiting day after floor-pacing day to hear about a job interview for the hospital was becoming increasingly stressful.

Carla had tried hard to give up smoking as part of her new clean, quiet image – *really* hard. But now she was agitated, and her eye had begun twitching. *It was always bad news when her eye began twitching.* She had nothing to calm her down till she got some drug access, and silly mistakes were always made when she became tense… *and twitchy.* Thus Carla was lighting up one cigarette after the other, consuming endless cups of black coffee, and repeatedly checking the blank inbox on the laptop.

It was three days later as she stood in the shower that she heard the ping. The laptop lay on the bathroom floor – *she nearly landed on it as she grabbed a towel and leapt out of the cubicle.* And there it was.

Gail Hanson:- gail.hanson@bellevuehosp.org
Fri 01/02/20

Dear Dr. Preston,

Thank you for submitting your application for one of our available medical positions at Bellevue. Whilst I appreciate you have practiced as an independent physician in the U.K. for the last seventeen years, unfortunately the B.M.A. qualifications differ from here in the U.S. There is a specific training, set of examinations and internship that has to be followed and undertaken prior to employment, either as an independent or hospital physician.

I'm sorry to have to disappoint you on this occasion and thank you for your interest in a position at Bellevue.

Yours sincerely,

Gail Hanson – Manager H.R. Bellevue Hospital

Carla stared at the screen in confused disbelief. This quickly turned to anger – *then cold, itching rage. How could she have not known this – this **ridiculous** rule? But why should she? It hadn't applied to a friend who'd spent a year in Australia.* Breathing slowly now… evenly, she sat eyes glazed… narrowed, and with one finger depressed the lid slowly until the machine's light extinguished. Leaning back against the shower glass Carla stared hard at the ceiling, only one thought in her head. *I must get inside that hospital.*

Gina threw herself into Molly's arms. She and Andrew had gone to the airport the following day to pick her up and they were now all together in JFK's arrivals hall.

"Molly it's *so* good to see you!" exclaimed Gina. "It feels like six *months* not six *weeks!*" Her friend hugged her back and Andrew put his arms round them both giving Molly a kiss on the cheek.

"Good to see you Molls," he said warmly. "You've got quite a bit to catch up on, hasn't she Gee?" Gina grinned.

"I told her about the baby on the phone Andy – sorry I just couldn't wait." Andrew rolled his eyes in mock annoyance.

"I should've guessed! Wonderful news though isn't it!"

"I'm ecstatic!" Molly replied, eyes like saucers. "Can't wait to be an aunty, I'll have her doing flying side-kicks by the time she's three!"

"How do you know it's definitely going to be a girl then?" said Gina teasingly.

"Gee – you *know* how I know…" replied Molly tapping her nose and laughing.

Gina and Andy could practically envisage their prospective daughter's little legs flying out at all angles, Andrew's cat Missy (now also Gina's cat) leaping up and away to safety somewhere. In reality, neither of them knew just how good Molly *actually* was.

The two girls walked arm-in-arm through the large hall, Gina asking for news of home, the pub and how Molly's parents were keeping, Molly asking Gina about morning sickness, cravings and baby names, declaring she was glad to hear her friend had ditched the whisky now she was drinking (healthily) for two. Andrew reached out to collect her main luggage from the wheel, and Gina took the opportunity to dive into the ladies' loo before the trip back.

"How is she really Andy?" asked Molly. She'd been concerned about her the last few days. "She seems fine now but on the phone the other day I definitely detected something, a kind of reticence, I didn't say anything but—"

"No, you're right," he replied. "It hadn't happened when she rang you actually, and we're still not sure but… look, let's get back to the house and we'll discuss it there."

"This isn't something to do with Charlotte Peterson is it?" asked Molly. The look on Andy's face told her all she needed to know. "You know she escaped don't you – on an away day from Rampton, her mother's funeral of all things."

"Well I didn't until I checked it online this morning, and I still haven't told Gee, but I can see I'm going to have to." At that moment Gina emerged from the washroom and Andrew changed the subject as they all walked through the massive glass entrance and out to the taxi rank.

"You are kidding me!" Andrew and Gina looked at Molly and shook their heads.

"'Fraid not," said Andrew gravely. "Gina still isn't a hundred percent sure it was her but—"

"In a coffee shop – *here* – *in New York?!*" Molly couldn't believe what she was hearing. They were back at the house, and after settling Molly in her room had made some coffee and were now sitting at the large breakfast table in the kitchen. Gina was close to tears.

"It was… *really* weird Molls, because the woman didn't look anything like her, and yet – the eye twitch thing, you know?"

"Well I never actually saw it if you remember – she got me from behind that evening in the park. When it was apparent she'd come to finish me off in the hospital but was interrupted and the chloroform pack was found under the bed, I was in the land of nod – *luckily not permanently.*" They sat there in silence, the only noise the clock ticking on the wall.

"It's going to start all over again isn't it?" Gina looked down and began stroking her stomach protectively – Andrew pulled her to him. He glanced at Molly across the table. She held his eyes and bit her bottom lip – *they both knew at that point neither of them could be sure it wasn't.*

Carla stood in front of the long bedroom mirror. She turned this way and that scrutinising the white coat with the name badge and bleeper, and the stethoscope that hung around her neck. *Quite amazing really, how realistic these fancy dress shops make their outfits – I'm impressed, very impressed.* She picked up the clipboard and held it under her arm – *yes, I think that will do nicely, very nicely indeed…*

NINE

LONDON
HEATHROW

Flying wasn't Harry's most favourite thing in the world, which was one reason he and Annie hadn't had many foreign holidays, something she'd regularly reminded him about, pretty much every year in fact. He'd even bought a bag of his much missed barley sugars to give him something to do – much missed because these days he regulated his sugar levels with insulin injections. *However they also helped with ears popping on planes or some such thing didn't they?*

Working with Fran again was pretty high on the things 'much missed' list too – it felt good to be back together as partners, the years seemed to have rolled away very easily these last few days. Planning and going on this trip was more than he could have hoped for, he had to keep reminding himself it wasn't exactly a *trip* in the holiday sense of the word.

When the Gale lad had rung him to say his fiancée thought she'd 'seen' Charlotte Peterson, without *actually seeing* her, Harry hadn't been able to make his mind up whether it was an early lead or her wild imagination. After their close connections with the Peterson murders two years ago, Harry and Andrew had kept their respective numbers. *It appeared the feisty psychic was out there with them as well – quite the case reunion then…* On a serious note, if it *was* her at least it was something to go on.

"Harry – we're boarding." D.I. Fran Taylor stood up and flicked off imaginary dust from her tailored jacket, and smoothed down non-existent creases from her tight black trousers. She looked good, she knew she looked good, and *no,* she told herself, *it was not for Harry's benefit.*

"You still do the 'flicky smoothy' thing then?" he quipped, head on one side as his hand disappeared into his barley sugar pocket. It was incredible how this woman always lightened his mood.

"Come on, we don't want to be at the back of the queue," she replied cynically ignoring his taunt – then over her shoulder… *"See you're still on the barley cubes!"* A playful smile danced across her face as she strode off jauntily towards the departure lounge.

BELLEVUE HOSPITAL
1ST AVENUE MANHATTAN

Manny Berkowitz had got careless. He'd driven a cab most of his adult life and was proud of the relatively few fender benders he'd had in that time. However, for some reason that woman's face had got hooked right inside his head like a bass angler's barb, and on the return journey to JFK the day he'd dropped her off in Brooklyn Heights, Manny had swerved to avoid back-ending a truck. He'd flipped his cab and was now hooked up to a morphine drip with a punctured lung, a head wound, one leg and both arms in plaster. All things considered he'd been pretty lucky – that was until today…

Dr. Carla Preston walked through the doors of Bellevue Hospital with all the confidence of having worked there for a decade. She looked plain and studious, no make-up, no heels no attitude – she looked like she *belonged* there. She'd done this once before two years ago at Kirkdale General in Cumbria. Her intention then was to finish off the Fields girl. Unfortunately it hadn't quite worked out. *It was also the night her beloved horses had been murdered.* Well, at least one person had got their come-uppance for that – *and his nauseating sister would soon be following suit, in as colourful a way as she could create.* A smirk slid over her lips as she realised the anorexic/bulimic joke she'd made at Jenny Flood's expense.

The reception area and walkways were absolutely enormous. It made Kirkdale General look like a Barbie and Ken hospital set. Carla saw lifts ahead of her, there was also a pharmacy on the ground floor which she assumed was for out-patient prescriptions. She walked through the wide corridor to the double bank of elevators and checked the departments on the directional boards. Nobody looked at her twice as she pressed the button, waited for one to arrive and walked in. Luckily with so many available, no one else followed. Good job, her mouth was so dry a conversation would have proved difficult.

She chose a floor and the doors closed. Carla breathed slowly and deeply as she gripped the clipboard. She had about three minutes before they re-opened and she'd be slap bang in the nucleus of medical activity, the throng of a busy Manhattan hospital. *Her eye began to twitch.*

The nurse had just left Manny's room having done his obs. (blood pressure, temperature, pulse and heart). She also checked his morphine feed. He wasn't feeling too clever and a bit sick at the thought his insurance was likely to get cranked up as well. The morphine wasn't exactly helping his breathing either given the punctured lung and his personal sensitivity to it – but it was helping with the pain.

He'd been drifting in and out of sleep whilst waiting for a visit from his family when he saw her through the window to the corridor. Manny blinked slowly, he was tired, the window had blinds, and although open his head was also still a bit fuzzy. He leant forward in concentration and screwed his eyes up…

Carla had stepped out onto the medical floor and pretended to check 'notes' on her clipboard as she walked. *Good job she'd remembered to stick it in her bag,* she thought, *it had given her something to do – look busy about.* All the time her eyes were searching for the goal, heart pounding, palms damp, smiling at various nurses – nobody challenged her. The bleeping of various monitors was all around, medical staff in consultations, conversations and occasionally castigations. A red-faced nurse who'd forgotten to fill in a patient's observation chart and check a drip; and an intern (first-year student doctor) who repeatedly got answers wrong in a consultant's *'Guess The Condition'* test. Not so different from her early days on the wards she thought ironically, *only then there wasn't a fake doctor walking through her teaching hospital looking for the drugs room.*

Then rounding a corner into C.C.U. (critical care unit) she saw it. There was hardly anyone nearby and those that were seemed engrossed in what they were doing. Tentatively she felt for the handle, with her back to the door, eyes split between checking the staff and the faithful clipboard. Of course it was locked, she hadn't really expected anything else – but at least she knew where the drugs were. And then... *all hell broke loose.*

When the siren sounded and several people started running towards her on a code blue (patient emergency), Carla immediately thought she'd been spotted as an 'unknown' on a CCTV camera, but quickly realised she hadn't seen any. Her stomach crunched in anxiety, she instinctively jumped away from the EDR (Emergency

Drugs Room) as a nurse produced keys on the run and head straight for its door. She was inside in a flash, grabbed a metal box and was out again, *not forgetting to lock it.* It took no more than a few seconds and then she was running on down the corridor with three other members of the crash team leaving the area comparably quiet.

It was then that Carla saw the man. Their eyes locked through the window of his room opposite, his looked a little scared – unsure. She knew she recognised him from somewhere, but irritatingly couldn't quite match the face with the event. Of course it had to be in the last few days, so when it dawned on her who he *was*, *she knew there had to be an extra despatch on this trip.*

She crossed the corridor, entered the room and closed the door behind her. This had to be done fast. The window blinds were flicked shut; nurse call buzzer knocked to the floor and morphine drip switched to maximum flow (with a squeeze on the bag for good measure). Manny the cab driver was in no fit state to fight back. He struggled valiantly beneath the pillow as Carla leant heavily across his broken limbs and pushed down hard. His torso bucked and twitched... then just stopped. She lifted the pillow, placed it back behind his head and plumped it up beautifully...

It wasn't difficult for Harry and Fran to silently relive past feelings when in constant close proximity for eight hours. Neither of them actually referred to it directly, but there was a charged energy nevertheless – it was most definitely the elephant in the plane even after seven years apart.

"What's the plan then?" he asked her, sipping a coffee – an infinitely better coffee he'd noted than any of the stations they'd worked at.

"Well… we've got rooms booked at a small hotel near the Stone residence. Given your contact's phone call and latest information it seemed the best option. Plus of course the finances from the powers that be don't stretch past three stars as you know. It looks okay though, and we can go and interview your three informants sometime tomorrow, get an official statement of what Miss. Rowlands actually saw." With no acknowledgement she turned her head to look at him – he was fast asleep with his coffee listing at an awkward angle. Fran gently removed the cup and replaced it in the tray holder. *Same old Harry, never could face a plane trip.* She rolled her eyes as she plugged in ear buds for the film. *Well at least it isn't a disaster movie*, she thought resignedly as Harry's breathing deepened, and his head slipped sideways on to her shoulder…

Back at the house Carla reflected on the day's achievements. At least she'd located the drugs room, *or one of them*, it was just unfortunate that the cabbie had got in the way of her 'research'. It was also quite handy that the little nurse, who'd been reprimanded for her lapse on obs. duty, would likely be first in line as suspect for the huge alteration in his morphine drip. She felt a bit guilty about that, reminded her of a past unfair situation as a junior doctor, but only for a fleeting moment. *Needs must after all.*

She cooked and ate a scratch meal and then logged into her email account. On seeing a second message from Bellevue Hospital's H.R. department she opened it hesitantly.

Gail Hanson:- gail.hanson@bellevuehosp.org
Fri 02/02/20

Dear Dr. Preston,

I am contacting you because a temporary non medical position has become available within the anaesthesia team here at Bellevue. I don't know if you would be interested, but we require an anaesthesia technician with a job description as follows;

Duties to include but not limited to – the re-stocking of anaesthesia supplies, turning rooms over for the next case, ordering supplies etc. for the operating room, bringing equipment to the room, fetching blood from the blood bank, and generally working to help the anaesthesia personnel. Other errands in the hospital are also required to be carried out as necessary.

It may be that you would feel this post is beneath your remit given that you are a trained British physician and would not be permitted to act medically. However, if think you might be interested and would not feel compromised by the duties and constraints required, please let me know in the next twenty-four to forty-eight hours.

Yours sincerely,

Gail Hanson – Manager H.R. Bellevue Hospital

Carla read it through three times. She seriously couldn't believe her luck – *the anaesthesia department!* Her smile was actually genuine, even nearly reached her eyes. *Now* she could get this wake started…

TEN

KIRKDALE
CUMBRIA

Annie Longbridge would have gone away somewhere hot and luxurious for a couple of weeks 'R & R' if it wasn't for a couple of anchors holding her at home. Her long-lost son Michael, who she'd met up with secretly a couple of times since he'd turned up on her doorstep… *and of course Baxter.* There was no way Harry would have allowed him to go into kennels, and if she was completely honest neither would she. Baxter may be a giant pain in the backside where redesigning of the garden was concerned, but even Annie didn't like the idea of him being away from home, away from people he knew and in a strange environment.

"You should've been called Monty or Alan," she told him as she ruffled his ears and put down his dinner. "Which one is the untidiest I wonder, Don or Titchmarsh?" Three seconds later Annie was picking the bowl up again, its silver inside refuting any signs of

85

previously held meat and biscuit. Baxter immediately began to slurp noisily from the other bowl, followed by swinging his happy face around, smiling as water flew from his mouth all over the floor... and Annie's pumps. Sighing, she fetched one of the many dog towels to clean up her feet and the floor just as her phone beeped a text. She pulled it from the back of her jeans pocket and read...

> Hi – thought I'd let you know I'd arrived safely. The B&B is fine and food quite good. We'll talk properly when I get back, please don't forget Baxter needs his walks. – H.

She stared at the screen for a moment before slowly shaking her head. It would be 1.00 p.m. there – he... *and she* had arrived the night before. *Unbelievable Harry – un-bloody – believable even for you.* She re-pocketed her mobile, took off her wet pumps and dried the floor. *He can sodding well wait for a reply*, she thought hotly.

MANHATTAN
NEW YORK

Harry and Fran had booked in at a small bed and breakfast in Manhattan across the other side of the river from Brooklyn, and 'The Maples', Narrows Avenue, home of Gareth and Emily Stone. Fran had noticed that Harry kept fishing his phone out of his jacket to check notifications then snapped it shut irritably, re-pocketing it with a disapproving grunt. *Things even worse than expected at home then,* she concluded. She staunched a brief tingly feeling and then immediately flushed out uncharitable thoughts – *the second part wasn't easy.*

They'd had a large and late cooked breakfast, followed by a lunch of hot jam custard doughnuts from a street seller (*or cart vendor as they'd discovered was the correct term*).

"Much more of this adjustment to my food diary and I'm going to be the size of this bloody town!" Fran rolled her eyes as she sucked sugar off her fingers. Harry glanced over the rim of the bulging warm bag, mouth around his second protruding doughnut, eyes taking in the fact she could eat ten bags of jam custards and Annie would say Fran *still* had a figure to die for. *Harry would say the same.* She hadn't changed a bit – that was the hardest part – it felt like nothing had changed, they were back in the 'Job' – *together.* If it wasn't for the New York scenery, they could be in the station car park at Canon Row about to go out in the area car. *He sensed she was back there too…*

They were sitting in a hired Ford Fusion outside The Harbor B&B in Edgewater Street. The Harbor sat at the corner of Edgewater and Hylan Boulevard. Fran was the designated driver, she'd driven in the U.S. several times before and Harry was more than happy to let her take the wheel – just as she'd always done. He may have had a reputation of being a tad sexist in some areas, but never when it came to Fran's driving. It was legendary. This was probably in no small part due to her brother being a semi-professional racing driver, Fran could certainly pull out all the stops in a chase if needs be, *and without feeding lamp posts.*

"Okay let's make a move." Fran scrunched her doughnut bag and cleaned her sticky fingers on a wet wipe. Harry had noticed she'd already stocked the car with other handy necessities including mints, tissues, adaptable chargers and a bin bag. *This was beginning to feel more like the Canon Row years by the hour.* "Have you got the address Harry?"

"8056 Narrows Avenue Brooklyn 11209," he replied, tapping it into the car's satnav as he checked the route by list. "You'll need to turn it around and go back up Hylan Boulevard towards Bay Street – think that's the same way we came too. We need to go over the Verrazzano Bridge back into Brooklyn, shouldn't take more than twenty, twenty-five minutes going by this." Fran turned the car around and they were soon heading back up Hylan. Harry was right about one thing, she was slipping easily back into their partnership, only this time Fran Taylor officially took seniority. Although it didn't really feel like it, she was sensing all the old comfortable familiarity returning, and she was enjoying it – *a lot…*

BELLEVUE HOSPITAL
1ST AVENUE MANHATTAN

"Welcome aboard. You do understand we can't use your British doctor title for the reasons I explained in my email?" Carla had just successfully passed her interview for anaesthesia technician at Bellevue and was feeling pretty damn smug, despite the loss of her medical title. After all, she hadn't used it for the best part of two years and had been stripped of it anyway.

Gail Hanson sat back in her black leather swing chair rolling an elaborate-looking pen between her fingers. Carla sat the opposite side of Gail's large neatly organised oak desk, in a very ordinary fixed grey material seat with a slightly worn patch on its arm. Yes she felt smug, but it still grated that not so long ago *she* would have been the one enjoying the luxury... *and with a very special pen.*

"Oh of course that's fine," she breezed. "I understand completely, just grateful for the opportunity to be able to work in a New York hospital, gain some acc... some *different* experience whilst I'm out here."

"Excellent, well we'll see you on Monday then Carla." Gail stood up, indicating the interview was at an end. "If you report to housekeeping before your shift they'll issue you with some technician scrubs." She held her hand out as Carla smiled and stood to receive the dismissal shake. Once outside the door she took a deep breath and exhaled slowly. A smile tugged at the side of her mouth, her eyes steely and cold. This was a major achievement. It meant access to hospital equipment, access to anaesthetics – *access to the mortuary*. Oh yes… definitely a major achievement…

She walked back towards the elevators, rode to the ground floor and was soon outside back into a busy New York working day. It was cold and windy. She pulled the collar of her coat up around her neck, acutely aware of the lack of thick waves that used to keep it warm, her ears red, supporting the unfamiliar black arms of her fake glasses.

It was when she crossed the road further down from the hospital to a small café for a much needed coffee and croissant, that Carla thought she'd noticed *him* again, *Mr. Hawk*. He'd been hanging around to the left of the building as she'd come out, and was now walking down parallel to her. Equally she wasn't entirely sure it *was* him, but had felt someone 'around' her, even in the enormous expanse of a New York high street. Her nickname for the man from the gangway on the plane, whose piercing glance however fleeting had still unnerved her, seemed to have stuck. In the absence of any knowledge as to exactly who he was, *Hawk* was as good a name as any.

Carla walked into the café and sat in a window booth. She picked up the menu and ordered when the waitress came, but then looked sideways through the glass across the street. He had followed her down on the hospital side and was now standing in a bus shelter checking his mobile. No wait – *now* he had a long-range camera and was taking a photo of the building opposite him – the Café Deli-Cious – the building she was *sitting* in. *He has to be with the 'people' who arranged everything for me,* she thought rationally. Who on earth else could it be? Carla couldn't work out if she was scared or not. It would make sense that with so much of their money invested in her they would want to keep an eye on where she was and what she was doing. Still, she admitted to feeling unnerved. Not something she was used to, and worse still couldn't do anything about. She could hardly 'despatch' one of their gang members, she wouldn't last five minutes.

Her croissant and coffee arrived, and the first bite stuck awkwardly in her throat as she considered the consequences of eradicating a gang member. She immediately washed it down with a gulp of her Americano. The road was far too wide to analyse his facial features, but when she exited the hospital she'd noticed he'd got a goatee beard and moustache that definitely weren't there on the plane *–but the dragon neck tattoo was.* His scarf had blown sideways in the wind revealing it clearly. Could the tattoo be a gang emblem? Could there be more than one of them following her? That thought *did* scare her. Carla ordered another coffee – *she needed to up her game, move it on quickly, flush out Emily and Jenny and get the hell out of this country – somewhere safe, somewhere she could hide. Maybe Brazil…*

BAY RIDGE
BROOKLYN

Harry, Fran, Andrew, Gina and Molly sat in the lounge of Emily and Gareth's Brooklyn home at Bay Ridge. Fran aside, it brought back uncomfortable memories to the rest of them of two years before. Emily and Gareth were at work at McCarthy Stone Publishing on Water Street, and Harry and Fran had just learnt Gina still hadn't told her mother she thought she'd seen Charlotte Peterson outside Honey's the day before. Fran was happy for Harry to take the lead…

"I think I'd like your mother here for this discussion to be honest Miss. Rowlands, and it might be an idea for Mr. Stone to be present as well. Is that possible?"

"Well I don't know how their diaries are panning out for today but I can give Emily a ring, I have her direct number," offered Gina.

"It would be good if you could try and get hold of her," Fran intercepted. "I don't want to alarm you, but we think you probably *did* see Charlotte yesterday, just that it's likely she looks very different. We have reason to believe she left the U.K. looking for your mother and her friend Jenny Flood. We're assuming she's living somewhere in the area, getting herself organised and will start searching where she believes they live and work." Gina shivered till Molly put a protective arm around her, and in the absence of his favoured '*KitKat*', Andrew pulled a '*Hershey*' bar from his pocket. Harry raised his eyebrows in anticipation. Breaking a line off, Andrew gave a wry smile as he lobbed it over to the retired D.C.I.

"Thanks son, getting to be a bit of a habit this!" He winked and they semi-laughed as paper came off, both remembering the '*KitKat*' incident at vet Josie Kinkaid's house, one of Charlotte's victims in 2018.

Gina went out into the kitchen to phone Emily as her mobile was plugged in and charging on the counter. Fran looked puzzled – "I'll tell you later," offered Harry, swallowing his chocolate – *"Actually that's not bad!"* Andrew smiled and threw him another piece, then saving a bit for Gina, shared the rest with Molly and Fran. Fran looked skyward and sighing patted her totally flat belly.

"That'll sit nicely on top of the custard doughnuts!" Harry was just about to say she'd nothing to worry about when Gina came back into the lounge.

"They're on their way. Jenny too – it's been a bit of a shock for them, I had to say something as Emily had a really important meeting and Jenny was attending with her. Gareth was free – *ish* but as soon as he realised what it was about…" She tailed off and sat back down next to Andrew where she glanced downwards lightly stroking her stomach. The action wasn't missed by Fran.

"Are you…?"

"Three months," interrupted Gina looking up at her… *"Not a great time to be meeting up with my kidnapper again…"*

ELEVEN

MANHATTAN: NEW YORK
McCARTHY STONE PUBLISHING

Jenny Flood had given up smoking and been eating better since that dark time two years ago when anorexia had raged during the summer of the *'Great Plan…'* She'd even been managing three small meals a day most days – now however she had a cigarette in her mouth and that old familiar *'friend'* nausea was rising up from her guts.

She grabbed her coat from the stand in her office and slipped it on quickly, flicking her long black hair up and over the faux fur collar. It streamed down the back of the tight-fitting red cashmere midi as she slung her black patent bag over her shoulder and walked from the room. Emily met her in the corridor and their eyes locked. She had rung through to Jenny five minutes earlier; it wasn't the call Jenny was expecting, to confirm their meeting with author Harper James was in fact going to be slightly earlier after all. Instead,

Emily had blown her right back into that nightmare where she'd loved and lost Miles for the second time, her brother Jason forever to that devil woman, and sent her careering downwards into another endless mind-altering spiral she'd not long come out of.

Feeling responsible, Emily had given her a good job and an apartment near them here in Brooklyn. She'd been getting there – *slowly. Now it looked like Charlotte Peterson was back.*

"Ready?" Emily Stone looked anxiously at her friend and colleague. She knew Jenny was not a mentally strong woman and had promised herself she would make damned sure she'd look out for her after what she'd put her through in trying to send Charlotte over the edge.

It had been an insane plan really – Emily had felt massively guilty it had gone so far that Charlie had flipped into full-on cuckoo mode and turned serial killer. No man was worth that, and at the end of the day Miles certainly wasn't, but it hadn't been all about Miles... Leaving Gina with her mother to raise had been the hardest thing of all – Emily would never forgive Charlotte for blackmailing her with her mother's life and forcing her to leave the U.K. after uni all those years ago, just because of her affair with her then fiancé, Miles. Now it seemed 'The Great Plan' may have been reversed, and come back to bite them both – *hard.*

Drawing heavily on her cigarette, the younger woman looked shakily at her now...

"As I'll ever be," replied Jenny. "Sorry about the ciga—"

"It's fine, inside the office this once won't hurt. Don't want to be getting back into the habit though, *so* bad for the skin." Emily winked and squeezed her elbow as Jenny smiled weakly, and the two women walked arm-in-arm to the elevators where they'd arranged to meet Gareth.

Carla had almost finished a third coffee in Café Deli-Cious whilst watching '*Mr. Hawk*' who was still standing at the bus stop opposite. Three buses had come and gone and he hadn't availed himself of any of them. *Definitely the guy on the plane then,* she thought. It was just as she was contemplating a fourth Americano when he put the mobile to his ear again for a few moments, then back into his pocket. Two minutes later he'd hailed a cab, got in and was driven off.

Carla drained her cup, got up and walked out of the door. It was time to be back at the house, online and locating Emily's whereabouts. She already knew she was likely to be in the vicinity, and that she was married to Gareth Stone of McCarthy Stone publishing. *Now she had access to medical supplies again, plans must be made to put them to good use.*

She didn't know for certain if Jenny Flood would be conveniently close to hand as well, but had a strong feeling that wherever she'd find her oldest adversary, *the latest one wouldn't be far away.* Jenny was weak, had no family left and needed strong female support – Emily would be able to provide that. Carla believed that was *exactly* what she'd been doing here in the US for the last two years. *Let's hope you've been working close, and/or buddying up together with your perfect little lives – enjoying all the 'Big Apple' has to offer, it will make it easier to find you. Enjoy it while you can girls, take your last bite – I'm coming.*

NARROWS AVENUE
BAY RIDGE, BROOKLYN

When she heard the key in the front door, Gina got up from the sofa, crossed the lounge and walked quickly out into the hall. Emily, Gareth and Jenny were already taking their coats off. As in the past, Gina noticed how amazing Jenny looked and felt an old stab of insecurity, although today her complexion had returned to the pale, wan colour of that terrible summer.

"I'll make some tea shall I?" This to Emily as her mother and Gareth made their way to the lounge with Jenny in tow.

"Thank you Gina – yes – I think we could all use some." She turned back from the lounge door and touched her shoulder. "You should have told me you know, that you thought you saw her the other day. I don't want you worrying – about *anything*, particularly now." She looked down at her daughter's waistline.

"Especially if it *is* Charlotte you saw." Gina managed a nervous smile and left them to go into the lounge whilst she headed off to the kitchen. Molly, sitting nearest to the hall, overheard and got up to join her friend, greeting Jenny on the way through. It was a large gathering – one full of past memories for most of them, or more accurately – *past nightmares…*

Harry and Fran stood up when Emily, Gareth and Jenny entered the room. Harry held out his hand to Jenny first. Her brother's murder that summer of 2018, and Jenny's witnessing of Susie Sarrandaire's horrific death (real name Danielle Mogg) had meant Harry had spent quite a bit of time with her two years ago. He noticed she was looking pretty anxious and just as thin today as she had back then.

"Miss. Flood," he said, shaking her hand warmly. "Good to see you again, although sadly not under the best of circumstances."

"D.C.I. Longbridge – I thought you'd retired?" said Jenny, accepting his handshake. Fran interjected and introduced herself…

"D.I. Fran Taylor – we're terribly overstretched as a service," she explained, holding out her own hand in greeting. "Harry's extremely experienced and was the Senior Investigating Officer with the Peterson murders as you know. He's back temporarily to help us with this new development." Emily and Gareth, who'd not met Harry before, although he'd attended her mother's (Gina's grandmother's) funeral at Gina's request and seen Emily there, had exchanged greetings and were now sitting down. Fran and Jenny were also now seated just as Gina walked back into the room with a large and very full tray. Once everyone had been settled with their teas, Fran addressed the room.

"Thank you for altering your work schedules Mr. and Mrs. Stone, Miss. Flood, we feel it's important that you're all here today to bring you up to speed with what we know about Charlotte Peterson's escape from Rampton Psychiatric Hospital in the U.K., and for us to learn exactly what happened the day Gina thought she may have seen her." Andrew had been quiet up to now but felt he needed some answers regarding what he saw as lax security.

"How the hell did she get away in the first place?" he said curtly. "Surely she would have been cuffed and with at least two officers present on the day of her mother's funeral?"

"She was lad," said Harry immediately, "she got sprung by an outside gang, God knows who arranged it but it must've been an inside job. It was pretty damned professional because she was whisked out of the North Midlands and gone before we could even get cars on the ground."

"But this was a couple of months ago, more, how come you haven't tracked her down in all that time?" This came from Gina who was protectively holding a cushion against her stomach.

"As I said Miss. Row—"

"Gina – call me Gina… *please* – I feel we all know each other well enough now." Harry smiled and relaxed the official approach.

"As I said, *Gina*," continued Harry, "we believe it must have been an extremely professional hit. The police van taking her to the funeral was ambushed *miles* from Rampton, on a quiet part of the route to the crematorium in Wilmslow Cheshire where her mother had lived. The two police officers in charge were shot dead. Whoever did this must be expecting a huge pay-off from someone as a reward. It's not like Ms. Peterson is a celebrity or a mafia gang leader… but her parents were millionaires, technically she *is* a very wealthy woman even if she currently has no access to her inheritance." Fran took it up from there…

"We think she was probably hidden up somewhere for a few weeks whilst a fake passport and other papers were being prepared, and it was likely of course she changed her appearance drastically for those. This is where you come in Gina, because although the woman you saw may not have *looked* like Charlotte, there would obviously be a very good reason for that. Can you describe the woman you saw that afternoon and explain exactly what happened? How she looked at you, where she was standing, what her mannerisms were like and why you felt it was her – that sort of thing." Gina took a long drink of her tea followed by a deep breath, Andrew stroked her shoulders and Emily waited. She hadn't even been aware of the woman outside Honey's that day – *how could she not have noticed her? She'd known Charlie so well for so many years. Whether in disguise or not, if she'd seen her she felt sure she would've recognised her.* Gina began hesitantly…

"Well… it was so strange really and… well *weird*. One minute Emily and I were just… chatting, having coffee and cake, talking about our wedding," she said briefly turning to Andrew, "then suddenly I saw this woman through the window on the street *staring* at us. She seemed to appear from nowhere, I think you had your back to her," this to Emily, "that's why you didn't see her."

"How did she seem Gina?" asked Harry. "In her behaviour for instance, was she quiet, did she say anything, knock on the window, or use threatening gestures?"

"No, nothing like that," replied Gina, "she just stood stock still and… well just stared hard – *right at me*. It felt creepy, but you can't exactly arrest someone for staring. That's why I didn't say anything – it all seemed a bit silly to bother anyone with it." Everyone in the room knew it was far from silly if it *had* been Charlotte, it was the not *knowing* that was making them all experience a distinct tightness in their chests. "There was *one* thing," added Gina, "I don't know if it's anything or not but…"

"Yes – what exactly?" shot back Harry and Fran in unison causing them to instantly exchange glances.

"Well although she had very short, straight black hair and glasses, not her usual shoulder-length auburn style, it was the eyes – they were the wrong colour. I could see them because we had a window seat. Charlotte Peterson has green eyes or maybe hazel, but definitely not blue. These were bright blue, *too* blue if you know what I mean, as if they were a *false* blue, and that woman looked at me in exactly the same way as—"

"*A lead-eyed, dead-eyed shark…*" Molly finished for her.

TWELVE

68ᵀᴴ PRECINCT, BROOKLYN
NEW YORK

The following morning Harry and Fran sat in the reception of N.Y.P.D.'s 68th Precinct waiting to see Detectives Frank Delaney and Terri (T.J.) Malone. The 68th was the closest to the Stones' house, and if possible they wanted to get some surveillance organised – *just in case.*

"So… do you reckon they'll play ball?" Harry whispered, leaning in close to Fran across the gap of the plastic bucket chairs.

"Well I certainly hope so," she whispered back. *"I rang the Chief Super and he arranged a call from the top through to their Commanding Officer."* Fran reached into her back pocket. She continued to keep her voice down and head close to Harry's. *"Name's Captain John Carline, at least he's agreed to send a couple of his officers down to see us. With a bit of—"*

"Sir – ma'am – I'm Detective Frank Delaney and this is Detective Terri Malone." Harry and Fran stood up as a tall well-built *(and Fran couldn't help noticing, rather fit looking)* officer who looked to be in his late thirties, walked towards them. A shorter, dark-haired olive-skinned female officer of about the same age accompanied him. Everyone briefly shook hands, and Det. Malone immediately invited them into an office away from the main reception area so they could speak privately. Once seated, Fran extended an arm out to Harry…

"Ex-Detective Chief Inspector Harry Longbridge and I'm Detective Inspector Fran Taylor of the U.K. Cumbrian Police."

"*Ex*-Detective?" quizzed Malone looking at Harry, clearly unsure of his authority.

"I got called back in for this case," Harry replied. I was Senior Investigating Officer two years ago – it was pretty grim."

"So we hear," added Terri, "how can we help exactly? I take it you've not tracked down your perp, a…" Det. Malone checked her notebook, "a Charlotte *Peterson? Another* ex by the looks of it." Terri exchanged a raised eyebrow with her colleague.

"Yeah… well we don't exactly allow our medical doctors to keep their titles once they turn serial killer," added Fran crisply.

"*Quite,*" replied Frank, flashing a *'that was pretty dumb'* expression at Terri. "Well you're in luck. We got a new Chief Commanding Officer July last year, Captain Carline. He rolled out a neighbourhood policing policy across the whole borough, recruited N.C.O.s, that's 'Neighbourhood Community Officers', and reduced crime in this area by double digits." *Delaney looks decidedly pleased at this*, thought Harry, *as if the whole thing had been his own idea...* "He certainly won't want any U.K. perps spoiling his numbers by adding to his load," continued Frank. *Sounds like our 'Hobby Bobbies'*, Harry summed up derisively, but he kept that to himself too.

"At the moment we just need twenty-four-seven surveillance on a private residence over at Narrows Avenue." This from Fran – Harry added...

"And if possible an officer keeping an eye around the corner of Water and South Street, on a company called *'McCarthy Stone Publishing'*. Is that doable do you think?"

"Should be, depends how long for, but we can probably manage a couple of weeks," replied Frank, looking at Terri questioningly.

"Yep – could cover that," she agreed.

"Thanks, we appreciate it," said Fran, smiling at Harry with relief. "Obviously we'll keep you informed if we locate our target, presumably we can call on you guys for help if need be?"

"Sure, here's my card." Frank passed a couple of official-looking *'Detective Frank A. Delaney N.Y.P.D. 68th Precinct'* contact cards across the table they were sitting at, as did Terri Malone. Fran reciprocated. Harry didn't feel it would enhance the U.K. U.S. relationship if he slapped his golf membership pass down, even if it did have his mobile on it. *God how he hated being retired…*

Molly was trying her level best, *and failing*, to interest Gina in her wedding preparations. Jenny had gone home to prepare for a date (*the first in a very long time*), Andrew was reading a crime novel (*typically*), and Gareth and Emily were throwing a spag bol together in the kitchen. The smell of ground beef, tomatoes, red wine, garlic and basil was absolute heaven, but even though it was an hour since Harry and Fran had left, a distinct tension still floated above the Italian infusion. It was as if they were all back there, back home in Kirkdale sitting in Andrew's flat waiting for murders to occur. Except that this time round Andrew didn't have anything to try and solve… *yet*.

"Come on *Gee*… it'll take your *mind* off it." Molly leant forward and waved a copy of *Brides* at her friend who wasn't exactly showing much enthusiasm for the big day. "You haven't even chosen a dress yet. Even though having it here in the grounds means you won't be booking a venue, you've still only got three weeks!" Gina looked up from picking at her fingers and attempted a smile.

"How can I plan the happiest day of my life, well, one of them," she looked down at her hands now covering her stomach, "with that… *insane… death bitch on the loose?!*"

Molly reluctantly dropped the glossy magazine back onto her lap and glanced over at Andrew, who, unusually, had not really been taking in much of what he was reading. He closed his book and leaving it on the chair, crossed the room, sat down next to his fiancée again and picking up both her hands kissed them gently.

"We don't even know for sure it *was* her yet sweetheart, don't let this, whatever *this* is, spoil our special day. We've come out here to get married, to celebrate with Molly, your mum and Gareth, and other members of your new family." He stroked her hair and tipped up her chin to make her look at him. "*Nothing* is going to happen to you." He turned to include Molly. "Not to any of us – *I won't let it.*"

BELLEVUE HOSPITAL
MANHATTAN

Carla looked down at the pale mauve scrubs top and trousers she'd just been issued with and grimaced. *Mauve is so not my colour* she thought acidly. Fact was Carla absolutely *hated* mauve, or any purple shades come to that. She favoured very deep clarets and maroon reds or blacks. Apart from complementing her hair and complexion *(her hair even when it was auburn and shoulder length)*, it didn't show the blood so easily… At the thought of more being spent, her lip sneered upwards on one side and she slowly brightened, put her bag in the locker and turned the key.

It was her first day. Things had to be fairly ordinary (sadly) but she knew she couldn't arouse any suspicion. She always remembered her fake glasses now. It was quite difficult at first as she'd never worn frames regularly before, only sunglasses, but now she was getting into the rhythm of her new character. Polite, quiet, studious, obliging, head slightly down in public areas and displaying very little personality. As the days go by and she meets and has conversations with work colleagues, she must agree with everyone rather than be confrontational, be helpful, focused, learn quickly, and after her shift appear practically invisible. *Such is the visage and behaviour of an accomplished assassin – stoic – silent – deadly.*

Her first morning passed without complication. Carla shadowed an experienced senior anaesthesia technician and was shown how to clean down and prep several O.R.s (operating rooms) so they were sterile and had the correct instruments, gowns, gloves, caps, masks, hand gels etcetera ready for each surgeon's case. She also kept her eyes open for where the muscle relaxant, anaesthetic and coma drugs were kept. So far she hadn't come across them… *but she would.* The annexe room where the pre-meds were given was going to be her first check in, as soon as she got the chance to be alone on her duties. It was the most obvious choice – she also wanted to 'acquire' a retractable scalpel. They were just too useful and handy at close quarters not to have one. It may be necessary to slip one of those in her pocket from another team's group of O.R.s though. *She didn't want to attract any unwanted attention to herself.*

During each break Carla spent some time acclimatising herself, learning her way around the hospital, using both the elevators and staircases to check out different floors – *different escape routes.* It was important to know the layout of the building especially the mortuary. *That* she made a priority. It was an absolutely enormous facility though – thankfully there were maps on every floor and she was in every day that week, plenty of time to avail herself of how the various departments were set out in one wing at least.

Today she also spent some time in the anaesthetists' '*Team Break Room*'. She was sitting with a coffee and a magazine when two nurses came in talking quickly and in earnest about a mutual friend…

"…But Leah *Chang? Never in a million years!!*" exclaimed one as she began to operate the coffee machine. "She's the most focused and detailed nurse I know, *even on zero sleep!*"

"*Exactly,* it's just *awful,*" replied her colleague whilst she waited, "she swears she's innocent but apparently the patient's wife Mrs. Berkowitz is pushing for a full-on external investigation. She's refusing to accept an internal one. Leah's worried sick, they've suspended her until it's been resolved which could obviously take ages. *And then what?*" The second girl took her turn at the machine.

"Thing is…" came the response, "his autopsy *did* reveal a discrepancy around it not just being a morphine overdose. Heard that from the chief herself – *Kay Winford…*"

Carla's eye began to twitch behind her glasses. She gulped down the rest of her coffee, got up and walked quickly from the room, the two nurses were too engrossed with their conversation about Leah Chang to particularly notice her.

Outside in the corridor she sagged against the wall, heart thumping, trying to get her breath. Leah Chang may well be her get-out-of-jail-free card regarding cabby Berkowitz – but Kay Winford? Kay Winford was the senior expat pathologist who'd worked a stint at Kirkdale General two years ago. The pathologist who'd opened up Carla's (Charlotte's) victims for a root around. The pathologist who'd given evidence at her trial… this was not good – this was not good at all.

Later that evening, after turning over and prepping the last O.R. of the day, Carla made an excuse to her senior tech about forgetting some cleaning materials, double backed from the locker area and returned to the operating room she'd last worked on. Luckily it was fairly quiet, it was usually used as a maternity O.R., and unless an emergency Caesarean turned up, she'd been told there were no others due that night. Carla let herself in to the pre-op room and shut the door quietly behind her.

She could of course just stab the pair of them to death with a nice big knife (*Emily and Jenny*), she thought logically, however, that would be far too simple… and these days a bit too ordinary. She had moved on – they had all moved on, and this time it was going to be altogether more… well, *interesting. For her old 'frenemy' Emily Stone at least.* She had been the instigator in her downfall, the planner, the mastermind… *now she was going to experience the worst and most feared of all hells.*

Carla's eyes flew around the drugs cupboards and prayed there would be some. She would need her trusty staple of course; a friendly bottle of chloroform, but what she was really looking for was something else entirely. Something much more effective. A drug that had been discovered recently quite by accident, one she'd read about in Rampton; a derivative of the coma drug Baclofen – *Baclovate*… It went beyond the uses of its usual coma-inducing 'sister'. *So deadly was it in the wrong hands – it may well not even be included in this hospital's drug arsenal.*

THIRTEEN

KIRKDALE
CUMBRIA U.K.

The snow had come down overnight. Annie could sense its heavy shadow behind the curtains from her position under the duvet and pulled a pillow on top of her head. She emerged and turned over slowly. Luxuriating in the comfort of snug warmth Annie groaned at the realisation of having to walk Baxter, despite the slippery wet stuff she hated so much... *and the fact the young Lab delighted in hauling her along the pavement like a Husky pulling a sled.*

She needed time to wake up, and not just due to the bottle of raspberry flavoured gin she'd half emptied the previous evening. Harry was right about one thing, she *was* drinking too much, and a lot of it on her own. Well that wasn't *her* fault. He wasn't in the bloody house most nights, and now he wasn't even in the fucking *country*. Annie groaned and punched the pillows as the muffled sound of Baxter's sporadic barking began to waft up through the floor from the kitchen. She sighed heavily and threw back the cover…

"*Com-ing Baaax!* Maybe a nice *old* cat next time Harry eh?" she announced to the dressing table mirror as she pulled on her slippers and dressing gown and stomped downstairs to the kitchen. She was greeted by a bouncing black whirligig, and after a reluctant smile followed by a sigh and a not so reluctant pat of his head, she opened the sliding door to the garden for him before gathering the necessities to wake herself up. *Full kettle, strong coffee, big mug. Very big mug.*

Annie Longbridge *did* love her husband's dog, well, *their* dog. It was just that she'd had no say in his arrival and even less in his living arrangements. If it was up to Harry, Baxy boy would be sleeping on their bed every night, muddy footprints and all. It just wasn't how Annie saw house sharing with eighty pounds of over-excited slobber-slinging muscle that Harry regarded as his best friend. Sometimes he was an absolute angel *(Baxter not Harry),* mainly when he was asleep in his basket.

She drank her coffee, grateful *that* at least was a constant, and fiddled with her mobile. There had been a brief conversation the night before, unfortunately *after* the raspberry gin had made its mark, where Harry had reiterated for the umpteenth time that she wasn't to let anyone know where he was and what he was doing, and to make sure she was following orders regarding their happy black dynamo. There was also some sheepish acknowledgement that he understood she was probably none too happy about who he was with and why, and that she mustn't worry about that. *Yeah right.* Annie stroked the side of the phone with her forefinger and bit her lip. Fran Taylor finally had Annie's husband exactly where she wanted him – a level below in seniority… *and away from her.*

The sound of scratching caused her to look up into Baxter's goofy black face, breath steaming on the glass door, head on one side. As their eyes met, Annie softened. She realised he was probably her one and only loyal friend at the moment, she should probably make the most of it. *He also hadn't dug anything up that morning…* Annie let him in having already laid the towels on the floor, and with his usual hopping dance still managed to pat him dry. She even remembered to check in between his pads for impacted snow – *Harry would be very impressed.* She fed him his breakfast and sat back down with a second cup of coffee.

Should she give Michael a call – invite him along for a dog walk? Annie still hadn't mentioned her long-lost son to anyone, not even Harry. To be honest she hadn't felt there'd been any time before he'd flown off into the blue to hunt down Cumbria's answer to Shipman. That made her shiver, despite the rads being on full and warming her hands on a second mug – *Charlotte Peterson made Harold Shipman look like Dennis the Menace…* She wasn't even sure she *wanted* to share anything with her husband about Michael at the moment, didn't feel close enough. Harry was so mentally absent these days, fifty percent absorbed by Fran Taylor and the other fifty with the Peterson woman – *again*. Princess Diana had said there were three of them in her marriage… *well Annie Longbridge knew exactly what she meant.*

Maybe she should go and visit her mother for a couple of weeks, she pondered, although the thought of the six-hour journey back south didn't exactly fill her with delight. The relationship with her parents, particularly her father, had not been easy over the years, following what they'd always referred to as *'The Incident'*. Michael's birth *(and loss to complete strangers)* had left Annie with a large part missing from her life, a very large part – it had not been easy to forgive, *and she could obviously never forget…*

Margaret Campbell, daughter of a strict Presbyterian Scotsman, had met Iain McMahon, son of an even stricter Scottish Presbyterian minister. After marrying they had moved down south from Inverness to look for work, and finally settled outside London in the Beckenham and Penge area, where Annie had been born.

Although her mother had relented a little over their Church's non-celebratory beliefs of Christmas, certainly when Annie was very young, a child out of wedlock could never be tolerated, or even be known to exist. Hence as a teenager Annie had been shipped off to an aunt in Whitstable, Kent to see out her pregnancy, give birth and subsequently give UP Michael. She swore at the time she

would never forgive any of them, but of course she had –
eventually. It was just unfortunate that the fibroids Annie
had endured later in life had scuppered any chance of
further children. Her mother had always felt very guilty
about that.

Annie looked over at Baxter, currently assuming angel status in his basket. She felt she just didn't have the energy to pack a suitcase for both of them, sort out the car to carry him safely and make the drive. She had to face facts. She was feeling old, lethargic, depressed and unloved. And a complete and utter business failure. *No wonder she was drinking.* Just then the phone rang – *it was her mother…*

Annie could never understand how her mother could actually *do* that. Pick up on her thoughts and ring at *exactly* the moment they were activated. Later that day after making arrangements to drive down to London, her mother having made a very good case for a visit *(basically not seeing her for six months),* Annie decided to spend the afternoon packing for a week's stay. This of course also had to include all of Baxter's needs. She would take him for an early evening walk in the woods at the end of the road, he could have a good run and then he'd sleep in the car on the way down. They wouldn't get there till about ten but at least she wouldn't be driving in the morning rush hour and could wake up in her childhood bedroom. Margaret McMahon spoiled her daughter these days so breakfast in bed was likely as well.

Annie was starting to brighten a little. It would be nice to be fussed over for a week or so, but she still hadn't decided whether to tell her parents about Michael yet. Maybe something at the back of her mind had partly instigated why she was going? Annie wasn't entirely sure. Her father would certainly not want her to be having anything to do with him... even now. As the son of a Presbyterian minister Iain McMahon's upbringing had not seen much in the way of softness and compromise, and at seventy-five he hadn't found it easy, or even *necessary*, to change. His wife on the other hand had mellowed over the years. Mainly because of their daughter not being able to have any more children, but with a minister's son for a husband it was like talking to a brick wall. Then there was the fact Annie's brother had been blown up in Iraq – *Margaret McMahon knew all about a mother's loss.*

Luckily the snow didn't lie too much, and as was typical of a Cumbrian January (actually most months in the Lakes), the rain had washed most of it away by tea time. This was good news, Annie didn't fancy getting caught in a snow drift before she even got anywhere near the M6, particularly with a dog in the car.

After she'd got back from letting the neighbours either side know they'd be away for a week (she'd had to imply Harry was with her on account of his 'secret mission'), Annie dug out her green hooded jacket from beneath the stairs, put it on and laced up her walking boots. Baxter's red collar and lead came next... Of course he ducked and dived his way through all of it (laughing), and what should have been a simple operation, took at least five minutes to connect dog to both, and finally clip up. Annie made a mental note that the next time she spoke to Harry, she really needed to remind him that he must double his training efforts when he got back, because like him, *Baxter* didn't listen to her either.

By the time she'd been dragged down the road and reached the woods, the sun had dipped low behind Kirkdale Pike and cast an eerie gold glow through the trees. There was still a little snow left on the dog walkers' trail but it was okay to walk and looked really pretty against the red Acers. Their tiny leaves fluttered on the branches, but those that had fallen spotted the white, earthy floor like an array of splattered bloody paw prints... Annie shivered then and yanked her hood up.

She found her pocketed gloves and pulled them on as the wind began to rush the foliage along the path and billow up into the air. Baxter ran ahead kicking up snow, chasing the tiny red flyers, jumping, twisting and bounding along the path as Annie smiled resignedly – *he was a good boy really and obviously having a whale of a time!*

It was surprising there were no other walkers in that part of the woods. Usually in the afternoons there were at least two or three. Not today though, today

Annie found herself quite alone... well apart from Baxter of course. The trees on the steep, rocky hillside to the left of the trail began to get denser, and redder. It reminded her of Kirkby Pike, just above Keeper's Cottage where the Peterson woman had been finally captured and brought down in cuffs to Harry and his team that autumn two years ago. Now she was on the run again. *Why was that woman always able to infiltrate Annie's mind so much?*

"Bax-*ter?* Bax-*eee!* Where *are* you?"

Was it because Harry was hunting Charlotte down again, albeit in New York? *Or was it because she and her had something in common...?*

"Bax-ter! Bax! Where are you? Here boy – come!" The path had wound round to the left as it went up a slope. Suddenly the dog was nowhere to be seen – *or heard* which in itself was doubly unusual, and actually a bit disquieting. Annie stopped walking for a moment and listened. She concentrated hard, scanned the closer grouped trees to her left up on the slope, and the sparser areas on the lower paths. She couldn't hear him snuffling and rustling amongst the bracken and twigs any more, couldn't hear his excitable panting or see his lovely, smiley, soppy black Baxtery face...

"BAX-TERRRRR!! I've got BIS BIS!" She was worried now, shouting, quickly turning this way and that, almost dancing full-on Baxter-style circles. The higher, shriller and more desperate the tone of her voice alerted her to the fact their favoured shortening of the

word biscuits just wasn't working. It always worked. It never failed to return the Lab in three seconds flat from wherever he was and whatever he was sniffing out. Yet there she remained – holding an empty lead with the light dimming, the red Acers blowing in the wind and their fallen leaves scattered in the snow – totally alone… *until she wasn't.*

FOURTEEN

KIRKDALE
CUMBRIA

When the scent of *'Paco Rabanne'* floated towards her through the trees and finally hit her nostrils, Annie's heart all but stopped. She was back in that lane behind the school dance hall, shoulders pushed up against jutting flint. She could sense him now, feel him, almost hear his breath against her cheek – *she just couldn't see him.*

Then she heard it. A muffled whimpering. The gut-wrenching thump of fear in her stomach took her by surprise. *If that bastard has hurt my dog I'll fucking kill him.* The brief feeling of surprise at a Harry-sized strength of love for the black Lab came and went. She was left with full-on converted devotion. Now she knew what it was to love a dog, but where *was* he – more to the point, *where was Kenny Drew...?* She didn't have to wait long.

"Hello Annie love – long time no see and all that." Kenny sidled out from behind a particularly wide trunk and now stood directly in front of her… holding a gun. Baxter was nowhere to be seen. Annie could feel tears building up along with adrenaline-filled rage, utter terror and (weird given the situation) an awareness that Kenny had barely changed. She would have recognised him anywhere.

"What have you done with my dog? *If you've hurt him I'll—*"

"You'll do *what* exactly? Don't think you're in any position to make threats do *you?*" he sneered, lifting the gun a little higher. Then he seemed to change tack. "Come on Annie, you know I'd never harm a dog, used to have two Dobermans as a kid – don't you remember?" She tried to think back; somewhere deep in the recesses of her mind she could recall him having a couple of darkish dogs, but until she actually saw Baxter was okay, wouldn't put anything past a man with a gun. Especially Kenny.

As she continued to scan the woods for the Lab, another figure suddenly emerged from the trees. He also had a gun, *but this one had his hand on a black dog's red collar*. Her relief was palpable, *it was Baxter!* Despite the fact Annie now had two guns pointing at her all she could think about was that her dog wasn't injured – *or worse.* He looked completely fine, but was wriggling this way and that, straining and bucking to get to her – and away from Michael Morton… *Annie's estranged son.*

"Think our boy turned out pretty well," smiled Kenny, puffing out his none too impressive pigeon chest, "considering we weren't around for him an' all. Well your parents saw to that *didn't* they Annie? *Made damn sure of it, and you didn't do anything to stop them!*" Annie wasn't really listening to Kenny's lies, she was still staring open-mouthed at the man she'd only just met a few days ago, the man who'd asked to be accepted back into her life. She just about managed to stammer out a reply before demanding an explanation…

"Th… they never… knew – I… I didn't tell them who ra—" she glanced at Michael uncertain of what his reaction might be, "I mean… who the father was. *Kenny – why are you DOING this? What's this about, why NOW!?*"

It was starting to get dark, the sky between the trees looked like it was becoming heavy with snow again; it was also getting colder. No chance of any other dog walkers now, no chance of any help. She began to shiver… *inside and out.* Michael was looking oddly at his father…

"*Fifteen years I did!*" Kenny spat at her. "*Fifteen sodding years! Have you any idea what that was like? Being locked up twenty-three hours out of twenty-four EVERY day, having to do 'deals' just to get the odd ciggie, sharing a small cell with a bent copper, watching your back ALL the time. I don't suppose your pig officer husband has ever given me a second thought since then has he?!*"

"*H-Harry?* What's *Harry* got to do with anything?" Annie replied, voice shaking, one eye on Baxter who, looking very morose, had finally sat still but with *his* eyes trained firmly on his mistress.

"Your *husband* Harry, D.C.I. *bastard* Longbridge, was the Senior Investigating Officer on a city bank raid in 2004. He got me sent down *for a fifteen-year stretch for aggravated robbery.* I got out six months ago. Michael here had been looking for me for *years*, finally traced me through online news reports. *So – Annie – now we're all back together again,*" he snarled – *"one BIG HAPPY family!"*

Michael had by now lowered his gun, and was facing Drew. His hold on Baxter's collar had loosened slightly in lapsed concentration, it was enough for the Lab to lunge forward and run hell for leather to Annie who immediately dropped to her knees, hugged him and attached his lead. She stood up and Bax swivelled his rear end into a perfectly heeled sit by her left leg. She looked down at him, astounded – *but mega proud.*

"Kenny…" this from Michael, "you told me that you two were engaged, that her parents refused to allow you to get married and she refused to leave with you."

"Exactly so son, exactly so," he replied looking at Annie, gun still level with her gut… "and now we're all going back to somewhere nice and comfy where we'll let Harry know we have his wife and faithful buddy. Let's see who he's worried about most. He owes me a decade and a half of wages. Reckon that's about… *what…?* Half a mill? *I'm here to collect.*"

Michael didn't seem entirely convinced after Annie's slip implying Kenny had raped her, but went along with his plan anyway. He'd spent a long time searching for and investing in his father's plight, writing to him in prison, believing he'd been the victim of a rotten upbringing that led to mixing with the wrong crowd at school, petty crime during and after, gambling and falling into debt in his twenties and thirties, and finally hooking up with a major league underworld gang. *That had really been a step up in his education* – it had led to the bank raid, half killing a security guard, a prison stretch and his wife divorcing him.

Mostly Michael had felt sorry for his father *(and himself)* when Kenny had assured him he'd begged Annie to run away with him and get married so they could keep Michael, raise him together and *'be a proper little family'.* It was Annie, he'd said, who had refused to disobey her parents and let their baby be taken away and adopted by strangers. Michael's own childhood hadn't been that rosy in the end either, despite his adoptive family's supposed desperation for a child. It was mainly this fact that had persuaded him to agree to the whole kidnapping plot. He had agreed to watch the Longbridge house for a couple of weeks, go along with turning up out of the blue to introduce himself to Annie, build a relationship with her and develop a trust between them. Thing was, Michael had genuinely liked Annie – *he now fervently hoped that Kenny was telling the truth…*

BUILDERS' LOCK-UP
STRATFORD - EAST LONDON

Annie still hadn't told Kenny or Michael that Harry wasn't in the U.K. Not just because she'd been told by her husband not to breathe a word to anyone, but because she wasn't sure if either man would believe her, and she still wasn't entirely convinced that despite what he'd said, if angry and frustrated enough, Kenny might still hurt Baxter.

She also had no idea where she was. Michael had blindfolded, gagged, and tied her hands behind her back before bundling her in the back of a vehicle. She'd assumed it was a van from the high step up, and it had felt like a large space around her – *that and the fact there was no seat…* Despite the obvious danger, she'd actually dropped off to sleep for a while as they'd been driving for hours.

Baxter had spent most of the journey snuggled up with his head in her lap. *Bless him,* she thought, *he probably thought the whole thing was a game once he'd been able to get back to her. If they ever got out of this alive she'd make sure he had steak for dinner for the rest of his life. At least Kenny had allowed her to keep Bax with her…* It was this fact that kept Annie sane because she wasn't entirely sure how she should be feeling. Whilst she was clearly in a ghastly situation, *she'd been kidnapped at gunpoint for God's sake (double gun point),* she knew the men concerned, albeit not in a good way, and there'd been the weakness over Bax. Somehow she sensed her life wasn't actually *threatened*.

The hard-backed chair she was tied to now though was as bloody uncomfortable as the floor of the van, but having Baxter lying across her feet was a comfort. Suddenly the blindfold was ripped off and the gag taken out of her mouth. Michael offered her a cup of water up to her lips. She drank awkwardly, thirstily, whilst her eyes flashed this way and that trying to gauge her surroundings. A very large dirty building, old and with high ceilings, graffiti-scrawled stone walls, decorating gear, paint-stained sheets and the distinct smell of turps. And it was cold, *really cold*. Baxter was given a bowl of water too – *so far so good*. Kenny was sitting opposite her smoking something disgusting and looking very smug. He flicked ash onto the floor and gesticulated in her direction with his cigarette as he spoke…

"As long as you do *exactly* as I say, you'll be fine. That means *no* yelling, *no* withholding information, and *no* trying anything stupid. You can't escape. Pointless screaming, nobody's going to hear you – these premises are way out of town and haven't been used for decades. You can start with telling me your husband's contact details." She looked around her again, trying to remember where the doors were in case she was re-blindfolded. He noticed. *"Oh and Annie –* whilst I really *do* love *dogs*, I won't hesitate to shoot *you* if you're not a good girl." Kenny inhaled deeply, lifted his head up a little, smiled broadly and then blew out a few smoke rings. *Still trying to impress,* she thought, *same as way back when. Well at least it looked like Baxter was safe, but now she had to tell him that Harry was in America. Would he believe her?*

Her other captor was now sitting at a table against a wall to the right of the chair where Annie was tied up. She looked over at him and noticed how he repeatedly rubbed his thumb over his bottom lip. Did she detect a slight frown? Annie wondered if he felt a bit uneasy with the way events were unfolding. She'd noticed it in the woods and felt he hadn't really been that rough when he'd bound and gagged her before shoving her in the van. It was as if the push he'd given her was carefully considered – *almost staged. No,* she concluded, *their son, if that's definitely who he was, was not entirely on board with this.*

Michael Morton fiddled absentmindedly with the mobile sat on the table in front of him, spinning it around and then stopping it, with the action on repeat. He certainly felt confused but didn't want to upset his father, especially after everything that had been planned over the last six months. There was going to be a big cut in it for him too, Kenny hadn't been too specific about just how much, but it was going to be enough to make it worth Michael staying on side. At the end of the day Annie and her parents had ruined his and Kenny's lives, and Harry Longbridge had sent Drew down for a long time. It wasn't difficult to draw the conclusion that whilst what they were doing was a criminal offence, it was nevertheless completely understandable. *But... if it went tits up... Michael shivered as he glanced over at his mother. He felt bad for her there was no getting away from it. He didn't relish sharing a cell with any of Kenny Drew's friends either – and his enemies even less.*

At that moment the mobile rang. Michael looked down. He stopped spinning when 'H' flashed up...

FIFTEEN

BROOKLYN
NEW YORK

Carla had indeed found a bottle of Baclovate in the pre–op room's drugs cabinet of the O.R. she'd prepped earlier for the morning. Only a small one, but then only a small dose was needed. Those dubious gods appeared to be with her yet again. It was now nestled safely in an underwear draw along with a pack of syringes (and some chloroform), *but of course no antidote.*

Unfortunately, there was none in the O.R.s that weren't assigned to her rota, she'd already checked. It would have been less risky if she could have accessed it away from her own floors but… well, needs must.

She'd been quite busy following her drugs raid. Night after night the evenings that followed had been spent at 'home' on the laptop, trawling through social media. Searching and sifting, tracking and tracing, matching up names, emails, telephone numbers, work places, who was friends with whom, where and when they were visiting or meeting up for dates and family events. It all began to fit together like a giant jigsaw. It all resulted in a perfect picture... *of precisely where both Emily and Jenny lived.*

"This!" Carla crowed out loud, waving her third glass of red triumphantly at the screen... *"This is exactly why people shouldn't play out their lives on Facebook and other social media sites!"* She slumped back into the sofa cushions victorious and took a triumphant sip, narrowly avoiding a slosh of wine over the keyboard. "It took me longer than I thought – but now I have you... *I – Have – You...* "

Molly was leaning against the alcove nursing a morning coffee and looking out of her guest bedroom window. Her attention was drawn to the car parked opposite the house.

The Narrows was a lovely tree-lined road with many other large properties like Emily and Gareth's, all set well back, all with wide, deep, grassy front lawns, some with pillared steps the same as theirs, some with sloping driveways. It was clearly a very sought-after neighbourhood. Why then, for the past forty-eight hours had there been a police car sitting outside? She tapped her nails on the mug, then put it down on the dressing table as she began to move around the room opening drawers, choosing clothes and laying them on the bed before going for a shower.

As the hot water ran over her hair and down her back, the inside of the cubicle steamed up quickly, and the inside of her head rattled away with reasons as to why there was a police presence outside the Stones' address. She supposed they could just be following someone who happened to have stopped their car nearby, or a neighbour could have reported something suspicious, even in Narrows Avenue. It *was* the U.S. after all. Maybe they were just having a cheeky spot of breakfast on the 'QT', a couple of bacon rolls and a quick read of the paper, *or maybe… maybe things were already hotting up regarding Charlotte Peterson.* She turned the shower off. Despite the warmth a shudder ran right through her.

Later, as Molly towel-dried her hair and flicked damp, dark waves out of the roll neck she'd just pulled on, she checked the street from the window again. The patrol car was still there – not only was it still there, along the road a little and leaning against a tree, she spotted a figure with their head hunched down inside a high collar, and hands plunged deep into the pockets of a black Reefa jacket. They were also looking up at the house – *at her window.*

A sudden sharp rap on her bedroom door made her jump. She left her 'lookout' position and crossed the room to open it to find Gina, who because of the pregnancy was as usual looking a little pale.

"Molls have you seen it – the patrol car?"

"Yes. Did you see the figure a couple of houses up – leaning against the tree?"

"No – no I didn't," replied Gina, automatically stroking her stomach.

"It was probably nothing," said Molly, noticing her friend's agitation and taking Gina's hand. "It just seemed like he, or *she*, was looking up at the house, at the windows."

"*Who* was? *Who* was looking up at the windows?" Andrew had passed by on the landing, overheard their conversation and entered the room. Gina turned to her fiancé and snuggled under his arm as he pulled her to him. "Molly?" he looked questioningly at her over Gina's head.

"There's a patrol car in the street opposite the house. Plus a figure, man or woman I'm not entirely sure which, in a black *Reefa*, collar pulled up and leaning against the tree outside the Denton's place – *and it isn't either of their kids because of the height.* Have a look." Andrew walked over to the window and checked the road. The patrol car was there – the *'Reefa' had gone.*

Jenny Flood had really settled quite well into Brooklyn life these last two years, considering what she'd had to hide, what she'd had to try and forget. Of course forgetting was impossible. How could she forget her brother had been murdered or that Emily had set up and engulfed them both in a crazy revenge plan – primarily due to a worthless man they'd both had a relationship with at different times? A man who'd been married to her brother's killer, a man in all likelihood she would have to meet again at Gina and Andrew's wedding, *given that it had become apparent he was the girl's father.*

She'd been grateful to Emily and Gareth for the job at McCarthy Stone and the apartment on 4th Avenue (only five minutes from them), but then Jenny figured it was the least they could do, well, the least *Emily* could do... Gareth knew nothing of their '*specific contribution*' to events two years ago in '*The Lakes*'. Still, since arriving from the U.K., it had been much easier for her than it might otherwise have been. As a vulnerable woman with mental health issues and no money, trying to start over in another country... she wouldn't have found it easy. *Especially whilst trying to hide a murky past.*

On the whole she'd managed to get the anorexia under control with help from a therapist at Bellevue Hospital, and had begun eating reasonably well. Now she was waiting for the new man in her life to arrive for a nice meal and a quiet night in. She checked her hair and make-up in the bedroom mirror and touched up her lipstick a little more before she left the room to return to the lounge dining area. This was in fact right in front of the miniscule kitchen complete with seventies serving hatch – but she loved it all the same. It certainly beat her grotty rented flat above the dress shop in Kirkdale, *and it was all hers.* Yes things were certainly looking up... *well... that was apart from the latest news Harry Longbridge had brought from the U.K.*

Jenny hadn't exactly spent much time cooking up a variety of amazing dishes in the last ten years, so there wasn't anything elaborately simmering away in the oven. However the aroma of a simple roast chicken and garlic sauté potatoes met her as she left the bedroom. With a tossed Italian salad and French bread, strawberries and cream for dessert and a bottle of white chilling in the fridge, she hoped it would do.

There was a last reassuring glimpse in the mirror as she crossed the tiny hall towards the lounge. Mike *was* very special after all. One hand passed nervously over her stomach, a tight breath caught in her throat, and a fervent hope that she could endure this… this full-on meal, fluttered in her chest. *It was then that she turned back towards the sound of the doorbell.*

Mid morning the following day, Andrew, Gina and Molly had taken a cab into New York and spent some time at McCarthy Stone to learn how various aspects of the business worked. This was something Andrew had been particularly looking forward to with his love of crime thrillers and all things *'booky'*, as he liked to describe his reading habits.

They hadn't ventured out much since Gina had thought she'd seen Charlotte outside Honey's café, and Harry and Fran had arrived from the U.K. to interview her the other day. Whilst acknowledging her escape from Rampton and Gina's experience that there was a real possibility of Charlotte being in the area, it *was* still only a possibility. They couldn't stay cooped up in the house forever. There was also still the matter of a wedding to arrange and not a great deal of time in which to do it.

Emily had suggested employing a professional wedding planner but Gina had insisted on doing everything herself, *with Molly's help of course*, whilst still sharing bits and pieces with her mother so she would feel included. To be honest although Emily didn't say so, work was full on at the moment, which was why she'd suggested the wedding planner in the first place. Now on top of everything else, Jenny had gone AWOL this morning and there was a huge literary fair to organise for April, the same month Gina and Andrew were getting married. She'd already rung through to Jenny's office twice since nine, now she was trying again. It was eleven o'clock and she'd still not put in an appearance. The internal phone connected and just rang incessantly. Impatient and feeling a little put out now, Emily left her desk and walked through to her P.A.'s office. Megan Calder stopped typing and looked up.

"Can I help Mrs. Stone?"

"Yes Megan, have you seen Jenny this morning? Has she rung in sick to H.R. do you know?"

"I haven't seen her today, I can check for you if you like?" She reached for her phone.

"No don't worry, I'll pop along to her office myself and then try her at home, thanks Megan." Emily's smile was not a confident one as she walked out of her

P.A.'s office into the corridor and turned left towards the 'Events' department where Jenny ran the P.R. and media side of the company. She was always in by 10.00 a.m. even if she'd had an early appointment at Bellevue with her counsellor. Emily knew of these as she'd set them up personally for her to help with her anorexia when she'd first arrived in New York. In any case these had become far less frequent of late as she'd been improving so much, especially since meeting Mike.

Arriving at Jenny's office, Emily knocked then waited out of courtesy in case she was having a conversation on an external phone. When it became apparent there was definitely no voices coming from inside, she opened the door and walked in. There was no coat on the stand, no bag by the desk, no evidence of consumed and much needed early morning coffee. *No Jenny.* Emily's heart began to beat a little faster – a lump was fast developing in her now dry throat. When she felt the blood rush through her ears she moved gingerly over to the leather couch and putting her hand out to steady herself, sat slowly down. Pulling her mobile from her pocket, she brought up Jenny's name from the contact list with unsteady fingers and pressed connect on her home number. She waited, eyes closed, head in her hands, knowing what it could mean as it rang, and rang, *and rang…* Then suddenly it picked up! Emily's eyes flew open, smiling, her head shot up, she could feel her anxiety plummet, it rushed out of her as she almost laughed with relief, Jenny was there, *she was there and she was okay! Thank God!* And then the sky fell in…

"Hello – this is Detective Frank Delaney of the N.Y.P.D. Who is this please?" *She dropped the phone.*

SIXTEEN

BUILDERS' LOCK-UP
STRATFORD - EAST LONDON

Michael had stopped spinning Annie's mobile as soon as it had rung, and after seeing the screen, chucked it over to Kenny whose eyebrows had raised a notch at the illuminated 'H'. His mouth twisted into a lopsided grin and his head nodded slowly. He swiped right and held it in mid air…

"Andrea? Andrea are you there?! It's your mother – where are you?? We expected you hours ago! As per usual you're so incon…" The scratchy, shrill and irritated tones of Annie's mother echoed around the empty lock-up, then cut dead as Kenny killed the call. Scowling he marched angrily over to Annie who was still seated and tied, but remained gag-less and able to see. Baxter rose slightly on his haunches and actually gave a low growl now detecting a very obvious threat. Drew smiled at him, took a deep breath and calmed down a little.

"Not mellowed any has she…" He stated this as a fact rather than a question. Annie shook her head. He looked back at the phone. "Why 'H' for the number?"

"'H'… for *'Home'* – I was… was going to drive down, to see them tonight – due around ten. I've no idea what time it is, it must be… *late*." Her voice tailed off and Annie sighed as she looked up at the roof in resignation of another failed visit. "It's… *it's been a while*. She's probably really pissed at me now."

"It's nearly midnight." He put the phone in his pocket. "Strange Harry hasn't rung you. Aren't you usually together in the evenings these days? I heard he'd been put out to grass, *collected a nice fat pension*," Kenny sneered. He inclined his head towards Michael implicating him as the information source. Now it was Annie's turn to breathe in deeply, and follow it with an anxious lip roll. *How long should she keep it from him? That Harry was in New York back on a major case, no grass involved anymore… That she had no idea when he'd be home? It could be weeks. How long would they be prepared to hold on to her, keep her alive?*

Kenny was scrutinising her now, *he was up really close.* One hand stroked Baxter's head gently, reassuringly. The other trailed the nose of his gun down her cheek and across her lips. The coldness of the metal left an icy threat. His face now nauseatingly close to hers, their skin inches apart, nostrils flooded with Paco Rabanne, memories on repeat… *she felt sick.* A tear slid down her cheek. Kenny wiped it away with the Glock before continuing on down to her throat towards her open shirt collar. He nudged the material to one side, kept going till it was taught – *a button strained*. Across the room Michael had raised himself slightly out of his chair in anticipation. He wasn't quite sure of what, or even what he was going to do, what *could* he do? He just knew it would be wrong to hurt her. The air was still. Even Baxter had quietened. Annie knew she had to tell him – *and tell him now*.

"Harry's… he's… he's out of the country." She faltered, whispering in a small voice, head down. "I – I honestly *don't* know when he'll be back." She rushed out the last bit with her head up, hopeful it sounded realistic, strong, *the truth* – because it was. Annie Longbridge truly had absolutely no idea when her husband would be leaving the U.S., what exactly he was doing day by day, and more to the point with whom. Except of course she did know *who*, she just wasn't sure how close the *'who'* was. *Or how often…*

"He's… *whaaat?!!"* Kenny swung round to Michael – face like thunder. "You said you'd *checked! Checked – everything – twice! Three times!"* The younger man coloured up quickly and began stammering – this he definitely *wasn't* expecting.

"W-Well she never gave – sh… she never said any—"

"*Nobody* knew, Kenny – *nobody*," Annie intervened. Drew swung back to face her, veins standing out at his temples. "Harry told me not to breathe a word," she continued – "I *haven't*… until now." Annie tried her best to stare him straight in the eye, appear confident. Kenny Drew ran an exasperated hand through his hair, Michael looked almost apologetically at her, and Baxter was back up on his feet. His mistress shushed him quietly under her breath, smoothed a hand over his back and ordered a near silent sit, *with an added pat to his rear end.*

"Right! Well let's see how fast he wants to get his arse on a plane when he's informed of the stakes back home!" Kenny yelled wildly as he stomped about. *"Number!"* When Annie told him to just look it up under *'Harry'*, the man snorted, holstered his gun inside his jacket and retrieved her phone from his pocket. Annie glanced over at Michael and saw him looking anxiously at her again. Kenny tapped out Harry's number – the line connected…

Everybody waited. All that could be heard bouncing off the walls was the ringing of Annie's phone. And then it stopped.

> *'The person you are trying to reach*
> *is not available to take your call*
> *at the moment. Please try later.*
> *Alternatively if you'd like to lea…'*

Annie wasn't sure if she was gutted Harry hadn't picked up or not. On the one hand she wanted him to rush home and rescue her, on the other she realised how entirely impractical that was, clearly not being able to just conjure up an instant flight and have it deliver him in the next half hour. Then there was the fact that he was three thousand miles away and would be out of his mind with worry. He would... *wouldn't he...?* Her thoughts had stopped there.

Kenny on the other hand was more livid than gutted and only just restrained himself from hurling the phone to the floor and grinding it with the heel of his boot. Instead he returned it to his pocket and looked at his watch. Twelve-fifteen. Seven-fifteen in New York then, early evening. Maybe he was at some swanky dinner. Even so, didn't stop him from answering his phone, nobody seemed to be able to stay away from the bloody things these days. He was still getting used to smart phones after spending fifteen years at Her Majesty's pleasure – *courtesy of the man he was trying very hard to blackmail.*

Michael stood up then and walked over to Kenny, turning his back to Annie he whispered something in his ear. Kenny nodded and Michael glanced over his shoulder at her before walking swiftly through the large eerie building and out into the night air.

Annie watched him leave. Even more concerned for her predicament now she'd been left alone with the man who'd raped her decades ago, whose company she'd been in the last few hours and in such close proximity to, that it made her feel like it was yesterday. Whatever the reason for Michael's involvement with this, and despite her disappointment and distrust of him, she still sensed he wouldn't let Kenny hurt her. Although Drew obviously needed to keep her alive for the ransom money he intended to demand from her husband, Annie couldn't help wondering if he felt things weren't going to plan, he'd have to kill her anyway. *She did after all know who he was.* She needn't have worried. A few minutes later Michael reappeared with a couple of large sports bags and placed them on the table. Then she remembered there had been something soft in the van on the floor near her head where she'd been lying, tied up, rolling back and forth for hours, all the way to wherever this was now.

Michael unzipped the first bag, pulled out several large blankets and placed them on the table. From the second he brought out some service station sandwiches and tins of Coke. He chucked a packet of sandwiches over to Kenny and followed it with a can, left his on the table and took one over to Annie. Pulling the cellophane off and lifting one half out of the cardboard container, Michael offered it up to her. She thought of refusing it for a moment but she was starving and certainly no martyr. Annie leant forward, opened her mouth and bit into it. She chewed and swallowed quickly, then looked down at Baxter who was whimpering and looked at Kenny. He'd already noticed.

"What about the dog? I told you to get some—"

Michael produced a large sausage roll from his pocket and unwrapped it. Baxter's ears had been up

145

and his mouth drooling since the sandwiches had come out. He was now full on fidgeting and whining until the pastry was handed to him.

The whole situation really was quite surreal, but as long as Kenny was playing the '*Dog Father*' and Bax was safe, fed and watered, Annie felt a little calmer. Cold, tired and very uncomfortable – *but calmer.* She couldn't help but notice the blankets on the table. Kenny followed her line of sight and looked at his watch. It was now 1 a.m., he was ready for his bed, and it most certainly wasn't going to be in this shit hole.

"Right… time we were off!" he said sharply, pulling out Annie's phone again. She immediately looked anxious, at first one then the other of her two captors, wide-eyed in alarm at the thought of being left alone, re-gagged and blindfolded, in a *cold, dark, lock-up…*

"But just before we go home to our nice comfy duvets," continued Kenny, with a glint in his eye, "I'm going to try my future benefactor one more time." He laughed loudly at his own joke and nodding wildly, looked over at Michael inviting him to join in. He felt obliged but it was half-hearted, and couldn't quite manage a similar full-on guffaw. Kenny made a disapproving face, dropped the mirth and tapped out Harry's number a second time. *Again it connected and rang out.*

"Damn you Longbridge, you elusive bastard!" he yelled uselessly at the mobile, eyes narrowing, lips pursed, puffing, panting and now pacing up and down in short bursts.

"Surely… surely you're not going to… *leave me – us – here?*" pleaded Annie. She looked primarily at Michael. Her most feared thought now was to be left in the dark, blindfolded and gagged again. *And what if they took Baxter?* She swivelled her head agitatedly, to and fro between the two men.

"You'll be fine." This was from Kenny who was already picking up the blankets from the table and taking them over to her.

"We can leave the gag and blindfold off can't we?" Michael asked. "We're miles from anywhere out here, the whole Stratford complex has been deser—" Michael suddenly reeled sideways from the back hander Kenny had delivered across his jaw having chucked the blankets.

"SHUT the FUCK… UP!!" he roared, fuming at the younger man for letting their location slip, or at least the town. Now it was clear to Annie that she was in a disused builders' lock-up, on a deserted complex full of similar buildings in Stratford. And he'd already said if she screamed no one would hear – *so well out of town then.*

Kenny turned back to the heap on the floor, picked them up and arranged one across her shoulders, one over her lap and round her legs, and folded the largest one into a square padded bed for Baxter at her feet. He then produced a lamp from one of the bags, set it on the table and plugged it in. It really was difficult to come to terms with a man who acted so ambivalently.

It was seriously messing with her head. One minute he was threatening to shoot her if she didn't behave and assaulting his accomplice, the next he was supplying food, light and blankets. She never felt sure what he would do next, whether or not she was safe. *And what if he couldn't get hold of Harry?*

Annie had been scared to ask earlier, she knew she should've said something but now she was desperate.

"Kenny... I... I need to... I gotta *pee*." Drew blew an irritated sigh and stood thoughtfully for a few moments, then looked at the exit door. It was clear he was impatient to reach his bed. He indicated to Michael with a flick of his head, to sort it out. Morton returned to her, took off the blankets and untied her hands and feet, then walked her to an area behind a stack of old fencing panels and found her a bucket. Baxter followed.

"Don't try anything Annie," whispered Michael. "I believe he *will* shoot you, even if it's only a flesh wound." She nodded and waited for him to turn his back. It was horribly embarrassing and she felt utterly degraded, but she had no choice. When she'd finished and hoisted her pants up, feeling damp and disgusting, Michael had the grace to look briefly uncomfortable before walking her back to the chair, retying her hands and feet, and wrapping the blankets about her again. Baxter settled on his bed having cocked his leg up the fence panels...

"I'll leave a low lamp on by the table," said Kenny, "it'll give you some light. We'll be back in the morning, *and you'd better pray I've managed to get hold of your husband."* He turned to go, but then appeared to have forgotten something. He walked back over to Annie and producing some tape from his pocket re-gagged her. She began to protest but he ignored her as the wide sticky band was wrapped around the back of her head in a full circle and then torn off the roll. When he'd finished she looked him dead in the eyes and begged with her own to remove it. *He didn't.*

"Just in case – *don't want to be making any more mistakes do we,*" he said, turning to Michael who had averted his eyes to the door. Michael Morton was beginning to wish he'd had no part in this. In fact he was beginning to wish he hadn't searched for his father at all.

With that, both men walked out of the lock-up and Annie was left in semi darkness, cold, damp, bound and gagged… *but at least she was alive and had the comfort of her best friend lying at her feet.*

SEVENTEEN

BROOKLYN
NEW YORK

The night before, Jenny had answered the door to Mike who had brought the holy trinity with him – *flowers, wine and chocolates.* She thought that had gone out in the eighties, it certainly wasn't something she was used to, but then Mike *was* quite a bit older and always made her feel special. At forty-five he was thirteen years her senior but as he always told her, *'age is just a number'.*

It had been a lovely evening. The food was perfect, Mike was perfect and Jenny had actually eaten three courses for the first time in years, *albeit small ones.* She put this down to how he made her feel, which was calm, happy and in charge of her life. No need to make food a control issue any longer, nothing to feel in turmoil over. It had never been about aesthetics – always about Miles and how powerless she'd felt in their relationship. Now all that was behind her.

After eating and talking about news and work *(Mike was a Brooklyn fire fighter with the N.Y.F.D.)*, laughing at his niece's antics the previous weekend at his sister's, and sharing ideas for a holiday together later in the year, they'd cuddled up on the couch under subdued lighting listening to a *Snow Patrol* compilation. Jenny had never been happier.

Mike couldn't stay over that night. He was on at seven the following day for a twenty-four-hour shift and wanted to get at least seven hours, so had left at ten-thirty. Carrying seventy-odd pounds of kit on your back when you're running into a fire required quality shut-eye, particularly when you're over forty. *This was the only time he'd acknowledge the age thing.*

Jenny was just clearing the dishes off the table after seeing him out, when the doorbell went for the second time that evening. *Forgotten your keys again I bet, or your wallet's fallen out of your back pocket like last time!* Smiling, she glanced quickly around the room but couldn't see evidence of either, so headed straight for the hall and the front door. The exterior porch light was still broken from three weeks ago, and her narrow hall not as bright as it might have been given the previous owner's love of deep grey, and the fact she'd still not got around to decorating everywhere yet. Jenny pulled the door open and began to joke about his memory...

"You forgotten your keys a—"

The force with which she felt her body fly backwards was just as much of a shock as the act itself. The side of

*her head smacked mercilessly against the left-hand wall as
she landed on the base of her spine, almost as far up as the
lounge door and crying out in agony!*

*The door slammed shut behind her attacker,
reverberated in its frame and there was a constant wet
stream dribbling down to her jaw. She could barely see
him. Apart from being slightly woozy from several glasses
of wine, she was now engulfed in a cracking headache. The
intruder had swiped at the hall light switch to avoid any
passer-by seeing through the glazed door, plunging them
into darkness. Dazed, Jenny still attempted to scrabble
backwards as he advanced. It wasn't quite pitch black
with the low light trying to seep in from the lounge, but
she could now sense him standing over her, tall, strong and
in control… It had taken a few seconds but then she could
hear someone's panic-stricken voice building to a crescendo,
screaming above Snow Patrol's 'Chasing Cars'…*

What happened next was pure evil. The stuff of
nightmares – one that Jenny Flood thought she would
never have to experience again. After the door was
locked and just enough chloroform delivered to her
nose and mouth to remove any resistance *(and to stop
that godawful screaming)*, she was dragged backwards
into the lounge by her arms and left on the floor by the
little dining table. It still bore the remnants of a happy
evening, a fun romantic meal for two… the beginning
of a new life.

Panting with the exertion, the intruder flopped on
to the couch and removed their balaclava. It was hot

and itchy, claustrophobia inducing… *she was glad to get it off.*

Charlotte sat quietly getting her breath back, staring at one of her two most hated enemies as the woman lay helpless and prostrate on the floor. Not quite unconscious *(where would the fun be in that?),* but not able to stop what was going to happen next either. She studied her carefully, head on one side as Jenny moaned and slowly brought her hand up to her head, felt the blood, her breathing laboured.

"Well now Jenny isn't this nice. You even laid a dinner table for me, shame I couldn't make it earlier, it all looks so pretty. Still, not to worry, I love strawberries and can always pop a few in a Tupperware container before I go. I'm sure you've got one somewhere, even in that doll's house of a kitchen."

That voice! Jenny tried to force her eyelids open, tried to lift her head but it still felt too heavy, she couldn't coordinate her limbs and her chest felt like it was caving under a sack of cement. Panic gripped her now – far more than if it had been a rapist. *Charlotte Peterson. She* **was** *in New York. And she was an assassin.* Jenny tried her hardest to lift herself up, but each time her herculean effort with miniscule result was rewarded with a foot pushing her back down.

"*No, no, no!* You don't want to be getting up, it's *way* past your bedtime and tonight you'll be getting your best sleep *ever.*" Charlotte pulled a pair of surgical gloves from her pocket and put them on. Next, out came a small, thin plastic container. Charlotte snapped it open and withdrew the syringe, which she held up for Jenny to see. Pre-loaded, the Baclovate gleamed... *pink and deadly*.

Jenny could just make out a blurred image that didn't match the voice. She began to open her mouth to beg, but Charlotte was bent over her now and placed a finger lightly on her lips... "Shhh... it'll be fine, you won't feel a thing. Well... you'll feel all your limbs begin to paralyse of course, but it won't hurt too much. Not until it gets in to your organs anyway, *that* might hurt. I'm not sure to be honest. It's a new drug you see, one I'm not entirely familiar with – *certainly not in this quantity anyway.*"

Jenny began to breathe in sharp rapid bursts, eyes wide in terror she tried to move it as Charlotte inserted the needle into her lead-heavy arm. She winced as helplessly, resignedly now she felt the neon-pink liquid sinister and cold, seep beneath her skin into her bloodstream, until its operator had pushed the plunger all the way to its base. Thoughts of Mike floated in her mind, of how happy she had been in those few short months, of what their future might have been, of children, of her first chance of real happiness... *And then it began*. It started with her feet, tingling at first then creeping, tight, hard, constricting. She could no longer feel them. The paralysis crept up her legs slowly at first – then it began to accelerate.

"Well I must be away now I'm afraid, things to do, people to track down, you know how it is." Charlotte bent down close to Jenny's face, her left eye twitching. *"You crossed me Jenny Flood – you and your husband-stealing mentor. And now you're both going to pay for it. The drug I've administered will crawl up your body like a boa constrictor – it will squeeze and paralyse every muscle, tendon and organ. When it reaches your lungs it will suffocate you... slowly. You are going to die Jenny – you are going to die tonight and you're going to die all alone. Say hello to that horse-murdering brother of yours for me!"*

Charlotte stood up, returned to the couch to retrieve and replace her balaclava mask, and then walked past her victim towards the hall. Suddenly she stopped. Turning around she walked back to the dining table, popped a strawberry in her mouth through the opening in the mask, sucked thoughtfully on the delicious fruit and swallowed. *Then she threw her head back and laughed, all the way to the front door.*

Detective Frank Delaney had C.S.I.s (Crime Scene Investigators) and forensics bursting the seams of the victim's tiny apartment.

"She was certainly a looker," he commented out loud, standing over the body of Jenny Flood. Unfortunately for him, Bellevue's chief forensic pathologist on that day was Kay Winford...

"So Frank, *would it have made any damn difference if she looked like Larry King on a bad day?*"

"No ma'am – no of course not I – er – apologise for appearing insensitive." Delaney flushed as he caught Det. Terri Malone's raised eyebrow. She was sat on the sofa supplying copious tissues as she gently questioned the neighbour who'd found the body and called 911.

Bellevue's finest obviously hadn't mellowed any during her two-year stint in the U.K.'s Lake District, and Delaney and Malone conveyed understanding of that in their single glance exchange. Terri though, in addition, was exasperated at Frank's lapse in trying to avoid old-school cop comments.

It was at exactly this point that Emily Stone had rung through to speak to the deceased, and it was Delaney who'd taken the call...

"Hello – this is Detective Frank Delaney of the N.Y.P.D. Who is this please?" There was no response. "Hello... ? Hello... ? *Hello – are you still there?*" There was a rustle and anxious voices in the background...

"Hello, err... sorry, *hello* this is Gareth Stone. I believe my wife was trying to contact our work colleague Miss. Jenny Flood? Are you there with her? Is everything... *is she okay?*" Frank hesitated for a moment before answering...

"Good morning sir – and you would be who *exactly* in relation to Miss. Flood?" replied Frank. This threw Gareth slightly.

"I'm her employer... and... friend I guess, well my wife is more so but... look is Jenny th—"

"Mr. Stone I'd like if possible for you and Mrs. Stone to come down to the 68th at 333 65 Street, Brook—"

"Yeah I know where it is Detective, it's my local station. Look is Jenny *okay*, that's what we need to know?"

"If you could just meet me at the station in say thirty minutes?" Delaney replied. "No, make that an hour. I've got a couple of British officers turning up here shortly. I'd rather not say anything over the phone sir if you don't mind."

Gareth agreed, but he wasn't happy. *And he wasn't stupid.* Something must've happened and this guy was going to play it by the book. It also looked like Harry Longbridge and Fran Taylor had been notified… *which could only mean one thing.*

Gareth Stone looked at his wife who was currently giving a good impression of a scared rabbit in the headlights of an eighteen-wheeler. He'd found her sitting on the sofa in Jenny's office, staring at a mobile on the carpet. Once he'd ascertained whose it was and what was going on, he'd picked up the phone and had the conversation with the officer at the other end. Now he understood why Emily was looking none too clever, and was now mirroring pretty much the same himself. *He also had a jagged rock in his guts as he feared for Jenny's wellbeing.*

"Em… they want us down at the 68th. I don't think it's going to be good news – we need to prepare ourselves."

"What's not going to be good news? Prepare for *what exactly? What's happened?!*" At the sound of Andrew's voice Emily snapped out of her trance and looked at the three of them standing in the doorway. Andrew, Gina and Molly had been with Gareth looking at some of the production issues McCarthy Stone had to deal with in the graphics department, when he'd disappeared. After wandering around for a bit and finally asking one or two people, they had discovered he'd come down to the media and events floor and followed him down.

"It's Jenny," Gareth answered. "She didn't come in today and it's very unusual for her not to call and let us know. With the suspicions we've had regarding, well, with whom Gina felt she saw... Emily had rung Jen at home and..." He tailed off for a moment noticing Gina and Molly's clasped hands. "The N.Y.P.D. is at her apartment now. They've asked us to meet them over at 65 Street – it's our local station." Andrew felt sick. He'd been here before. *Exactly here.* The same call, the same reason, the same event two years ago when his friend and colleague Rachel Dern hadn't turned up for work. His mind was racing ahead. It's how it all started... her murderous campaign, her inevitable capture, and her incarceration at Rampton. She'd been sprung on the day release, flown to New York under a new identity – *and now she was taking her revenge.* It *must* be that. There was no doubt about it...

Charlotte was back.

EIGHTEEN

STATEN ISLAND
NEW YORK

Harry Longbridge was looking at his mobile. He'd had it on charge in his room at their B&B, The Harbor, the night before, whilst they'd been downstairs at dinner. Hence he'd missed the two calls from Annie. He was just about to return them when his phone suddenly sprung into life with his new *'Law & Order'* ringtone *(just a bit of fun to offset the deep stuff)*. Fran had of course tried telling him it was nearly ten years out of date, but it had been his favourite show at the time and there was just no dissuading him…

He took the call ignoring the two missed ones from Annie – he'd ring her later… she'd understand. *Wouldn't she?*

"Detective Longbridge?" Harry recognised the voice.

"*D.C.I.* Longbridge, *yes, kind of* – is that Detective Delaney?"

"It is. Sorry, yeah D.C.I. Look – we have an incident over at 4th Avenue Bay Ridge, *the apartments there?* Actually you probably wouldn't be familiar with… Anyway, we believe it could be linked to your female U.K. absconder you came to see us about."

"*4th Avenue?* Is it Jen… I mean is it *Miss. Jennifer Flood's address?*" It rang a bell. Harry had taken Jenny's contact details when he and Fran had been at the Stones' place a few days back. He threw out a guess shot.

"Yeah – 'fraid it looks that way. Do you want to come over and I.D. the…" Harry flinched.

"*I.D. Detective… ?*"

"Yeah – sorry, it's not great. We've got forensics going over the place now. If you can make it in the next fifteen minutes, only I've got to leave here for a meeting in an hour back at the station."

"We'll be there," replied Harry crisply. He said goodbye and rang off, then immediately phoned through to Fran's room, updated her and arranged to meet in reception. She wasn't exactly thrilled Delaney had contacted Harry instead of her – *male dominant syndrome clearly alive and well.* Of course guilt then immediately swept through her. A woman had likely been murdered or at the very least attacked, and on top of that it was someone Harry knew.

They left the building in silence. Harry felt like shit, he knew she did too. *They'd fallen down on this job big time.*

They turned in to 4th Avenue and cruised slowly towards Jenny's apartment. There were emergency vehicles and officialdom everywhere – they couldn't get near the place. Fran parked several doors down and they got out of the car and walked back to the address. She lifted the yellow cordon tape, showed her warrant card at the door and explained Harry's advisory presence to the posted detective (given his absence of a warrant). The officer had already been briefed however and waved them inside after ensuring they'd both dressed in shoe guards and cover suits.

C.S.I. and forensics were everywhere, and Harry immediately picked up on the smell of chloroform. The blood smear across the low part of the left-hand wall opposite an open door didn't escape either. *Still got it 'Magpie',* he thought, *just wish it wasn't here.*

Frank had seen them arrive through the large lounge window that fronted the street. The curtains were closed when the team had arrived, but after forensics had completed those checks, they'd been drawn back. He came out to greet them in the hall.

"D.C.I. Longbridge, D.I. Taylor. Sorry we have to meet again under these circumstances." Fran waved her hand and shook her head dismissively…

"Please, first names are fine. You okay with that Harry?"

"Sure," he nodded, looking at Delaney. "Detective?" Frank acknowledged assent and extended a hand towards the lounge where they slowly filed in. It was even busier in there. Shuffling into the small, elongated room full of white coats felt like being stuck on the Tube in a forensics-only rush hour.

"So what've you discovered so far – anything conclusive?" Harry asked Frank as he looked about the room and took in the remnants of the cosy meal for two on the table, the flowers and opened box of chocolates on the coffee table.

"My God – Harry Longbridge!! What the hell are you doing this side of the pond, and at this crime scene?" Kay Winford had been standing with her back to the newcomers, but on hearing Harry's voice had swung round, dropped her mouth mask and pushed back her white forensics hood. She was still as he remembered her, stout, buxom, bright-eyed and forthright. He'd held a great deal of respect for Kay Winford during the time they'd worked together, and now seeing him again her face was a picture. Harry's matched.

"Kay! Well I'll be bug—" He grinned and held out a hand, then felt the automatic broad smile inappropriate. "*Good* to see you Kay, although…"

"Yes – it's bad Harry," she said accepting the handshake and guessing his thoughts. "About as bad as it gets actually, by my reckoning some form of injectable paralysing drug." She pointed to the needle mark on the victim's arm. "I won't know what exactly till we get her back to the lab. There's a lot more here than just rigor [mortis] though. It would have been extremely unpleasant to say the least…" She tailed off with a slow head-shake and frowned expression.

"You two know each other?" This from Frank, clearly surprised his forensic pathologist knew a *'British Bobby'* who'd just walked off the street as far as she was concerned – or so he thought.

"Those two years at Kirkdale General in the U.K.'s Lake District," Kay replied. "Thought you were up for retirement that Christmas though Harry, what happened? *Wouldn't they let you out?"* They both gave a wry laugh.

"Oh yeah, I retired alright – didn't appreciate how bored senseless I'd be though. So when Fran here, an ex-London colleague, relocated to Kirkdale, she asked for me to come back in on this case."

"*This* case, how does—?"

"Remember Charlotte Peterson, serial killer the summer of 2018?" Kay nodded and *'hmmed'* acknowledgement. "She got sprung from Rampton during a day release for her mother's funeral. We lost her Kay. Not one officer in the U.K. could track her down, she just went to ground. Then we got a tip-off she was out here looking for revenge on two specific people, maybe more. Jenny was one of them."

"I thought the surname 'Flood' sounded familiar – she had a brother didn't she? Young lad, purple hair – *never forget crazy hair!* Sadly ended up on my table too…"

"Exactly so… another of that crazy bitch's victims, which all things considered, leads to me think this is her work too – although clearly a massively different M.O. *[method of operation]*, despite the obvious chloroform connection." He lifted his head and wrinkled his nose. "Don't think I'll ever forget that smell now as long as I live."

"We can't just jump to conclusions that this *is* this perp of yours Harry," Frank interrupted, "there's clear evidence here of a romantic evening and firstly I'll be looking for the man, *or woman* [this directed at Kay] who shared that meal with Miss. Flood last night."

"Oh Jenny was definitely straight officer, I'd stake my life on it," chipped in Harry. "Kay? You met her in the U.K.?" The pathologist nodded.

"Definitely straight – no question… *Doesn't mean her boyfriend killed her though…*" Harry and Frank looked at each other and nodded in unison.

"Well when you lot have finished reminiscing and summing up…" Fran was standing arms crossed and glaring a little.

"Sorry Fran." Harry reverted to official introductions. "Kay Winford – D.I. Fran Taylor, Fran – Kay Winford, forensic pathologist. Kay and I worked together at Kirkdale General on more than one occasion." The two women shook hands. "Fran is up from '*Canon Row*' in London, now working out of '*Kirkdale Nick*' and heading up the new Peterson case which we believe has turned Stateside." At this point Frank Delaney took his opportunity to ask about the differences in the U.K. murders.

"How different *was* the M.O. exactly?" he asked. Harry and Kay looked at each other, the pathologist displayed a *'you'd never believe me if I told you'* expression as she pulled a specimen bag from her pocket.

"I'll leave that one with you Harry – good to see you again. If this *does* turn out to be one of yours, let me know if I can help with anything. You'll find me at Bellevue if I'm not out and about." She gave him her card.

"*Actually* it's one of... *oh never mind.*" Fran rolled her eyes in defeat. Harry sighed and Frank's interest increased.

"Come on Fran," Harry said passively, "we're a team again and I *am* the one with the history on this. It's why you brought me in from the cold remember?"

"True," she conceded, head on one side. "Right then *D.C.I. Longbridge* tell the detective here exactly what Peterson *did* to those girls back home." At this, most of the team in the lounge seemed to stop what they were doing and turned to look at Harry. He was just about to open his mouth to respond when the theme to *'Law & Order'* began to fill the air...

Harry had excused himself and edged back out into the hall when he saw Annie's number on his mobile screen. He pressed the receive button and immediately began talking...

"Hold on love, just finding somewhere quieter. Be with you in a sec." He swiftly removed the shoe covers, wrestled with the forensic suit, which took longer, then finally stepped outside into the fresh air. It had grown colder as the day approached the afternoon, snow threatened as he pulled his jacket collar up around his ears. Fran had followed him to the door, stopped and waited at the threshold. Harry walked up the street towards their hired car, irritated on remembering Fran had been driving so had the keys, and turned back round.

"Annie? I'm here now just had to—"

"SHUT THE FUCK UP AND LISTEN!" Harry nearly tripped over the ornamental stones that edged the neat grass squares fronting the apartments.

"What the... *who the hell—?*"

"I suggest you rest your mouth and open your fucking ears Longbridge. I have your wife – I have Annie. I actually also have your dog, nice boy – he's safe. She isn't." Fran had begun to strip off the forensic suit and shoe covers as soon as she saw the expression on Harry's face – it didn't look like he was on a sweet call from home. It didn't even look like a *nagging* call from home. Harry's eyes found hers as she advanced up the street.

"Who *is* this? If you've *harm*—"

"I don't think you're in any position to be making threats mate, *do you?*" Harry absentmindedly felt behind him for something to sit down on, but obviously being in the street found nothing. Fran had picked up the pace and was now running – *he looked as if he was about to faint.* She flashed the key at the car as she ran, and once beside him, turned him round again to walk back to it, opened the door and literally put him in. Then she ran round to the driver's side and was sat next to him in an instant. Harry put the phone on loudspeaker…

"Do you remember the City's Nat West Bank heist in 2004?" continued the caller. "The biggest case of your career I reckon. You got me sent down for a fifteen stretch Longbridge, *fifteen sodding years*. Well now I'm out – and I want my fifteen years of lost dosh. By my reckoning that's about half a million *including interest*."

"Kenny… Drew." It was so quiet Fran could barely hear him whisper it into the phone. All his years of grittiness and surety had vanished instantly. Harry rubbed his forehead and leant against the side window, eyes suddenly tired. He noticed the snow *had* started up again, stared through the windscreen as the flakes fell outside and wondered if it was snowing in Cumbria, London, *or wherever the hell else Drew had got his wife incarcerated.*

"So…" Kenny continued, "Annie is comfortable – *for now.* But it's up to you. If you want her to remain that way, *if you're sensible*, then this is what you're gonna—"

Harry took a deep breath, licked his lips and sat bolt upright. Suddenly the bulldog was back, tenacity firing through his blood — *basically because he knew he needed to show it.*

"Kenny? *Now you listen to me and you listen good. I don't have half a million and even if I did I wouldn't give it to you or any other bastard con. I have a few connections of my own from the Canon Row days, and if you so much as BREATHE on my wife I'll see to it one of them finds you, rips your fucking balls off and feeds them to you in a McDonalds bap!!* **DO YOU UNDERSTAND?***"*

There was a long silence followed by a click. Fran realised she'd been holding her breath and hadn't remembered to breathe out. She did so now with her eyes wide, a torrent of questions spewing from her lips after the air rush. Harry just stared silently through the windscreen... *and watched as the snow fell faster.*

NINETEEN

BROOKLYN
NEW YORK

"Harry?" Fran touched his arm as he sat staring out of the window. The snow was coming down thick and fast now and looked like it might actually start to settle. He turned to her then looked back down at his phone.

"Kenny Drew is a *filthy, snivelling little piece of…"* He exhaled loudly and smashed the side of his fist into the door. "I'm going to have to call him back. He knows that. He's also obviously got Annie's phone."

"Harry you've got to call it in – now! And you're going to have to fly back to the U.K., there's nothing else for it!" Harry pulled at and chewed on the side of his mouth as he tapped the mobile on his leg between intermittently looking out of his passenger window, the windscreen and finally back at Fran's *'you know I'm right'* face. He didn't even feel his hand throbbing.

"I can't. Call it in that is. He'll kill her. Obviously I'll *have* to go back though." Harry looked down at his mobile before continuing. "I'm going to ring him, tell him what he wants to hear… then fly home, track him down – *and bust his ugly face wide open!*"

Carla had turned up for work at the hospital as usual the day after her 'visit' to Jenny. She was preparing O.R.3 for a booked C-section and felt good, *very good.* Probably the best she'd felt in a very long while. *One down one to go… well apart from the nosey cab driver patient of course and I might also just be tempted to…* Abruptly her self-congratulatory thoughts were interrupted by her senior anaesthesia technician Jodi Denton, who from nowhere was suddenly standing right behind her. Jodi was her main 'trainer' even though she'd only been doing the job herself for a couple of years. At thirty-seven although only a few years younger, as far as Carla was concerned Jodi was frankly lacking in the *'seriously intelligent'* department. She certainly wasn't a trained medic – and Carla was already beginning to feel the rub regarding the banned use of her U.K. credentials…

"*Carla*… can I speak with you a moment please?" Jodi sounded curt, impatient and unlike herself, *not very happy at all.* Carla sighed and turned around from the instruments she was preparing. She now saw that Jodi's expression matched her voice – it was not a happy one. Considering she was usually a bit *'full on'* for Carla's tastes, this was definitely a deviation from the norm. Carla smiled – *barely.*

"Yes Jodi – how can I help?" Her expression displayed feigned interest.

"The drugs cabinet in O.R.2; I carried out a stocktake last thing before going off this morning as I've been on a late. There were some items missing."

"Well I expect they've been *used* then Jodi," replied Carla, the sarcasm only just apparent, but lingering all the same and with Jodi only just realising. Although she still wasn't *quite* sure.

"There were no requests for chloroform from O.R.2 yesterday, and certainly none for Baclovate. That's a rare use and dangerous med. That drug is on a majorly strict control list, *it has to be signed out – **in triplicate!***"

"Sooo…" Carla palmed her hands upwards in a puzzled manner with matching expression. "What are you saying here Jodi, that I whipped a few bottles out of the cabinet for some kind of *weird* party?" The younger woman stood holding her stocktake clipboard as their eyes held each other for a moment. Carla waited.

"No… well… not *exactly*, it's just that these—"

"It's just that *I'm the newest member of the team* and as such you're quizzing me first?" Carla's intended newfound *'keep your head down, meek and mild, yes ma'am no ma'am'* persona was looking and sounding a little thin on the ground at that moment – and what's more she knew it. She bit her lip and reverted to a major climb down… "Look – Jodi. I'm *reaaally* sorry, I honestly didn't mean to sound… *awkward* or… *rude* or anything, it's just that I wasn't feeling too good yesterday, and knocked some bottles over when I was replenishing a drugs cart for an op, and… well I felt emb—"

"You should've come to me and filled out a damage and loss form. This is *very* serious, we can't have drugs just *disappearing* you know!" said Jodi, steely eyed now as she made a note, and more than a little suspicious at Carla's climb down. However, Jodi'd had a hard shift, was tired, due to go off duty in twenty minutes and wasn't about to delay that with an official warning report. She wanted to get her head down for a few hours so she could pick the twins up herself for a change. Her mother-in-law was really helpful and the kids loved her, but she liked to collect Max and Ava herself whenever possible. They had an after-school group finishing at five that day which meant she should be able to get a good seven hours in beforehand if she left now.

"Yes of course. I apologise. It won't happen again." Carla allowed herself to look suitably demure and completely in the wrong now, accepting of her reprimand.

"Right… well… we'll leave it there then," said Jodi who still felt a little surprised at Carla's sudden personality change, but shook it aside and walked off down the corridor to put in her stocktake form with an explanatory note before leaving for the day.

Carla watched her go and smirked as she turned back to continue with the prepping of O.R.3. *That one will never see what's right under her nose as long as she's breathing through it,* she thought dryly. *Which of course, will probably turn out to be her safety net…*

Emily was numb. She and Gareth had just arrived home from the meeting with Detective Delaney at the station. They took their shoes and coats off in silence, shaking the snow from their clothes through the open front door. Pointless really as the wind blew more back in than they were trying to shake outside, but Emily barely noticed. She stood almost trance-like in the hall as if she were waiting for something. Gareth put a guiding arm around her waist to help her towards the kitchen and she put one foot in front of the other without really thinking.

Andrew, Gina and Molly had been filled in on the terrible events regarding Jenny's death whilst still at the publishing office. They'd made their own way home when Emily and Gareth had driven over to 68th precinct, and all three were now sitting round the kitchen table cradling mugs of hot chocolate and brandy, *even Gina had guiltily accepted a splash of alcohol.* The weather had taken a turn for the worse, they were in shock and the drink gave some small comfort. All three looked towards the doorway as Emily and Gareth walked in. Andrew was the first to get up. He noticed immediately how awful his future mother-in-law looked in that moment. It was natural for her to be horrified, shocked and devastated about what had happened to Jenny, of course it was, but there was something else too. He just couldn't quite put his finger on it.

"Can I get you both anything?" he asked gently. "Coffee; chocolate; brandy; something to eat?"

"I think… I think I'll just take some pills… lie down for a bit," said Emily rubbing her forehead. "I can't… I just can't *cope* with this at the moment." Gareth kissed the side of her head as she turned around, walked back out of the room to the hall and went upstairs, then nodded to Andrew to acknowledge his offer of a drink before sitting down.

"A black coffee – *with a very large whisky in it.*"

Emily lay on the bed but couldn't sleep. Her thoughts were a tangled, electrified and disassembled confusion. *How long would it be before someone worked out she'd orchestrated the whole horrible mess? Well, Charlotte's altered mindset and subsequent descent into serial killer delinquency of two years ago anyway.* She felt guilty then, thinking of herself when Jenny was lying cold and still in a hospital morgue. *Jenny dead… it was too awful to even contemplate let alone accept and face up to. Face up to the fact it was all her fault. That she, Emily, had started the ball rolling the day she'd first met Jenny at that literary event in Carlisle five years ago, then spent the following three persuading her to do her dirty work for her. Thank God Ethan was in Canada visiting his parents. He was the only other person in the link that connected her to the culmination of that summer's Cumbrian killing spree.* Emily had not intended it to go that far obviously, *neither of them had.*

She lay staring up at the ceiling remembering the nine-millimetre Luger she'd unwrapped in her bathroom at the Grange Hotel. The gun Ethan James had flown into Cumbria on his private Cessna, landing at a deserted airstrip in Kendal and driving down to her in Kirkdale. Not that he'd known what he was carrying… *as far as she'd been aware*. Emily had trusted Ethan implicitly, *mainly because she had far too much on him*. His affair with Jodi Denton for a start, *his* wife's and *her* best friend Faithe's younger sister. Plus the odd diamond heist and deliveries he'd been dabbling with on the side… She just prayed that with him being out of the country, he'd literally be flying under the radar and not front and centre if any of that particular pile of shit was going to hit the fan.

Emily *had* intended to kill Charlotte that day by the lake in Keeper's Cottage at the bottom of Kirkby Pike, despite their few moments of teenage memories. It was only the shock of police sirens sounding so close that had made her shoot wide, hitting her arm and necessitating a fast exit. Yet Charlie had never mentioned it to the police; at least, Emily had never been interviewed about it.

So much hatred – so many deaths… and now poor Jenny, *poor, dear darling Jenny,* who had never wanted to be involved in the first place, and by all accounts had just started to find a little happiness with a new man… was gone.

After the whole crazy scheme involving Charlotte's husband Miles was over, the man they'd both loved wildly and lost at different times, of the two of them, Jenny was the least guilty – yet she was the one who'd paid the highest price. And the only person Emily had shared any of this godawful mess with. *Now she was on her own with it.*

She felt a tear slide down her cheek as her eyes closed and she turned to bury her head in the pillows. Sleep came fitfully for a few hours until nightmares lurched her awake. It was late afternoon. She fell back onto the pillows with beads of sweat popping across her forehead as slowly the hazy February light struggled in through the window. It was dim and the snow was still falling heavily. She lay perfectly still, knowing now that without a shadow of a doubt, Charlotte was here in New York. She could feel it. She could feel the venom. Charlie was here – *and she was coming for her.*

TWENTY

BUILDERS' LOCK-UP
STRATFORD - EAST LONDON

The following morning Kenny drew back the heavy door to the lock-up and a huge shaft of natural light poured in. Annie instinctively shut her eyes and dropped her head sharply against the brightness, unable to shield her face with her hands bound behind the chair. The lamp was still on, although redundant now as the illuminated room lit up and the murky damp interior sprang to life around her once more.

Michael followed his father in and pulled the door across behind them. He looked over at Annie… her head low, bound, gagged and with smudged day-before make-up. The woman that had birthed him and let him go, the woman he'd grown up without but had thought about all his life, the woman he'd harboured bitter confused feelings for as long as he could remember, certainly since the time he'd been told of his adoption. She had lifted her head slowly as the door slid shut and

Michael noticed the tearstains on her cheek, saw the harrowed look in her eyes. He dropped his own away as Kenny swaggered towards her, *phone in hand.*

"So Mrs. Longbridge, not *too* uncomfortable a night I hope?" He now stood right in front of her, bent down, one hand resting on a thigh fingers squeezing, his morning breath both evident and crude. She glared at him heart thumping whilst Baxter had switched quickly from lying with eyes faced towards the door, to sitting up alert as Kenny approached. The dog's throat spoke a low warning then his muzzle knocked Kenny's hand smartly off his mistress's leg. The man looked surprised, even annoyed at first, and then roared with laughter, held his hands high and stood up.

"I love that dog of yours!" he cried, now smacking his own thigh in appreciation. *"What a cracking lad!"* He looked over at Michael, his eyes wide and laughing exaggeratedly, then suddenly his face dropped like a ventriloquist's dummy as he swiftly swung back round to Annie… *"But…* unfortunately for you, great though he is, *young Baxter here is going to be of zero help if your husband doesn't call very soo—"* He looked pointedly at the mobile as it immediately began ringing in his hand. With a grin on his face he twisted it dance-like from side to side, then made a dramatic arched sweep with his arm, swiped the screen and landed a finger on the green phone key…

"Harry. Had a little think have we?" *He pushed the loudspeaker on as he grabbed a chair from the table, placed it in front of Annie and sat down.*

"Drew? *I want to speak to my wife*. I want to speak to Annie – *right now!*" Annie's eyes flared wide at the sound of Harry's voice as she made urgent throaty noises behind the silver tape across her mouth. Kenny reached forward and unsympathetically ripped the tape half off. She winced at the pain but then used her opportunity...

"*HA – RYYYYYY!!!!*" Annie screamed at the top of her voice before her mouth was instantly resealed. Baxter began barking profusely and leaping about at the sound of his 'dad's' voice and Annie's screaming. Kenny spoke calmly back into the phone...

"She's very alive Harry as you can hear. Now what are you proposing to do about your little cash flow problem?"

"I can't just magic up half a million from nowhere and you damn well know it. It's going to take *ti*—"

"*Time* isn't something I've got a lot of Longbridge, and frankly I don't think your wife fancies her current '*home*' for the next few weeks either. You're gonna need to get your act together pretty damned quick. And it'd better not include any of your old mates in blue either, or Annie here is going to find herself... *hmmmm... how shall I put this...? Deep under cover!*" He sniggered at the correlation.

"*Look*... I'm not even in the U.K. at the moment as you may or may not be aware," replied Harry earnestly. "I'll be on the first available flight back – just... *please... don't hurt her.*" Harry hated having to plead it wasn't in his nature, and never with a con. But he was sitting in a hired car three thousand miles across the Atlantic and feeling pretty useless.

"Three days Longbridge. *You've got three days.*" Kenny stabbed his finger at the red phone icon and it fell silent.

Annie's shoulders began to shake as she started to cry. The tape across her mouth was hampering her breathing as it grew faster and more distraught. Michael got up from the table where he'd been sitting, watching uncomfortably throughout, and shoved it away from him. He marched over to her and eased the sticky tape off a good deal more carefully than Kenny had, which didn't go unnoticed. Michael was rewarded with a narrow-eyed stare followed by a raised eyebrow from his father, who was now beginning to sense maybe his newfound son wasn't entirely on side. With his back to the older man, Michael gave Annie a tiny hint of a sympathetic smile.

"Just remember where your future lies Morton," snarled Kenny. *"If you want one that is."* Michael turned round slowly and thought carefully before speaking.

"She was having breathing difficulties, and no matter what you told *him* – she's no good to us dead. I'm going for food and something to drink as we didn't pick anything up on the way over." Kenny grunted an acknowledgement that summed up acceptance of what he'd said, and the fact his stomach was in need of sustenance. Annie looked at Michael in the hope of another compassionate smile, but whilst his face was in full view of Kenny's now scrutinising gaze, found none. He turned on his heel, walked towards the heavy lock-up door and heaved it open. She watched intensely as he disappeared after dragging it shut behind him. Now she was alone again with Kenny – *and the expression on his face made her shudder as it swept her head to foot.*

"I wouldn't take what our boy says too much to heart by the way," said Kenny meaningfully as he turned back to Annie, stroking her jawline with his forefinger, his face now only inches from hers. Suddenly her head was pulled onto his mouth and he was kissing her hard on the lips as she frantically tried to turn away in disgust. *He back handed her cheek in anger and followed it fast with a second in the other direction.* A red weal delivered from a signet ring on the return swipe began to smart under her eye. She groaned in pain. "Be *very* careful lady – I *will* kill you if Harry doesn't come up with the money. Make no mistake about that. *I can hardly do anything else now can I…?*"

BROOKLYN
NEW YORK

Harry and Fran were still in the car and sat silently for a moment. The snow remained in a steady fall and the last of the forensic investigations at Jenny Flood's apartment down the street behind them were coming to a close. Finally Harry looked up from the mobile he'd been flipping over and over in his hands since Kenny Drew had cut the call. He watched through the windscreen as the weather began to deteriorate rapidly, and then with a grim expression turned to Fran.

"What do you reckon the chances are of a flight in this?" he said tipping his head towards the window. She sighed and bit the inside of her lip, swallowing hard, her eyes darted all over his face, one she was extremely fond of despite her haranguing at times.

"It's not looking good," she said tensely. It was getting really heavy now. "You're going to *have* to call Hitchings, Harry." *(Ch. Superintendant Chris Hitchings – Kirkdale.)*

"I've told you… I *can't*. You don't know Kenny Drew, Fran. I remember what he was like back then and I don't suppose prison has helped sweeten his temperament any. He's a nutter. *And he's a nutter who's got my Annie…*" Fran felt a twinge of jealousy then, she knew she shouldn't but she did. She could see he was tearing up and he looked wrecked. She suggested they went back to their B&B at the corner of Hylan and Edgewater. They both needed a decent meal, particularly Harry with his blood sugar issues, and then they could thrash out exactly what he was going to do.

It was a long, slow drive back to The Harbor B&B. The snow just wouldn't let up and the flakes seemed enormous, like a million exploded feather duvets. Fran had to use every ounce of concentration to get them back safely, especially as there were more than a couple of 'sliders' on the road. They finally turned the corner into Edgewater Street which The Harbor fronted and she parked up. Harry had been fidgety all the way back and looked a little clammy too, which was strange as he'd told her he'd got the sugar thing under control.

"Harry… *you okay?*"

"Not great. Forgot my jab this morning, I need to inject." Fran told him to stay put as she unclipped her belt, got out and walked gingerly in the snow round the car to the passenger door to help him out. She had her right arm around his waist and was holding his left elbow.

"This is bloody embarrassing," he said, eyes tired and beads of sweat well pronounced across his forehead, *he looked as a weak as a kitten.*

"Never mind that," said Fran warmly. "Lean on me and take it easy, you'll be fine. Let's get you inside, *all 'jabbed up' good and proper.* We'll check your levels, get a nice hot meal – you'll be as good as new. " He looked at her grinning at him and managed a weak smile back, their faces only a few inches apart. She looked and smelt wonderful as always, despite an arduous and distressing day. Even with everything that was going on it felt so *good* to be back with Fran. Maybe it was especially *because* of everything… He loved his wife and he was worried sick about her, but there was no denying the old Harry/Fran connection was there… it had always been there. It started at the Canon Row station in London, and although nothing had actually happened, it had very nearly finished his marriage. Seven years apart had changed nothing, and as Fran helped him up the snow-covered steps to the front door *he knew he wouldn't want it any other way.*

Carla could do the work at Bellevue standing on her head, eyes shut and with her hands tied behind her back. It was boring. The people she worked with were boring. *She* was bored. The strain of pretending to be something she wasn't was also increasing, and resembling a dark-haired version of Mia Farrow in *'Rosemary's Baby' (with glasses)*, was seriously wearing a bit thin.

At first it was quite fun to act the part of a completely different personality, now she just wanted to get the job done, *or jobs, depending on how many loopholes appeared,* and move on to pastures new. Mr. Berkowitz had just been unfortunate. Well, unfortunate for him, Carla wasn't really bothered either way, but she obviously didn't want to get caught. Hopefully there wouldn't be any more 'additional necessities' to attend to. At least she'd completed another shift and was now almost home – *thank the Lord!* A nice hot bubble bath, a plate of tagliatelle and a glass or two of red would improve her mood significantly.

She took the key out of her purse in readiness as she walked, and was just about to climb the steps to the front of the house in Cranberry Street when she saw it… Her white door with the Georgian squared window glass was clearly ajar, and from the large pieces of splintered wood on the ground, *it looked like it had been heavily jemmied.*

TWENTY-ONE

BROOKLYN
NEW YORK

Carla stopped dead in her tracks as she absorbed the scene in front of her. There were no footprints up to the door. Whoever had broken in must have done so before the snow had really got going, which of course meant either they'd gone out the back or... *they were still there.*

She felt in her pocket for the small knife she'd kept there ever since her visit to the Café Deli-Cious. The day the man she'd dubbed *Mr. Hawk* had stood at the bus stop opposite and pointed a camera directly at her. He had also shared her flight out to New York, she was positive of that.

Carla's fingers closed tightly over its handle now as she began to climb the steps to the jemmied door. Her heart was racing and hand almost numb from the fierceness with which she grasped the weapon. When she reached the top step her lungs could barely work and her ears pounded – *she knew she was taking a risk.*

For once the hunter really did feel like the hunted… it was not a feeling she wanted to maintain.

She took a deep breath and shook herself down. With a guarded glance both ways to check for any close pedestrians, Carla drew the knife from her pocket and pushed the point gently against the open door. It moved slowly to reveal wood chippings on the hall floor as well, big ones, plus the busted lock. It was very clear now just how damaged it actually was. In broad daylight as well – *that took balls*.

The actual hallway was all in good order, the stairs ahead of her too, and she ignored the upper level to press on with checking the lounge at the end of the hall, and the kitchen to the right. There was a breeze coming from somewhere and it definitely wasn't behind her. As she entered the lounge the distinctive scents hit – *mint, sage and thyme*. The little herb garden that grew in various large tubs in the yard outside was well stocked. Despite the snow, their aroma was now filling the room easily. Her heart was thumping wildly now but Carla knew she had to keep herself fully focused and in control.

The vivid red and black curtains were not as she'd left them that morning, open to reveal the French windows to the small but pretty courtyard garden. Someone had drawn them – now they covered the glass but billowed gently at the bottom. She stopped for a moment clenching and unclenching the knife, flipping it over in her hand, round and round, hesitating in front of the huge red and black swirl-patterned drapes. Then from nowhere came a huge gust of wind that blew the left curtain high and into the room revealing nobody behind it, and the door open. The tubs and the yard were fully accessible as she'd suspected. Nevertheless, Carla walked slowly and carefully towards the window with the knife held out in front of her, intermittently swinging it behind to prevent a surprise attack.

On reaching the open doors it was clear there was nobody in the high-walled garden. Taking care not to slip she checked all around, behind snow-covered firs and the larger shrubs anyway. The tall black gate to the right had been opened though, and its padlocked chain hung limp and unused. *She wouldn't make that mistake again.*

Carla returned inside and ignoring her wet shoes, marched back through the lounge, this time at a smarter pace, back out into the hall and turned left for the kitchen. After a swift check she literally ran to the stairs. *The dollars in the briefcase!!* The stash left for her when she arrived in Brooklyn suddenly burned its way through the tension to front and centre in her mind. At the top Carla paused. Now she could hear something, and it wasn't the breeze through an open door or window. A soft *phut… phut… phut* was clearly audible. *Something dripping?*

The knot that had formed in her stomach when she'd remembered the dollars, now doubled in size at the top of the stairs. *How could her bloody heart beat any louder?* But it did. Her mouth, now a desert, craved moisture, yet her hairline gleamed with sweat as she wiped the back of a hand across first one eye then the other. She licked her lips – it didn't help. *Phut… phut… phut…* The dripping sounded louder as she advanced along the landing towards the bedroom she was using, the door slightly ajar. Carla stood outside for a moment wondering whether she should rush in, slam the door open to the wall or creep in quietly. ***Phut… phut… phut…*** So much louder now. She took a deep breath, flung the door to the side and plunged in like a Japanese warrior swishing the knife this way and that, twisting her head and body in different directions to take in the whole room. Nothing. Not a thing. No wardrobe doors open, no drawers open, nothing disturbed at all. Suddenly her eyes widened. A pot of bright red paint lay across the dressing table and dripped regimentally – ***phut… phut… phut*** onto the carpet. Then she saw it. The message scrawled in capitals across the centre of the mirror… *in red.*

I KNOW!!

She dropped the knife! Her hands flew to her mouth and lungs gave an inward gasp as Carla staggered backwards. Shaking more violently now she spun this way and that, convinced *he* was going to pounce on her from somewhere, but she had no idea where or how.

She fell to the floor in a crouch, head still up and on a switch, eyes like a half-starved urchin scanned every inch of the room and the open door to the landing. Both hands scrabbled desperately across the carpet in different directions for the dropped knife, but without the benefit of sight as she dared not look down. Finally her fingers found it and once found snatched it up as she jumped to a quick stand, knife back in defence and her back to the wall. The only noise her hyperventilated breathing and the paint dripping on the carpet. It was only then she realised. *It wasn't paint.*

When Emily came downstairs after a fitful sleep it was 7.00 p.m. She showered, changed into a velour lounge suit and poured herself a very large G&T in the kitchen. A large gulp followed by a second was downed before she topped it up and joined the others in the sitting room.

"Em sweetheart, come and sit down." Gareth got up from his chair opposite the door as he noticed her enter the room. He had begun to walk towards her, arms outstretched, but Emily held up her free hand and shook her head to indicate no fuss or touching. He sat back down – crushed. She was feeling vulnerable, exhausted and *guilty.* Four pairs of eyes watched her then looked at each other as she lowered herself into the nearest sofa, drank deeply and stared into the fire Gareth had lit earlier.

"It's certainly been a... a *terrible* day, just *awful*," he said carefully, trying to gauge her reaction. She carried on staring into the flames, just drinking, as if she was the only one in the room. Andrew, Gina and Molly looked to Gareth for guidance but found none, and it was only the doorbell that broke the heavy silence.

"Shall I—" started Andrew, who was sitting nearest to the door. Gareth shook his head and held up a palmed hand to signal his intention to go. Sighing heavily he got up and walked through to the hall and down the long, oak passageway to the front door. He opened it to see Detective Delaney standing on the porch, hunched against what had now become a blizzard, into the tall collar of his jacket.

"Good evening sir, sorry to disturb you this late. Would it be possible to come in for a moment? Something's come up with regard to Miss. Flood's death since our meeting earlier, and I believe it might be important." In one look, Gareth's expression said it wasn't at all convenient. His wife had just lost a close friend and he had chosen nine-fifteen at night to come round to continue with their meeting at the station. He replied slightly irritated with:

"I – er... well... *yes, yes* I suppose so. My wife is extremely upset though, not good at all in fact. We'll talk in the kitchen if you don't mind?"

"Of course," replied Frank Delaney as he inclined his head and stepped into the hall, brushing snow off his coat and then looking slightly embarrassed about it. "Although…" he continued firmly, "I'm afraid I'm going to need to speak to Mrs. Stone as well… *if* that's okay?" Raising an eyebrow, Gareth lifted his head in query. There was the slight narrowing of his eyes, a concentration, a wondering… The two men walked down the hall and into the kitchen.

In the lounge it had remained extremely tense. Gina had tried to comfort her mother as a friend would, still not entirely comfortable or used to their mother–daughter relationship. Andrew and Molly remained quiet. Molly through a mixture of shock at the day's events, the embarrassment of knowing Emily even less than Gina, and also feeling very much the guest. Despite the fact she'd suffered a key part in the Peterson murders two years before (given Charlotte had tried her level best to despatch her 'to the other side' on a park bench in her own town), at that moment she still felt like a fish out of water.

Ten minutes had passed since the 'visitor' had arrived but not been brought through to the lounge. It felt like a couple of hours. Then suddenly the door opened and Gareth walked in and straight over to Emily who'd actually begun to at least acknowledge Gina's attempts at comfort. Considering her early stages of pregnancy, Gina was holding up pretty well, despite not being able to join her mother in a drink to steady her own nerves, which would have helped considerably.

"Em, Detective Delaney has some news. He'd like to ask you some questions regarding some personal property of Jenny's."

"*Property?* What do you mean *property?* I don't know anything about her personal things." Gareth wasn't exactly glaring at his wife but he didn't look happy.

"Emily… Jenny wrote a diary. There's one for 2018, the year you went to the U.K. for your mother's funeral. The year tha—"

"Yes I know what happened that year Gareth! We all bloody know what happened which is why it's all happening again now!!" Her sudden switch in a nano second from silent morose flame watcher, to full-on fish wife sent sparks flying around the room. Gina gasped, as did Molly. Andrew however watched her steadily, surprised at her outburst, but with something still knocking at the back of his mind. A few rusty sleuthing cogs began to slowly tick over in his memory of that summer…

Emily placed the empty glass she'd been nursing for at least half an hour onto the table and followed Gareth out of the room. In the kitchen Det. Frank Delaney was sitting opposite the door and watched her closely as she entered with Gareth behind her. He noticed she would not hold his eye line but immediately went for the bottle of gin on the side, picked up a crystal glass from the draining board and poured herself a very large measure. He watched her slowly move about the kitchen putting the drink together, and only after she'd added a splash of tonic, a slice of lemon and some ice, did she sit down opposite him at the table and look him in the eye.

"So Detective, what's this property of Jenny's you want to ask me about that's so important it couldn't wait till morning?" She drank deeply and held his gaze. Frank Delaney put his hand into his jacket pocket and pulled out a black leather journal. It had a gold 2018 stamped on the front of it and two red ribbons each marking a section of the year inside. Placing it on the table, he opened it to where one of the ribbons marked a page in August, and slid it across the surface to her.

"Mrs. Stone, can you tell me why Jenny Flood would have written that paragraph?"

Emily looked hesitantly down at the diary. As she read the entry her heart faltered, her drink fell from her hand, and as if in slow motion, sailed south to the flagstone floor smashing into a million pieces.

This was exactly what she'd been afraid of.

TWENTY-TWO

HARBOR B&B - STATEN ISLAND
NEW YORK

Harry was feeling a whole lot less sloth-like after his insulin shot and a good meal. He and Fran were now sitting in the tiny lounge area off her suite, the large super-king bed out of view *but still the proverbial elephant in the room…* Of the two available on booking, this room was the largest and Harry being a gentleman had insisted she have it. They were again discussing the problem of his wife being held by Kenny Drew, but at least now he could think clearly.

"I need to book a flight home ASAP," said Harry, pouring them both a coffee from the pot on the welcome tray and handing her one. "The weather could stick her oar in on that one though." As he brought the cup to his lips, he looked grimly out of the window to be met with a zillion side-skimming white discs.

"It's not really let up all day has it?" Fran pressed. "The long-range forecast is worse Harry, you're going to *have* to ring Hitchings." She hadn't even looked at the coffee he'd handed her. She was staring at *him* trying to impress upon him the only choice he'd got.

"And if Drew thinks I'm not back in the U.K. to amass his half a million? *He's not stupid Fran.* No – I need to try and book a flight and I need to do it *now*." With that he began to twist around in his chair searching for his iPad, then realised he wasn't in his own room. Fran got up from the sofa, walked through to the bedroom to get hers from the bedside table, brought it back and handed it to him.

"I still think you should be contacting Ch. Superintendant Hitchings. He was the one who sanctioned your being on this trip Harry. You wouldn't even *be* here if it wasn't for him, he needs to know. I couldn't have swung it on my…" She fell silent then, looked down at her coffee on the table and immediately made use of it, drinking keenly now as she felt her cheeks flush hotly. Harry smiled softly and watched her for a minute as he waited for the iPad to come on. Despite everything he couldn't help being pleased she'd put in a request for him to come back for this case.

He was soon tapping a search into Google for JFK to London flights, and immediately met with cancellations for the following forty-eight to seventy-two hours due to severe weather conditions. Sighing, he shook his head wearily. Looking up from the iPad he saw Fran was now staring directly at him.

"So what are you going to do?" she asked.

"I'm going to ring Kenny Drew and try to buy some time," came the reply.

25 CRANBERRY STREET
BROOKLYN

After she'd cleared up the mess in the bedroom, called an emergency locksmith and had a bath to get the stress out of her system *(not easy),* Carla really didn't feel like cooking.

On closer inspection the 'paint' that had been dripping from the tin on the dressing table – definitely wasn't. She knew blood when she saw it, although she assumed it was from some kind of animal rather than human. At least she *hoped* it was… Even so, it had been a shock and no doubt a warning. The whole damn thing had been extremely unsettling, *she wasn't used to being the target.*

Once she'd eaten the pizza she'd had delivered and dumped the box in the bin, Carla settled in the living room with the rest of a bottle of white wine and a packet of chocolate chip cookies. After the blood-pouring incident in the bedroom, she really couldn't face the red. What she couldn't understand though was *why the break-in? Why* should *'Hawk'* be out to try and scare and threaten her? If he was part of the gang who was funding her little 'project' till she got her inheritance, all that would be necessary would be to keep an eye on her to make sure she completed her 'work' and they got paid out. She could understand *that*, it made perfect sense and would at least be logical. The rest of it didn't make any sense at all. But if he *wasn't* part of the gang – it might. She took a large gulp of the Prosecco and began to run her finger around the rim of the glass. But if he wasn't part of the gang… *then who the hell was he?*

Carla leant forward for her cigarettes, shook one out of the packet on to the coffee table, and reaching for the lighter alongside lit up and inhaled. She'd been trying to cut down since having to work in the hospital, but was now feeling distinctly uptight and uncomfortable. *Strange how taking a life had always had the opposite effect.* She'd always wondered about that.

She dropped the slim black and gold lighter through her fingers onto the sofa flipping it over to do it again on a repeating loop as she tried to work out the unworkable. The simple message on the dressing table mirror kept flashing up in her thoughts *large, red and jagged…*

I KNOW!! What did he know – *exactly?* Or could he be a she? Her eyebrows lifted seemingly of their own accord at that question, her mouth opening wide in company. *Surely Emily wouldn't have the gall to break in and do all this?* Another large mouthful of Prosecco didn't help the thought process much – she'd nearly finished the bottle now and after such a fractious and eventful evening felt exhausted. Much as Carla hated to fall asleep alone after the night's events, she really had no option, and at least the door was secure again. It was past twelve, time to get some shut-eye before she chickened out and tried to sit up all night on the couch.

After double-checking the lounge's French doors to the courtyard garden, she went into the kitchen and drew a large carving knife from the block on the work surface. There was something infinitely satisfying, even comforting about the singing, swishing sound that accompanied the pulling of it. Carla went back out into the hall and began to climb the stairs, then stopped. She went back down and re-checked the new lock and draw bolt on the front door. All good. She looked down at the blade she was carrying now. It made the small knife in her jacket pocket look pathetic. Through the window the moon caught its edge – it glinted as she admired it this way and that. There was something quite fascinating, even beautiful about it. *And as Carla let it hang by her side, as she re-climbed the stairs, she even managed a smile…*

BUILDERS' LOCK-UP – STRATFORD EAST LONDON

When Michael had returned with the day's supplies and seen the cut on Annie's face he was angry – *very angry.* As he placed the bags on the table and looked over at her tied and bound to the chair with that faithful Lab at her feet, he knew. He knew he was going to have to help her.

Kenny had placed one of the chairs in front of Annie and was slouching on it with his left foot up on his right knee. The mobile sat on his right thigh in complete silence as he picked at his nails with a penknife. The '*tick tick*' of the blade point sounded hollow in the dank air of the huge lock-up, and every now and then he looked up at her before dropping his eyes back to the phone. He eventually put the knife away and held the phone up to her – shaking it…

"That husband of yours is running out of time me thinks. He's down to two days before the local vegetation benefits. *Benefits from your body feeding it!*" Annie's eyes shot wide above the silver duct tape, crossing her mouth so high it reached up to the base of her cheekbone. They darted wildly over at Michael who was pulling sandwiches, cans of beer, plastic cups and bottles of water out of the first carrier bag. A newspaper followed last. He glanced at her covertly, head slightly down not wanting to attract Drew's attention with any sympathy in his expression. He waved a triangular pre-packed sandwich in the air and Kenny held both hands out to catch it. Michael tipped his head towards Annie and Drew nodded.

Out of the second bag came a box of dog biscuits and a couple of plastic bowls. He filled one with water, the other with some biscuits and took them over to

Baxter who fell on both immediately, switching from one to the other noisily.

Gently he pulled the tape off Annie's mouth. His calm eyes held her scared ones steadily, evenly, as he tried to relay a message of hope.

"Can I untie her hands Kenny? She's not exactly going to go anywhere is she with her feet strapped to the chair legs."

"Yeah okay, just whilst she eats – undo the leg ties as well, she's gonna need a piss anyway." Michael untied her feet and Annie stretched out all her limbs, grateful for their freedom, rubbing her wrists and ankles in turn. He went back to the table for another sandwich and a cup of water and took them back to her. She tore the plastic off the packet, pulled the food out and ate hungrily – *how much longer could she stand this for? What must her mother be thinking?*

Having cleared both bowls, Baxter snuggled up closely to his mistress and looked up at her. She stroked his head and broke off a corner of her cheese and pickle and gave it to him. He gobbled it up and put a paw up on her lap tapping it softly on her hands. Kenny watched him, mesmerised for a moment at the dog's devotion. He really did love animals – *it was his only redeeming feature.*

It was nearly eleven that evening before the mobile rang. It was sudden and shrill – and Kenny who'd dropped off after trying the *Sun* crossword, *and failing*, flung the paper off his lap and across the floor in shock. Annie had been allowed several loo breaks and was now re-tied to the chair, although the tape had been left off her mouth. Michael had assured Drew he would watch her. Kenny felt in his pocket for the phone having replaced it there earlier.

"Yeah?" his voice growled sharply down the phone. He wasn't ready for the reply.

"I – I don't know who you are but if you've got my Ann—"

"MUUUUUMMMMM!!!!" Annie screamed at the top of her voice as Michael dashed from his chair by the table and although fumbling badly, managed to slap fresh tape across her mouth.

"Shut *up* you *stupid* bitch!" he yelled angrily. Then with his back to Kenny and under the cover of Baxter's instant barking at Annie's screaming and his yelling, whispered, *"I'm going to help you – just don't scream."* She stared pleadingly at him as tears flowed down her cheeks at the thought of him helping her and the sound of her mother's voice. Annie knew her mother must have been worried sick when her daughter hadn't turned up the night before, the strange phone call she'd experienced when she'd rung Annie but heard Kenny's voice before he'd hung up. *Now she was hearing it again...*

"Why don't you just *fuck... right... off Mrs. McMahon – Annie's not coming home!"* He stabbed at the phone with his finger, slammed it on his chair and jumped to his feet. Even Baxter shied behind his 'mum' realising this was no longer a game. At that moment with Annie looking desperate at the initial hope then loss of hearing her mother's voice, Kenny glaring, the whites of his eyes rapidly becoming bloodshot, and Michael not quite sure what he was going to do to remedy the entire craziness of the situation… a shrill ring filled the air once more…

TWENTY-THREE

HARBOR B&B - STATEN ISLAND
NEW YORK

Harry sat facing the phone in his hand. He had it on loudspeaker as it connected to Annie's mobile. Fran realised she was clutching her now empty cup and put it quietly back on the tray. Suddenly the phone stopped ringing and the call answered...

"This had better be you Longbridge 'cos I'm getting mightily pissed off with your mother-in-law!"

"It is me Kenny. And what the fu... *what's my mother-in-law got to do with anything?"*

"She was expecting the lovely Annie to arrive last night, of course she didn't 'cos she was dining in with me!!" A loud guffaw rang out from the other end. Harry and Fran looked cynically at each other and then wearily away. "She keeps bloody ringing this mobile. Forget about her Longbridge, *waddya gonna do about my money!?"*

"Look... Kenny... I... the sky's haemorrhaging

snow over here, all the airports are closed for a minimum of seventy-two hours, *there's no way I ca*—"

"Three days I gave you Longbridge," replied Kenny Drew menacingly. "You've got two left."

Harry heard someone scuffing across what sounded like a stone floor… Kenny had sauntered over to Annie and ripped off the duct tape.

"Tell him Annie – tell your husband what's at stake here."

"HARRY FOR GOD'S SAKE!! Pleeease Harry I—" There was the sound of a sharp slap and a woman crying out. Fran dropped her head. Harry jumped up from his chair and started striding in and out of the sitting room area to the bedroom and back again, flinging his free arm around in anger and frustration. Finally he stopped, whipped round and spoke low into the phone through gritted teeth…

"One hair Drew… one fucking damned hair of her head – *I'll know.*" His face was twisted into a shape and expression that Fran had never seen, and never wanted to see again.

After the phone had cut off the other end, Harry slumped down into a chair. Leaning forward with his head beneath his hands he felt utterly spent. It left a hopeless, useless silence in the space between them that neither felt able to fill, and whilst knowing what *should* happen, Fran knew it was unlikely he'd agree – *even now*. Eventually he lifted his head.

"Don't look at me like that. I don't *have* the answer

Fran." He stared back at the table, eyes glazed. "I simply don't have it this time…"

25 CRANBERRY STREET
BROOKLYN

Carla knew exactly where Emily lived and had intended to deal with her first, make her the first port of call so to speak. However, with the entire round-the-clock police attention the Stone address had been given, it had been simpler to rid herself of the anorexic first. Of course since that little job had been completed, police presence at the Stone household was likely to be even heavier. She'd yet to discover whether this was or wasn't true, but it was highly likely given the fact that Harry Longbridge was in New York.

Carla had picked the local paper off the mat in the hall when she'd come downstairs that morning. Jenny's murder had made the front page and there'd been a mention of U.K. officers at the scene. That could mean only one thing. *Longbridge.*

She threw the paper on to the table as she entered the kitchen and began to gather breakfast items together to join it. Her favourite muesli and granola got poured into a bowl, and as she added the milk had one eye on the paper. Carla ran over a few details in her mind. Since the break-in the night before, which of course, not wanting to attract law enforcement attention, she hadn't reported, it suddenly occurred to her that neighbours might have heard or seen something. Carla hadn't really had anything to do with either side yet, trying hard to keep herself to herself, but it wouldn't be impossible for someone to have heard breaking glass and splintering wood. They may well approach her about it, particularly as she'd been able to get an emergency locksmith out to fix the door despite the weather.

After she'd finished her breakfast, Carla fixed some coffee, picked up the paper and took both through to the lounge. This Friday to Sunday it was her long weekend off – she was going to make the most of it… *planning the next strike.*

Twenty minutes away, Andrew also picked up the paper from the Stones' hall floor and began to walk through to the kitchen. Gareth had gone in to work, Emily was still in bed and Gina was also having a lie-in. He stopped midway to the kitchen door. Jenny's face was plastered all over the front page of the *The Bay Ridge Courier. So soon*, he thought. *It's only been a few days.* He carried on down the elaborate hall and through to the kitchen, something tap-tap-tapping remorselessly at the back of his consciousness. Andrew still couldn't get out of his mind that Emily was hiding something. However he didn't feel he could talk to Gina about it, not least because of her fledgling relationship with her mother. This meant it was back to chewing over conspiracy theories with the one person he could rely on not to fall apart at the moment... *Molly*.

He put the pot on, prepared Gina some grapefruit for when she came down, and glanced up at the clock; it was eight-thirty. Ten minutes later he was nursing a black coffee and reading the report of Jenny's murder when Molly walked in. She left the door open and Andrew indicated for her to close it. He held up the paper to her, desolation on his face.

"Oh God it's not in there *already?*" Molly shut the door and sat down at the table as Andrew swivelled the tabloid round to her. She grabbed it, mouth and eyes wide open.

"*Coffee?*" he said tensely. "I've just made some." Molly nodded as she ran her eyes over the front page.

"Yeah – yes usual... thanks Andy," she replied almost absently as she read. "This is just... *awful! It's hideous!* It's saying they think some kind of drug was injected into her. But that's not a Charlotte Peterson trait is it – maybe it's *not* her?"

"Not easy to replicate what she did last time though is it Molls," suggested Andrew, putting a mug down in front of her. "Maybe it was just a case of '*needs must*' in her eyes. It looks like a medically induced death judging by the write-up, some kind of heart-stopping drug maybe?"

"They've not given any real details here, it's too early. What about that strange man, or woman? You know – the one we saw standing outside watching the house the other day? We never told anyone Andy. Well

208

I didn't – did you? It was the morning we went into Gareth and Emily's offices I think."

"No I didn't – that was the day when everything kicked off with Jenny. I think so anyway, I can't even remember now with the avalanche of events that's followed since. I'm going to be hard pressed to remember my own name soon!"

"Speaking of avalanches…" Molly gestured with her mug towards the far window at the utility end of the kitchen. It was now overlooking a huge white expanse where landscaped lawns and flowerbeds used to be. "Have you seen outside this morning?" Andrew got up and walked over to the other end of the room and looked out. It was still snowing. He could also see the depth of it already about two feet up the back wall of the house, and still coming down.

"Not exactly looking great for the wedding is it?" He sighed heavily. "Not unless a heat wave suddenly descends anyway. God what a mess…" Andrew came back to the table, passed it, and on reaching the door to the hall opened it a little and checked for movement upstairs as he listened carefully. Hearing nothing, he waited a moment more and then shut it quietly. With his voice lowered slightly Andrew sat back down and made sure he was facing the door.

"Molls… Gina and Emily aren't up yet. I can't talk about this to either of them." Molly raised both eyebrows behind her mug and then placed it back on the table.

"Go on…" she encouraged, intrigued now.

"I feel really bad about this but… *Emily*. What do we really *know* about her? With regard to Charlotte I mean. Charlotte Peterson used to be a respected G.P. in a small Cumbrian town, stroppy self-serving and up herself, granted, but never to the elderly… never to them. They all loved her. Why did she suddenly turn into a psychotic serial killer of the young – mainly women?" Molly nodded, eyes wide slowly absorbing this revelation, one they'd never thought of back then. She started air pointing with her forefinger…

"We never really heard all the reasons why did we?" she said thoughtfully. "Yes there was a connection to Jenny because of Miles' playing away, and with Emily and Miles right back to their youth, but… could that *really* have sent someone into a murder spree? *And why at that precise time?*"

"I always felt that Jenny was hiding something back then, do you remember?" replied Andrew. He glanced up at the door, and turned his head slightly as if he'd heard something. Molly nodded again in agreement.

"Yes I remember. You had that awkward questioning session in your office one morning, she was really *cagey*." Andrew nodded.

"We know about her affair with Miles, but I always felt there was something more, something deeper," he continued. "Emily's reaction to Jenny's death doesn't seem like just shock and sadness to me. It's *way* beyond that. She looked scared last night, *really scared.* After her interview in here with the police – *she looked positively grey…*"

CONFERENCE ROOM
68TH PRECINCT, BROOKLYN

Det. Frank Delaney stood in front of the huge crime boards. Pictures of Jenny Flood's body, her apartment and various people she'd associated with covered the white expanse. Included in that crime pic collage was her new boyfriend of not that many months, fire officer Mike Hyland.

"Okaaay… we've all been briefed on the appalling murder of Miss. Jenny Flood." He turned to the largest photo of her in the centre of the board and pointed to it. "So far… and I know it's early, but we *all* know that the first twenty-four to forty-eight hours are critical for evidence gathering… so far we've turned up very little." A lone voice called out from the back…

"What about the diary?" asked Det. Terri-Jane Malone, (T.J.), who'd found the diary herself in the dead girl's bedroom.

"Yes – that's the *very little* I was referring to T.J.," replied Frank pointedly. "It's *something*, and I've interviewed Mrs. Stone with regard to the pages that mention her. However, she has a cast-iron alibi for the evening the murder took place and the twenty-four hours either side."

"Yeah, because Casey and I, Randy and Geoff have been taking twelve-hour shifts over at the Stones' place this past week."

"Precisely Malone... plus the fact there are other witnesses who can bear out her whereabouts, albeit they are family and friends. The diary *does* however make interesting reading, and we'll come back to that later." A hand went up in the front row. Frank pointed to the officer and indicated for him to speak.

"What about the boyfriend – *Hyland*. Has anyone actually interviewed him yet? I hear he's a fire fighter, likely to be reasonably strong, easily able to overcome a woman, particularly this victim. She was real slight from what I hear, maybe only ninety five pounds?"

"*Quinnel*... and that goes for all of you... can we please stop referring to those murdered as *'the victim'*? Her name was Jenny – Jenny Flood, and she'd only been out here from the U.K. a couple of years."

"Yeah Casey lay off the 'vic' stuff, that lady sure got unlucky. *Use her goddamn name!*" Casey Quinnel flushed red as Detective Randy Summers, a big Jamaican cop, jumped out of his seat pretty irate. He always got pretty irate when women got murdered, especially when they weren't given proper respect. Not surprising since both his mother and sister lost their lives to an intruder at their home twenty-five years previously. Randy had just past his fifteenth birthday. He'd been the only one to escape, something he'd never gotten over, never stopped feeling guilty about. It was one reason he'd joined the N.Y.P.D., probably the main one.

"Okay Summers – he's had the talk!" blasted Delaney. Randy sat back down as an officer behind him patted his shoulder. They all knew his story.

Frank Delaney turned back to the board and tapped on a picture of Mike Hyland that was found at the scene on a display shelf in the lounge.

"This is Mike Hyland," he said looking directly at Quinnel. We want to interview him to rule him out as much as anything. Neighbours have already said he'd been there on a number of occasions, one or two mentioned he seemed a really nice guy and there had never been any raised voices overheard. Still, we obviously have to speak to him, so Quinnel – I'll leave that one with you." Casey Quinnel held up his pocket book in acknowledgement.

"And Quinnel…"

"Sir?"

"No bloody snowmen squads this season." Casey snorted and was joined by a few similar noises from the room as he turned round to greet their approval.

"No sir, definitely no snowmen squads – *sir…*"

"Hmmm… right – the rest of you split up into two teams, one on door-to-door again over at 4th Avenue, the other at Miss. Flood's work and on her medical history. *Let's get to it!"* Several eyes rolled at the repeat of the door-to-door as they began to get up and make their way to the exit.

That just left Jenny Flood's diary. Frank Delaney still wasn't quite sure what to do with that little find. T.J. hadn't forgotten though, and this time she stood up and walked straight down to the front instead of making her way to the side door and leaving with the rest.

"Sir... *the diary?*" Terri had a hunch that little book was going to prove crucial. She was also determined the fact she found it wasn't going to get lost in the following evidence gathering weeks. T.J. fully intended to ensure that top notch was decorating *her* belt and not Quinnel's. Delaney smiled, he knew she was keen, he also knew she was one of his best up-and-coming officers.

"Call the U.K. detectives Taylor and Longbridge," said Delaney. "I think this is something they're gonna find acutely interesting."

TWENTY-FOUR

BUILDERS' LOCK-UP
STRATFORD - EAST LONDON

Annie was dozing on and off. It was her third night in the lock-up and she was cold, dirty and knew she smelt awful. That was what she hated most, the indignity of not being clean – sometimes not even being able to prevent wetting herself.

Her hatred for Kenny Drew was only surpassed by her fear of what he would do if Harry couldn't get home. *If he couldn't save her.* And Baxter, dear precious Baxter who'd remained faithfully by her side throughout their whole ordeal, when presumably he could have run off at the first sign of that huge sliding door opening every morning… w*hat would become of him?* No doubt Kenny would take him. At least he seemed to have a genuine love of dogs, despite being a total utter shit-faced bastard. One prepared to kill people for money without blinking twice.

She was seriously cold, shivering with the bite of it. Her head was banging like a drum and she couldn't feel her hands or feet. Dozing in and out of sleep had become impossible now, and her neck hurt like hell from hanging downwards or backwards when she dropped off. Annie had reached the point where she felt she'd no fight left in her anymore. There was only twenty-four hours left for Harry to give Kenny what he wanted, and there was no way he was going to be able to do that. Even if he could get home there was no possibility of raising half a million in a day. Hell, he couldn't raise a quarter of that without selling the house, the whole thing was absurd... *and terrifying.*

She shivered, her teeth were chattering. The weather had taken a turn for the worse in the U.K. too, and with the lock-up being so large, empty and having no heating, Annie had no hope of keeping warm even during the day. The nights were doubly awful. The place must have stood unused for years. She looked around her for the millionth time – Kenny was right, nobody would ever find her here. Her only warmth was Baxter occasionally jumping onto her lap and laying his body across her legs, or his head on her knees if he wasn't sleeping across her shackled feet. He jumped up now and rubbed a black velvet head against her face, a large, wet Labby tongue swished across her left cheek. How close they had become him and her, how much better she'd come to understand this dog, to connect and bond with him. If she ever got out of this alive she would tell Harry how she now understood this special relationship with his Lab, *his best friend.*

Suddenly Annie heard the familiar sound of the huge gate grinding across the stone. Cold air rushed in sending brick dust, empty cans and sandwich wrappers tumbling across the floor. She closed her eyes against the red cloud that always wafted up each time the lock-up was opened to the outside. When she opened them she saw Michael had slipped in through the gap. It was dark but she could still tell by the younger man's slimmer size and height it wasn't Drew. He turned round to look out into the black and appeared to be listening to, or *for* something. He was. Unbeknown to Annie, at that moment Michael Morton had to make sure there was nothing that could cause them a threat, *basically make certain he hadn't been followed.*

Annie watched curiously, intrigued as he stood absolutely still then heaved the sliding door shut. Her eyes widened. She flexed her numb fingers and pulled at her stuck wrists as he turned round to face her. In the shadows of the entrance he put a finger to his lips. Baxter was alert and had immediately stood foursquare facing the door the minute it had opened.

"It's okay, don't be scared," he said keeping his voice low. "My car's outside. I'm going to get you out of here to your parents' place." Annie's eyes closed slowly and then opened in relief as tears began to well up. She now shook at the ropes and tape that bound her arms and ankles in anticipation of being free. Her heart triple thumped – then briefly missed entirely as he walked out of the gloom. She winced when he reached her and peeled back the silver duct tape from her mouth. Despite his best attempts at being gentle, her face still hurt from Kenny's backhander. She didn't hold back when the tape finally came off…

"Thank *GOD! Why* Michael, *why did you do this!?*" Annie burst out loud.

"*Shhhh!!!!* Not *now* Annie, we *have* to get away. If Kenny finds out he'll kill us both." She paled significantly and nodded silently in agreement. She knew he wasn't exaggerating. The man may love his animals but he was a rapist, a kidnapper and a potential killer. For all she knew he could have already killed.

As swiftly as he could, Michael unwrapped the duct tape from her ankles, untied the rope beneath it and repeated the exercise with her hands. He was all fingers and thumbs as he worked, but soon Annie was rubbing her wrists and Michael ran over to the table to fetch Baxter's lead where it had been slung on the first day. He stuck it in his jacket pocket and held a hand out to Annie gesturing fervently at her to move towards him, but when she got up her legs felt wobbly and she fell back down on the chair. Michael ran back to her and quickly rubbed some life into her cold limbs, all the time looking anxiously over his shoulder at the door, heart banging. Being the son of Kenny Drew would offer no protection whatsoever now.

"Okay? Do you think you can run?"

"Y-Yes I… I think so, Annie faltered, still not quite sure why he was helping her. Michael placed his hands under her arms and pulled her up off the chair. She wavered a moment as he held her steady, but sheer self preservation got her legs working, and together they ran for the exit with Baxter at their heels somehow knowing he needed to be obedient. *Obedient fast and quiet.*

Michael opened the door as small a crack as he could manage given it needed a heave to move and then it always shot sideways with the momentum.

"Wait here a moment. Let me do a quick check outside again first." He started to go forward when Annie pulled him back.

"Be careful," she whispered. He half-smiled and squeezed her arm.

"Stay here, I'll be fine. Bax, you watch your mum eh?" The dog held up a paw and looked straight into his eyes. Michael shook it, a lump in his throat, and with that slipped out into the night. Annie felt for Baxter's head and found a wet tongue licking her hand. She looked down and with shaky fingers scrunched an ear. They both remained silent. The only sound their breathing, both fast, both anxious, as frosty clouds swept across the black outside.

Then from nowhere Michael was beside her again and yanking her out of the lock-up.

"Quick – we need to run – *see? Over there!*" Michael pointed across the yard. She'd been blindfolded when they brought her three nights ago so wasn't familiar with the layout, and it was dark. There were huge containers and disused building equipment lying around, together with old waste units and rusty scaffolding. She nodded frantically and as they all ran to the car, his eyes were flashing everywhere.

Annie could see a red Volvo parked on the road beyond the high mesh gates, one of which was now open and had a redundant padlock dangling on one side. The automatic key fob made a comforting clunk-clunk sound as Michael extended an arm to open the locks on the run. With a dry mouth and shaky legs, he, Annie and Baxter half-stumbled, half-ran across the yard, but were soon through the gate to the quiet road – *and freedom*. Luckily the snow hadn't had much affect in East London. *There was no stopping them now.*

He opened the door, helped Annie into the passenger seat and was just opening the back for Baxter – when suddenly the yard lit up like a football stadium…

"Did you think I wouldn't follow you Morton!?" yelled Kenny Drew as he leapt from his van, gun in hand with it pointed directly at Michael. Annie twisted round in her seat and pushed opened the door. Michael shoved it shut again flicking the lock.

"Stay in the fucking car!" he yelled angrily!

Helpless she screamed for Baxter who was intermittently barking and whining madly, twisting and jumping this way and that. She tried to clamber over to the driver's door but what happened next shocked her back into her seat.

"You omitted to mention filthy lock-ups and degradation in your plans Kenny! Well I'm not a totally heartless bastard – it's not my style. Not where women are concerned and certainly not where my own moth—"

Annie heard a gun fire and saw Michael drop like a stone beside her window. She screamed as he slumped on a thin veil of snow, his body now leaning against her door, one hand clutched at a burgeoning red shoulder, the other holding the keys and streaked with blood. She froze, unable to think of anything but watch in horror at what was exploding only inches away, the other side of a thin sheet of metal.

Baxter was going demented now, running in circles round the vehicle first one way then the other. Annie just stared open-mouthed, head following him *Exorcist* style, heart trying to burst through her chest!

Suddenly Kenny erupted in a loud guffaw at the young Lab's antics and fell forwards, hands on his knees shaking with laughter. At the sound of his loud hollering, Annie used the few seconds break in tension to frantically search the car for a weapon. She felt inside the door and glove compartments, ran her hands under the front seats, above the visors and inside the rear pockets on the back of the front seats – *nothing!* Kenny was now pointing helplessly at Baxter. He thought it hilarious the dog was performing circus tricks (for want of a better description), at such a tense moment! *Then from nowhere on the third run, no warning at all, the young Lab came hurtling around the front of the car and launched himself at Kenny's head as the man swiftly resumed a stand to see him sail through the air towards him. Annie's face formed a stellar scream from inside the car...*

"Bax – NOOOOOO!!" And as she yelled, fought with the weight of Michael's body against the door and pummelled against the window – *a second shot rang out...*

TWENTY-FIVE

BUILDERS' LOCK-UP
STRATFORD - EAST LONDON

Annie sucked in so much air when that second shot exploded she nearly choked on absolutely nothing. At first there was an eerie silence. She had shut her eyes and covered her face when the gun had gone off again, barely dared to open them and remove her hands. When a goofy black face appeared at her window, tongue lolling out and with that huge sloppy grin, she burst into tears shoulders shaking with heaving grateful sobs.

"Bax… oh Bax!!" Annie fumbled with the lock as Michael pressed the key and pushed himself upright, leaning on his canine accomplice. With the door finally open, Baxter leapt all over his mistress whining and licking her face faster than a drug-crazed lizard! Annie was so confused now but just felt thoroughly relieved her dog was safe and well. And, she had to admit… *Michael too.*

"Kenny?" she asked with an anxious glance at Michael.

"Have a look," he replied flatly, leaning heavily on the roof. Annie leant out of the car to see her captor and high-school rapist clutching his stomach as he bled out into the snow-covered slip road. He was moaning in agony and clutching his guts, the gun now snug in Morton's good hand.

Michael let Baxter into the back seat of the Volvo and shut the door.

"I hope you rot in hell Drew!" He spat derisively at Kenny before walking round to the driver's side. He stopped for a moment then reversed his steps till he was standing over his 'father'. "I'll get an ambulance sent, won't be in any kind of hurry though. Bye… *Dad.*"

By the time they reached the Blackwall Tunnel, Michael was seriously losing blood and beginning to feel really weak. When Baxter had leapt at Drew's head he'd knocked the gun out of his hand, Kenny had lost his balance and ended up on the ground. Michael saw this one and only chance, crawled over to where the gun lay, swiped it out of Drew's reach, and just as his father had regained a half stand, managed to fire off a wild shot. The bullet was lodged somewhere in the man's internal organs, and frankly he wasn't bothered where.

Eyelids now drooping as he drove, slowly and painfully he pulled a mobile out of his left pocket and dropped it into Annie's lap.

"Yours I believe. You'd better call your husband... *and* your mother. Let them know you're okay. Well, not okay exac... but... *uhhhh... God I'm so sorry...*" His head dropped slightly, partly because of the pain his shoulder was in, a lot more because of the shame he felt. They were in the tunnel now and it caused him to drift sideways perilously close to the wall.

"Michael look out!!" Annie yelled as his head jolted back up and he gripped the wheel with his good hand, the fingers of the left merely resting on the base of it. He reacted and re-adjusted in the nick of time.

"I need to take over the driving," she demanded. "Pull over as soon as you can... before we *all* get killed."

Michael just about managed to keep going with the help of the radio and an open window, until a twenty-four-hour BP garage appeared on the Kidbrooke Park Road. He turned onto the forecourt and pulled up away from the pumps at the furthest part of the site. It was quieter here with less consumer activity. Even though it was 4 a.m. there were still a few people about. With hoods up on the coats Michael had brought with him as protection, against any possible CCTV as much as the cold, they both got out of the car and swapped seats. Now Annie was driving and at last able to head unhindered for her parents' home in Kelsey Park. She pulled out into the traffic and Michael relaxed as best he could with his seat reclined as far as possible.

"We need to get you to a hospital Michael," she said firmly, checking her rear view mirror. "I don't know what you're going to say to them but you've got to get that bullet out."

"No! No hospitals!" he snapped back angrily. Then more softly, "Sorry... *sorry...*" He paused. "Can't *you* do something?"

"For God's sake Michael I'm a hairdresser not a surgeon! There's only so much a pair of Diamond Edge scissors and a Denman brush can achieve!" He looked helplessly up at her from his laid-back position. She thought in that moment he looked nearer thirteen than thirty-two. As she indicated to turn left onto the Catford Road she asked him...

"So... am I *really* your mother?"

"You saw the birth certificate," he said quietly. A pause...

"It could have been fake," she replied low, almost whispering.

"It wasn't... and you *are*. My mother that is, not a fake." They both looked at each other then – and smiled as Baxter deposited a large Labby kiss on Michael's head.

KELSEY PARK AVENUE - BECKENHAM SOUTH LONDON

Annie pulled into the drive and parked up behind the large conifers at the back of the house. The drive ran right around the property and the height of the trees provided a screen against ground views from the rear bedrooms. She turned off the engine. Michael was asleep and Baxter's head lay on his paws with half an eye open – *just in case.* Annie gently shook her son. There was no response. She tried again more firmly and still he didn't wake up. She was beginning to panic when Baxter barked loudly in his right ear and suddenly Michael's eyes flew open. He jumped in shock then held his shoulder as he winced in pain.

"Sorry," she said, automatically wincing in sympathy. Annie reached round to the back seat for a bag of medical supplies she'd managed to buy from another all-night garage after finding a wallet in his glove compartment. A very basic selection but they would have to do for now.

"It's okay," Michael replied, eyes closed. "It's just that it's really agony, not feeling too great to be honest." Annie opened the bag and pulled out some bandages, disinfectant, scissors and cotton wool.

"I picked these up whilst you slept. Let's get your top off and I'll do what I can. Then we need to get you to a doctor." With Annie's help, very slowly and very awkwardly Michael managed to get his good arm out of the right sleeve, but his injured left shoulder was proving a lot harder. She turned in her seat to try and help with the difficult angle and his obvious pain, when suddenly the air was filled with the sound of an ear splitting car horn – *theirs!*

"*Shit!!...* Shit!! Shit!! ***Shit!!***" Annie hissed under her breath. She folded her arms, sat back in her seat and waited. It didn't take long. A light flared in one of the upstairs windows followed by one on the ground level. Then the back door opened and in two minutes flat her father was standing in front of the bonnet with *his* arms crossed and her mother in hot pursuit. *It was going to be a long and difficult discussion…*

HARBOUR B&B - STATEN ISLAND NEW YORK

When the theme tune to *Law & Order* went off in his left ear, Harry wasn't even asleep. It was 1.00 a.m. and he felt like he hadn't slept for a month. He stuck his arm out to pick it up, and seeing it was Annie's mobile was ready for an onslaught of abuse from Kenny Drew. He pressed the green phone icon…

"We've got no weather change here Drew – I can't *force* them to fly me out, now let me speak to her, I *demand* you let me spe—"

"Harry… it's me. It's okay, I'm okay. It's a long story but—"

"Annie?!! Annie!! Thank God!! Are you sure you're… where are you? What happened, how did you get…" He was now sat bolt upright in bed and wide-awake. His heart was thumping like a drum solo and the utter relief was immeasurable.

"All in good time Harry. I'm at my parents' house. We're safe and well, showered and fed."

"We? You said 'we're safe and well'. Ohhh… oh yes of course Baxter. You *do* mean Baxter don't you? He *is* okay isn't he?"

"Baxy's fine. He's been amazing Harry… absol—" He heard sniffing and sobbing sounds and waited. "Sorry…" Annie sniffed again then continued. "I love that dizzy dog as much as you do now – put it that way."

Harry paused a second before answering, sensing there must be more. *A) It was unlikely his wife had escaped without help, even with Baxter's protection, and B) She mentioned they'd both had a shower. Dogs don't do showers… do they?*

"So who got you out… and *how? And what about Kenny Drew? Where is he? Have you rung the police?*"

"Harry, *please*, I can't go into it all again right now, I've just gone over everything with my parents and I'm *so* tired. I'm just ringing to reassure you that it's all over and I'm fine." Annie had in fact given quite a watered-down version of events to her parents that excluded who Michael Morton actually was, and more to the point his initial involvement. Her father, being very grateful Michael had *'rescued'* his daughter *when he'd 'heard her screams as he drove past the lock-up',* was at that very moment driving him to the local hospital to get treatment for his shoulder. His wife was fluffing around Annie like a mother hen, all starchiness and stiffness a thing of the past.

"You *are* coming home as soon as the weather improves aren't you Harry? Dad checked the advance forecast for New York online. It's supposed to improve in the next couple of days." Harry took a deep breath before he answered that one... She was now safe and well and being looked after by her parents. Whilst he knew he should really be on the next available flight out of JFK, Harry also knew he had a job to do. He didn't want to be sitting alone on that plane, without Charlotte Peterson securely handcuffed between him and Fran. As usual Annie had already sensed what was coming but let him say it anyway...

"Well let's see how it plays out eh love? You're home safe and sound now and you're not injured at all... *are you?*" He at least had the good grace to flush as the words fell out of his mouth.

"No but—" she began...

"Well not physically anyway," he continued over her. "I know you've gone through a terrible time love, *really* terrible, *dreadful,* but you're with your folks now and I'm sure your mum especially will enjoy having you all to herself, running around and fussing over you. It'll be good for you both to have this time together, make *her* feel better too."

"Yes Harry," she replied flatly. *He's clearly forgotten what Mum used to be like,* Annie thought drily, although her mother's reaction since she'd arrived home certainly seemed to have wiped all that out. Funny how tragic circumstances can change a person... well... *some* people.

"I'll be home as *soon* as I can and I promise I'll drive straight down to Kelsey Park. And Annie... I-I love you—"

Well I wasn't expecting that, she thought, tearing up.

"– It's just that I really need to see this through to the end," he continued quickly. "It's Charlotte *Peterson* – that makes it a personal thing. You *do* understand don't you? I've got to find her, get her back, and before she strikes again."

That's as may be, thought Annie Longbridge nursing a large brandy at her mother's kitchen table. *But it's not just Charlotte Peterson that's a personal thing though is it Harry...*

TWENTY-SIX

BELLEVUE HOSPITAL
MANHATTAN: NEW YORK

The night shift always presented opportunities, and the seven that followed the break-in at Cranberry Street were no different. Carla was on 10 p.m. till 6 a.m. for a week and intended to make good use of it.

There were no visitors at night. It was still busy medically speaking, but not enough to stop chances of learning more about the layout of the building. Where she could temporarily stash stolen drugs in an emergency, where the mortuary and pathology labs were, where the best places to dispose of a body might be...

This particular night Carla was checking out the quickest routes to various areas she thought might prove useful, and found herself on the other side of a lower floor, close to some O.R.s that weren't within her remit. With all the operating rooms came the pre-op rooms. *With all pre-op rooms came drug storage cabinets.*

She couldn't help swinging her hair in the mirror of the rest room as she prepared for her 'tour'. The blonde wig bought with the white coat and stethoscope from the fancy dress store a few weeks ago now sat firmly in place and covered her black pixie cut. She also removed her non-prescription fake glasses.

Carla walked the length of the corridor and counted doors as she went. By the time she'd reached the end of the O.R. section she'd learned there were the same number of operating rooms as on her own floor, and that they were set in the same places beneath the ones above.

It was an extra quiet night being a Monday. No weekend accidents and emergencies from drunk drivers and bar fights, although O.R.s 3 and 7 *were* being used which *was* likely to be some kind of emergency, so gave them a wide berth. O.R.10 though at the end of a long line, was definitely empty and fairly isolated being situated nearest the corner. This meant it was also close to the stairs and lifts. *Perfect*. Carla pushed the door open whilst still checking over her shoulder, despite it being totally deserted and secluded at that end. *Can't be too careful even at 2 a.m…*

She went inside and closed the door quietly behind her. It was too risky to turn the light on and she had no torch, but there was just enough light from the corridor through the central window to find the prize. Her eyes swiftly scanned the room, she was getting used to their layout now as they were all pretty much the same. *A surgical scalpel or two might come in handy* she thought – *well it would be ungrateful to leave them behind if they were laid out ready and waiting.* She still had the small knife in her pocket since 'Mr. Hawk' had watched her from opposite the café, but a proper piece of surgical kit was so much more... *satisfying in use.*

Carla covered her mouth and stifled a smug laugh as it rose in her throat. *This game was even more fun than the last, especially as there'd been no real interference so far, well apart from the cabby, and Leah Chang was still out for the count under gross negligence on that one. Shame – she was a sweet little thing.*

As she reached to open the larger of the two stainless steel supply cabinets, Carla noticed it was the smaller one to the side that housed the scalpels. *Thank you kindly, don't mind if I do,* she thought, and pocketed two of the larger-bladed knives. It was as the second one slipped into her pocket – *that she heard it...*

Jodi Denton was the senior anaesthesia technician responsible for three floors of O.R. surgical drugs and equipment. With all that had been going on in her private life (*basically Ethan James being more off than on since the U.K. Cessna trip two years ago*), her mind had been very much elsewhere.

Ethan would be very distant for months at a time, and then he'd call out of the blue. The whole relationship, if it could even be *called* that, had become untenable... *and it hurt like hell.* The not knowing why when everything had been going so well, albeit she was cheating on her husband with her brother-in-law, made it even more stressful. Add to that her best friend, police officer Terri–Jane Malone, was continually pressing her to give him up, and it was no surprise she'd forgotten to stocktake O.R.s 8, 9 and 10 on floor 3. Now Jodi was hurrying and not really thinking straight. That stocktake was a day behind and she had to decide what needed re-ordering, as well as preparing the sheets, get those figures in for the following day, plus her designated work for that shift.

Her new rubber-soled flats squeaked noisily on the shiny floor as she marched swiftly down the corridor towards O.R.10, her last 'missed' check for the night. Even as she turned the paper from O.R.9 on her clipboard and pushed the door open to O.R.10, she was thinking of Ethan and the last time they'd been together…

Jodi stood rooted to the spot. Her eyes fixed open for just a second, in surprise more than anything. The turquoise room in the beach hotel where Ethan had last made love to her began to splash red with indoor rain as his face slipped further and further away, until he faded altogether – *and then she fell.*

This wasn't a special 'despatch' and she didn't have any Baclovate on her anyway. So when Carla emerged from behind the door, slid the scalpel into Jodi's right kidney and yanked – there were no regrets about not being able to use her new *'injectable toy'.*

As the woman dropped her clipboard and folded forward a lead weight in her arms, Carla simply let her slip to the floor in a heap. The burgundy seeped slowly at first then spread like a map across her pale mauve scrubs. Jodi Denton's astonished expression seen only by the previously unblemished floor as she slumped face-down in a corner.

Carla's hand began to shake. She watched transfixed as the blood dripped down the handle and snaked her wrist. As usual when faced with a *messy* impromptu despatch… anxiety struck, so with all the self-control she could muster, she placed the scalpel into her pocket and tried to breathe. Normal 'in and ex' halation had stopped briefly when her victim had fallen to the floor. Now Carla entered racing recovery mode, thoughts shifted swiftly into strict methodical order. Bed linen cart/clean up/elevator/basement – *begin*.

Harry Longbridge couldn't sleep. It was 3 a.m. and he was on his back staring at flaky cream paint around a bedroom ceiling light at The Harbor B&B. He was agitated and stressed, *and felt as guilty as hell.* Although he knew he couldn't just *walk* across the Atlantic, he also knew he *could* get a flight to London in the next couple of days if the weather held. He also suspected Annie would never forgive him if he stayed out in Brooklyn, particularly with Fran – nobody would blame him for not finishing the job given what had happened to his wife. But *he* would. *The Magpie would blame himself.* Harry Longbridge *always* finished a job.

He turned over, sighed heavily again and faced the curtains, not peeling but not exactly shouting this decade either. If it was the other way around he knew he'd be absolutely livid if Annie hadn't abandoned *her* job, and no doubt his wife would be pointing that out when he finally got home. He wasn't looking forward to a lecture from his in-laws either, especially as it would be justified and he was going to end up looking a prize shit of a husband. One that Annie's strict Presbyterian father Iain McMahon would not miss the opportunity of giving a dressing down… he was absolutely certain of that.

He hated not being able to sleep it always interfered with his insulin problem. Bad enough trying to balance food choices and everything that went with it, plus getting his shots right (something he rarely managed correctly), but when he didn't get eight hours either it just fucked everything right up.

Wide-awake now, he threw back the covers made his way to the tea tray and flicked the kettle on. It had just boiled when he thought he heard a knock at the door. He stopped with the teabag mid air over a cup and listened again. A second rap followed. He dropped the bag into the cup and walked to the door one hand ready to open it, when he stopped. It was after all gone three in the morning, and he wasn't wearing anything…

"Who is it?" he asked guardedly.

"For God's sake Harry who do you *think* it is – *Santa?*" hissed Fran on the other side. *"Open up it's me!"*

"Hold on… with you in a minute…" He looked around haphazardly for something to make him decent, and settled for a bath towel round his waist and yesterday's sweatshirt from the back of the chair. Catching himself in the only long mirror in the room wasn't pretty.

When he finally opened the door Fran had her *'I told you so'* face on – right before the smirking started. Harry gave her the *'don't even go there'* look and then noticed the outwardly held screen on her mobile. Ch. Inspector Chris Hitchings' face was smack bang in the middle – *and it didn't look happy.*

Carla scrubbed her hands and arms over and over until her skin was clear of Jodi's blood. She watched it spin round and round with the water in the sink until it finally disappeared and left it silver again. She dried her hands, pulled the sheet off the pre-op bed and threw it over the body, then made sure it was covered before leaving the room to find a linen cart. Pointless cleaning up the floor and splashed cupboards until she got back.

She was just about to open the door when she saw a spatter of Jodi's blood on her own scrubs. Groaning, she pulled the top over her head taking care not to disturb the wig, rolled it into a ball and desperately scanned the room for a spare or a white coat. Carla almost laughed when her eyes went full circle and noticed that behind the door hung a lab coat, a bit on the large side but it would have to do. She put it on and rammed her stained top deep into one of the large patch pockets. *Should've brought in my own fake whites,* she thought crossly, *but to be fair this **was** an extra and unexpected job.* Finally she opened the door.

Her head pounded with every controlled step along the corridor to the corner, the 'cul-de-sac' and the elevators. She must not run, she must not flap she must not attract attention. *It was so much easier in private houses, in their homes.* Deep long, slow breaths moved in and out of her lungs imitating a pair of old bellows trying to breathe life into a dying fire. She dare not let herself lose control, she dare not let them come quickly – *she could not hyperventilate.*

As Carla arrived at the elevators, footsteps sounded in the main corridor. Two sets. Her breathing quickened as she hit the button, swivelled her head right to the corner wall and wracked her brains to unlock a memory. *The housekeeping area!! Third floor or fourth floor? **Third floor or fourth floor?!*** She was on the fifth. The elevator car whirred from deep below. She hit the button again.

"Come on come on come on!!"

Voices now – male, and some laughter…

"God I need coffee about a gallon I'm parched and absolutely *knackered*. A plate of cheesy fries would go down nicely too."

"*Don't!* The other half has threatened *divorce* if I don't get rid of this belly!" Laughter ensued as the owners of the conversation closed in on the corner area just as the elevator pinged its arrival and doors opened. Carla leapt inside and stabbed mentally at the fourth floor button just as the two surgeons from O.R.3 rounded the corner. They saw the doors about to close and called out as they hastened their step.

"Hey – hold the ride please?!"

A second sooner and Carla might have needed more than one cart. She just prayed they weren't aiming for the fourth floor. The elevator slowed down, gave a bounce back to level up with the ground outside and announced its arrival. The doors opened and she gingerly looked out. All seemed quiet and the elevators either side weren't arriving. Now she needed to recall the exact location of the housekeeping department where the sheets, blankets, towels and more importantly – carts were stored. *If there was one on the fourth floor...*

Carla swallowed repeatedly in an attempt to keep her mind off her breathing and her now thumping headache. *She shouldn't have killed Jodi Denton. What the hell was she thinking of for Chrissake? She could've just knocked her out and run! Her blonde wig was very realistic and she had no glasses on. Jodi would never have recognised her in the dim light!* As she berated herself over her impetuousness and stupidity, with nobody about, Carla moved faster towards where she believed the housekeeping area might be. With her mind teeming, she passed it on a left corner and had to turn back. The heavy double doors swung inward when she shoulder barged them, now she really needed to get this thing done.

Luckily she could see all the carts lined up together and within easy reach. Carla picked one quickly and was about to push it through the door *when a wheel started to squeak like a stuck pig!* Shoving it to one side she chose another and tested it first. All good. It felt like ten hours but took less than ten minutes to get back to O.R.10, although she thought her heart would give out whilst wheeling it round the corner from the elevators. Tired surgeons from the other O.R. may well have finished and be heading that way to go down to the coffee lounge and meet their colleagues.

Her luck held and Carla breathed a sigh of relief when she was safely back inside the pre-op room of O.R.10, the door closed safely behind her. The only problem now was – *Jodi wasn't there.*

TWENTY-SEVEN

BELLEVUE HOSPITAL
MANHATTAN: NEW YORK

If Carla's head could have spun a full three-hundred-and-sixty degrees it would have. Now she *had* to switch the light on. The illuminated room soon revealed what had happened as the evidence was laid bare of a person bleeding out who'd dragged themselves slowly across the floor.

Jodi hadn't been able to stand but she'd managed to manoeuvre herself using her good side, on her left arm and shoulder, over to the actual operating room door. The hallway outside the pre-op was obviously where she'd wanted to get to, but in the dark, bleeding heavily and in her agony and confusion, she had misjudged her way to the correct door that led to the outside – *and help...*

The O.R. door opened inwards, and with a huge effort derived from sheer self-preservation, Jodi had heaved her mutilated body inch by searing inch, through the opening into the second room. On the other side she'd tried her best to feel around in the dark for a cabinet or anything to use as a screen, had somehow achieved that and managed to curl herself up in the dark behind one.

And that's where Carla found her.

At The Harbor B&B Harry took the phone from Fran and sat on the bed whilst she made them tea. Chief Super Chris Hitchings had no misgivings about ringing them at 3 a.m. it seemed, and neither did he have any qualms about yelling his head off in the middle of *their* night from across the pond. He also had a complexion resembling beetroot…

"Longbridge – what the hell is going on? I've just had South Norwood on telling me your wife's been rescued tonight from a lock-up in Stratford! Shots were fired, one man down one injured, and you knew all about it but didn't report it – to any damn station – ANYWHERE!! And it was Kenny bloody Drew Harry! Kenny bloody Drew!! He hasn't been out five minutes! Like to enlighten me??"

"Yes sir well with regard to my wi—"

"Not only that Longbridge, you've been out there swanning around with D.I. Taylor and I've no updates on the Peterson woman either. It's just not good enough Harry you know damn well it isn't." Fran smarted at this last considering it was *her* case and Harry was *not* the Senior Investigating Officer anymore. But as usual everybody

forgot or assumed he was. *Oh what the hell…* She knew she should've reported in more regularly though, and began chewing on her lip as she walked back from the tea tray – Harry still trying to get a word in…

"No sir, you see the thi—"

"You're not even officially back in the job dammit! This was a very special case – I laid my neck on the line with the Yard because of your history with Charlotte Peterson. You can't just make it up as you go along anymore Harry. And what about Annie for fuck's sake?!"

Fran handed Harry a tea, sat on the bed next to him and took the phone.

"It wasn't Harry's fault sir, he was being blackmailed by Drew who threatened to kill Mrs. Longbridge if he contacted police."

"To the tune of half a million Chris," added Harry, who was now pretty peed off with calling him 'sir'. "I couldn't get a flight out either because the weather over here is shite and they've closed all the airports."

"You've got another two weeks to track Peterson down and that's it, then Scotland Yard is taking over. I've been hauled over the coals for this already – and D.I. Taylor… I want an ongoing *daily* report – *as* of tomorrow. *Do – you –understand?* You *are* an officially serving officer *and I don't want you picking up bad habits from my ex-D.C.I.!*"

"Sir…" This meekly from Fran, Harry was now in the bathroom making use of its main item. Hitchings ended the call even redder than he'd started, and apart from the loo flushing, the sudden silence was deafening. Harry emerged holding tightly onto his towel. He noticed that despite her support of him and explanation to Hitchings, Fran had another 'I told you so' face on.

"Yes, yes okay – he's a bit miffed," said Harry avoiding her stare.

"A bit… *miffed?* He's bloody *furious Harry!!*" replied Fran, snatching her phone up and waving it violently in the air. "I *told* you we should have called Annie's hostage situation in, and she *is* your wife Harry! *For God's sake!*" She was now standing up and running her phone-free hand through her hair.

"*Look…* I made my decision and I'm sticking by it. You never met Kenny Drew back then Fran so don't give me the old 'I told you so' routine. He's an evil dangerous bastard. It's turned out okay hasn't it? Annie's safely with her parents and South Norwood are dealing with it. The main thing that's bugging Hitchings is *you* not keeping him up to date with what's going down out here."

Fran narrowed her eyes and marched to the door. She knew he was right and she hated him for it. Although of course she didn't hate him at all – and that was the problem.

"*Fine! I hope you choke on your bloody tea!*" came flying out angrily under her breath before she swept out of the room and slammed the door. Harry sighed, picked up his cup and rolled his eyes. It was probably for the best. Having Fran Taylor in his bedroom in the middle of the night was probably not a good idea. Scrap that, it was *definitely* not a good idea. Particularly when he was only wearing a bath towel…

BELLEVUE HOSPITAL
MANHATTAN

Carla stared at Jodi's foetus-like body. Coiled and pressed against a wheeled supplies cabinet, it was very badly hidden in a corner. She'd tried to drag a screen across her but it was clear by then that she couldn't manage anything more.

Once Carla had seen the direction of the blood smears on the floor of the pre-op room, she'd turned out the light, pushed open the door to the O.R., slipped inside and listened. All she could hear was her own breathing, which meant that out of the two of them, *only she was alive.*

She went back into the pre-op room and pushed the bed linen cart into the O.R. wheeling it right up to the body. It took more effort getting Jodi Denton into that cart than she could have possibly imagined. After one or two failed starts she finally managed to heave her in and cover her with the used bedding. Now all she needed to do was get her down to the boiler room…

Harry wasn't the only one who wasn't sleeping that night. Andrew had been lying awake the last few, in fact he'd not had much sleep at all since Jenny's murder. He was seriously beginning to wonder why he, Gina, and Molly were even still in the States given what was going on. He was also starting to feel distinctly uncomfortable where Emily was concerned. Andrew wasn't a police officer and had no professional experience as any kind of investigator *(well apart from his dire involvement with the Peterson case)*, but what he did have was a nose for things that didn't quite *'fit'*. And Emily Stone was definitely in that category. Something… *somewhere* regarding her and Jenny, didn't quite fit.

If it wasn't for the fact that the airports were closed due to the weather, he would have suggested they went home and arranged a small wedding in Kirkdale after the baby was born. *In fact*, he thought decisively, *as soon as it's light and Gina wakes up I may well mention it.* Andrew turned his head to check the bedside clock – 5 a.m.… He sighed impatiently… *We're all holed up in this house most of the time now. I'm not sure if any one of us could be a target or if Charlotte Peterson was even responsible for Jenny's death. The police haven't come up with anything and the not knowing and not being any further forward is driving me nuts.*

Andrew never was much good at coping with 'cabin fever'. His decision was made. *As soon as she wakes up I'm going to tell her we should go home as soon as we can get a flight out of here.*

When morning came, the sky was still dark and heavy with snow, and Gina wasn't feeling too good at all. She'd woken with griping pains in her stomach and Andrew was concerned the whole Charlotte business was getting to her. He wondered if she might even need to see a doctor, but Gina being Gina wanted to see if it wore off. She had a serious dislike of doctors and hospitals, and frankly all things considered, nobody could really blame her. Andrew however didn't want to ignore it.

"Gee I think we should get you checked out, take a cab to the hospital, it won't take that long and you'll feel better once you know for sure."

"I really don't want to move at the moment Andy, it's not that bad just some griping, think I might have eaten something that hasn't agreed with me."

"Like what? You've been so careful and not even had any alcohol. Well apart from that little shot of brandy in your coffee the other night and that wouldn't have done it."

"Look… if it's still there by lunchtime I promise I'll go. Just leave me to have a lie-in till then eh?" she said, holding her stomach.

"Okay you win," he said smiling and stroking her hair. He planted a kiss on her forehead, threw the quilt back and got out of bed. He pulled on some sweat pants and made for the door.

"Andy!?" she called after him as he was about to leave the room.

"*Yes – what!? Are you okay? Has it got worse? I told you we shou—*"

"The quilt…" She pointed to the haphazard mess he'd left it in when he got out and he immediately returned to the bed to arrange it perfectly around her.

"Sorry sweetheart, you rest now and I'll bring you a tea up in a while. You haven't gone off it or anything have—"

"*Noooo…* go on… *shoo!* I'll be *fine*. I'll just have a little lie-in and doze for a couple of hours. But you could leave me some grapefruit ready for later please, that would be lovely." Andrew thought he'd never get used to his carb-loving fiancée asking for grapefruit, or any kind of fruit come to that. Amazing how hormones could affect a woman.

"Right okay then I'll see you in a bit." He leant across the bed and gave her another kiss then headed off to the bathroom for a shower. And despite his wonder at learning about female pregnancy cravings, as he stood with the hot spray washing over his body, Andrew Gale, senior crime reporter at a small Cumbrian paper *felt very troubled indeed.*

Carla had not found it easy. Not easy at all. She was now in a cab on the way home after the nightshift from hell, and still didn't know how she'd got through it…

Down in the boiler room it had been hot *and absolutely enormous.* There were gigantic pipes everywhere painted in all sorts of colours, greens whites and reds, running floor to ceiling and wall to wall in every direction. There were smaller ones too and many with big spoke wheels, *to open and close valves* she assumed. It was like spaghetti junction with boilers and various incinerators dotted here and there as well.

Carla had never actually seen inside such a place anywhere before, but she'd searched for it at the hospital on a previous nightshift, so she'd know exactly where it was and how long it would take to get there. Just in case. But she didn't think she'd actually need it – well… not for the circumstance she found herself in anyway.

For whatever reason, the boiler room technician had not been about when she pushed the cart through that door. It was a gigantic complex that had to run the whole hospital above it, so she'd guessed there must have been more than one operative, but still saw nobody in the area she'd entered.

It had been hard-going pushing the bed-linen cart with Jodi's body concealed between the sheets, slowly up and down lanes, between all manner of square and tubular engineering containers as she'd searched for the right incinerator. Finally after about five minutes, the longest five minutes of her life… she had found it. Carla wiped her forehead with the back of her forearm and leant against the bar of the cart to get her breath, all the while her eyes had looked furtively around the vast pipe world that had become a maze encased around her.

The controls and dials had looked self-explanatory. She'd noticed the temperature gauges and written operative explanations. That hadn't been the hard part. The hard part had been heaving Jodi's body up from the bottom of the cart even though she'd tied her body into the sheets like a caul first, to make containment easier. Then it had been a second heave up onto the metal tray of the incinerator, followed by the rest of the linen. *Never ever would she be doing this again…*

Once the deed had been done and the heavy metal door clanged shut, Carla had spun the temperature up to the highest level and set it to the longest possible time. Never having worked in a crematorium before, she'd decided to play it safe. The flames had roared and the bile in her stomach had all but followed suit, but at least all the physical evidence would now be gone… *or so she thought.*

TWENTY-EIGHT

BELLEVUE HOSPITAL
MANHATTAN: NEW YORK

Kay Winford had been a forensic pathologist for nearly twenty-five years. Nothing, however, had prepared her for what she was looking at right now.

Jenny Flood's cadaver lay stretched out on the table. A long line from the bottom of her collarbone to the top of her pubic bone, newly incised, had glared up at her. After the top layer of skin and very small quantity of subcutaneous fat had been peeled back, what was revealed was utterly astonishing. Every single one of the organs looked withered... *and black*. Whatever drug had been injected into her that night must either have been one Kay had no knowledge of, or one that was rarely used, and/or heavily restricted. *And used in a completely different way for a different reason... and in a much smaller quantity.* The heart, lungs, liver, kidneys, bowel, bladder, uterus – every single piece of visible flesh beneath the surface, was shrivelled, charcoal black and of an irregular shape.

She knew when she'd examined her body at the scene it wasn't just in a state of rigor mortis, and Kay had found the needle mark. Her job now was to discover what had been injected to cause that damage to the organs of this poor woman, and the onset of it, *whilst she'd still been alive.*

ENGINE 210
CARLTON AVENUE - FORT GREENE. F.D.

Det. Casey Quinnel had paid fire officer Mike Hyland a visit at his place of work, Fort Greene's Carlton Avenue – *Engine 210 of the Brooklyn Fire Dept.* He'd commandeered a room to interview the man who'd insisted on working even though his new girlfriend had just been horrifically murdered. Quinnel had suggested there was more than a whiff of suspicion over this until he felt the wrath of Hyland's colleagues, who clearly thought the man was a god – every last one of them. It was also obvious to the most cynical cop (a group to which Quinnel was proud to belong) that Mike Hyland had loved Jenny Flood totally and completely, despite only having been in a relationship with her for a few months. He was working because facing a fire and saving other people was the only way he could get through the day. *I couldn't save Jenny,* he'd said tearfully, *I'll be damned if I'll let anyone else die by me not doing my job.* The nights however were another thing altogether…

The facts were that Hyland had no access to restricted medical drugs, intravenous or otherwise, no motive to kill her, there was nothing in the infamous diary to suggest there had been any problems between them, and most of all he'd told him a neighbour had seen Jenny, very much alive and kissing him goodbye at the door on the night she'd died. Satisfied the guy was not a suspect Casey gave him his condolences, and said he'd be in touch if he needed to speak to him again, although he wouldn't have been doing *his* job if he hadn't asked him not to leave the State whilst investigations were ongoing. *And he still intended to check up on that neighbour.*

The two men shook hands, and Quinnel left feeling distinctly lucky his own girlfriend Leah Chang was alive and well. Even if she'd got her problems at the hospital with the gross negligence case at the moment, at least she was safe and robustly healthy. Casey would also make sure he was there for her a lot more now. Lay off the late nights with the boys for a bit, including with his colleague, her brother Eddie Chang – *just till it was all sorted.*

Det. Terri-Jane Malone had pulled up outside The Harbor B&B. Jenny Flood's 2018 black leather diary sat on the seat beside her, the two distinctive red tail markers keeping those important paragraphs easily to hand. Terri had been refreshing her memory of it before going in to meet the British officers, now she picked it up and slipped it inside her case-notes bag. *This was going to be interesting,* she thought.

Inside, Harry and Fran were already waiting in the lounge with a pot of coffee and some biscuits. Fran was more than a little prickly with him over the Chris Hitchings call in the middle of the night and they were both tired, although Harry was doing his level best to smooth things over.

"Cookie?" he said brightly, holding up the plate.

Fran ignored him. She sat drinking her coffee and staring studiously towards the hallway over the rim of her cup. She prayed Detective Malone would turn up soon.

"Come on Fran," Harry pleaded, putting the plate back on the table. "I've said I'm sorry. You know I couldn't call in Annie's kidnap to the Super, for God's sake she *is* my wife, don't you think *I* wanted to get her out of that lock-up?"

Fran turned from looking at the hallway, and sighing heavily, held his gaze. She sat looking ultra calm with her chin resting between her left forefinger and thumb, and right foot on her left knee. Dressed entirely in black, she looked relaxed yet efficient, but didn't feel either. She swore this man who could bring out every emotion, from exasperation to adoration and everything in between, *would quite literally end up being the death of her.* She tipped her head at the plate of biscuits. Harry smiled broadly and re-offered the chocolate chips. Fran took one just as T.J. Malone walked into the room.

"Good morning, Detectives Longbridge and Taylor? We met at 68th Precinct and also at Miss. Flood's home. I'm Detective Malone – T.J."

Harry stood up and shook her hand followed by Fran who quickly pocketed the cookie first, and then they all sat down.

"As I explained on the phone earlier," said T.J., "we – *I* – found something of great interest at Miss. Flood's house which we think will have a direct bearing on your original case in the U.K. with the Cumbrian killings, and so your reason for being out here."

"Go on," said Fran, leaning forward now, desperate to learn all she could about that summer if she was ever going to be seen as the Senior Investigating Officer. Terri-Jane sensed her need. *They were two of a kind, Fran and her.*

T.J. pulled a book out of the case she'd brought with her, and moving the tray over slightly, placed it on the table. Harry immediately realised they hadn't offered her a coffee and held up the pot to her quizzically.

"Yes… thank you, cream no sugar," Terri said smiling as she opened the book at the first red marker and pushed it towards Fran. She picked it up and read the paragraph that had been highlighted in yellow…

'Saturday September 15th 2018
…Things are just getting too hot. I'm going to have to ring Emily and tell her I can't cope with this anymore and want out. Getting involved

with Miles again is just too heartbreaking, and Charlotte is getting more and more suspicious. Andrew Gale, the guy I'm working with at the paper is now asking all sorts of questions, and with Jason being here as well… it's just all too much. I should never have gone along with Emily's crazy plan after we met at the 2015 Carlisle conference. I should have kept saying no, but she wanted to send that bitch over the edge and into a nuthouse. No matter what she'd done to us – well her mainly, I should have just refused!'

Fran slid the diary over to Harry as he passed a cup of coffee to T.J. He then picked up the book and read the entry whilst crunching and dropping crumbs. Sweeping them off the page with both eyebrows arched significantly, his head leant in. Jenny had never mentioned this association with Emily to him back then when he'd interviewed her. Their relationship hadn't come to light until more recently. That day at Margaret Rowlands' *(Gina's grandmother's)* funeral, Harry had only ever seen Emily from a distance. He hadn't been aware who she was although her rich auburn hair had matched Gina's exactly, and knowing the younger woman's history, he'd had a damned good guess at who she was. The fact Jenny had left for Brooklyn immediately after her brother Jason's funeral had only become common knowledge much later. He turned to Fran.

"This is evidence of a pre-meditated act. Of what crime exactly I'm not sure – *yet*. Coercion certainly, but I can't imagine Mrs. Stone wanted to incense Charlotte Peterson into committing *murder?*"

Fran narrowed her eyes in thought as Harry put the diary back on the table and reached for his coffee.

"What do we really *know* about her though Harry?" she pointed out.

"There's more," said T.J. as she swiped the pages over to a few weeks later at the second red marker. *"And this is a killer if you'll pardon the pun."* This time it was Fran's turn to raise a brow.

"Here." Terri prodded at the second piece of highlighted text. Harry picked the diary up with his free hand, and with heads together he and Fran read in tense silence.

'Friday October 26th 2018

Oh my God I can't believe I'm writing this!! She's had me following her all over the place for weeks, I'm sleeping with Miles again, lying to new colleagues, and today, today I actually SAW her murder my old school friend Danni Mogg!! Sweet innocent Danni!! It was just horrible, horrible! I don't know what to do! What the fuck is going on in my life??? I've had it now, that's it, that's IT!! I can't go on with this mad fucking plan of hers! Emily's GOT to come home – put a stop to it, she's GOT to! Nobody was supposed to DIE for God's sake! Nobody's bloody safe anymore, NOBODY – I'M not safe…'

Harry knew about Danielle Mogg because Jenny had told him. It had been central to the C.P.S.'s case that had got Charlotte Peterson sent to Rampton Psychiatric Hospital. Danielle Mogg had been an aspiring young actress going by the name of Susie Sarrandaire. What Harry *hadn't* been told by Jenny, was that Emily Stone had been manipulating her into following Charlotte *anywhere*. She'd told him Danni was an old friend, and had witnessed her murder through a window because they'd met up purely by chance when Jenny had recently moved into the area. Danni had said to drop in for a coffee.

"Detective Malone this is a very important document. I take it Detective Delaney's seen this?" Fran could see from Harry's face how shocked he was and for once had no objection to him taking the lead.

"Yes, and although it's part of our crime scene he thought you'd want to see it."

"Indeed. I'm – *we're* grateful," said Harry, briefly glancing at Fran. T.J. inclined her head in acknowledgement and leant forward to pick up the diary.

"Detective Delaney *did* pay Mrs. Stone a visit regarding this information, following Miss. Flood's murder," she said, placing the book back in her bag. "I believe she declined to comment, and went upstairs to lie down claiming stress and upset due to Miss. Flood's death as she was a close friend and colleague."

"Will you be inviting her in for an interview

considering she didn't answer Detective Delaney's questions?" asked Harry.

"Yes, I'm sure the boss will be doing that at some point soon. I think given she's got an alibi for the actual murder, and Miss. Flood was a friend of longstanding, he's giving her some space at the moment."

"I assume the N.Y.P.D. will want to keep the diary until you've caught the killer?" asked Fran. At that moment a call came through on her radio and T.J. motioned to her to hold on as she walked out into the hall to receive it. Fran poured herself another coffee.

"What do you think Harry?"

"I think Emily Stone engineered a plan to ensure a susceptible woman that she knew had a serious psychological mental history, toppled right over the edge. And I think she pressured a vulnerable young girl into doing her dirty work from three thousand miles away."

"Me too… *What are we going to do about it?*"

CHAPTER TWENTY-NINE

KELSEY PARK AVENUE
BECKENHAM: SOUTH LONDON

Annie Longbridge was keeping a close eye on the weather in Brooklyn. She wasn't quite sure why really as she'd already had her answer from her husband, and Harry wasn't flying home till he'd found the Peterson woman.

For the first few days since the escape, she'd also been torn between telling her parents the truth about Michael, versus leaving them in blissful ignorance. That he'd simply happened along at the right moment, played *'Superman'* for an hour or two and probably saved their daughter's life. In the end Annie had decided to let them remain happily grateful in the dark, it was kinder and would avoid so much trouble – and they would have to tell the police that anyway. Telling Harry of course was going to be a complete nightmare… *which was why she wasn't going to tell him either.*

The police had interviewed them in separate rooms at South Norwood station the morning after they'd turned up at Annie's parents' house. Michael had explained how he'd heard Annie's screams because his satnav had taken him off course up a slip road, and during the rescue had initially been shot in the shoulder by Kenny when he'd returned to check on her. Later in a tussle for the gun, Michael had said he'd had no choice but to shoot Drew in self-defence. He'd aimed for his knees but fell backwards over Annie's dog and the gun went high. This second part was a lie, but he and Annie had already worked out the story and he knew she'd back him up in the other interview room. As neither of them had remembered to send an ambulance to the builders' yard, they'd both agreed to say that when Kenny went down they just took their chance and made their escape.

Annie had to explain about her history with Kenny Drew of course. About Harry's connection as the Senior Investigating Officer who'd put him away for the bank job fifteen years before, and that was why he'd tracked them down and kidnapped her for a ransom when he'd got out. They were both told they would need to be available for further questioning once Kenny had been found, whether that was dead or alive, and then they'd been allowed to leave. Armed police and ambulance were to be sent to the builders' yard at Stratford. *They both knew what they were likely to find, and armed police was almost certainly unwarranted.*

Michael had stayed at her parent's home in Kelsey Park for a few days until his shoulder had improved enough to travel more comfortably, and then got a cab back to his place which strangely wasn't that far from Annie's parents' house. There was no way he was going to be able to drive for weeks, so he'd told her to keep the Volvo, then she could get back home. It was the least he could do for her under the circumstances. When the cab came to take him back to Lewisham it had been an awkward goodbye at the door…

"Will you tell Harry about me being…" Michael looked down and then to the cab waiting in the road before looking back at Annie.

"Probably not," she said softly. He nodded, breathing a long sigh of relief.

"I'll never forgive myself for my part in… *everything*, you do know that don't you? If I could just turn the cl—"

"Don't. It's okay, it's… it's okay," she said hesitantly rubbing his good arm. "You came through in the end Michael and for that I'm grateful. Kenny Drew always was a bully and a control freak. I've no doubt he also managed to persuade you that everything was my fault." Michael chewed the inside of his mouth and looked across the lawn.

"When I'd started to try and find my real parents, I did find him, quite easily in fact. I lied that day in the pub. When I told you it was another Kenneth Drew. He said you'd thrown away a chance of you and him being together and living with his parents. That he'd wanted to look after you, keep us all together as a family." Michael looked back at her as Annie smiled wryly. A small, sharp sigh escaped as she raised an eyebrow in disbelief and shook her head.

"No. That's not what happened at all." She looked over her shoulder and stepping outside pulled the door almost shut behind her in case either of her parents came into the hall. "He raped me Michael. He raped me against a flint wall at a school disco when I was just sixteen. My parents sent me away to an aunt's in Whitstable until you were born. Then the social took you away a week later and gave you to your adoptive parents. I thought I would cry for the rest of my life." Her eyes glistened then, tears shone large and threatened to fall. She wiped them away quickly as Michael pulled her close and hugged her as best he could with his left arm.

"I hate him for what he did to you. I'm staggered you don't hate me for being the result of it and my part in your second hell this last week. I should go…" He turned and walked a few steps down to the cab, but Annie stepped off the porch and reached out to him.

"Michael!!" He turned round to see the alarm on her face. "I know our reunion hasn't exactly been normal but…" she took a deep breath,… "I don't want to lose you again Michael – I *can't* lose you again." He walked back up the path as Annie came forward and put her

arms around him. She kissed his cheek and then smiled awkwardly. *He* was smiling broadly, eyes glazed, full of hope.

"I can't believe you're being so *wonderful* about it all," he said incredulously.

"It's quite simple," she said, wiping his tears. "You're my son... *and I never stopped loving you...*"

HOME OF PATHOLOGIST KAY WINFORD
BROOKLYN, NEW YORK

Kay put the last book down and felt her heart kick off like a machine gun. *The Little Black Book of Hospital Medicine, Mosby's Drug Reference* and *Robins Pathological Basis of Disease* were her top three 'go to' for checking any theories. They had never let her down yet, and *Mosby's* hadn't let her down now, but the thought that someone who shouldn't be, was out there with access to Baclovate... She shivered.

Kay was a strong woman. Some might even say hard and not least a little flippant sometimes in the autopsy room, although never disrespectful. Not much shocked or affected her anymore; she'd seen most things. Well except kiddies, she always hated to see a child on her table. But mostly, mostly she found it fascinating and just got on with the job the best way she knew how in order to stay sane. *This however was something else entirely.*

Her partner Rebecca Larson put a large whisky and ice on the oak table beside her.

"*Enough Kay.* You never let up, it's time to relax now." Kay looked at her partner, and catching her hand as she walked past, smiled briefly before dropping it and picking up the glass.

"Thanks Bex, I could really do with this." She brought the drink to her lips and took a large gulp, savouring its distinct flavour. As she closed her eyes and leant back into her chair the spirit warmed her throat and soothed her soul. And as Rebecca drank her wine watching in concern from the sofa opposite, Kay wondered if she would ever truly relax again…

After having taken Gina a coffee and some toast about eleven, Andrew had left her to rest for the afternoon. She was still refusing to go to hospital and insisted her pain wasn't so bad now, just felt a bit tired and wanted to sleep. Emily was also out of it (with sleeping tablets), but Gareth had to go in to work. That left him and Molly alone. With an improvement in the weather, he suggested they take a walk to get some fresh air and maybe some brunch. He needed to talk to her privately, and what he wanted to discuss he wasn't about to risk letting out in the Stones' residence for a second time. He left a note for Gina on the kitchen table and then they both left the house.

Well wrapped up, they walked down the steps to the street. Andrew nudged Molly and tipped his head towards the police car opposite the house.

"Still got us under protection then," he said. *"Or surveillance…"*

"What do you mean *surveillance?*" replied Molly as they reached the street and began to walk down Narrows Avenue, avoiding the slush that was now all that remained of the snow.

"I'll tell you when we get some coffee and something to eat – I need your insight on this."

"Not so sure I've got much of that out here Andy, don't forget I never got a vision about Jenny's murder. Unless my ability's completely vanished, I think it's only apparent when I'm in my own surroundings."

"Well I meant more your gut instincts Molls, rather than the other thing, strange that you didn't have the slightest warning though given what happened last time."

It was only a few minutes to the Narrows Coffee Shop and Molly was now more than a little intrigued. She increased her step to match his and soon they were seated in a corner away from the window. This tiny family café of just ten tables was packed; they were lucky a couple had just vacated theirs. With its bright orange walls and mottled brown tiles beneath a mahogany dado rail, along with non matching sage green seats, its decor belied the amazing smells, fabulous coffee and delicious all-day breakfasts on offer. And the seats *were* at least squashy thought Molly, although she was secretly thinking how much nicer The Carpenters was decked out at home.

"So what's all this about?" she asked Andrew as her eyes roamed hungrily all over her cheese and bacon omelette, chips and beans. "You'd better hurry up 'cos I'm not going to be able to contribute to this conversation in a minute!" Andrew laughed, not so long ago that would definitely have been a Gina comment, but her appetite had been on the wane with all the morning sickness. "Well you—" started Andrew...

"Too late," teased Molly as she fell on it like she'd not eaten for a week. After the first mouthful, her fork waved around in a fast circular motion indicating he should start the story whilst he waited for his food to arrive. Having known Molly for years now, he'd picked up on her 'cutlery language'. Andrew took a deep breath, looked around him as if there were radio wires in the closest diners, and spoke in as low a voice as he could manage but so Molly could still hear.

"I know she's Gina's mother, and I know I've mentioned this before... but I think Emily's hiding something. I think it's something really big and I also think the police may have found some evidence that connects Emily to Charlotte Peterson and Jenny's murder."

Molly's eyes widened significantly, and not just because of Andrew's theory. She swallowed awkwardly and followed it with a gulp of coffee.

"Jeez Andy where are you *getting* this stuff from?!" She rubbed and patted the top of her chest to help the food go down, and drank some more coffee to aid it as

Andrew's all-day breakfast was put in front of him. He thanked the waitress and waited for her to move across to a window table before answering.

"She's not left the house since Jenny got murdered, she keeps sleeping late and I took a peek in her en-suite and saw some sleeping tablets. I'd stake my life on it they're not Gareth's."

"Yes but is that *really* all that strange? It could just be because of her losing a close friend couldn't it?"

"I overheard some of the talk in the kitchen the night the two officers came to speak to her and Gareth. Remember Gareth mentioned they'd said Jenny kept a diary?" Molly nodded.

"Yes it was right before they left the lounge for the interview in the kitchen wasn't it?" she replied, fork stationary in mid air.

"And it wasn't just *any* diary was it, it was from *that* year. Emily must have been shown something pretty incriminating in it, because shortly after they left the lounge – *I heard a glass smash on the floor.*

CHAPTER THIRTY

BROOKLYN
NEW YORK

At first Kisle Denton was concerned when wife Jodi hadn't returned home after her nightshift at the hospital, but now he was beside himself with worry. Jodi often popped to the store to pick up some bits before coming in, but she'd finished hours ago. It was now noon and he'd not heard a thing. She was always very precise with her daily routines since working at Bellevue, but hadn't rung and her phone wasn't connecting either. He'd tried more than a dozen times. He'd also rung work, a few friends they both shared, and even been across the road to her sister Faithe's friend, Emily Stone, but there was no answer there either. *It was like she'd disappeared off the face of the earth.*

By two o'clock Kisle had made a decision. Their children Max and Ava were due out of school at 3.30 p.m., they would need picking up. Jodi tried to do that when she could, but often his mother would help out.

He'd get her to collect the kids and take them back to his parents' place.

Jodi's folks lived in Seattle, Washington so weren't around, and her sister Faithe was currently out there visiting them. Kisle knew he needed to report his wife as a missing person, and tell her family too, he just couldn't believe the whole situation was actually *real*. And now he was sweating and his stomach crunched at the possibilities his mind was delivering. He also knew the police would probably make various comments like it hadn't been twenty-four hours yet; she was an adult, a free agent, and start digging into their private life. The implication of some other guy being on the scene was standard fare for the N.Y.P.D. He'd heard it all before on the cop shows, and whilst a lot of stuff on TV wasn't accurate, he was pretty sure that *would* be. *He just never thought he'd hear it being spoken about Jodi.* He pulled his cell phone from his pocket and dialled 911.

BOILER ROOM - BELLEVUE HOSPITAL MANHATTAN

It was always hot working in a boiler room but Joe Suarez was used to it by now having worked in various hospital boiler rooms for the last twenty years. What he wasn't used to was finding human remains inside any of his incinerators.

The medical waste cart sat idly by whilst he stood open-mouthed in disbelief. His eyes initially stared hard, then blinked slowly and thoughtfully through his face guard as he inched his head forward to try and process what he was actually looking at...

Joe hadn't seen them at first. As normal he'd just been getting on with his work fetching the first cart in line against the wall, singing absentmindedly as he pushed it over to *'Incinerator MW1'*. That morning it was a song from a favourite retro radio station whilst driving into work. It had been playing hits from the 80s and now he couldn't get Queen's *'Another One Bites The Dust'* out of his head.

As he strolled back with the cart and hit the chorus, he chicken-jerked his head back and forth and tapped out the beat on its landscape handle. Although relaxed, he knew his job inside out and would still adhere strictly to the rules when actually operating any incinerator. Joe was always very studious and detailed with all his checks, and had made sure the controls on the one in front of him had returned to the automatic reset position from its last use. He'd just opened the door and reached round to his cart to begin loading the first pile of soiled operating materials, when something had made him turn back. Something that wasn't dark... something that caught the corner of his eye...

It was then that he saw the teeth.

Det. Frank Delaney put down the phone and was just about to call Terri, Det. T.J. Malone, when it rang again. He answered somewhat irritably.

"Officer Delaney!"

"Good morning Officer Delaney, I'm sorry if this is a bad time bu—"

"No, no, it's fine – sorry, just a bit full on here. How can I help?"

"It's Celia, Celia Dawson… *from the club?* You may remember I'm also Senior Management Co-ordinator at Bellevue?"

"Oh hi Celia, yes, yes of course, how's it going?" Delaney looked at his watch. He liked Celia and knew her from a mutual jazz club they both belonged to. Sometimes she took a little while to get to the point about anything though, and he *really* didn't have time to chat right now. However, she'd never called him at work before…

"We have a… an incident Frank. Well, potentially a very serious… errm… I'm not… it's a bit…" She was doing her 'thing' and Frank was already beginning to get impatient. He'd just had a Misper (missing person) phoned in and wanted Celia sorted pdq, albeit politely, and then off his line.

"Celia, could you get to the point?" She took a deep breath…

"I think we have a homicide situation at Bellevue… but I'm not entirely sure, that's to say, I'm not certain anyone's actually *dead but*—"

"What?" He was seriously pissed now… *"How do you mean you're not entirely sure anyone's dead?* You're running a *hospital* Celia – *it's your job to be sure."* He was now standing up, looking through and tapping on his office window to front reception, right arm in the air trying to attract a free officer. It was crucial to get feet on the ground ASAP for the Misper, and a hundred percent attention definitely wasn't going down the line to his jazz club associate at the other end.

"Our boiler room technician found some teeth."

"Excuse me?" said Delaney, exasperated now as he scanned a busy reception.

"They were in one of the medical waste incinerators. *They're human teeth Frank."* Delaney stopped arm waving and held a palm up to the rookie officer who now stood outside his window peering in quizzically. Suddenly he was looking at the phone in his hand with more than a hundred percent attention. He sat back down.

"Go ahead – *I'm listening…"*

"We have C.S.I. arriving any minute. A Bellevue staff member living in your district worked a nightshift last night, name's Jodi Denton. I believe she's very close with one of your young female officers, *Terri something?* Well Jodi's husband called in this afternoon. I thought you'd like to know Frank, given that Jodi didn't return home… *and our senior pathologist tells me we already gained a body of another young woman from your patch only last week."*

Carla knew she'd overstepped the mark this time. To fry a member of staff probably wasn't her finest hour even if it was, for her at least, unique. She was actually sweating as realisation dawned that dopey Jodi had a husband who would be wondering why she hadn't come home, and a senior management personnel they both shared who would have the work rota for that nightshift. *She had even started to bite her nails.*

It was two o'clock the following day when the hospital rang to ask her when she'd last seen Jodi Denton on her shift the previous evening. Carla knew the call would come and she'd sat in the lounge waiting with a black coffee, a packet of Marlboro Gold and a lighter... *sweating.*

"*...No, I hardly saw her to be honest, only at the beginning of the shift around ten and we were on different floors last night anyway. I thought I might see her in the coffee room at break time but she wasn't there, and after I'd completed my last two O.R. rooms it was time to leave...*"

To be fair it had surprised her how easily the lies had fallen out of her mouth and into the phone given the amount of salt water running down her back, but she'd managed it. It was done. She would now need to stick to that simple story no matter what – especially when the cops arrived.

Carla breathed a sigh of relief but it was short lived. She realised all she needed now was an eagle-eyed 'jobsworth' boiler technician, ash sifting and running to management. Irritated, she edgily lit up another cigarette and punched out a search of her favourite *Rachmaninoff* on YouTube. As she leant back against the cushions and drew in heavily, the music filled the room and the lighter twirled and flipped through her fingers, repeatedly dropping down on to the arm of the sofa. She screwed her eyes up against the smoke. She had come for Jenny and Emily, and there was still Emily to deal with. All these other people just kept distracting her, getting in the way of her objectives, interrupting her schedule. Well no more. It was time to up the ante. But before she could make a new plan, *the new plan was made for her.*

He'd been watching her for two years, waiting for months and following her for weeks. It had been easy, all of it. She thought she was in control but… no. He was enjoying the whole process even more than he ever thought he would. The substitution of the hairdresser in London, the faint glance in her direction on the plane, standing outside the hospital in Manhattan and at the bus stop opposite the café…

Breaking in to where she was staying had been satisfying too. Quite enjoyable seeing exactly how she was living, how far she had fallen from the fancy house and land in Cumbria, letting her know she wasn't the one in control anymore. He wasn't certain why she was out here, but he could fathom a guess. People like her always had a dirty job to do, a person to track, a killing to complete. What was it she called them? Despatches? Yes that was it, despatches. And she must have been desperate to get to whoever it was she wanted to despatch this time. Desperate enough to cut a deal with the 'Zandini' mob, that they had sprung her from a Rampton security van and set her up in New York. But then it was quite likely she didn't even know who her temporary benefactors actually were. If she did she'd probably be looking a lot more worried than he could see at that moment. They would want their money back – all of it. And she was going to have to get access to her mother's Will to do that. Unfortunately for her that was never going to happen – he would make sure of that.

He watched her now through the black wrought-iron gate in the wall of the little courtyard garden, at the back of the Cranberry Street house. This time he had waited for her to return from work. All the curtains and windows were closed tight, all except the lounge ones. They were only roughly drawn and left enough of a gap to see a glimpse of her on the sofa and hear the strains of Rachmaninoff… She looked tense. He noticed her hands were shaking as she held her cigarette. Maybe not quite the assassin she thought she was then? Well the message he'd left scrawled across her dressing table mirror a few nights ago could have contributed to her angst – he certainly hoped so. He wanted her to feel anxiety, to feel unsure, to feel someone was watching her, waiting for her, for his right time. His perfect time.

Two years. Two whole years he'd had to wait for this. Now everything was going to culminate in the perfect ending, the perfect revenge. If she only knew. He could easily take her now but it wouldn't be the same, he needed her to fall from her highest personal point, to fail... and fail publicly.

The old Cumbrian newspaper lay in his right hand, well read and rolled tight. He gripped it firmly and his eyes narrowed... like a hawk.

THIRTY-ONE

MANHATTAN
NEW YORK

With no events organiser at McCarthy Stone, Emily had no choice but to get out of her 'grief bed' and back to work. Jenny had left a big hole in the company and it had yet to be filled. Emily would have to oversee her deputy, probably promote her to the job after token internal and external interviews, *depending on who applied,* and arrange for, or interview for a replacement trainee.

She didn't want to be there, she didn't want to be doing anything at all frankly. Her guilt over Jenny's death was going nowhere, *would* go nowhere, would probably *never* leave her… she knew that. Maybe if she threw herself into work it would take the edge off it? Whilst that was doubtful it was hopefully not impossible… eventually.

There was also another U.K. event to set up for the autumn. She wasn't entirely sure about that either – too many memories. At least it was going to be a venue in Norwich, Norfolk rather than that fateful one in Carlisle, Cumbria. The one that had re-started the whole bloody nightmare, *but even so…*

"Mrs. Stone?" Megan Calder popped her head into the office holding a red file. Emily lifted an arm and ushered her over.

"The internal applicants, you've already collated them Megan?"

"Yes Mrs. Stone. I knew you'd need to proceed as quickly as… well… decently possible."

"And that's why you've been my P.A. for the last five years Megan – *thank* you." Her assistant smiled and placed the folder on her desk.

"Coffee?" she asked.

"Always Megan… always," her boss replied returning the smile. Megan left the room and soon returned with a filtered coffee.

"Oh I nearly forgot Mrs. Stone, you had a call yesterday from a new agent pitching for a debut author, name of Jaycee Jordan? I said you wouldn't be in till next week though as I thought tha—"

"That's strange, they normally email," interrupted Emily. "Name doesn't ring a bell either." She thought for a moment… "Okay, just send me through her contact details, I'll get back to her as and when." The younger woman nodded her head in acknowledgement and left for her own office, leaving Emily with the start of a new week, *and a new and very different life without Jenny.*

The twenty-four-hour split-shift watch outside the Stones' house in Narrows Avenue, and McCarthy Stone Publishing on Water and South Street, had been stood down. Casey, T.J. Randy and Geoff had been on twelve hour paired shifts, with some occasional help from colleague Eddie Chang over at the publishing house, for the past three weeks. There had been no suspicious activity either going in or coming out. Apart from one guy a week ago who looked as if he was hanging around a bit too long on the footway opposite, there was basically nothing to raise concern. He hadn't returned either, and although Geoff Nelms had had a quick word and made a brief note in his pocket book, just to be on the safe side (and to basically cover their backs), the guy seemed legit. He wasn't drunk or high on anything, not carrying a weapon, and they could hardly book him for standing innocently on the sidewalk. It was decided they *would* be continuing with random daily checks however.

The boss had also ordered enquiries into the murdered girl Jenny Flood's medical history. It had turned out a local M.D. had records of her attending Bellevue pretty regularly for a longstanding anorexic condition. Nothing else found had been of special interest medically, but it all had to be followed up, checked, logged and filed. Eddie Chang had taken that one on given his sister Leah worked there, and had now returned to duty following her completely unjust and unfounded negligence investigation. It had been a pretty short enquiry, basically because she was totally innocent of any wrongdoing and held a hundred percent clean sheet. Her reinstatement had given him a chance to catch up with her, and grab a sneaky coffee in the nurses' lounge…

"I don't know what's going on here Eddie but something doesn't feel right."

"How'd you mean Lea?" he asked, as always using his sibling name for her.

"I'm not sure. It's just that… well… the chat on the wards is the autopsy on the murdered British girl, the one on *your* patch – *Jenny Flood?* Well *that* wasn't normal – not by any stretch of the imagination. And now Jodi Denton's gone missing."

"Who's Jodi Denton, what's she got to do with the British girl? Has this been phoned in? Are you *sure* she's missing?" Eddie was beginning to think there was a lot more to find here than a dead girl's shrink reports.

"She's a senior anaesthesia tech, runs all the O.R. turnovers, general cleaning and drug orders etc. on my floors. She's definitely missing Eddie… her husband rang in this afternoon."

"Have you spoken to Casey about all this? All your uneasy feelings?"

"Not seen much of him lately, he's been on lates and nights."

"Oh yeah, course, over at Narrows in Brooklyn. I've done a couple of watches with him to help out. It's a favour to a couple of British cops over from the U.K.

They've got an escaped serial killer and reckon she's in New York targeting a woman at that address, maybe more. Not that *I* told you that of course Lea." Leah looked thoughtful for a moment…

"I was going to tell him when he changes shift. I think that's at the weekend. You know… *all* this started the day that cab driver Mr. Berkowitz died and I got hauled in to management for suspected negligence."

Eddie remembered Leah had then wrapped her hands around her mug and stared at him anxiously across the lounge table. *He was beginning to think she was on to something… and it wasn't good.*

Before the call had come in, Det. Frank Delaney had fully intended to get boots on the street for the missing Denton woman. That was of course until he'd spoken with Celia Dawson from Bellevue. The Manhattan C.S.I. would be dealing with the case now, and given the information she'd imparted earlier that day it wasn't looking good for her lost employee. He grimaced at the thought of teeth being found in an incinerator. Frank couldn't recall any investigation in his twenty-year career where that had happened.

Glancing at the clock to check his shift was well over, *and that eyes were elsewhere*, he pulled a bottle of whisky and a glass from his file drawer. He still hadn't got any leads on the Flood murder and it was bugging him. As his favourite spirit slid down he thought of the British girl, Mrs. Stone… and *that diary*. It was a U.K. crime those two women had been on the edges of two years ago, not a U.S. one. To be honest he wasn't even sure how to play this one out. He had a British body in the morgue from his ground at Bellevue, with suspicions but no proof this U.K. killer Charlotte Peterson *could* be responsible, but no clue as to her whereabouts. There were clearly deeper connections between those three women than he first thought. Terri (T.J.) had confirmed the U.K. officers Fran Taylor and Harry Longbridge had had no idea about that deeper connection either. Maybe it was time to interview Mrs. Stone again... and officially this time. Perhaps he'd also include the British cops on that. Frank picked up the bottle, swirled the last of the liquor in his glass, knocked it back and returned both to the drawer.

He pushed his chair away from the desk and got up. Grabbing his jacket off the wall, he walked to the door and turned out the office light. Hopefully he could hitch a ride home with Eddie Chang, better to be safe than sorry, and he needed to be seen to do the right thing anyway. Eddie could fill him in on his Bellevue visit on the ride home and pick him up in the morning. Two birds – one stone and all that.

He caught up with his young officer in the front hall and cadged a lift, Eddie was more than happy to drop him off as they only lived a short block from each other in Brooklyn so quite close by. As the two men walked up the stairs to the street, Frank Delaney thought about

Kisle Denton and his family. Like many times before, he felt abundantly grateful *he* had a wife to go home to. One who was neither dead *nor* missing…

Molly had found a local advanced Taekwondo 'Dojang' (class) to go to whilst she was in New York. She'd been out there for three weeks now and missing her double weekly sessions. As Gina had felt a lot better that day she'd persuaded Andrew she was well enough to go along and watch, and as he hadn't exactly relished the thought of being stuck indoors with Emily and Gareth, he'd gone along too.

It was literally only a few minutes away at Ovington Avenue. *It surely wouldn't be a problem? Even at night,* he'd reasoned to himself. *No, it would be fine. Well… as long as he was with them.* Until that night though Andrew had never actually *seen* his friend in action…

Molly didn't have her dobuk with her (the white uniform worn by Taekwondo students), but when she'd rung the contact number in the local paper to enquire about class space, she'd explained why and asked if they carried spares should she attend. The 'sabom' (instructor) told her she'd be very welcome and that they kept a few dobuks for people just trying out, so may well have something to fit.

Andrew and Gina sat on chairs at the side of the hall and watched as Molly joined the others on the padded blue mats. What followed left them speechless. They knew she'd had an interest over the last two years or so, well, since Charlotte's attack on her in the park that day really, but had no idea to what extent. It appeared that Molly Anne Fields had been a very busy girl on a Monday and Wednesday evening back home in Kirkdale since her ordeal. She kicked, leapt and spun with such speed, precision, height and uniformity that both Andrew and Gina had to pick their jaws off the floor – *several times.*

"How could we not have known about this Gee?" He was speaking *to* her but staring at Molly on the mats. His head moved up and down and side to side like it was on strings from above as he watched every move his friend made. "*You're* her best friend, didn't you have any idea how *fantastic* she was at this oriental thing?"

"It's Korean – and nope, never had a clue. Once I'd moved out of the pub and in with you, we weren't really so… well, in each other's pockets I guess."

"She's absolutely awesome…" said Andrew, mouth open, as he shook his head slowly in disbelief, eyes glued to *all* the students' abilities, but particularly Molly's.

"Yep, and I for one am *pret-ty* grateful she stuck with it," replied Gina, looking at her friend with awe. "I remember she gave up a few other similar things she started, self-defence, kick boxing and some other thing. Maybe she was just trying to find the right '*fit*' for her." She tapped his arm then. "And have you noticed something *else* Andy, something rather special?"

"Special? *Everything's bloody special,* what bit are you picking *out* here!?" He asked incredulously not able to tear his eyes away.

"She's wearing a black belt…" Gina whispered almost reverently, also still watching in complete fascination.

They turned to each other then… *and smiled slowly.*

THIRTY-TWO

68TH PRECINCT

BROOKLYN, NEW YORK

They had just finished breakfast in The Harbor B&B when D.I. Fran Taylor took the call from Det. Delaney. She put her phone on loudspeaker as it moved to interesting so Harry could hear…

"… so in view of what was revealed in Miss. Flood's diary, I thought you'd want to be in on the interview. I'm going to request Mrs. Stone comes in today or tomorrow." Fran raised her eyebrows at Harry questioningly and he nodded.

"Yes Det. Delaney," she replied. "We certainly would, and appreciate you calling us."

"No problem – I'll be in touch with the details. Bye for now."

"Thanks again, bye now." Fran flipped it off and pocketed her phone.

"Well, looks like the decision regarding Emily Stone's input into Peterson's sanity collapse has been sorted for us," said Harry, picking up the coffee pot for the third run.

"Yeah, but we're still no closer to finding her *are* we. *Damn that woman!*" She thumped the table and cutlery jumped up and jangled back down as several shocked patrons in the breakfast room turned round. Harry waved both hands at their newly acquired audience, gave a nervous laugh and an 'everything's fine folks' expression before turning back to a marginally embarrassed Fran. "Keep it *dowwwn...*" he said under his breath. "She was a hard villain to crack the first time around and that was when she was a novice, a clever one most of the time I'll grant you, but a novice nonetheless. She won't be easy to find a second time."

"We've been out here nearly *three* weeks Harry," Fran replied, quieter and more controlled. "A lot's happened in that time. Superintendant Hitchings is *not* going to be happy about us flunking out on this. We... *I* could well get pulled from this operation, not only that, I could end up with egg on my face if I don't find her and take her ba—"

"Op – *o p e r a t i o n...*" interrupted Harry, saying the word slowly, thoughtfully...

"What?" hissed Fran, palms up wearing a confused look and feeling irritated at having to keep her voice low.

"Operation, doctors, hospitals, medical stuff... she's a G.P. for Chrissake *why didn't we think of it before?!*"

"*What?* – think of *what* before?" Fran's voice started climbing again.

"Charlotte Peterson. And *please…* try and stay off the ceiling…" He gave a second awkward and placatory smile to the other diners whilst she responded with a loud – '*hmm!*' Fran then poured herself another coffee which probably wasn't the best idea, given she was already wired. Harry continued. "Maybe she's set herself up as a doctor over here, some kind of medic, shrink, something *anything* – maybe in a clinic… or a *hospital?*" Fran dropped the attitude and let a smile spread slowly across her really quite beautiful face as she lifted her cup. As possibilities of leads danced through her mind she literally glowed. Harry smiled and thought she had never looked more captivating…

Having felt better the previous evening at Molly's Taekwondo, Gina was finally persuaded by her friend to take a trip into Manhattan and visit Gabriella's Bridal in Wooster Street. She'd seen some dresses in a magazine the store was stocking, but with all that had been going on still hadn't done anything about it. Now Molly was pressing her to get this important part, the *most* important part of her and Andrew's wedding sorted.

Gina was still a bit apprehensive and Andrew certainly was, considering it wasn't really an outing he could join them on. However he was at least a little happier having seen Molly's performance at her class the night before.

"How long do you think you'll be?" he asked, buttering his rye toast, still a favourite and even more easily available in New York…

"Two or three hours I guess – no more," said Molly raising her eyes at Gina (who was finishing a second bowl of grapefruit), and receiving a positive response, got up from the table gave a quick spin and a leg strike, sending the toaster off the counter top. Being the nearest, Gina automatically flung her arms out and caught it before it landed on the floor, causing hysterics all round. It felt good. There hadn't been a lot of laughter lately. "Don't worry we'll be *fine*," Molly continued, standing back to back with Gina now in a *'Charlie's Angels'* pose.

"I wasn't too keen to start with, Andy," added Gina, reaching for her cup on the table and downing the last of her coffee, "but it *is* getting boring just sitting about feeling like we can't do anything or go anywhere. I'd really like to check out Gabriella's I've simply *got* to get my dress sorted. I'm already worried sick I've left it too late as it is. You *know* we've not got long to go, it's all got completely out of hand now." Andrew folded his arms and sat looking at the pair of them, now standing by the door clearly determined and ready to get their day's plan into action.

"Okay you've both convinced me," he said sighing. "Make sure you've got your phones and stay together though. And cab it there and back. I might have a mooch around locally whilst you're—"

"*Love* you my crime crazy little bookworm!" said Gina, blowing him a kiss as the two girls disappeared into the hall chatting all over each other. *Well at least she seems a lot happier and more upbeat* he thought, *thank God for that!*

Emily Stone knew exactly why she'd been asked to attend a meeting at her local police station. Which is why although she'd agreed to be there at two o'clock that afternoon (from a choice of two dates), she had absolutely no intention of turning up – *to either of them.* Coincidentally she *did* have a gynaecological appointment that day at two. That's why she chose the exact same day and time to attend at the station.

Jenny's diary had been a shock. She wasn't sure how it was going to affect her yet or just how seriously the law would take it, but right at this moment she just couldn't face any more Charlie stuff. Even now her childhood name for her crept in despite the very real chance she was out there to kill her.

So this was why she was now sitting in Bellevue's gynaecological department waiting to see her consultant. The reason was genuine enough. She'd been having some strange stabbing pains lately, much worse than during her monthly cycle, and what was really worrying her was that it was completely sporadic and not always connected to her period. Her M.D. had advised further investigation.

Emily picked up a magazine and flipped through it, not really reading anything, put it down and picked up another one. She followed this up with at least three more before starting all over again. Her mind couldn't concentrate on anything. Every dark-haired woman looked like Jenny and every auburn-haired 'floppy mop' reminded her of Charlie. Especially the latter, especially from their school days…

She glanced up at the clock. Ten past two. The woman opposite had been crying softly and trying not to for the last twenty minutes. She sat with a soggy tissue clutching some paperwork. Emily couldn't help noticing she was alone, but didn't like to say anything. *Poor cow,* she'd thought as she looked up at her under her fringe, *must've been given some really bad news.* She bit her lip then and remembered why she was there, or why she thought she *might* be there.

Her mobile buzzed. Taking it from her pocket she flipped the screen over and let it leave a message. No surprise as to who it would be, she was pretty sure of that. Her suspicions proved correct when she checked her voicemail, *Det. Delaney asking why she hadn't arrived.* Emily ended the message, turned the phone off and looked up at the clock again. Two-twenty. An apology that appointments were running late ran across the ticker board. She was wearing a watch but it was easier to just look up at the wall.

The tannoy system was getting a fair battering, calling doctors to various places and reminding visitors not to smoke, lifts were opening and closing their doors, and the nurses at the reception desk pinging and dinging the 'next patient please' announcement. Just not ping announcing her own bloody appointment…

A young nurse came in and sat down next to the girl who'd been crying, gave her a cup of something and relieved her of her paperwork. She just caught the name Lucy when the nurse addressed her, and Emily began to wonder what was going on in Lucy's life. Maybe she was married with kids, maybe not. Perhaps she was a teacher or a cake decorator or a pianist… Obviously not so great on the health side clearly, *but then she doubted very much anyone was trying to track her down and kill her…*

Finally it came. "Mrs. Stone to room five please – Mrs. Stone to—"

"Yes I'm here…" Emily announced back to the nurse on the microphone, one hand aloft as she picked up her bag and walked over to room five to knock on the door. She hesitated for a moment as she thought of Lucy. *Now she'd find out if she'd been right all along.*

When Carla had seen Emily in the gynae section on the way to her lunch break, she nearly did a double take. In fact she was so surprised she nearly dropped her sandwich and Pepsi, as well as having to swallow a loud gasp. Looked like she wasn't going to have to take on the role of fake literary agent *'Jaycee Jordan'* after all then. To have Emily served up on a plate at her place of work was more than good luck, it was surely a sign from her oh-so black and evil gods.

She wasn't prepared however. The Baclovate was back at Cranberry Street and there was very little left of it anyway due to her over-excitability and relative ignorance of the drug when despatching Jenny. And of course with no Jodi around to complete the re-stock… *Damn it!* There was only one thing for it. She had to leave work right now, feign sickness, get home, get the Baclovate, her wig, white coat and stethoscope, and get back to the hospital as quickly as she could. And pray the gynae list was a long one, *and behind schedule.* That there would be enough of the deadly pink liquid left to complete the second job was a major add to her prayers.

It took less than ten minutes to get back to her locker, get her bag, jacket, outdoor shoes and phone, and plead with the new temporary senior O.R. tech to let her go home with a migraine. She called for a cab on the way to the lift and it was there waiting as she walked out of the building. Her excitement was at frenzy level. The need to get her breathing under control had never been so strong. *This was it! This* was going to be the most fulfilling and creative kill of her career. That thought had almost pulled her up short as she walked across the entry hall. A tiny little woodpecker in the back of her head tried hard to remind her she'd trained to save life not take it…

And it was as Cumbrian serial killer Dr. Charlotte Peterson posing as O.R. technician Carla Preston walked quickly out of Bellevue Hospital and into her waiting New York cab… she saw her ex-husband's daughter Gina Rowlands being rolled in on a gurney. Her eyes popped wide as the cab pulled from the kerb and she looked over her shoulder in utter disbelief.

This day just got better and better.

THIRTY-THREE

MANHATTAN: NEW YORK
GABRIELLA'S BRIDAL: WOOSTER STREET

Molly and Gina had taken a cab straight to Gabriella's Bridal, and as promised, not hung about town window shopping or dropping into cake shops beforehand.

Gabriella's was a dream for any bride, and although they hadn't called ahead for an appointment, something they discovered they definitely *should* have done, the store director didn't turn them away. A bridal consultant led them to a private room and Gina was able to lose herself in another world for a while. She actually began to enjoy planning her wedding. In fact for an hour or two they both almost forgot the hideous situation surrounding them.

Lifting a couple off the rails and holding them up to her, even Molly felt like trying on a couple of dresses, and she wasn't even seriously involved with anyone. Her cheeks flushed at the thought of the guy she'd shared a mat and swapped numbers with at Taekwondo the other night, then pushed his handsome face out of her mind. This was *Gina's* time.

After trying three or four beautiful gowns, her friend came out of the luxury dressing room in an ivory cloud of lace, satin and tulle.

"What about this one?" Gina swept across the floor in a stunning Romona Keveža design. The others had been gorgeous, and given that Gina never wore a dress of any description, she'd looked amazing in all of them. This one though, this one had Molly thinking she might actually start blubbing. She stood up slowly from the velvet couch putting a hand out behind her on the arm for support…

"Oh Gee… that's… that's …"

"It is a bit isn't it…" she said with a slightly shocked smile. Looking down she still automatically smoothed her hands over her hip line. Gina walked carefully over to the larger mirror holding up the enormous skirt so as not to trip, and stopping suddenly just for a second, turned her head away from Molly to wince in pain. On reaching the mirror she looked over her shoulder at the delicate lace pointed back, and run of tiny buttons that led down to the waistband. *For the first time ever I actually feel pretty,* she thought, facing front again and gazing at all the satin that swam about her feet… *as she fought to ignore the second stomach contraction.*

Knowing her best friend like a sister because in a way she was, Molly spoke the words everyone was thinking.

"You look absolutely *beautiful*. Andy's going to literally melt when he sees you in that."

"Oh I hope not!" Gina laughed self-consciously, pink tingeing her cheeks. "But I know what you're saying. I absolutely love it," she breathed, hardly able to take her eyes off her reflection, the pain easing slightly now. She was literally glowing, and Molly could see what people meant when they described a pregnant woman as blooming, *because she definitely was…*

"That particular dress is part of our sale collection to make way for new inventory," encouraged the bridal consultant. "So if you'd like to, you can pay for it and take it today?" Gina looked at Molly excitedly, whilst gritting her teeth against the returning waves.

"Yes then?" she beamed, biting her bottom lip in anticipation, and trying to displace the pain…

"*Of course yes then!*" laughed Molly. "Are you *kidding?* You'll never beat it and we can take it *now!*" She went over to her friend and gave her a hug and a kiss on both cheeks. Gina sucked a small intake of breath. "Good things start now!" She winked. *Only Molly was wrong…*

When they heard the guttural groan and floor thump from the dressing room, *all hell broke loose!* Molly rushed over to the curtain dragging it open to see Gina collapsed and clutching her stomach in obvious agony.

"*Get an ambulance – she's pregnant!*" The shocked consultant stood open-mouthed dithering. "*Now dammit!!!*" shrieked Molly, bending over Gina as her friend groaned and gasped for breath.

"It... it *hurts...* " Gina whispered, breathing in small bursts through her mouth. "Baby... my ba— "

"It's okay... it's *okay* sweetheart, it'll be fine, *she'll* be *fine*, they're calling an ambulance now. Try to be calm – breathe *s l o w l y*." Checking her watch, Molly smoothed the now damp hair away from Gina's forehead as her friend grimaced for the umpteenth time and automatically cradled her stomach, wanting to bring her knees up, but the voluminous dress made it difficult.

"We need to get this off – *now!*" Molly directed to the consultant. It wasn't easy, but between the two of them they managed to prop her up and get the dress unbuttoned and off.

The sirens sounded in the distance as they sat Gina down on the dressing room chair so they could re-clothe her in her stretch jeans and baggy top. By the time her ankle boots were back on, sirens were blasting through the store and consultants running everywhere opening doors and directing paramedics to the emergency.

Once Molly was sure Gina was being looked after she cast a quick eye over the bottom half of the dress before the consultant took it away. She caught her arm...

"Can you put that aside please? I'll sort it for you later." The young girl nodded as Molly quickly gave her their details before following the medics who were now helping Gina outside to the waiting ambulance.

The flashing rear blue lights, whilst different from home, set off a hazy memory locked somewhere at the back of her mind. She shook it away and climbed into the back of the vehicle. As the doors closed and the double thump sounded to let the driver know it was okay to go, she sat on the bench opposite the trolley holding her best friend and watched the paramedic monitor her responses. *At least she's conscious* she thought… *at least she's alive.*

Harry and Fran were waiting at 68th Precinct for Emily Stone to turn up and Frank Delaney was getting markedly impatient. It was already half-past two and he didn't have time to waste with a missing person to deal with. Despite the fact that Manhattan C.S.I. had attended at Bellevue and taken charge of the teeth found in the incinerator for forensic DNA analysis, he still had a desperate husband waiting on news of his missing wife. One who coincidentally, *or not,* lived opposite Emily Stone. All three were in Frank's office, all three becoming decidedly twitchy.

"I take it you've tried to ring her?" Fran asked tapping her foot.

"Several times," replied a harassed Delaney. "Plus I've left messages. As you both know she's not actually under arrest for anything so it's purely a request to help with enquires at this stage, but if I don't hear anything from her today I *will* be paying her a visit later."

"Just to deviate slightly," said Harry. "Charlotte Peterson, our reason for being out here…"

"Have you made any headway with that?" asked Frank.

"It occurred to me earlier that considering our escapee was a doctor for seventeen years, if she's over here, and I'm convinced she is, then she'll presumably need money, but more than that… *drugs.* She'll be after chloroform for a start it's part of her trademark."

"And the other part?" asked Frank.

"Ice…" Frank's eyebrows flew up. "It's a long story," said Harry checking his watch and beginning to stand. "Look, it doesn't appear Mrs. Stone is going to turn up." He turned to Fran. "I think we should start checking out a few hospitals and medical centres. See if she's applied to any for work."

"*Whoa…* wait a minute. She won't be able to work as an M.D. out *here.*" Harry and Fran looked at each other. "However long she's been working as a medic in the U.K., British training won't count for anything in the U.S. All our medical staff has to go through their training in *this* country." Harry looked crestfallen. *Fran looked worse.*

"Great… that's just *great!*" she said getting up and beginning to pace Frank's office. Harry sat back down and steepled his hands…

"Doesn't mean she can't *clean* in a hospital though *does it?*"

Carla leapt out of the cab, paid the fare and ran up the steps of the Cranberry Street house. She didn't want the driver for the return trip, better not to spend too much time with one person. She would ring for another when she'd got what she came for.

Unlocking the door Carla hesitated for a second. Ever since the break-in, coming 'home' hadn't been so easy. She stood still and listened before entering the hallway. *Silence.* With the door closed behind her she tore up the stairs to her bedroom, crossed the floor to the dresser in three quick strides and yanked at the top drawer. Pushing her underwear aside she found the chloroform immediately, pulled it out and put it in her pocket. Then she looked for it – *or what was left of it. The pink one,* the one she reserved for the special despatches. She knew it was in there, she knew it *had* to *be* there. She rummaged for it… top bottom left side right side – nothing. She yanked the draw from the cabinet and threw everything onto the floor, where *was* it? *Where the fuck was it?*

Her head was all over the place now, heart thumping in her ears. She looked at the bedside clock, already two-fifty. If she didn't find it soon the golden hour would be over. *Think for God's sake THINK!* Carla tried to slow her breathing but the hoarse oxygen gulps kept coming one after the other. Wheeling round she swiped everything off the dressing table with a guttural scream as the items flew across the room peppering the walls and crashing to the floor.

Panting hard, she stopped suddenly bent at the waist leaning on her thighs forcing herself to exhale slowly. Then her hands flew to her face as she made herself think clearly. Slowly they fell away, she stood up, opened her eyes – and her line of sight hit. *The second one, it must be the second drawer down.*

Carla grasped both handles and opened it. Slowly this time almost scared she was wrong. But there it was… glowing. Gleaming through fine lace of a cream camisole was that beautiful neon pink. It was her lack of time that hadn't allowed her to remember. It *had* been in the top drawer, but the night she'd used it on Jenny she'd replaced it in the one below.

She snatched up the bottle, pocketed it and slammed the drawer shut. The white doctor's coat, stethoscope, meds chart and blonde wig were dragged from the next one down, the mess on the floor left where it was as she stormed from the room heading for the stairs. She ran down so fast she nearly fell and had to grab the banister to save herself.

At the bottom the wig was pulled on, straightened and checked in the hall mirror, as she turned this way and that to be sure it looked natural. The white coat was next, then she wrenched the mobile from her pocket to ring for the second cab in an hour praying for two things – one it would arrive quickly and two… *two that the gynaecological department were running late as usual.*

When Carla walked back into Bellevue calm as you like, nobody but nobody looked at her twice. She headed for the elevators and pressed the button for gynaecological outpatients. The lift sounded its arrival and took her to the second floor. As she walked out of it, confidently rounding the corner to the gynae area and holding her breath in anticipation… *Carla saw the empty chair.* She was too late. Her eye began to twitch and she tasted blood in her mouth from the tooth now buried in her lip. The disappointment was crushing, unbearable. She had come *so close, so close…*

Turning from her scene of abject failure, eyes like grit and hatred scarring even deeper, she clasped the chart to her chest till her knuckles were white.

And then Emily Stone came waltzing out of a consulting room.

THIRTY-FOUR

BELLEVUE HOSPITAL
MANHATTAN: NEW YORK

Molly was walking alongside the gurney holding Gina's hand as the paramedics wheeled her into the E.R. She was still cramping and finding it difficult to talk when a nurse came to see her in a side bay, so Molly explained what had happened in the bridal shop, and about the previous episodes she'd had.

"It seems to be quite random, and when it's not happening she's completely normal, it's crazy."

"Does it start after any particular foods do you know? Has she got any cravings yet?"

"I don't think so, although... well she's started eating a lot of grapefruit lately and I don't remember her *ever* eating it before. She's more of a biscuit and cake person." The nurse smiled...

"Like me then!" she said rolling her eyes and patting her wide waistline. "It's quite possible with the grapefruit being acidic, eating a lot of it and the womb expanding, the rise in pregnancy hormones… all this can cause stomach cramps, it's quite normal in early pregnancy. Better that you did call an ambulance though, especially as she's in so much discomfort."

"Well she collapsed in the bridal changing room *we didn't have much choice!*" replied Molly a little sharper than she'd intended.

"Quite. Well, the doctor will come and see her soon to reassure you both." Molly patted Gina's hand as she groaned and clutched her stomach again.

"Has she had any stress, or any blood loss at all?" asked the nurse a little more concerned now. Molly hesitated. There wasn't an easy answer to the first question, certainly not with any detail. She played it down…

"Well, yes… a *bit*. Stress that is, no blood loss though. She's not long found out who her real parents are *[a slight exaggeration but…]* and planning a wedding on top of discovering she's pregnant, although they are… her and Andy, her fiancé, they're really happy about the b…" Molly tailed off just as the curtain swished open and a dark-haired doctor with a neat razor-sharp beard and moustache stepped inside. He had heard much of the conversation before entering the cubicle.

"And who do we have here Nurse Cafferty?"

"Afternoon Doctor Garcia," said Cafferty, eyes glued to his and glad it was Garcia who'd attended. *Spanish guys with beards always did it for her…* "This is Gina Rowlands, twenty-two, blue light admittance not long ago, three months pregnant, presenting with severe abdominal cramping. Currently has a thing for grapefruit and experiencing some short- and long-term stress."

"Ah. That might explain things then," he said, smiling at her patient. "Mind if I examine you Miss. Rowlands? Or may I call you Gina?" Gina was breathing a little more easily now the pain had passed again and was able to speak.

"Yes… that's fine… on both counts," she said a little breathlessly. Gina lifted her top to expose her stomach and Dr. Garcia felt gently all around the area, which produced instant squeals of pain.

"Well it's obviously tender. I'll give you something to line your stomach and I recommend no acidic or fried foods, no hot flavoured and spicy foods and definitely *no* stress. Bland and boring is the order of the day for the foreseeable I'm afraid. I think Nurse Cafferty had it spot on. Nothing to worry about but if it doesn't settle down you *must* contact your primary care doctor or come back in, okay? I take it there has been no blood loss?"

"Yes – I will, thank you Doctor, and no, no blood loss," replied Gina, relieved but not totally reassured. "Would it be possible to… umm… have a scan? It would make me feel less anxious to actually *see* my baby's okay. *Keep my stress down…?*" Dr. Garcia smiled.

"I'll see what I can do. I take it you have insurance?"

"Yes that's no problem."

"Good. Well I'll get your prescription sorted and Nurse Cafferty will see if we can squeeze you in."

"Thank you. That's great isn't it Molly?" she said turning to her excitedly. However, Molly, who had also been glad it was Garcia doing the rounds, wasn't entirely in earshot…

An hour later, Gina had an uncomfortably full bladder and was lying on a bed with jelly smeared all over her stomach. An ultrasound transducer was moving slowly across her lower abdomen.

The sonographer watched the monitor very closely as Molly held Gina's hand trying to look confident and not let her eyes leak, and Gina was anxious and tearful but feeling better since the pain had stopped. Both had benefitted somewhat from Dr. Garcia's attention, and neither had rung Andrew yet…

"There you go," said Hayley smiling, "there's your baby, see?" She pointed to a black and white hazy splodge on the screen, turning it slightly so Gina could see more easily. "And that's his or her heartbeat – right… *there.*"

"*Her* heartbeat," said Molly, grinning stupidly at Gina and squeezing her hand. Gina lifted herself up and turned her head to see the screen.

"Are… are you… sh… sure? That everything, that she's okay?"

"Well I can't tell you it's a girl at only three months gestation, but… yes, everything looks completely normal."

"My friend's convinced it's a girl," said Gina looking at Molly, relief spread all over her face.

"How are you feeling now?" asked Hayley. "Have you been able to take the medicine the E.R. doctor gave you for the cramping?"

"Yes thank you, although it's probably been diluted somewhat with all the water I had to drink." This caused a ripple of much-needed laughter.

"Who did you see?" asked Hayley, reaching for tissues and handing them to Gina.

"A Doctor Garcia – he was really nice," Gina replied, wiping the gel from her stomach as Molly enjoyed recalling blue eyes and a rich Latino voice.

"Mmm… *yes he definitely is, isn't he?*" Hayley agreed replacing the transducer back into its holder. "And *I'm* going to ensure he knows how lucky he is *that I'm single!*" A louder burst of laughter filled the room this time as Gina winced and held her stomach at the same time.

When Harry Longbridge and Fran Taylor were presented with a printout of Brooklyn and Manhattan hospitals alone, Harry's *'doctor turned hospital cleaner'* idea with regard to Charlotte presented itself as several hours of exhausting phone calls. When T.J. Malone brought in a wider list of medical centres, specialists and M.D. offices, they both looked visibly pale.

"I'll get a couple of our guys on it with you," offered Delaney, "it'll help break the back of it anyway."

"Well at least we're not checking the entire country," said Fran picking up the Brooklyn list and pulling the phone towards her, "something to be grateful for I suppose." Harry picked up the Manhattan sheets.

"We know that Miss. Rowlands saw a woman she felt had that special *'look'* of Charlotte Peterson, standing outside a Manhattan coffee shop called Honey's. "

"Honey's? That's cake *heaven!*" said T.J., still in the room. "I often meet friends there on a day off. Best lemon drizzle anywhere in New York, Honey gets her friend Julie to batch bake it for her."

"And *now…* I'm hungry…" groaned Harry.

"No worries," said Frank smiling broadly at Malone, "we'll send T.J. for take out!"

Having duly sorted a late lunch for his 'guests', Delaney borrowed another office and put in a call to Kisle Denton to find Manhattan C.S.I. were at his home questioning him over the last time he'd seen or spoken to his wife. Frank had a short conversation with the Chief Investigating Officer, and established that what Celia Dawson had told him about the teeth in the Bellevue incinerator was indeed true. Not that he believed she would lie to him, but Celia *did* have a bit of an elaborate imagination at times, and a tendency to flap when under pressure. He often wondered how she managed the two traits in her position as Senior Hospital Manager, although understood she was generally well thought of.

Kisle Denton had not been informed of the incinerator incident yet, but Frank was told hair samples had been collected and bagged for DNA purposes from one of Jodi's brushes in order for forensics to run tests alongside the burned teeth. It occurred to him that if there *was* a match, it might be worth pushing Bellevue to the top of the phone list for U.K. detectives Longbridge and Taylor.

He could hear Mr. Denton's voice intermittently in the background. One minute he was shouting questions at the officers as to why there was no news of his wife, and why weren't they out there searching for her, the next he could hear heavy wracking sobs as the man clearly couldn't cope with what was almost certainly becoming a serious missing persons investigation. One his wife was at the centre of. Not for the first time did Frank Delaney find himself thanking his god he'd never had a family member suffer as a victim of crime.

After ending the call, he reflected on the drive home the night before and the one into work that morning with his officer Eddie Chang. He'd hitched the rides after a drink at the end of his shift and the information from Eddie's sister Leah had proved more than interesting. The British girl's autopsy, Nurse Leah's ordeal regarding a dead patient she'd been initially suspended for, and the fact she'd worked with Jodi Denton, all proved very thought-provoking. Frank never jumped to conclusions, but Bellevue had certainly had more than its fair share of strange events recently. *Yes – it definitely needed to be first on the check list...*

Carla had watched Emily walk out of the consulting room and straight into the ladies' room. It was three-fifteen, and her lip was throbbing from biting it so hard when she'd thought Emily had already left.

Holding her clipboard and papers as if she were reading, Carla hung around outside and waited. Around her a world of doctors, patients, visitors, clerical staff and cleaners got on with their day. Interacting with each other, they worked, chatted mopped up tears and handled phone calls and small children whilst Carla just heard a general buzz. Her eyes momentarily flicked up from the clipboard, she pretended to make a call one moment and read a text in another. She thought her head would explode with the tension of what she had planned. *And then she had an idea.*

Carla walked straight into the ladies' room, concentrated hard on summoning up a believable Irish accent, and pretended to be talking to someone on her phone as Emily stood at the mirror applying lipstick...

"...yes of *carrse* noorse, I'll surely be down as soon as I've finished up here. A Miss. Roorwlands in E.R. you say? Can you be giving me the cubicle number there?"

The 'conversation' had the desired effect. Emily's head switched sharply left towards Carla as soon as she heard Gina's surname. Carla was just finishing up as she tentatively approached.

"Excuse me um… I know this sounds a bit… er… strange, but did they mention the Christian name at all? It's probably a long shot but… it's just that…" Carla looked directly at Emily. There was not a hint of recognition, not one in the other woman's eyes. The accent and disguise was holding true, it was then she knew for sure she had the upper hand, *she was safe.*

"Well she did now actually, and who would you be thinking it might be?"

"It could be my daughter Gina, she's pregnant you see and I've just got to know for sure it's *not* her, or if it *is* her. Oh God… what if it *is* her and she's hurt? The wedding… the baby… I just—"

"Nyow, don't you be worryin' yeself… Missus…?"

"Stone – Emily, can you take me to her, just in case, just so I can be sure it's not her?"

"Of *carrse* Missus Stoorn, I'm shur she'll be just grand, it'll ahhl be foin." Carla forced a wide smile and taking Emily's elbow guided her out of the ladies' rest room, staggered at her *'frenemy'* not recognising her, and even more surprised at her own not-so-terrible melodic Irish accent. *Another golden nugget of information learned in that moment – Miles' and Emily's brat Gina wasn't only pregnant with their grandchild, she was also planning a wedding. Presumably to that journalist she failed to finish off when she cut his brakes in Kirkdale – somebody Gale? Well maybe we can bring their 'wedding' forward a little…*

Emily couldn't possibly have known her obvious relief she'd either soon be with *Gina,* or find it was someone else entirely, would be as short lived as Carla's forced smile. This had already dissipated as they walked down the corridor to the waiting elevator...

THIRTY-FIVE

BELLEVUE HOSPITAL
MANHATTAN: NEW YORK

When the man shouted Charlotte's name loudly in the corridor just once, neither of them saw him. Carla's reaction however gave a stunned Emily the shock of her life. Unaware of any danger, a loaded penny dropped scarily into place.

Carla's head had swung round the instant she'd heard the man shouting her real name. Emily had at first looked quizzically at her. It had taken a few seconds but then… *wham!* Realisation flew across her face as the scream she tried to release but couldn't get out, jammed awkwardly in her throat. Her eyes took in the blonde hair, blue lenses (behind the glasses), *and that out of place 'off' Irish accent.* The man who yelled *"Charlotte!"* was nowhere to be seen and the knifepoint now in Emily's side kept that scream from escaping.

Having abandoned the clipboard face down on a spare trolley, Carla now had her right arm around

Emily pulling her in close, the small knife she kept in her pocket in her left hand. She steered her swiftly towards the elevator bank and made it abundantly clear her captive should do exactly as she was told.

"One silly move and you'll be wearing your left kidney as an accessory," she said through a weak smile over gritted teeth. Emily felt sick. There were people all around but she was too scared to scream. She tried to use her eyes but the sheer industrious energy of the hospital meant everyone was focused on their own day, their own responsibilities. If they ended up in a lift with no one else, Emily felt sure she would also end up dead. Maybe there was nothing else to do but try and plead with her, remind her of their early childhood friendship, although that would lead to the university years when she'd taken Miles from her, got pregnant with Gina and… well, the rest was history. It was why she now had a knife in her side. *It was why it wouldn't help.*

The elevator arrived with a ping and a flash of orange. Carla walked her quickly inside, pushed 'B' for basement and the doors closed before anyone else could slip through. The absence of conversation was deafening as the soft whir of the elevator's mechanical workings took them downwards, their breathing the only human sound. With a maximum of three floors to travel, the journey didn't take long and the jolt back of the floor came too fast for Emily to act. No time to think of an escape, no time to think of how to talk

Charlie down. *Still she thought of her with that same adolescent nickname.*

When the doors opened all was quiet at first. A slight chemical smell met them as they walked out of the lift and Carla noticed Emily's nose wrinkle.

"Formaldehyde and formalin," she said knowingly. *"Keep walking."* A couple of male pathologists deep in conversation barely acknowledged the two women as they strode towards them heading for the elevators. Carla knew exactly where she was going but prayed Kay Winford wouldn't be on duty *just* yet. Emily's despatch had not been planned for that specific day. Seeing her in the gynae reception had been a complete fluke and she had yet to check out Kay's shift patterns.

As they rounded a corner the chemical smell grew stronger and Emily's fear grew faster. She was now breathing rapidly eyes darting everywhere looking for someone or somewhere to escape to. It was just as a white coat walked across the end of the corridor and she'd decided to risk being stabbed, that Emily pushed her sideways through a set of swing doors into a room with a wall of silver squares in front of them. Nobody was there. Well... nobody *living* was there. Carla's luck was with her, the pathologists near the elevator had knocked off for a break and Kay appeared not to be on, *but she had to be quick.*

Before Emily realised what was happening, Carla had switched the knife for the pre-loaded Baclovate and rammed it home deep, just under her ribs. Emily shrieked in pain and leapt away, pressing a hand against her side in shock. Eyes shot alarm at her attacker as terror and adrenaline spread quickly. Only it wasn't merely terror and adrenaline that was seeping insidiously into her bloodstream and around her body.

She was surprised at first that Carla had just let her go. That was until her feet had begun to feel numb. Then her calves. *By the time it had reached her thighs she was terrified!*

"Wha… what's happening… what've you done to me? What's…" She didn't get any further and Carla moved quickly to catch her as she fell to the floor.

"I know you can hear me so listen up," Carla purred sadistically as she leant over her. "Unfortunately I only had half a dose left after dealing with Jenny," *Emily's eyes widened in horror…* "This means I'm not entirely sure how long it will take. By now though I expect your limbs are feeling pretty stiff and your head is extremely fuzzy. You may even be feeling warm, who knows, but that won't last long once you're… *in there.*" She extended an arm to the silver wall. Emily could do nothing. Move nothing. Say nothing. Only her eyes remained open – and horrified.

"Oh, I nearly forgot to say, Baclovate won't actually *kill* you, at least I don't think so, not that amount anyway." She sniggered quietly and leant closer to her ear… "*Your autopsy will see to that.*"

The next few minutes Carla sped up ten-fold. She pulled out an un-named bottom draw and dragged a now stripped, muscle-stiff Emily onto the tray. This required massive effort and she'd had to stop several times. Removing her rings had proved particularly difficult especially her wedding ring, but it was a damned sight easier than it had been getting Jodi in and out of that bloody laundry cart.

Once she was on the tray head first, she pushed the drawer front away from her and Emily slid silently into a chilled void. The thump shut seemed to startle Carla as she stood looking at it for a few seconds, almost as if shocked by her actions. But no, she was thinking. A quick check of the mortuary door first, then glancing at the other drawers she began checking some of the name tickets. Most wouldn't do at all (including of course Jenny Flood's), but she finally found a female one that was close enough… *'Melissa Jackson – 44 – auburn hair – narcotics suicide – 6.45 p.m. – 03/03/20.'* It took two minutes to remove the ticket from the drawer front, and on opening it, the one tied to Melissa Jackson's big toe. She transferred both along with the evidence sheet which she tucked carefully around her, then after stuffing Emily's clothes, shoes, jewellery and bag into a bin liner, walked straight out of the morgue with it and didn't look back.

Inside her 'silver coffin', cold and numb in the dark, Emily's eyelids became heavier and heavier… *until so weak and useless they closed completely.*

Andrew looked at his watch. He had expected Gina and Molly back at least an hour before and was beginning to feel slightly anxious. Had they been at home in Kirkdale he wouldn't have given it a second thought. Here though was something else entirely. He'd been into town to check out some bookshops, had a general wander and grabbed a coffee, but was now back and still found the house empty.

He was just going to ring Gina when the landline chimed noisily. Andrew looked around and saw it on the arm of Gareth's chair.

"Hello?"

"Hi – this is Detective Delaney from the 68th. Is that Mr. Stone?"

"No it's Andrew, Andrew Gale. My fiancée and I are staying with the Stones."

"Ah yes I remember. I wonder if you could help me Mr. Gale... Is Mrs. Stone there?"

"No, no she's not. In fact nobody's here. I was just starting to get a bit concerned about Gina, my fiancée – that's Mrs. Stone's daughter, and our friend Molly. They went into Manhattan this morning and it's now five o'clock. They should've been back ages ago."

"Have you tried phoning either of them?"

"Yes their phones were either switched off or had no—" At that moment Andrew's mobile rang. "Hold on Detective, I think that's them now."

"Andy it's me, Molly. We're on our way back, had a bit of a scare but—"

"What do you *mean* you had a bit of a scare? Are you okay, is Gee—"

"She's *fine* Andy just some stomach cramps. We needed to get her checked out at the hospital but—"

"Hospital??? Hospital???" Andrew's voice was now raised significantly and picked up by Frank Delaney on the other phone…

"Are your friends okay Mr. Gale, which hospital are they at right now?"

"Molls, where are you? I've got the police on the other line looking for *Emily*, which hospital are you at?"

"Bellevue in First Avenue, it's a good one – she's been thoroughly—"

"It's Bellevue, Detective. Is that particularly relevant?"

"I don't know at the moment," replied Frank, "please get Mrs. Stone to ring me as soon as she makes contact or arrives home could you? Glad you've caught up with your friends."

"Right – okay will do." Andrew said goodbye, hung up and returned to Molly.

"Molls, can I speak to Gina, I take it she's right there?"

"In the loo, she had to drink loads for a scan, now she's getting rid of it all."

"Okay well… *shit!* You mean I've missed her first *scan?*" He sighed as he realised things were not going to plan at all and was now running a frustrated hand through his hair whilst pacing the lounge. He wasn't used to being so stressed, he was known for calm thinking, solving problems and looking out for people.

He didn't like this feeling at all. *More than ever since they'd arrived he wanted to get them all safely on a plane and fly straight back to the U.K.*

Molly had been queuing for at least fifteen minutes after her call to Andrew. They hadn't eaten since breakfast and were both pretty hungry, so she was picking up snacks from a nearby cafeteria whilst Gina was in the washroom.

As she walked back across the wide hall juggling food and drinks, she was scanning the seating where they'd agreed to meet, but Gina was nowhere to be seen. Sitting down she plonked the snacks on a table, ripped open a sandwich pack and began to eat whilst keeping an eye on the door. After about ten minutes and checking her watch three times, Molly left the food and headed over to the ladies' room. Her tummy did a triple flip as she pushed the door open and saw three women using the basins mirror and driers. Gina wasn't one of them. There were six cubicles available and only two were occupied.

"*Gee?* Are you *okay?*" Molly spoke hesitantly into the air… The other women looked at her and each other, one older lady explained her sister was in one of the cubicles and asked who she was looking for. Another younger woman then exited the only other one. Molly felt sick, very… *very* sick…

"*Have you seen a young woman – twenties?*" she asked urgently of the now four women standing in front of her. "She's about *so* height [indicating with her hand] long auburn hair and she's—" The older lady's sister then exited the only remaining cubicle and spoke to her.

"I saw someone like that leave as I walked in," she said looking concerned, "seemed in an awful hurry, pushed past me on the way out." Molly stood with her back to the mirror holding onto the basin surround. None of it made any sense. Gina would never have run out on her like that.

"I *have* to find her," Molly whispered under breath. "She's pregnant, she's not been well… things aren't—" With that she pushed herself off the surround and with confused eyes behind her and heart pounding, walked quickly from the ladies' room searching Gina's I.D. on her mobile.

Heading towards a nursing station to get help, her phone rang before she could bring up the number. Checking the screen she saw Gina's photo come up. *Thank God!*

"Gee where the *hell* are you I've been worried *si*—" Molly heard a muffled sob followed by a shaky voice…

"Mm… *Molls?* She's… she's *got* me. Charl—" There was the sound of footsteps on a rough concrete floor, a heavy rustle followed by a shriek. Then another voice came on the line.

"Well if it isn't the little psychic *sorceress*. Didn't see any of *this* coming *did you?*" Molly froze in the middle of the hallway trying to process the ear poison. People passed by in all directions. They became a blur of blues, whites and mauves, a whole sea of underwater colours as she blinked several times, massaged her temple whilst her brain tried to acknowledge the words she was hearing and make her eyes focus normally. She dropped onto the nearest chair and tried to control the anxiety now mixed with rage that fixed itself deep into her core.

"Where – are – you?" Somehow her voice held level and true without a hint of tremor. Surprisingly there was tinkling laughter at the other end. Then Carla breathed heavily into the phone…

"Now that would be telling wouldn't it *dear*… as they say, it's for me to know and you to find out."

"If you lay *one* fing—"

"I don't think you're *exactly* in a position to be making any demands do *you? Now **shut** it and listen…*"

THIRTY-SIX

BELLEVUE HOSPITAL
MANHATTAN: NEW YORK

Kay Winford pushed the doors open to her pathology lab and threw a cheese sandwich and a three pack of chocolate chip cookies on her autopsy table before hanging her coat up. She then swore as she realised she'd forgotten her black coffee…

It was five-thirty and lunch was getting later and later. It had got to the point where three meals a day were beginning to merge, and the chance of eating anything healthy went out the window decades ago. Such was the life of anyone remotely connected to a medical profession, especially in a large hospital. Thank God her partner Bex was a great cook, it was the only place she'd see anything remotely close to a salad or containing vegetables.

She checked the next in line whilst she fed her *'gut gremlins'* as she called them, and then her eyes fell on Jenny Flood's drawer. Suddenly the gremlins weren't demanding anything at all. Never in the history of her career had she been so affected by an autopsy than the shrivelled black organs she'd found inside that woman. Kay swallowed awkwardly at the memory of it and removed her lunch to a spare cupboard that had become a bit of a larder on the quiet. She knew she may or may not catch up with it later.

There were two autopsies that needed to be done within the next twenty-four-hour period. A Dean Coleman (bungled burglary incident), fifty-three with a bullet wound to the chest, and a Melissa Jackson, forty-four, a suspected narcotics suicide but an autopsy was required to discover if that was actually the case. Both were within the optimum time, but she'd been receiving pressure from the police on the bullet wound autopsy that had come in that morning. 'Melissa' had been waiting from the previous night according to the log and drawer tag, and Kay felt a pull towards attending to her first. She couldn't quite fathom the reason, maybe because of young Jenny Flood. That girl's death had seriously rattled her, God knows why, although it was almost as though she'd known her when she hadn't any *real* connection at all. Kay had worked with Harry Longbridge on the Peterson case in the U.K., and had only met Jenny once when she'd had to identify her brother's body. Jason had been the only male out of Charlotte Peterson's five victims.

Her hand rested on 'Melissa's' drawer. Inside, Emily lay numb from head to foot. Her lungs were at below visible function and her limbs cataleptic. She was unable to see, move or speak. But she could hear *everything*...

At that moment Kay's mobile buzzed. She fished it out of her pocket and retrieved the text. It was the third requesting forensic information on Dean the shot burglar. She sighed and walked to the other end of the silver-walled fridge and pulled on the relevant drawer. *Sorry Melissa love, you'll have to wait...*

68TH PRECINCT
BROOKLYN

Harry and Fran had spent the last three and a half hours phoning hospitals, medical centres and M.D.'s offices in Brooklyn and Manhattan, asking if they'd employed any female British doctors in the last three months. So far they hadn't turned up anything, and reams of paper cascaded over the floor. When Frank came back after speaking to the Chief Investigating Officer at Kisle Denton's place, suggesting that based on *that* conversation plus Eddie Chang's chat with sister Leah regarding the dead cabbie, the fact she worked with missing technician Jodi Denton, *and* heard details of the British girl's autopsy (admittedly rumours), they all looked at each other and chorused – *"Bellevue!"*

"I think it would be worth calling them next before trawling through the rest," said Frank Delaney looking hopeful. Fran's expression clearly showed excitement at finally getting somewhere.

"Hell so do I!" she gushed, reaching for the phone. Harry was quiet for a moment and then asked Frank a question.

"Did you get hold of Mrs. Stone yet?"

"No I left two texts and then rang her at home. Spoke to that young lad, *Gale?* The future son-in-law? Said there was nobody at home. He's going to pass on the message when she gets back." Harry started to feel distinctly uneasy. He wasn't sure why, he had no insight into any of their movements so didn't know what they were all doing on a day-to-day basis, but somehow he felt responsible for this 'family'.

"Where's Gina and Mol – err... Miss. Rowlands and Miss. Fields? Did he say?"

"They went into Manhattan this morning. Actually he *was* a bit concerned they hadn't turned up yet, but then got a call on his mobile whilst I was on the other line saying they were on their way back." Fran had had her hand on the phone to ring Bellevue ever since Frank's recent tip-offs, and was looking perplexed at Harry. *Why was he worrying about two girls on a shopping trip, when they should be concentrating on that hospital?*

"Hmm... think I'll give Mr. Gale a call," he said. "Fran, ring Bellevue, find out if they've had any enquiries from or actually employed any British G.P.s recently." Fran arched her eyebrows and opened her mouth in sheer disbelief that yet *again*, he was taking the lead and giving her instructions, especially when she'd been waiting for his focus on it. Harry however had already left the room to speak to Andrew on his own and already had the connection by the time the door closed behind him...

"Andrew – it's Harry. Detective Delaney just told me Gina and Molly have been in Manhattan today, are they back?"

"Hi Harry, no, not yet. I was getting a bit concerned actually, but Molly rang to say Gina had a bit of a turn with her stomach again so they got her checked out in hospital to be on the safe side. It's all to do with the baby – you know?" He didn't actually as Annie hadn't been able to have children with the fibroids, but he could hazard a guess.

"What hospital lad? Where did they get her checked out?"

"Bellev— *Harry*... that officer asked the same question. Is there a *problem* with that place?"

"No... not in general lad no..." He hesitated now not sure how much to say. "Let me know if they're not back in say... *the next hour?*"

"If I don't hear from them in the next thirty minutes I'm getting a cab into Manhattan *myself.*" Harry smiled. He knew that was exactly what he'd say.

"We'll talk later then – bye for now." Harry shut his phone and was just about to walk back into Frank's office when he heard a massive thump on the desk. His heart raced just a little as he opened the door...

"Harry it's *Bellevue!!* She got in to *Bellevue!!*" Whilst his brain sang, his heart and guts felt cold. *If Gina and Molly weren't home in the next hour…*

"What's the exact situation? What did they tell you?"

"I spoke to their H.R. department, someone called…" She flipped the paper up on her notebook. "Hanson… Gail Hanson, she's head of H.R. said they took on a Dr. Carla Preston in early February, but only as a technician. As Frank told us, she also explained they don't hire doctors that haven't been trained in the U.S."

"Carla *Preston?*" repeated Harry incredulously. "*C.P.?!!*"

"Oh my God – *yes! I hadn't picked up on that!*" Frank Delaney looked from one to the other… *"Charlotte Peterson – Carla Preston?"* repeated Fran, palms up and hands shooting forward. "*Same initials!* And get this – she's a technician in the *anaesthesia* department!" Harry was apoplectic at that comment.

"Let's get over there – *now!*"

"Whoa… now *hang on!*" interjected Frank. "There's protocol to follow here, you both *know* that *right?*" Delaney now had his hands up. "We'll need to inform Manhattan P.D. for a start."

"Of course," said Harry, "meanwhile, we're going to pick up *OUR U.K. serial killer!*" He held out his arm as he opened the door and shot Fran a 'get moving' look, but she was already out of her seat. As Fran followed Harry through the door she called over her shoulder;

"Tell Manhattan we'd certainly appreciate their help!"

Outside as they walked super fast over to the hired Ford Fusion, Harry sensed her increased eagerness to apprehend their escapee. Mainly because although *he* was the one to tell Delaney they were going there and then and to basically stuff his protocol, it was Fran who was practically running to the car. Whilst he was used to, and very happy at her being his driver from the old days, he could also sense when a race was in the offing. All perfectly fine and legit on London streets, but this was New York – *and it wasn't a police vehicle.* As he opened the door he shared his thoughts…

"Just remember this is a hired car Fran and you're driving on the other side of the road."

"Don't worry Harry, you know I've got my brother's blood running through my veins, he's been doing rather well at Silverstone lately." She fist pumped the air as she zapped the lock.

"*Has* he…" replied Harry sceptically, all too aware of the traffic swishing behind the police station. "Not in a hired car paid for by the Met. or the Cumbrian constabulary I'll warrant. *No card pun intended.*"

"Come on Longbridge don't tell me you've lost your bottle? I *was* your driver back in the day remember?"

"I remember," said Harry smiling, "but we didn't have Hitchings *'back in the day' did* we!" Fran laughed as she held his eyes, her hand now resting on his thigh.

"Buckle up – let's go get the witch!" she said wickedly. Her face was radiant in anticipation. Images of Canon Row flashed through his mind as she looked at him, a warm feeling of reminiscence flooded his body. He picked up her hand, squeezed it gently and holding her eyes and their past a moment longer, placed it on to the wheel.

"Drive the damn car Taylor!" Harry mock ordered as he looked straight ahead trying to keep a straight face. Fran smiled as she turned the ignition – *they both knew 'it' was still there.*

BELLEVUE HOSPITAL
MANHATTAN

Molly was panic stricken. She'd been warned to say nothing to anyone, particularly the police, or Charlotte (Carla) would kill Gina. She'd said she was waiting for something, and once that something had occurred she might, just *might* let Gina go. She'd only come for two people. Gina wasn't one of them, but she wouldn't rule out a little extra if she needed bargaining power later. It would be under certain circumstances and agreements from them both if she were to go free. If they didn't comply with *everything* however… then it would be curtains for her friend, and then she would come for her as well. As she saw it, that left Molly with little to no options, which was why she was still sitting outside the ladies' washroom in the restaurant area staring at her phone.

"Are you okay Miss. err …?" Nurse Leah Chang had popped down to the cafeteria to get something to eat. She had just started a late shift and was stocking up with snacks for later. Whilst in the queue she'd noticed Molly was looking really distressed and alone. After paying for her chocolate stash she'd walked over to where the girl was sitting.

"I… er… no I'm fine," replied Molly. "That's to say I'm…" she looked around hesitantly, "yes I'm… I'm fine." It was obvious she looked anything *but*, so Leah pressed her gently…

"Have you had some upsetting test results today, is that it?" Molly shook her head, eyes staring, biting her lip nervously. Her mind was somersaulting. This was not in character for her, like Andrew, she was the strong one, the feisty one. It was them that took care of *Gina*, always had always would. Now though, now she felt helpless, because she *was*. A watery mist began to skew her vision and she immediately looked away. Swallowing hard, Molly tried to hold back the tears and failed miserably.

"I'm sorry…" she said voice breaking, feeding her bag onto her shoulder, "I have to go, I have to…" She got up and headed straight for the elevator. She'd been instructed to leave the building within ten minutes of receiving Charlotte's call on Gina's phone. However, as Molly walked across the huge tiled floor, heart fighting brain, it occurred to her Charlotte wouldn't necessarily know whether she'd left or not. It was a gamble that insane bitch wasn't watching her, but as she reached for the button – *Molly knew she wasn't going anywhere.*

THIRTY-SEVEN

BELLEVUE HOSPITAL
MANHATTAN: NEW YORK

It was dark. So very, very dark... *and cold.* Emily had no idea how long she'd been in there but it felt like forever. Was this death? Had she already died and gone to some kind of alternative hell, one with no flames?

Breathing was barely possible now. It felt as if there was an elephant on her chest, her lung capacity must have dropped to about ten percent and there was no feeling anywhere at all. Strangely though, muffled sounds filtered through the box. She'd been able to hear before Charlotte had slid her into the chilled blackness where panic had eventually subsided to be replaced with acceptance...

"... . Yes I've not long completed it... It is yes. The bullet's sealed in an evidence bag for the lab and I'll have a full report for you in the morning." Kay rolled her eyes... "Nope... definitely only *one* bullet and no other external damage other than bruising to the knees you know about, and gravel grazing to the palms… Yep, yep, okay, I'll expect someone around nine then, bye… bye." She shut off the phone and smiled a thank you at her assistant who'd cleaned up after Dean Coleman's autopsy, and was now preparing fresh instruments for the next one.

"Take a break and go get yourself a coffee when you've set that one up Ash, you look like you could do with one." Ashley Suarez fetched a few more steel trays, a scalpel and pair of rib cutters, laid them on the tool table with the rest and grabbed her purse.

"Thanks Doctor Winford, I'll be about twenty minutes if that's okay, I need to pop down to see Dad in the boiler room."

"Say hi to Joe for me," said Kay, *"and remind him he owes me ten bucks!"* she called out as Ashley disappeared through the door with a laugh and wave of acknowledgement.

Kay surveyed the freshly decked instrument table and then cast a glance at the fridge. Always aware of Jenny Flood's body being held inside it, she was beginning to wonder if she was getting too old for the job. She spoke out loud…

"Pull yourself together Winford you've at least another ten years before you can retire, you'd only be bored anyway. Right Melissa love, let's find out what happened, get you sorted." She walked towards 'Melissa Jackson's' (the suspected suicide's) drawer.

Inside Emily lay completely immobile. She was vaguely aware of some words through a heady haze and the metal walls that surrounded her. Then suddenly… suddenly she was *moving!* Sliding into the open she sensed the light through the delicate skin of her lids, but still couldn't open her eyes. She couldn't move… she couldn't *speak*.

Kay wheeled the autopsy table over to 'Melissa' and married it up under the mortuary tray beneath her. Now she eased her down carefully on to the table, and pulling it away from the fridge, shut the drawer door and rolled the trolley back into position. Reaching up for the switch, she flipped the giant overhead light on, and then with one hand each side, angled it to gain the most effective use for the job. With the evidence sheet pulled down to expose the body to the waist, she was ready to begin. Kay turned to the instrument table and selected her scalpel…

Fran Taylor had not forgotten her brother's 'off road' driving lessons. They were programmed in the back of her mind to retrieve when needs must. *Now was needs must*. Whilst Harry was looking for the G.P.S. in the glove compartment she slipped her arm out of the window, up and above, before swinging right onto Belt Parkway.

Even in New York Harry noticed she was handling the Fusion like a Ferrari, skimming past traffic along the highway like Lewis Hamilton, and eating up unfamiliar interstate routes as if she 'flew' them daily. Harry was both impressed and thought her bat-shit crazy at the same time. She glanced sideways grinning…

"Looking a little green Harry, you *did* remember your shots this morning didn't you?"

"My shots have absolutely nothing to do with my current complexion D.I. Taylor *as well you know.*" Fran fished around her side pocket, pulled out a pack of cherry cookies and deposited them in Harry's lap whilst she took the road for the tunnel one handed. Old habits died hard.

"Eat. We don't know what's going to happen when we get there, I don't want you collapsing on me." Harry snorted in disgust. He hated his diabetic condition, having to juggle jabs and different types of food at different times drove him nuts. However he unwrapped and ate all four biscuits. She was right of course, they had no idea what they'd find at the hospital and he wouldn't necessarily have the opportunity to grab anything. They didn't help his complexion though – Fran doing a Lewis Hamilton anywhere other than the U.K. still had him covertly gripping the door handle.

The G.P.S. was set for the fastest route from the station in 65th Street Brooklyn, to Bellevue Hospital in 1st Avenue Manhattan, but it had tolls at the Hugh L. Carey tunnel that took them under the East River. Luckily Fran had pre-arranged a visitors' automatic toll pass account with the car rental, so they wouldn't have to stop at a booth. As they'd entered she'd 'kindly' informed him the tunnel had flooded in 2012. *Harry rolled his eyes and sincerely hoped there'd still be enough of a car to give back to them (pass or no pass) let alone themselves.* He wasn't massively keen on going through the Dartford tunnel back home let alone under an estuary of the Hudson. At least everywhere was mostly straight…

The speeds she was reaching once out of the tunnel, Harry was convinced the N.Y.P.D. would be right behind them. Staggeringly they'd not heard any sirens on their tail, and it wasn't until they'd arrived and got out at the hospital he'd realised why. She'd placed a portable flashing light on top of the car. He looked at her over the roof and then pointedly at the siren. Fran took it off and stuck it on the back seat. Slamming the door and walking swiftly round to where he was standing she paused very close to him.

"'Ever Ready' didn't *actually* mean what everyone *thought* it meant back in the day Longbridge."

"Never thought it did D.I. Taylor… never thought it did."

Kay carefully drew out a Y incision with a marker pen, put the *'Sharpie'* back on the instrument trolley and picked up her scalpel. Looking down at 'Melissa', she sighed deeply then shaking her head, paused for a moment and leant back, the knife hovering in mid air gleaming in the overhead light…

"Such a shame, I wonder why you felt the need to, well, if you *did* take your life of course. That's why we're here now isn't it." She sighed again and leant forward over the body.

Emily was helpless. She knew what was coming next and began to pray to a god, anybody's god. There were minute sensory feelings returning but her entire body was rigid… that small amount of Baclovate had done its job. There was nothing left for her to do. As she felt the point of the blade, just a small pressure above her right breast… *a tear escaped and ran down her cheek.* Kay jumped back in horror, nearly taking a nick out of her own arm.

"Jesus Christ! What the…?!" She bent over 'Melissa' and listened very closely. Nothing. *Or was there?* She got a mirror from her handbag and held it close to the woman's nose. The tiniest cloud of condensation appeared on the surface. "Oh my God…" she whispered. "Dead girls don't cry…" Then more loudly as she ran to the door of the mortuary… ***"Dead girls don't cry!"***

Having read up on the positives and perils of Baclovate only a few weeks ago, she knew she needed some Bacliscind to reverse it… *and quickly.* When Jenny Flood's autopsy findings had sent her to study her top three reference books, the latest *Mosby's* had given her the information she'd needed. Baclovate was a new drug discovered by accident as a spin-off from the active ingredient *Sildenafil Citrate* in Viagra. It was exceedingly potent stuff. In very tiny quantities it had begun to be used as an extreme numbing agent in major deep-tissue work where anaesthetic would be dangerous to the patient. As in most drugs, huge amounts could kill. In Jenny's case, her shrivelled blackened organs had alerted Kay to research her findings. However, without its antidote, a half or quarter dose above normal would cause radical adverse changes to the body, *prior to a slower death.*

Now she prayed there would be some Bacliscind upstairs in one of the pre-op rooms, or anywhere come to that. Technically it would need to be signed out but she wasn't going to let a little thing like that come between her and potentially saving a woman's life. Despite being a generous size eighteen, pathologist Kay Winford ran like a gold medallist for the elevator and punched the button, then put a call out for Ashley Suarez to return whilst she waited for the cage to descend.

Charlotte sat cross-legged filing her nails as she studied her captive in the low light of a small side lamp. There were no side windows and there was only the blackness of a winter's evening falling through the skylight.

An almost tired look crossed her face as though having to kidnap Gina for a second time in two years really was quite tedious.

She looked a lot like her mother. Well like her mother *used* to look given she probably had a large, long Y shape stitched down her torso by now. Still, the hair would be the same, the nose, the high cheekbones, the slight freckling...

Gina was lying in a drowsy state on an old mattress Charlotte had dragged into a corner. Her head was swimming. She felt pressure on her mouth as a damp musty smell reached her nostrils which slowly brought her round. Then she heard the rustling. Her first thought was rats. The sheer terror of that made her sit up quickly but her head was so woozy she fell back on to the mattress again. The same crackly noise sounded and she tried to focus her eyes ahead of her. At this point she realised her hands were bound and it was duct tape across her mouth.

"Finally she wakes up," Charlotte sneered. She was still wearing her blonde wig and white coat. Even the stethoscope remained around her neck and the clipboard lay beside her on a table. "I didn't plan for this to happen you know Gina. Despite the fact your mother, my *oldest* and *closest* friend, slept with my husband when we were at university and *you* were the result. Despite all that, I didn't come to the States to kill *you*. Unfortunately though you've got in the way for a *second* time and so it's quite likely I may have to." Gina struggled at the bonds on her wrists and tried hard to scream under the tape across her face, but it died in her throat a screechy weak grunt.

Her vision was still a little blurry from whatever drugs she'd been given to knock her out and she panicked then remembering the baby. Tears came quickly which only made her vision worse, but not before she finally realised where the rustling was coming from. A light snigger filtered through the haze. Gina looked down and realised her own clothes had completely disappeared. She wiped the tears away with both hands, and confused, strained to focus more clearly. Then wished she hadn't. In their place from head to foot, was a full-length, wide-skirted lace wedding dress... *in pitch black.*

THIRTY-EIGHT

BELLEVUE HOSPITAL
MANHATTAN: NEW YORK

Gina's eyes widened in disbelief. She could feel nausea building which wasn't good considering the tape across her mouth, and tried desperately to calm herself internally whilst frowning questioningly at her captor.

"*Oh…* the *dress?*" Charlotte asked sarcastically, waving the nail file in the air and guessing at the question. "The copy of '*Brides*' or '*Weddings*' or whatever it was you and your man-stealing mother were looking at in Honey's that day. I was outside looking in through the window – remember? I was… *am* a doctor, that makes me *very* observant. Which is *also* why, when I saw you enter the washroom earlier, I made sure your friend didn't see you exit, jabbed you with a pre-med and helped you up here." Charlotte tilted her head on one side and gave her famous half smile… *"Nobody suspects a doctor helping a woman who feels faint."*

She put the nail file down and checked her watch as Gina's phone rang. Charlotte pulled it from her pocket and saw Andrew's name flash up on the screen. Moving closer she turned the phone to face its owner and let it ring out. Gina dropped her head and forced down the rise of sobbing that threatened to overwhelm her. Charlotte put it back in her pocket.

"That man of yours is very persistent isn't he, must've rung at least a dozen times in the last hour. I'd call that a tad controlling, best not give in to that is my advice. Oh… I forgot. *Probably won't make a lot of difference in the long run will it…*"

Molly knew she'd been taking chances. She still hadn't rung anyone after Charlotte's threat to kill Gina if she did, and was torn between sticking with that and dialling 911, or at least phoning Andrew and getting Harry involved. That *was* why he and his colleague Fran Taylor were in the States after all, and after Andy there was nobody she trusted more.

As she took elevators to various non-ward floors to check out where Charlotte could be hiding Gina, and getting absolutely nowhere, it suddenly occurred to her they may not be in the hospital at all.

She'd already received some strange looks, especially at below ground levels of the hospital. Not surprising given the fact she was running a lot and almost certainly looking worried sick. There had been questions from a couple of staff at one point, where a story of her sister about to give birth and herself unable to find the maternity ward, had tumbled out far too easily. And then on higher floors there were the drug addicts fighting with physicians, and more than one violent drunk who nearly knocked her over with a wild punch in the air as they staggered down the hallway. When she saw a couple of young male teenagers having to be restrained and kept apart in one room, and a woman thrashing about screaming whilst coming off heroin in another, Molly had had enough.

She really wasn't sure how much longer she could hold out not calling for help. Looking at her mobile there wasn't much of a signal now anyway, and the battery was down to fifteen percent. If Andrew had been trying to get hold of her he probably wouldn't have been able to get through. After an hour of trying to find Gina and realising she wasn't even sure how she'd approach a rescue single handed, Molly made the decision to ring him at least, and for that it might be best to go to the lobby of the hospital and use a pay phone. Decision made she ran to the nearest elevator and smacked the call button hard. Now she was desperate to contact Andy and get Harry and the N.Y.P.D. on scene. She just prayed that doing so was the best thing for Gina. If Charlotte had *any* way of seeing her on CCTV, *she may just be signing her best friend's death warrant.*

As she walked out of the lift and was running for the hospital reception area Harry Longbridge and Fran

Taylor came out of the revolving glass doors and saw a crazed dark-haired young woman, hurtling towards them.

It was nearly time. He'd been on her trail for so long now it felt like it had been his life's work. Well in a way it was. She still hadn't twigged though. Of course she knew there was someone out there, he'd made sure of that with the break-in and message in blood across the dressing table mirror. But she hadn't worked out who he was and how he'd found her... or why. Why the hunter was now the hunted... And that made it all the more satisfying. The shock when she found out, the incredulity, the disbelief... it would make all the sacrifice, this obsession that had shattered his marriage, almost cost him his job – it would make it all worthwhile.

His latest disguise was not so dissimilar to hers. A doctor's uniform worn in a hospital. Amateur dramatics had come in handy as a hobby, not surprising when your regular job was so dull. In his white coat pocket he had a gun instead of an emergency bleeper though, inside of which there was a cartridge. With her name on it.

He was close now, very close. But he would wait for the grand finale. It had to be right.

Kay Winford had never run so fast in her life as in the previous ten minutes. As soon as the elevator door had opened on the nearest O.R. floor, she'd careered down the hall, flat pumps landing heavily on the shiny floor, white tails flying behind, leaving surprised faces and open mouths in her wake. Kay never *ran* anywhere… *ever*. She had managed to contact Ashley Suarez sharing a coffee break with her dad Joe in the boiler room, and got her to return to be with 'Melissa', or who she'd *assumed* was Melissa but was now not so sure.

Kay practically slid round the corner to the nearest set of O.R. rooms on the first of the operating floors and prayed they were up to date with supplies from the pharmacy store. Even so, officially the chief pharmacist really *would* need to sign out the Bacliscind and need to know why she was requesting it, despite Kay being a trained physician. *Unless… unless she could get a 'hall pass'…* She took out her phone.

It took an awful lot of persuading, even with their past history, but she managed to get Chief Pharmacist Kerry Sanger to agree to release a file of Bacliscind and waive the prescription. She and Kay had lived together for two years but parted on good terms. They'd always promised to have each other's back. Despite this she had to agree to meet her with a full explanation at the O.R. where she was waiting agitatedly outside. *Luckily it was O.R.12 and not one that Jodi had been responsible for prior to her 'disappearance', or stocks may well not have been up to date.*

Kerry arrived within five minutes and her eyes bulged as Kay related what had happened. She immediately shooed the on-duty pre-op staff away from the drugs cabinet, unlocked it and the two women searched desperately for the drug Kay needed whilst the surprised anaesthetist and O.R. nurses looked on.

"There!" exclaimed Kay pointing to the silver and blue labelled bottle on the top shelf. Kerry reached up and grabbed the precious drug off the shelf before re-locking the cabinet. She held out the Bacliscind then just as quickly snatched it back.

"You *do* know how to administer this don't you Kay, because if you don't both our jo—"

"The woman's going to be *dead* if I don't get back with this Kez – she was one teardrop away from an *autopsy!*" Kerry nodded, smiling briefly at her old pet name, and handed it to her in silent agreement. Kay didn't hang around.

"I'll phone through to critical and prepare them for an extreme and unusual emergency," Kerry yelled to Kay who'd already taken off towards the elevators. *"Good luck!!"* she called out as her pathologist and dearest ex disappeared into a lift.

Molly ran straight across the enormous tiled hall into Harry's arms babbling about Gina being kidnapped, she just *knew* it had to be Charlotte and to *please* save her, all as Andrew charged through the doors a couple of minutes behind them. Molly was right. He'd been trying to get hold of them both for the last hour and a half and was now experiencing anxiety levels way beyond his personal norm. To then hear his fiancée was back in the clutches of Cumbria's most dangerous psychopath had him clutching his hands behind his head and twisting left and right not knowing which way to turn.

"Okay son just *calm down.*" Harry passed Molly gently to Fran, put his hands on Andrew's shoulders and held them firmly. "We'll *find* her – we'll get her back just like we did last time. And she'll be alive – *I promise!*" Fran stared at him hard. Harry felt her eyes bore into his temples. He couldn't promise to save her and he knew it. Strangely though, Fran had a feeling he was going to. She looked around at the sheer size of the place. Bellevue was bloody *enormous.* God knows how Harry was going to pull this one off but somehow she knew he would – it was after all why she'd brought him. Well... *one of the reasons...*

"Fran you spoke to the head of Human Resources didn't you? A Gail someone, Hanson wasn't it?" he asked now.

"Yeah, said they'd taken on a Carla Preston beginning of Feb."

"Right, we'll start by going to see her, get some shift info and her home address." He turned back to Molly and Andrew. "I know it's completely pointless telling you to go home or find some coffee so I won't bother. But you do *exactly* as I say, understand?" They both nodded. Molly felt mentally a lot stronger now they were here. Harry especially. She breathed deeply and smiled confidently at Andrew. *Now* things would get done.

Charlotte had discovered the old O.R. floor on her latest night duty. She'd read something about old hospitals having all the operating rooms set right on the top floors pre-1980s. Bellevue was a very old hospital, the oldest public hospital in the States. Although a great deal of modernisation had obviously and continuously taken place, the remnants of the sky-lit O.R.s on the highest floor had proved to be a useful find.

Gina woke up on the mattress in one of these disused operating rooms set right at the top of the hospital and realised she was no longer drugged and heady. She also noticed she was alone. An old clock on the wall had only one hand, there were panels missing from the ceiling and there was dust and bits of old medical equipment everywhere.

She tried again to twist her hands free from the tape but Charlotte had tied her wrists with bandages underneath as well. It was hopeless. Tears began to streak her make-up and she was *so* hungry. She had no idea of time but judging by her stomach it must be at least seven o'clock. Andrew must be worried *sick*, she thought, *and where was Molly?* It was only then that it occurred to her that Charlotte may have hurt her. Her shoulders began to shake then and crying began properly but she knew this was dangerous with her mouth taped up and forced herself to stop. There was nothing she could do but wait, and lie there in that disgusting black dress that now also stunk of her urine…

Charlotte wasn't quite sure what she was going to do with Gina yet. She was technically due on a late split shift at seven, so had removed the blonde wig and white coat to change into her mauve technician scrubs at her locker. She took her fake glasses from the white coat pocket, rolled the disguise items into a ball, and hid them under a black jacket at the back of the tall metal unit. Then after closing and locking the door, turned to the mirror to check her short black pixie crop and put the glasses back on. Smiling at her 'Carla' reflection, she walked back out into the hallway and nearly bumped into a senior doctor.

"Oh I'm so sorry, do excuse me," she said, eyes down, playing her 'plain Jane' part perfectly.

"That's *quite* alright, no problem at all," replied the ginger-haired doctor, smiling and thumbing his matching neat goatee. And as Charlotte hurried off in the opposite direction, he smoothed the pocket that concealed the nine-millimetre Glock 43, and turned round to follow her…

THIRTY-NINE

BELLEVUE HOSPITAL
MANHATTAN: NEW YORK

Kay Winford arrived back in her autopsy unit to find Ashley waiting nervously by 'Melissa'.

"Dr. Winford! Thank goodness you're back!" she whispered urgently, as if she didn't want anyone to hear, particularly the *'dead'* body. "She's... she's—"

"Not dead. Yes I know," replied Kay quickly, placing the Bacliscind on the counter. She selected a 50 ml syringe from a drawer, drew up a full file of the yellow liquid and injected the lot into the left arm of the woman on the table, then stood back. "I don't think her name's Melissa Jackson either, I have strong suspicion this is—"

"Em... I'm... I'm..." Emily opened her eyes as Ashley leapt back so fast she collided with the instrument trolley sending it crashing into the sink cabinets. Emily's left arm jumped at the noise as the runners for the crash team came shooting through the double doors with a trolley.

"Okay guys get this one up to C.C.U. *A-SAP!!*" ordered Kay. "I'll be right behind you to fill them in. Kerry Sanger's already rung ahead." The four techs got Emily onto the trolley and out of the door as Ashley remained flattened against the sink, eyes and mouth fixed open. Kay turned to her young trainee…

"And *you* young lady…" Ashley was worried, she'd hardly responded professionally to the situation and she knew it…

"I'm *so* sorry Doctor Winford I shouldn't have—"

"Go home Ash, take the day off tomorrow. It's been a hell of a shock for us both *and I've been in the job for darn sight longer than you have.* I'll see you in a couple of days, and don't worry I'll square it with H.R."

"Thank you," replied Ashley relieved, "I really hope the lady recovers… whoever she is." Kay smiled and passed Ashley's coat and bag to her. She'd never met the woman on her way up to the critical care unit, but Kay had been in Cumbria in 2018, and was Kirkdale's senior pathologist that year. She was pretty sure she knew who 'Melissa' *really* was. *It was time to contact her favourite D.C.I.*

Fran and Harry were in Gail Hanson's office whilst Andrew and Molly waited outside.

"There, that's Carla Preston – anaesthesia technician. Said she was a British doctor. I did think it strange she was prepared to take such a menial position given her training." She turned the computer screen round to them as she printed out the file complete with photo. Harry and Fran leaned in to look at it. "She originally applied for an E.R. vacancy we had end of Jan beginning of Feb," Gail continued, "I explained the U.S. training requirements and why we couldn't accept her application. It was purely by chance a tech job came up and I emailed her back to ask if she'd be interested. She jumped at it." *I bet she did,* thought Harry.

"Well none of us have seen our absconder who we believe is your Carla Preston, looking like that," said Harry pointing at the photograph. "Only one person has and we think Peterson's kidnapped and holding her somewhere, possibly in this hospital."

"Carla's immediate boss was Jodi Denton," said Gail, "and *she's* still missing." Fran and Harry looked at each other. "Her shift rota's the same but we had to engage another supervisor. Looking at this they should both be on now." At that moment Harry's phone went. He answered irritably at the interruption and didn't check the name...

"Yep – Longbridge."

"It's your *wife*. You *do* remember me do you Harry? About five five, dark blonde wavy hair, not a bad body, failed businesswoman and newfound Labrador enthusiast." Harry sighed rubbed his forehead and rolled his lips. Her timing was, *as usual*, impeccable. Nevertheless the guilt hit him like a sledgehammer. He'd not rung Annie in a week and had barely noticed. Now of course he was deeply involved. He turned away from the others and spoke more quietly into the phone.

"Annie... I'm... now's *not* the time. I – I know it's—"

"Well *what* a surprise – *not!* I take it the fact I was kidnapped, kept in an old builders' yard as a result of *another* of your past cases, *under the threat of death for several days and nights I might add*, just isn't enough to get your attention. What *does* a woman have to do Harry? Eh? *Murder someone?*" Harry could hear another call trying to come through and apologised as he put Annie on hold. This time he saw the caller. It was Kay Winford...

"Kay, I'm here at Bellevue where are *you?*"

"On the way to CCU, that's why I'm ringing, I think I've just sent Emily Stone up there." Harry swung round to Fran and Gail Hanson, eyes wide.

"What the hell is—"

"You remember the Flood girl? I told you I thought it wasn't regular rigor mortis at the scene?"

"Yeah yeah... *so?*"

"Similar outward presentation must have been a lower dose. She was in my fridge tagged up with another woman's details, same sort of age and description. I'd not met her before so..."

"Christ! Is she *okay?* You didn't...?" *No wonder she never turned up for her interview with Frank Delaney,* he thought drily.

"Who knows, this is unknown territory Harry, new drug. I certainly hope so, in *time*. If she even *makes* it, God knows what the lasting effects will be, physically *and* mentally. What are you doing here anyway?"

"We've got a serious situation Kay. Now you've told me what's happened with Mrs. Stone I'm convinced Charlotte Peterson *is* at the back of this. Emily Stone's daughter Miss. Rowlands is missing. She, *Gina*, came in to the E.R. earlier with stomach cramps. She was with her friend Molly who's safe with us, but Gina disappeared after having a scan – *she's pregnant* Kay. We're pretty sure she's been kidnapped and it's Peterson – I *know* it." Then he thought for a moment. "Long shot – have you come across a tech assistant called Carla Preston?"

"No sorry Harry, I'm mostly in the autopsy unit, see doctors on various wards of course but it's a big place."

"Yes of course. Look I've got to go. We need to locate Miss. Rowlands as quickly as possible. You and I both know what… well…" There was a pause.

"Indeed. Might see you later in CCU then? Bye for now." Kay rang off and completely forgetting Annie had been put on hold, Harry shut his phone and turned back to Fran and Gail.

"I'll let Celia Dawson know what's going on as well," said Gail, picking up her phone. Fran looked questioningly. "She basically runs this place," she said opening her office door for them all to exit into the corridor and re-join Andrew and Molly. *"Although she's almost certainly googling her next jazz concert..."*

Nurse Leah Chang was on the phone and juggling a ham roll, Coke and a packet of crisps. She was in the cafeteria queue for the second time during her shift, and completely unaware the woman who'd caused her negligence suspension was within touching distance. It was busy and they'd been there for fifteen minutes. Leah recognised Carla as the new English O.R. tech assistant or cleaner and store stacker for want of a better description, but was blissfully unaware of anything else. They didn't speak. In fact the nurse rarely spoke to her, something about Carla made her feel uncomfortable.

Leah had received a call from her brother, Officer Eddie Chang who'd rung to tell her to expect an influx of police very soon... *and why.* He shouldn't have done so but he did. She was his little sister, if there was a nutter running around that hospital he was going to warn her. As he spoke, Leah's mouth got wider and wider. She scanned the cafeteria wondering who and where this psycho was, just as Charlotte paid for her items and walked quickly away.

One by one the snacks slipped from Leah's fingers.

Charlotte had no intention of actually doing any work. Once she'd picked up the sandwiches and cans from the cafeteria she intended to take an elevator back to the top floor. It was a little unnerving she didn't actually have a plan in mind for Emily's child, although she realised whatever she'd told that Fields girl, it was clear she'd have to kill Gina. She knew who she was. The thought of another exhausting trip down to the boiler room wasn't exactly enticing though. This would need some thought.

As she was crossing the reception area along the walkway above, a commotion below caught her eye and she saw a group of police run in to the hall. Charlotte moved closer to the rail and looked down. They had already approached several of the security officers who in turn started speaking into their radios and looking up. She automatically drew back sharply from the balcony rail and began to walk swiftly towards the elevators. *This wasn't good. This wasn't good at all.* If she'd been on the ground floor she could've slipped out and got away. To where exactly was anybody's guess that would have to come later. As it was, she was on the first floor gallery landing, *and they were on their way up.* Charlotte had no choice but to head back to the top floor where she had Gina held captive, and use her as a hostage.

She felt in her pockets. Her kitchen knife and scalpel were still there as always but she had very little in the way of various drugs and needles left. There were more in her stash at the house, but obviously getting there was out of the question, and it was far too busy to steal this time of day.

Once in the elevator Charlotte pressed the button for the top floor, but of course half a dozen other people got in and out and stopped the ride at various levels on the way. She started to get very agitated. Her mouth set in a thin line and her eye began to twitch. The sandwich she'd bought was being squeezed to a pulp as cream cheese oozed out of the sides under its plastic wrapping. Her knuckles turned white and her breathing intensified. She was attracting some very odd looks now and people were shuffling their feet as they moved closer to the elevator wall. Charlotte hadn't realised it but her face had twisted into something quite hideous, quite *vile*…

Gail Hanson had spoken with the Chief Administrator Celia Dawson and been told the N.Y.P.D. were downstairs. She related this information to Harry and Fran, after they'd checked with Charlotte's supervisor, *or Carla as her new supervisor knew her*, if she'd been seen that evening. The answer was no, she hadn't turned up.

Andrew and Molly were still in the group but their anxiety for Gina's welfare was now shot, especially after hearing from Harry about Emily's horrific near death. Fran was not keen on them staying and was just about to say so when a young Chinese nurse approached them. She saw they were holding a photo of the British O.R. technician who worked on her floor, and were asking staff if they'd seen her.

"Excuse me, is there something going on with Carla Preston?" Leah Chang pointed hesitantly to the photo Fran had been showing to a group of doctors.

"Do you *know* her, have you seen her *this evening*?" asked Fran urgently.

"She was in the cafeteria earlier… she was in front of me. Is… is she the one that—" Leah stopped herself, aware of dropping Eddy in it. She knew he really shouldn't have divulged police information.

"The one that *what* Nurse?" asked Gail Hanson narrowing her eyes. She hadn't forgotten Leah was not long reinstated following a negligence claim over a patient's death.

"Nothing, it's just… there's been rumours. You know… about Jodi, they were always bickering and stuff. We still don't know where she is, and ever since Carla's arrived things haven't felt right on our floors. She's not one of us, she doesn't make friends – she doesn't even smile much." A look that spoke volumes passed between Harry, Molly and Andrew – they knew exactly what she meant.

"Where would be the best place to hide someone in a massive building like this?" asked Harry.

"Almost anywhere," replied Gail, "even *I* haven't been in *every* room on *every* floor."

"There is… *one* place that could be used." This was from Leah who wasn't entirely sure if she was allowed to leave yet. All eyes were now on her.

"Go on," said Harry studying her closely almost holding his breath…

"The very top floor where the old operating rooms used to be, the ones that never got renovated." Leah bit her lip. "Sometimes the students go up there to… er… to make out… *a bit*," she finished awkwardly. Harry looked straight at Gail Hanson.

"Where's the nearest lift?"

FORTY

BELLEVUE HOSPITAL
MANHATTAN: NEW YORK

The 'doctor' scratched his chin. It was pure chance he'd managed to slip inside the elevator shielded by a couple of larger people before it had left the gallery floor. And more importantly, unseen by the one who had so much on her mind.

During his days following her around the hospital, he'd actually been called upon to attend patients by genuine staff. A young lad in the E.R. who'd badly sprained an ankle outside and had been carried in by his dad, an elderly lady who'd been having breathing difficulties, hardly surprising given her obvious cigarette habit, and a man who'd got a really weird rash. Almost thought about changing his job he'd enjoyed it that much. Not until he'd finished this one though.

The elevator seemed to stop and start a hundred times. People got in, people got out people got back in again. The journey seemed to take forever. He needed it to be full though, didn't want her remembering their collision in the corridor earlier. She was sharp that one, too sharp, but hopefully not sharp enough now she was under pressure.

He'd seen the police swarming beneath the gallery walk as well. You could hardly miss them there were at least twenty. He assumed they were there for her too, and would soon be on their way filtering upwards to begin their search on each floor. But they couldn't have her. She was his and he didn't care if he went down for it.

Harry, Fran, Leah, Andrew and Molly were on their way to the top of the building. It was agreed Leah was to go as far as the O.R. hallway to show the two officers where the old operating rooms were, and then return to her duties. Gail Hanson had received a message from Cynthia Dawson to meet her and the police on the first floor in order to advise re layout and send them up to join the U.K. officers.

Fran was trying to catch Harry's attention. They were standing in front of the others and she let her hand briefly touch his hoping it wouldn't get noticed. He turned his head towards hers and flushed slightly but said nothing. She rolled her eyes back and left indicating a reference to Andrew, Molly and Leah's presence, rather than any attempt at romantic finger brushing in an elevator. He didn't click at first, then realised she wanted them anywhere but near a psychotic killer. Harry knew she was right of course, but he also knew Andrew Gale. A studious, 'booky', small-town crime reporter with a passion for reading thrillers he may be, but he was also remarkably stubborn. He could be like a terrier on a trouser leg if he wanted, and with Gina at the centre of this… *Harry knew he'd never be able to shake him off.* There was also a special understanding between them. The boy had driven him mad two years ago turning up at every one of Peterson's murder scenes, but their 'truce' in that vet's house when Andrew had spotted his sugar problem… that lad had good natural instincts. No – *he stayed.* Molly on the other hand… he'd get the nurse to take her back down with her.

The elevator had stopped at the twentieth floor. There were five to go. He was getting a little tetchy now – she was so close to him and yet… He had to wait. When the doors opened pandemonium ensued! Staff could be seen running up and down shouting; "Double code blue rooms seven and eight!" And "Get the crash team in NOW!" Three people got out and stood flat to the wall to let relevant equipment trolleys rush through. When a nurse running past saw him before the doors closed, she shouted "Stop!! Doctor!! We need you we're short up here!!" He froze. This wasn't part of the plan. "Doctor we need you – please come now!!" Her look of surprise at his reluctance stalled her for a few seconds before she reached in to the elevator and pulled on his coat sleeve, her face

alarmed and desperate. "Sir? We need senior residents in
seven and eight – immediately!!"

Charlotte was staring at him strangely now. He had
no choice but to exit the elevator and follow the nurse.
He would have to extricate himself from the code blue as
soon as he could. He could hardly join in with anything
contributory… not as a Nottinghamshire solicitor…

The elevator finally arrived on the twenty-fifth after a
fair few stops on the way, and with only themselves
left the doors finally opened. Fran held the button to
prevent it being called back down as Harry stuck his
head out and listened. It was remarkably quiet for a
hospital floor, but then it wasn't used anymore – well
apart from those students sneaking off for their own
private shift.

He walked out tentatively followed by Fran and
the others. Leah Chang pointed left down the corridor
and they began to walk forwards. All were nervous,
all walked as if they had something uncomfortable
in their shoes, even Harry. Anyone would be very
foolish not to be uneasy, this was Charlotte Peterson
they were about to come up against, there was no
knowing what she would unleash. And then there
was Gina. Nobody knew if she was alive or dead, and
where Andrew was concerned that *was* the bit Harry
was jumpy about. He had a feeling the quiet booky
lad behind him could well turn into a murdering
lunatic if his fiancée was hurt – *or worse*. And despite

her flinging herself into his arms in reception earlier, he remembered Molly Fields as being pretty tenacious when push came to shove.

Leah Chang had stopped walking.

"The old O.R.s start from—"

"Shhh… *just in case.*" Fran shot her brows up and put fingers to her lips. Leah nodded and lowered her voice to a whisper…

"They start from here on the left and go all the way down to the end. There are also two round the corner, but I think there's an old meds storage room in between them as well." Fran smiled encouragingly.

"Okay thanks Leah, you've been super helpful. You should go back down now and take Andrew and Moll—"

"No way!!" they exclaimed together.

"Shhhhhhh!!!" hissed Harry and Fran in tune, protesting with eyes, brows and everything else going north. Andrew pinned Harry with a look that said *'you know you can't do this, we have history'*.

"Pleeease Harry? I may even come in handy these days," whispered Molly and gave a couple of high kicks and a double Taekwondo flip twist. Harry blinked slowly, head jerking forward. *She kept that bloody quiet.* He then shrugged at Fran palms out. She rolled her eyes and turned away as an impatient sigh escaped.

"Okay, but you remember this. We are *not* the bloody 'A' Team – *have you got that?*" All three youngsters looked totally confused and even Fran swung back round with an uncertain look on her face. Feeling his age Harry shook his head and turned to Leah…

"Off you go now and thanks for your help. Straight back down to your colleagues though, *okay Nurse?*" Leah nodded, got back in the same elevator and closed the doors. Meanwhile the others all looked at each other, and swallowing hard began to advance towards the door of the first disused operating room wondering where their back-up was…

It had been very close. She had no knowledge of it, but Charlotte had arrived on the top floor about five minutes ahead of Harry and Fran. She was now back inside the O.R. room around the corner at the end of the hall where she still had Gina bound and gagged.

After dumping the squished cream cheese on brown in the sink and the cans on the side, she turned to face the girl lying on the mattress. Gina was not looking great. Even allowing for low lighting, and the fact she was wearing a black Goth wedding dress and still feeling the effects of the injected pre-med, her general pallor was pale and her skin looked damp. Her eyelids were also flickering half closed and her head lolling.

Despite being stripped of her title Charlotte was still technically a doctor, she still knew how much or how little to inject for the result she required. She needed a hostage. If she was going to get out of there a free woman, a dead one wouldn't be much use. A check was definitely in order and she resignedly walked over to do it.

Hearts thumping, Harry, Fran, Andrew and Molly each took an O.R. door to press an ear to for verification of any voices or sounds of movement. There were small square windows in the double doors, but with no light inside they couldn't see a thing. All shook their heads, checking with each other in silence and moved on to the next four. This they did in sequence until they came to the corner at the end of the corridor and were left with the final two with a meds store between them. It was all laid out exactly as Leah had described. Harry put a finger to his lips then motioned for Andrew and Molly to stand back, although given her martial arts performance earlier would rather have kept her front and centre. At the end of the day though she was still a member of the public so was now looking at his raised hand that said 'stop there'.

Fran flattened her ear to the left-hand door whilst Harry checked his watch… *where the hell were those police officers? Gail Hanson got word from Celia Dawson they were in the lobby fifteen minutes ago!*

"Still no sign of their damn SWAT team," he whispered to Fran. "I'm assuming Delaney sent for some of their specialist guys?"

"*Shh!* I can hear something," said Fran sharply. Harry waited for a moment. "Look can you see? There's a low light as well. Someone's *definitely* in there."

"For fuck's sake!" hissed Andrew, marching towards the door. "I'm not leaving Gee a minute longer she's *preg*—" Harry swung round exasperated and barricaded him from getting any nearer.

"Shut it Gale for God's sake!"

Charlotte was kneeling on the floor beside the mattress. She pulled up Gina's eyelids. The girl was nearly out of it from the second shot she'd given her before going for the snacks. Pulse was okay though – she'd do. Good enough for hostage material anyway… she was still breathing…

Suddenly Charlotte heard something – *whispering?* She stood up and looked around the room but the light was so dim over most of it she couldn't see. The main light would obviously help, but to have the place lit up like a Christmas tree would hardly be sensible even on a supposedly disused floor.

All she could hear now was *her* shaky breathing. Charlotte walked gingerly across the shadowed room, barely inhaling. The wind created an eerie whistling from a loose pane in the skylight, and old medical equipment threw weird shapes in the gloom. As she moved further from the lamp's glow she suddenly collided with something tall and thin on wheels sending it crashing to the floor. Gina moaned at the noise and Charlotte turned towards her… *at which point the room exploded…!*

When Harry and the others heard the crash, everything happened at once.

"Now Harry!" yelled Andrew from behind as he ran forward. At that moment Harry's own assumption of what had likely occurred behind the doors fast tracked him into action, and he shoulder barged through them followed by Fran and Molly.

"Find the light!" yelled Fran heart pounding and body full of adrenalin hands out in defence pose, but Molly had already swept the walls both sides and found the switch. The room lit up to reveal a steely-eyed shorn dark-haired woman nobody recognised, holding a scalpel to the throat of someone they all *did*.

FORTY-ONE

BELLEVUE HOSPITAL
MANHATTAN: NEW YORK

Charlotte sneered and tipped her head to one side before speaking. The scene that had opened up before them had shocked everyone.

"*Well, well, well*, D.C.I. Longbridge no less. Surely you haven't come *all* this way just for little old me? I'm flattered, *really*." Harry stiffened.

"Don't be. Where you're going you'll be—"

"I don't think Gina here would appreciate your being disrespectful to me, do you?" She lifted the girl's head up and stroked her neck with the flat of the scalpel.

"I'll rip your fu—" Andrew had taken a step forward as he spoke, but Charlotte quickly flipped the scalpel on its edge and yanked Gina's head back further, exposing the tautness and vulnerability of her throat. Harry held his arm across him.

"Leave it son we need to—"

"*He may have come for you, you murdering bitch, but you'll never see the U.K. again!*" At the sound of a strange voice everyone facing Charlotte and Gina swung round. A ginger-haired, bearded doctor stood behind them with a gun trained on Charlotte.

"What the—" Fran and Harry were both taken aback especially as they were unarmed. Although it appeared the man was technically on their side, much as they'd like to, they couldn't allow him to *kill* her. *Where the hell was that back-up?* Harry narrowed his eyes then, something was floating about in the soup of a memory somewhere...

The man kept the gun levelled at Charlotte, and taking tissues from his pocket wiped firmly over the side of his neck to reveal a large tattoo. He then lifted his free arm to his face. Slowly the ginger beard was peeled off, and the matching ginger hair pulled from his head.

"Oh... my... God... *Christopher Mogg!*" exclaimed Harry. "*Susie Sarrandaire's brother!*" Fran turned to him eyes shocked and staring in *who the hell are they?* mode.

"Got it in one Longbridge," said Mogg, eyes still on Charlotte, who was also now in shock remembering the man with a tattoo outside the hospital. "You killed my little sister Danni two years ago Peterson, she was an aspiring actress on the brink of her career, my *baby* sister my *best* friend." Molly and Andrew's mouths fell open this was one *massive* turn up. They both

374

remembered Jenny talking about witnessing her friend Danni's murder. Susie (Danni) had been her best friend at school.

"Mr. Mogg… *Christopher*…" began Harry, "I get how you feel, you have *every* right to—"

"*And* I was your mother's solicitor," interrupted Mogg, eyes and gun still on Charlotte, "you'll never see your inheritance, your mother saw to that. Which means you'll never be able to pay off the Zandini mob for your little trip out here. *Now drop the fucking knife!*" Charlotte was the one looking pale now, so much so she let the scalpel drop a little. Gina had been swallowing, terrified throughout, too terrified even to cry. Then Charlotte's expression changed…

"Looks like I've got nothing left then," she said, "nothing to lose." She brought the scalpel back up level with Gina's throat and moved her hand across left to begin the slash. *Molly screamed!* Andrew, Harry and Fran all yelled *"No!"*

"*Drop* the gun sir and put your hands in the air – *now!*" From the doorway six of New York's finest had appeared with side arms drawn and ready to fire. Now fanned out, two had guns pointed at Christopher Mogg, two at Charlotte and two at Harry, Fran, Molly and Andrew. To say she was surprised was an understatement. The room was getting decidedly overfull, it was almost funny. She nearly laughed… *but not quite.*

"Who are the British detectives Taylor and Longbridge?" Harry and Fran disclosed themselves then

Harry quietly explained who Andrew and Molly were, whereupon they were taken outside. Fran and Harry were allowed to stay as their involvement had already been substantiated by Det. Frank Delaney and the two hospital officials, Gail Hanson and Celia Dawson.

"Ma'am… put the knife down please, nice and slowly and kick it away from you – do it *now.*" She and Christopher looked at each other, neither had dropped their weapons. The air was thick with fear and unbearable memories on all sides.

"Sir… *Ma'am*… put your weapons *down* please. We don't want to be here all night do we?" Christopher turned to the officer who spoke, the Glock was shaking in his hand he had tears in his eyes…

"But… she's *mine… she's mine! I planned it. I* planned it all so *perfectly!*" He was looking between Charlotte and the officer now, head moving quickly back and forth. "The switch of the Zandini mob's mobile hairdresser to *my girlfriend,* she works with her, I paid off the Zandini girl to keep *quiet.* My partner took the passport photo, gave it to me so I'd recognise her on the plane, *two whole years of waiting!* Longbridge… *tell* them! *Tell them what that fucking bitch did!!*" The gun was wobbling badly. Christopher Mogg dropped his head a broken man as Harry gently took the pistol from his hand. Using forefinger and thumb he passed it to the nearest officer as Mogg slipped down the wall and sobbed heavily into his hands on the floor. Fran dropped to her knees and put her arm around his shoulders before two officers cuffed him and took him out into the corridor.

"Very entertaining, sorry I can't *clap*," said Charlotte still holding the scalpel to Gina's throat. Four guns were still facing her as one of the officers tried again.

"Mrs. Peterson, we really need you to put the scalpel *down*." Gina almost fully round now and totally aware, realised Andrew was no longer in the room. Her eyes searched frantically and Fran picked up on it.

"He's outside Gina, you'll see him soon," she said smiling. Charlotte scoffed and then let her face fall into line.

"I wouldn't bet on it. Who *are* you anyway Taylor?" She looked at Harry and then back at Fran and smiled slowly. The highlighter on Fran's cheeks glowed a little stronger... "Ah... *got it!*"

"The knife please ma'am? Drop it on the floor and kick it this way," tried the officer calmly again.

"How does Mrs. H. feel about *you* then Taylor? Bet that didn't go down too well did it, you coming out here with him?"

"She's not out here with me I'm out here with her. I'm retired Dr. Peterson, they called me back in because I was on your previous case." At being addressed as Doctor, Charlotte hesitated for a moment. *Nobody had acknowledged her true status for two years. They'd taken it away, seventeen years a G.P. and they'd taken it away. To hear it again had dislodged something in her mind, like a jigsaw puzzle that was trying to reassemble in a different format, from a different era. This was the second time she'd been cornered, and this time there was no forest-covered pike above a lake to try and make her escape. For the second time… it was over.*

She dropped the scalpel. Harry sensed the fight had gone out of her in exactly the same way as when they'd brought her down from the Kirkby Pike to Keeper's Cottage. She gave a huge sigh and slumped back, removing her arm from around Gina. As the girl moved slightly to get off the mattress following hand instructions from one of the officers, Harry automatically went forward to reach the scalpel and slid it across the floor. *The syringe was stabbed viciously into his calf before he'd even stood upright.* Fran jumped forwards to catch him and Charlotte glared into his eyes as he keeled over.

"Not this time Harry… *not this time…*"

At that point all hell broke loose. Fran was shouting at and shaking Harry who'd collapsed on the mattress but wasn't responding. Charlotte was cuffed and marched from the room sneering defiantly, and Gina was helped outside to fall into a frustrated Andrew's arms. Police radioed officers waiting below with Gail Hanson and Celia Dawson to alert them they had an officer down and therefore a medical emergency. A code blue was called. Nobody knew what Harry had been injected with and he was completely out of it. The medical team arrived, took him off to the C.C.U. with Fran accompanying and fighting back tears. Andrew and Molly went with Gina for her to be thoroughly checked over, especially with regard to the baby. How long her mental state would take to recover was anybody's guess, *and she hadn't been told about her mother yet either…*

Gareth Stone sat by his wife's bed in utter disbelief. He simply couldn't process what he'd just been told, but he did understand he'd very nearly lost Emily in the most grotesque and sickening way possible.

Not being able to contact her for hours on end had been frightening enough, although Gareth had guiltily admitted to himself he'd thought she could be with another man.

He held her hand in both of his and kissed the inside of her wrist as her fingers traced his cheek. Emily lay there smiling up at him grateful for two things. One she was alive and had regained most of her muscle movement after Kay had injected her with the reversal drug Bacliscind, and two that in spite of everything she couldn't have wanted for a more loving and devoted husband. Then she realised that was three and gave a little laugh. What the hell… *they were together.*

"What's funny? I nearly *lost* you, you nearly *died!*" Gareth exclaimed with tears in his eyes.

"Oh nothing… just relieved I can still laugh," she replied smiling.

Luckily for Harry he'd only been stuck with a pre-filled syringe of diazepam Charlotte still had capped in her pocket, and not the deadly Baclovate. Fran was sitting very close by *his* bed in the critical care unit, desperate to, but controlling herself not to hold *his* hand.

"I thought you were a goner there for a minute D.C.I. Longbridge," she said throatily, eyes glassy. Harry picked up her hand and stroked the back softly. As he became lost in her gaze waiting for the tear to fall, Fran swallowed hard and looked away. With her free hand she dabbed a tissue carefully at mascara-laden eyelashes.

"It'll take a lot more than the likes of Charlotte Peterson to get rid of *me* D.I. Taylor," said Harry squeezing it warmly, *"there's still far too much I intend to do…"*.

Gina and the baby had checked out physically safe and well, although it would remain to be seen how her ordeal would affect her mentally in the long term. Afterwards they had briefly checked in on Harry, *who was now more a friend than anything,* and noticed Detective Delaney was just leaving. They then went on to see Emily who was being detained under observation for a week given the horrific experience she'd gone through. The fact the drug was new, and nobody could say for sure what the lasting effects would be with the quantities she'd been subjected to, was a worry for everyone. When they'd arrived to see her, much to Gareth's disgust *and despite the time*, Detective Frank Delaney was in the room. They waited on chairs outside, Andrew and Molly exchanging knowing glances over Gina's head.

"Mrs. Stone, I am so glad to see you looking remarkably well given your *terrifying* ordeal. I won't keep you of course and we can do this properly when you're fully recovered. But briefly, just for my records, the diary we found at the address of Miss. Flood. It had certain passages relating to your correspondence with her between 2013 and 2018. Can you—"

"I'm... I'm *sorry*... Miss. *who?*" asked Emily puzzled. Frank Delaney hesitated for a moment and Gareth's head did a fast swivel to meet his wife's querying expression...

"Miss. Flood... Mrs. Stone. Miss. *Jenny* Flood?" He looked at Gareth. "Your friend and colleague at McCarthy Stone Publishing?" Delaney waited.

"Sorry officer – never heard of her." Emily held a steady eye contact with Frank until he finally looked away. Gareth shifted uncomfortably not sure exactly what to think. He assumed she must have some kind of amnesia from the drug onslaught but...

"Okay, well... we'll leave it there for now. I'll let you rest. Thank you Mrs. Stone, Mr. Stone." And at that point, as Frank left, Andrew Molly and Gina filed in to see her. Andrew looked over his shoulder to see him watching between the open window blinds.

Delaney caught his eye as he observed Emily Stone smiling widely, arms outstretched and recognising *all* of them... *instantly*.

FORTY-TWO

KIRKDALE: CUMBRIA U.K.
TWO MONTHS LATER

Annie Longbridge had found it quite difficult when her husband first arrived back from the States. He'd been away six long weeks chasing his favourite psycho case, and not only that, he'd been doing it with his favourite ex-D.I. Now he was out of the 'Job', with no intention of returning to golf (or any other of the dreaded ball games he'd come to hate), and hanging round the house bored rigid.

This had made things difficult where keeping in contact with her son Michael was concerned, and frankly, the way she was feeling at the moment, Michael was the person who was most important to her. They had kept in touch since the escape from Kenny Drew at the disused builders' yard, and even met up a couple of times despite the distance. She still hadn't told Harry about him being her son, even though he'd obviously asked about the whole abduction episode within *minutes* of arriving home. Well... *interrogated* was probably a better description of the conversations they'd had, although she realised deep down it at least showed he *had* been worried.

Yes, it had been difficult between them over the previous two months since his return, but it wasn't just that. She hadn't been feeling all that great either. To be honest, there had been large amounts of tears, stress and anxiety, and to be fair to Harry, when her edginess, panic attacks and raised blood pressure had started he'd been quite sympathetic... at first. Thing with PTSD though... *it doesn't disappear after a few cups of tea and a packet of Bourbons.* And Annie being Annie, despite nagging Harry into sorting his diabetes two years ago, wasn't of a mind to sort her own issues out. This meant the current situation at home as she saw it was *'jealous failed businesswoman, with post-traumatic stress',* versus *'frustrated, displaced, work obsessed ex-police officer'.* It wasn't good. She was watching him at that moment from the opposite side of the lounge, endlessly checking his messages...

Harry sat intently scrolling emails hoping against hope he may have one from Fran, or even Chris Hitchings, asking if he wanted to come out of retirement permanently, or at least for a reasonable stretch. He was only fifty-one for God's sake, *it wasn't exactly old.*

He'd checked his mobile a million times in the last eight weeks hoping for *'the one'.* Although there was the odd message from Fran asking if he was still okay after stupidly putting himself in reach of being diazepam-jabbed by Charlotte Peterson, there were no requests to return either by text or email.

Baxter came up and nuzzled his hand until his head was beneath it for a stroke, something he'd done from a small puppy. He'd missed his best buddy in those six weeks, and although Harry had now been back for longer than he'd been away, Bax had kept him under very close watch since his return. Harry gave him a ruffle and bent down to kiss the top of his head. *Annie noticed the kiss.*

At that moment a new email came in from Frank Delaney. He'd promised to keep Harry in the loop over findings in the murder of Jenny Flood and the disappearance of Jodi Denton. Frank had already told him they'd found no actual proof of Charlotte's involvement with the death of cabby Manny Berkowitz, but given the timing of her arrival, it had been assumed she was likely to be responsible for his murder too. Exactly *why* she would be they still had no idea.

Frank Delaney:- det.frank.delaney@nypd.org
Fri 01/05/20

Hi Harry,

Hope you're well and completely recovered with no ill effects from the hostage situation at Bellevue.

Thought you'd like to know forensics came up with a match on the hair from Jodi Denton's brush, and the teeth found in the Bellevue boiler room incinerator. There were finger prints on the incinerator's controls that matched your escaped perp Charlotte Peterson, and CCTV footage came to light of them working on that last shift together near a pre-op and O.R. room. When forensics swept them, blood showed up under luminal and it was found to be Mrs. Denton's, along with Peterson's fingerprints there too.

There was a family service in her memory and I understand Mr. and Mrs. Stone were in attendance.

With regards to Miss. Flood, your pathologist friend Kay Winford confirmed the same drug was used on her as Mrs. Stone, only to a far higher degree which ultimately killed her. Mrs. Stone told us Peterson kidnapped her from within the hospital following an appointment, and injected her with something. (She remembered that!) She was extremely lucky, and that includes her wiped memory with regard to Miss. Flood's diary... and it appears, Miss. Flood herself. We noticed both Mr. and Mrs. Stone attended her funeral though...

Sorry for the delay on this – forensics takes at least five weeks and I've been on vacation for the last three. (Took in some great jazz concerts!)

Glad to hear Peterson is back in your secure unit in Nottinghamshire and Mr. Mogg is getting the help he needs with regard to his recovery over his sister's murder in 2018.

Please give my regards to Det. Taylor – it was good to work with you both.

Keep in touch,

All the best,

Frank

Det. Frank Delaney 68th Precinct – Brooklyn NYPD

Harry looked at Baxter.

"Time for a walk eh Bax? What do you think?" The Lab wagged his tail enthusiastically and not for the first time since his 'dad' had been back. Baxter ran over to Annie looked up at her and then back over at Harry. He knew what the dog was saying as did she. *They also knew Harry would do the park run on his own.*

On the second lap of Kirkdale rec., Harry's mobile bleeped a text.

"Hold up Bax there's a good lad." He pulled on the lead and Baxter sat dutifully. Then lay down… in a puddle. Groaning, Harry moved him along a bit till they reached the nearest bench and he managed to get Bax *not* to jump up beside him. His heart skipped a beat when he saw who the text was from…

Looks like Charlotte Peterson wasn't the only person we brought back with us from New York Harry…

He read it twice, looked across the park and then back at the phone as if the text would change if he didn't keep staring at it. Part of his heart sang like a bird, the other part, the part that belonged to Annie, felt crushed. Crushed because he knew it would finish her. Not only because he'd slept with Fran, her nemesis for most of his career, but because Annie couldn't have children herself.

It had only been the once, at the B&B after he'd been discharged from the hospital. They had both thought they'd lost each other, and for the first time in all those years had allowed themselves just one act of total loving connection.

He reached down to Baxter, slung an arm round his shoulders and put his head close to his sighing heavily.

"So how are we going to deal with this one then eh lad?" A long wet and warm tongue slathered his face.

Molly Fields had just finished a call from an elated Gina. She'd rung to thank her closest friend for the overwhelmingly kind gift arranged during their recent horrendous few weeks. There had just been a delivery at Gina and Andrew's place from Gabriella's in New York, and Gina was beyond ecstatic.

Molly smiled. She loved to give surprises and had hugged that secret to herself all the way home on the plane. There was no way her dearest friend, who was more like a sister, was going to miss out on her dream wedding dress because of *Charlotte bloody Peterson*. She had already caused her the nightmare from hell... *for the second time.*

The wedding had been postponed until after the baby was due. Ellena Rose Gale's arrival was expected the beginning of September, and Molly was thrilled she'd predicted the sex correctly. The dress would fit Gina just fine for their Christmas wedding in the beautiful Kirkdale parish church, *as long as she could keep Gee away from her favourite carbs!*

Now she was sitting on her bed biting her lip in anticipation. Fran Taylor wasn't the only one peeing on a stick that morning. Molly had closed her eyes for the entire time she'd been waiting, thinking about the gorgeous guy she'd got close to at the Bay Ridge 'Taekwondo nights'. And now it was time to see just how close... She opened them slowly, and with her heart leaping all over the place, looked down at the 'Clear Blue' test in her hands. *"Looks like we're going to be*

sharing some big girl stuff again Gee. This time though...
it's going to be all good."

EPILOGUE

RAMPTON HIGH SECURITY HOSPITAL

Charlotte was a little perplexed she had a visitor at all. She never had visitors. Not surprising really, it's something she'd come to get used to… *again*. But not today. Today the request sent out many times before had finally been accepted, and she'd agreed to see her. *Two months of secret correspondence had paid off.* Well, secret as far as one person was concerned anyway.

When the door to the lounge area opened and the woman walked into the room, for the first time in a good number of years, it was Charlotte Peterson who looked surprised – *or maybe not…* They weren't so different she and her.

The orderly indicated a chair for the woman to sit down, there were other people in the lounge and she acknowledged a thank you with a slight nervous snatch of her head. She looked about her and took a seat opposite the patient she'd come to see. The two women initially observed each other silently, an oblong table set between them. For a few moments the orderly stood to one side, and then left them to observe from a desk further away.

"H-Hello Charlotte," said the visitor, picking at her nails, eyes now darting between their misshapen edges and Charlotte's waiting stare. "I've been... I've... it's..."

The former doctor eased forward slowly, leant elbows on knees and made a bridge with her hands against her mouth. She then looked closely into the very soul of her. Closely enough to see it was severely emotionally scarred, *and thus vulnerable. Vulnerable ripe and ready.* The corner of her lips tugged into that famous half smile, her eyes remained cold. Charlotte breathed a whispered slow reply into her hands so as not to alert anyone nearby.

"Hello Annie... what took you so long?" And as Annie Longbridge smiled nervously, biting her lip, beginning to wish she'd never come, never written that letter, never got involved in *any* way whatsoever... Charlotte Peterson knew she'd found her. She had found *'the one'*. Exactly the *right* one for her very, very important work – ***The Delegate...***

ACKNOWLEDGEMENTS
HUGE THANKS MUST GO TO...

John Benedict M.D. – O.R. Anaesthetist, PA U.S.A.

For generously helping with regard to U.S. employment law pertaining to jobs able to be filled by medical foreign nationals, untrained in the United States. Despite constant research, I was unable to find this information and without it would literally have been facing a second huge writer's block as I did for *Blood List*. John is also author of several great medical thrillers, which I can thoroughly recommend.

Dr. David Turnbull – Sheffield Teaching Hospital U.K. For critical information regarding coma-inducing drugs, and ideas for eliciting further possibilities regarding drugs yet to be created in order to fulfil the plot line – this helped me enormously with a major part of the story.

Nick Burrows – My long-suffering I.T. guy

For maintaining my laptop, keeping me connected to the internet and generally helping me not go into meltdown! I couldn't write any of my books without you!

Dawn Wood (Dawnie) – A dear friend, past colleague and long time diabetic

For all the detailed information you gave me with regard to diabetes, which helped considerably with being accurate when referring to my D.C.I. Harry Longbridge and his own condition.

Patrick J O'Donnell – A dedicated U.S. cop and writer

For so generously gifting me a copy of his *Cops And Writers – From The Academy To The Street* which has been a godsend in helping me link in to the American police system. Anything I have written that departs from his factual information is purely to 'help my story along' and make it more enjoyable. *(It is fiction after all!)*

Jo Moss – My dear author friend and 'booky' companion!

For literally nagging me to dig *Blood List* out of my laptop in early 2018 after letting it 'sleep' for ten years, bring it up to date and finish it. Without Jo, *Dead Girls Don't Cry* wouldn't be in your hands now...

Everyone at Matador – For simply being the best!

Grateful thanks for running the most professional set-up in the business giving authors worldwide choice and control.

Bruce – For his belief in me

And of course not forgetting my husband Bruce, who has to spend a lot of his time living with someone who creates murder and mayhem!

DISCLAIMER/INFO

Having checked with medical professionals, and as far as I am aware is still the case, at the time of writing there are no such drugs named or otherwise similar to, that are or will be available or acting in the way *'Baclovate'* and *'Bacliscind'* have been suggested to by me in this book. They are both *purely fictional* in name and use, and I have invented them to create and enable exciting and crucial parts of the story.

AUTHOR'S LICENCE

Whilst trying to be as realistic as possible, in order to write an enjoyable *fictional* story, despite research, the specific layouts of both the Bellevue Hospital and the 68th Precinct in Brooklyn, their specific daily routines and methods of working, are unlikely to be accurate. I hope this fact won't have spoiled the story for those readers who are, or have been a patient or worked at Bellevue, or who are or have been employed in the N.Y.P.D. as an officer at the 68th, or the Manhattan P.D. at any time.

For exclusive discounts on Matador titles,
sign up to our occasional newsletter at
troubador.co.uk/bookshop